ENOUGH ROPE

Also by Barbara Nadel

The Hakim and Arnold series
A Private Business
An Act of Kindness
Poisoned Ground

The Inspector Ikmen series
Belshazzar's Daughter
A Chemical Prison
Arabesk
Deep Waters
Harem
Petrified
Deadly Web
Dance with Death
A Passion for Killing
Pretty Dead Things
River of the Dead
Dead of Night
Death by Design
A Noble Killing
Deadline
Body Count
Land of the Blind

The Hancock series
Last Rights
After the Mourning
Ashes to Ashes
Sure and Certain Death

BARBARA NADEL

ENOUGH ROPE

A Hakim and Arnold Mystery

Quercus

First published in Great Britain in 2015 by

Quercus Publishing Ltd
Carmelite House
50 Victoria Embankment
London EC4Y 0DZ

An Hachette UK company

A CIP catalogue record for this book is available
from the British Library

HB ISBN 978 1 84866 423 4
TPB ISBN 978 1 84866 424 1
EBOOK ISBN 978 178429 2447

10 9 8 7 6 5 4 3 2 1

Typeset by CC Book Production

Printed and bound in Great Britain by Clays Ltd, St Ives plc

To my wonderful editor, Jane Wood,
and to the memory of Eve & Trix

Prologue

All the accoutrements of the last stages of alcoholism were there. Empty bottles, faeces, boots with thin soles, an anorexic ankle. There was also some gear that took DI Kevin Thorpe back to the start of his career in the seventies. When was the last time he'd seen even the most desperate alkie heat up solid polish? Over a bonfire?

The twenty-something constable at his side said, 'What's the polish about, then?'

Such innocence, and yet the boy had probably seen more pornography than Thorpe had ever had dinners, hot or cold.

'They heat it up so they can drink it,' Thorpe said. 'Meths Boys was what we used to call them, back when this sort of thing was common. Blokes so poor and desperate they'd drink anything. Polish, methylated spirit, white spirit . . .'

'Christ.'

Thorpe had hoped he'd seen the last of the Meths Boys back in the early eighties, but in the new shiny London of the twenty-first century, apparently some remnants of the past remained.

'So, did he set himself on fire?'

The body had been found by a runner. Shaven-headed, he'd looked like a member of the BNP, except he spoke as if he'd been to Eton. Poplar was a funny place in 2014.

'No,' Thorpe said.

'How can you be so sure?' the kid asked.

The smell was a cross between scorched earth and burnt pork. The sight was worse. The body sprawled out in front of the Children's Memorial in Poplar Recreation Ground had been damaged by fire, but it was the short-handled knife in his chest that had killed the man. Thorpe pointed at it.

'Oh.'

'This is one alcoholic who didn't kill himself,' Thorpe said.

Eighteen pupils at Great North Street School in Poplar were commemorated on the Children's Memorial. They'd died in the first daylight bombing raid on London in 1917. The Memorial had been paid for by public subscription. It was a place Thorpe had always found incredibly touching. That generosity, and a love that some would call sentimentality, was something he'd always taken for granted in the East End of London. Here it was made solid in a white memorial listing eighteen names, underneath a standing angel with its wings outstretched.

Now someone had been killed in front of it, and there was even a mark in what looked like blood on the plinth. Thorpe wondered what kind of person would murder a hopeless drunk in front of a memorial to dead children.

Then, behind the memorial, he saw what looked like a bundle of rags in the middle of a flower bed. All the hairs on his neck stood up.

1

Eleven days earlier

'I've paid your friggin' rent!'

Yelling down over a set of rusting banisters at your landlord is not the best way to negotiate financial differences, but Lee Arnold was pissed off. Without any notice his landlord, George Papadakis, had put up the rent on his office.

'You owe me three hundred pounds!' the landlord countered.

'Yeah, so you say. But who's improved this shithole, eh? Not you, George. When I moved in here, the bog was like something out of the Ark. But you didn't give a toss, did you? I had a new one—'

'Only since Mrs Hakim came to work for you. Only then did you put that new toilet in. You didn't give a shit about it until then!' George spoke with a typical East End accent, but he waved his arms around as if he were declaiming from the steps of the Acropolis.

'I've painted the place, had the wiring done, and if you've

noticed, George, my sink don't drip down into your shop any more!' Lee said. 'Three hundred quid? You owe me that, mate!'

George clicked his tongue impatiently. 'I could get twice the rent you pay from one of these rich people moving into this area. You wanna watch it, Lee, the East End is trendy now for the young people. I could make your office into a luxury flat, just like that!' He clicked his fingers.

'Then do it,' Lee said. 'If you think you can tempt some knob-head hipster kid from Shoreditch all the way out to Upton Park, then knock yourself out.'

Up in his office, Lee's phone began to ring. He threw the butt of the cigarette he'd been smoking onto the stair he'd been standing on and stepped on it.

'And stop smoking!' George said.

'When you do, I will.'

Lee ran inside his small, stuffy office and picked up the ringing phone. 'Arnold Agency.'

There was a pause. In the years since he'd left the police and started running the agency, Lee Arnold had discovered that private detection services attracted the odd and sometimes the very very timid, as well as the desperate.

'Arnold Agency. Hello?'

He didn't like answering the phone. That was one of the reasons why he'd eventually caved in and employed an assistant. But now that the woman he'd taken on to do the 'officey' things was frequently busier looking for errant daughters and dodgy husbands than he was, Lee often had to answer his own calls.

'Mr Arnold?'

It was a man. Well spoken.

'Yes.'

There was another pause and then, 'Mr Arnold, I have a problem.'

'People who ring here usually do,' Lee said. There was something familiar about the voice, but he couldn't place it. He knew a lot of people, even some posh ones. 'What can we help you with?'

'I don't know whether you can help me at all,' the man said. 'But if we could meet somewhere – I don't want to do this over the phone – then we could discuss it.'

'We could,' Lee said. 'Although I have to tell you that I won't meet anyone in a dark alley, for obvious reasons.'

'Of course not. There's a pub near your office called the Boleyn. How about that?'

If he knew Newham's most famous pub he might be local. But the Boleyn was also West Ham United's boozer – and he was a bit posh even for the most gentrified bits of the borough.

'OK, when?' Lee asked.

'Can you meet me this evening? At five?'

'Yeah.' Lee flicked the desk diary open and began to write. 'Mr . . . ?'

'Smith.'

It was almost certainly something to do with his marriage. They were always 'Smith' or 'Brown'. Lee could see him in his mind: middle-aged, white, miserable. The wife was probably having an email affair with a waiter she'd met in Morocco.

'And how will I recognise you, Mr Smith?'

There was another pause. Then, 'Oh, you'll recognise me, Mr Arnold,' and he put the phone down.

Lee Arnold went outside and lit a cigarette to steady his nerves. That 'Mr Smith' had said he'd recognise him felt ominous.

Although she didn't like to give too much credence to the fantastical theories that some of her clients had about their husbands'/ sons'/daughters' behaviour, when Mumtaz Hakim found herself following Mr Ali to Broadway Market in Hackney she had been surprised. One of the great centres of East End urban cool was not a place she would have associated with a forty-seven-year-old imam from Manor Park. Girls in ripped tights and hipsters on fixed-wheel bicycles were not obviously the kind of company Mr Ali would want to keep. Had he come to the market to taste the forbidden fruit of the excellent pork with crackling Lee Arnold had told her they sold there? She doubted it, though anything was possible. Perhaps Mr Ali had a fancy for outsized lavender cupcakes. His wife was clearly worried enough to pay good money to find out.

As a girl, if anyone had told Mumtaz that overtly religious people did anything wrong, she wouldn't have believed it. But even at the relatively tender age of thirty-three, she'd experienced enough to know that wasn't true. Her late husband had been a 'good' Muslim, but he had also been a drunk, a gambler, and had sexually abused both his own daughter and Mumtaz. Now there were other 'good' men in her life who wore their religious credentials on their sleeves while concealing the foulest sins in their corrupted hearts. Was Mr Ali one of those?

She followed him to a second-hand shop that seemed to be full of industrial artefacts – metal filing cabinets, factory lamps and furniture made from what looked like railway sleepers. It was fascinating; she could see why Mr Ali was spending so much time looking around. But then he made straight for Regent's Canal.

When she'd been a child, Regent's Canal had been a drab, smelly and forbidding waterway. Mumtaz and her two brothers had often lurked around it to throw stones at rats and jump out at unsuspecting walkers. But when a young woman was raped and thrown into the canal in 1997, Mumtaz's parents forbade the children to go. They took no notice, but their adventures hadn't been the same. In recent years, however, the canal, just like Broadway Market, had undergone a renaissance. Filled with colourful barges, some of which doubled as floating shops, it was like a holiday destination. Mr Ali, smiling as he walked towards one of the barges, obviously thought so too.

She saw him get on board, to be greeted by a middle-aged white woman who addressed him by his first name and said, 'We've got some lovely stuff for you. Really different.'

Was she some kind of madam? Mumtaz cringed. She heard a male laugh that was probably his and wondered what the 'stuff' the woman had alluded to might be. Was it new young girls brought in for his pleasure? Or some peculiar sex toy? It was only when Mumtaz saw Mr Ali and the woman emerge fully clothed onto the deck in the sunshine, carrying bulging plastic bags, that she began to get a clue that maybe she had misjudged them. Then she saw the name of the boat, *The Knitty Nora*.

She heard him say, 'I take your point about the hand-painted cashmere, Dora, but my wife wants a sweater like the one in *The Killing*, so what can I do? Twenty years we have been together. I want to give her something she will love.'

Mumtaz wondered how she was going to start the conversation she had to have with his wife.

Lee Arnold was the same build as Superintendent Paul Venus. Tall and slim, Venus was in mufti when Lee found him sitting in one of the far dark corners of the Boleyn, nursing a whisky.

'I'm assuming it's you I'm here for, Mr Smith?' Lee said. Superintendent Venus had come to Forest Gate nick after Lee had left the force, but he had made his acquaintance and still had old mates who worked for him. None of them liked him.

'Yes.' Venus looked up. In his mid-fifties, he was almost ten years older than Lee, but his skin was smooth and his hair thick, which made him look younger. On this occasion, however, he had very dark circles underneath his eyes. 'Can I get you a drink, Mr Arnold?'

Lee asked for a Diet Pepsi. Venus went to the bar.

The Boleyn, inasmuch as it advertised itself at all, promoted an image of a real East End boozer. And that was no lie. But what it meant in the twenty-first century was not what it had meant when Lee was a kid. Back in the seventies the Boleyn had heaved with boozed-up, white, working-class blokes singing West Ham songs and having punch-ups. Now, although it still retained its early Edwardian décor, plus a faint air of chirpy cockneyism, it was a bit of a quiet billet, with the exception of home-game Saturdays.

But even though it was a shadow of its former self and he hadn't taken a drink for years, Lee Arnold loved it.

When Venus returned he said, 'I'm aware of the fact that you're friends with several of my officers, Mr Arnold. Specifically DI Collins and DS Bracci.'

Lee had worked with them both years before. He even had an ongoing, ad hoc, fuck-buddy thing happening with Violet Collins. He hoped that Venus didn't want to talk to him about that.

'But what I am going to tell you, you mustn't tell them, or anyone else. Not even your assistant,' Venus said. 'I can't stress that enough.'

Lee frowned.

'Can you give me an assurance that you will adhere to these conditions, Mr Arnold?'

Vi Collins had a theory that Venus was bent. As she perceived it, he was soft on organised crime in the borough and she speculated he was taking backhanders. Other people in the nick saw him more as a cautious operator. He was, after all, a posh type from out of the area, so fitting in was always going to be difficult.

Lee took a drink. 'Depends what it's about,' he said.

'Well, I can tell you it's not about any of my officers.'

'That's a good start.'

'And it doesn't have anything to do with any of DI Collins's theories about me either,' he said. He moved closer, leaning across the scarred pub table. 'So please put any notions you may have about my being on the make out of your mind. This is a personal matter.'

Another story that went around about Venus was that he was

shagging women in the station who were half his age. He was married, to a soap star who had a great big gaff in the country that he rarely visited, but he also had a flat in Islington. Had he been taking little PCs there for some extra-curricular? Was he about to get caught?

'I need your help. I need someone who knows about being a police officer, but who isn't one. I need . . .'

He stopped. This *was* serious. The shadowed eyes, together with the tears Lee could see in them, made the private investigator lean in towards the policeman. 'OK,' he said, 'just between you and me.'

Venus threw what remained of his whisky down his throat. He said, 'I've got a son. Harry. He's sixteen, attends a public school in Berkshire where he's a boarder. He's bright and his mother and I love him very much.'

'That's good.'

Venus was crying, tears falling down his cheeks. What was it with Harry? Drugs? Girls? Boys?

Venus said, 'He's been kidnapped.'

Lee hadn't been expecting that.

'His mother received a phone call the day Harry disappeared and then a written demand from the kidnappers was sent to our family home in Henley-on-Thames last Friday. They, whoever they are, want a hundred thousand pounds for Harry's safe return. But if I use my police contacts, if I so much as tell the police, Harry will die. I have complied with that. My wife and I are in the process of assembling the money in the required denominations. Would you mind if I got another drink? Would you like one?'

'No, but you go for it,' Lee said.

Venus went to the bar.

His wife was an actress called Tina Wilton. Lee remembered her from vaguely saucy comedy programmes in the seventies. Blonde, curvy and a bit tarty, she'd gone on to land a role in the long-running soap *Londoners*, back in the nineties. She played a tough matriarch, head of a crime family who, Lee always thought, were some of the worst caricatures of East End 'types' he'd ever come across. But a lot of people loved Tina Wilton and she was a regular on many panel and reality shows. Every time he saw her, Lee mourned for the way she had looked in the past, pre-Botox and plastic surgery. Had she done all that to enhance her career, or to try to please her husband?

Venus returned. 'We have to deliver the money to a PO box address on Brick Lane,' he said.

'Hold on,' Lee said. 'Do you have any proof these people have Harry?'

'Proof? What do you mean?'

'Did your wife ask to speak to Harry when they called? Have they called since? Have you spoken to them?'

'No, no.' He put his head in his hands. 'Look, I should have, but I didn't. I just need to deliver the money they've asked for.'

Lee sighed. OK, it was his son, but Venus's copper's instinct should have told him to ask for proof of life. He said, 'When?'

'Monday morning at ten.' He downed his latest whisky. 'I have to do it and I'm fine with that. I just want my son back unharmed.'

'But . . .'

If that had been all he had wanted, there would have been no need to tell anyone, let alone Lee Arnold.

'I also want to know who they are,' Venus said. 'My wife picked Harry up from school last week. Two days later he left on his bike to go and visit his friend George in Twyford, but he never arrived. Then came the phone call and the following day his mother received the demand.'

Harry was sixteen. Lee could remember being sixteen. He said, 'Look, I have to ask this – have you or your wife been having, well, issues with your son lately? Forgive me, Mr Venus, but I know you and your wife live apart. I'm just wondering how that's affected Harry. Whether it's made him—'

'Harry wouldn't put his mother and myself through something like this!' Venus said.

'I have to—'

'My wife and I haven't lived together, apart from the occasional week during school holidays, for a decade. He is accustomed to our separation. Nothing has changed for him, and in fact I would venture to guess that he has probably done very well out of having a father in London and a mother in the country.'

People often spoilt kids when their marriages failed. Lee wondered whether Harry had learned to exploit his situation. Or whether the boy, secretly unhappy, had just decided to take off with a heap of his parents' money.

'Something happened to my son between Henley and Twyford and I want you to go over there and find out what,' Venus said. 'I also want you to follow me when I drop the money on Brick Lane. I'll pay you whatever it takes. You can rip me off to your heart's content, Mr Arnold. I really don't care.'

'I won't, Mr Venus. I'm not like that.'

'I'm sorry.'

Lee could have done with a fag to help him think it over, but that meant going outside, and he didn't want to leave Venus on his own. Much as he was indifferent to him, this man was clearly very vulnerable.

'When would you want me to start?'

'Tomorrow,' Venus said, 'and I've got five hundred pounds for your immediate expenses on me now.'

'You want me in Henley-on-Thames tomorrow?'

Venus took a folder out of his briefcase and pushed it across the table. 'Yes. Here's some information about Harry, his friend George and significant locations like our family home. Plus my wife's mobile numbers and the address of the hotel I've booked you into tomorrow night.'

'You're very confident I'll say yes, aren't you?' Lee said.

Venus leaned back in his chair. 'I know you've not got a lot of work commitments, that your landlord has just put up your rent and that your assistant doesn't usually work at weekends. Your friend DI Collins has, as you know, a very penetrating voice.'

She could hear Lee's mynah bird going through his usual reper-toire of West Ham United songs and lists of players as she picked up the phone. Mumtaz heard Lee yell, 'Shut up, Chronus!'

She laughed. She was in a good mood. Mr Ali had not been playing around with a long-legged blonde in Hackney, which had curtailed her job, but she'd enjoyed telling his wife about the *Killing* sweater. It was an unusual thing to do, and yet Mumtaz could see how it could happen. Some Muslim men, her own father included, had a masculine image to uphold, but inside they were really soft as butter. Mr Ali had so wanted to make something for his wife that she would treasure, that he had resorted to clandestine knitting classes. When she told Lee, she thought he'd be disappointed that the job hadn't lasted longer. But oddly, he wasn't.

'Sometimes it goes that way,' he said. 'Don't worry about it.'

'Yes, but with the office rent . . .'

'Oh, don't worry about that either,' Lee said. 'That'll get sorted. Look, the reason I phoned was to ask if you or Shazia could feed Chronus for me this weekend.'

Until recently, DS Tony Bracci had lived in Lee's spare room. His wife had thrown him out in favour of a younger man, but she'd just taken him back and so Tony was no longer available for bird-sitting.

'Yes, that'll be fine,' she said.

'Just tomorrow,' Lee said. 'I'll be back Sunday night.'

'No problem.'

'Great. Thanks.'

She didn't ask why he wouldn't be around to feed Chronus at the weekend and Lee didn't volunteer the information. It wasn't her business.

Just as the call ended, Mumtaz heard the front door open, then close, followed by the sound of her stepdaughter going to her bedroom.

'Shazia?'

The girl, a bright, tall, skinny seventeen-year-old, didn't answer.

Mumtaz left the kitchen and walked the few steps to Shazia's room. After living in a five-bedroom house, the flat they shared now was cramped. It felt like living in a doll's house.

Shazia's door wasn't closed and so Mumtaz walked into her room. 'How long is this going to last?' she asked the girl.

Shazia, who was sitting on her bed emptying her bag, did not look up.

'Well?'

'I told you, as long as you insist on playing the victim, I don't want to talk to you,' the girl said. 'Go to the police or speak to Lee and I'll talk to you.'

'You know I can't do that.'

Shazia looked up. Her eyes, which were dark and huge, were also very heavily made up. She looked stunning. She said, 'I saw that Naz Sheikh today. He watched me get on the bus to college. He was smirking. Next time I see him, why don't I just punch him, eh?'

'Oh no! No!'

'Why not? He deserves it.'

Mumtaz felt her heart flutter. 'Shazia, you mustn't.'

'Mustn't?' She went back to looking at the stuff in her bag. 'Oh, just go away, Amma,' she snapped. 'Go away and leave me alone in my little rabbit hutch.'

Shazia hadn't had an easy life. Her mother had died when she was a child and her father, while fulfilling her every material whim, had sexually abused her. After his death and despite Mumtaz's best efforts, she'd also had to suffer the trauma of having to move from their lovely family home to a tiny flat so that her father's debts could be paid.

15

In his ignominious career as a gambler, Ahmet Hakim had got himself in hock to a local crime family. The Sheikhs did it all. Slum-landlording, money-laundering, illegal gambling, people-trafficking and blackmail. And when the need arose to give their errant clients the occasional reminder about money owed, the Sheikh family were not backwards in coming forwards. Naz Sheikh, the youngest member of the clan, hadn't so much as flinched as he'd stabbed Ahmet Hakim to death in front of his wife on Wanstead Flats almost two years before.

'I can't believe my father still owes those people money,' Shazia said. 'They're ripping you off!'

They were. The debt Ahmet Hakim had died for had been paid in full, with interest, when Mumtaz had sold their old house. But what Shazia didn't know was that Mumtaz herself was in debt to the Sheikhs. When Naz Sheikh had killed Ahmet she'd seen him so clearly she would have easily been able to give his description to the police. But she hadn't. Instead, she'd watched her husband bleed to death into the scrubby Wanstead Flats grass. And the Sheikhs knew why. She'd hated Ahmet. He'd made her life unbearable. Naz Sheikh had been her hero, and he knew it. He played on it. But no one else knew, especially not Shazia.

'These people add interest payments onto interest payments,' Mumtaz said. 'As long as they say I owe them money, then I owe them money.'

'That's insane. You should stop paying them.'

'I can't.'

'Why not?'

'You know why not, Shazia.'

They'd talked about this.

'Because they'll hurt us? Amma, if you told the police, if you told Lee—'

'It wouldn't get any better!' Mumtaz was yelling now. She didn't like to yell. She made a conscious effort to slow her breathing. 'Just leave it to me, Shazia. Leave it to me.'

Naz Sheikh, her one-time hero, had her. The deal – pay up or Shazia gets told her precious amma had a hand in killing her own father – was unbreakable. Even though the girl had suffered so badly at her father's hands he had still been her abba. Shazia would never forgive her. She would never get over it.

Mumtaz changed the subject. 'Lee wants us to feed Chronus tomorrow,' she said. 'He's away for the weekend.'

'With a girlfriend?'

'I don't know. I didn't ask.'

Mumtaz walked towards Shazia's bedroom door.

'You know you're forcing him to look elsewhere because you won't acknowledge what's happening,' Shazia said.

The girl had some notion that Lee Arnold had romantic feelings for her. It was absurd.

'Don't be silly, Shazia. I've told you about romanticising.'

'What, because he's a white man? What does that mean, Amma? My father, the one who got us into this mess in the first place, was a Bangladeshi Muslim, and look how well he turned out. Eh? God, you're so thick sometimes. Love is rare and you should never just ignore it. I know that and I'm only a kid.'

Mumtaz dismissed her with a wave of her hand. Then she went back into the kitchen and put the radio on.

2

Lee Arnold had not been the sort of kid who willingly read Enid Blyton books. In fact, any sort of book was a rarity in his parental home and his older brother usually used those that did get in as missiles. But he did get exposed to the Famous Five and the Secret Seven at school.

In an age of Glam Rock and skinheads, the characters had seemed like beings from another planet. All picnics and affectionate dogs, kids like George and Julian never said 'fuck' and certainly never got smacked by their alcoholic dad. Custom House was then one of the poorest parts of the London Borough of Newham. With the Royal Docks dying around them, none of the locals could afford holidays to Dorset or anywhere else. Lee and his brother Roy were lucky to get a day out to Southend-on-Sea and a hotdog while their father got pissed in a seafront pub.

Now he was in Blyton land, and it was weird.

Venus had booked him into a country pub, the Flowerpot, at a place just outside Henley-on-Thames called Remenham. He'd arrived early in the morning, wanting to get a jump on the day so that he could get to know the area and meet the missing Harry's mother. When he'd first rolled up, the Flowerpot hadn't even been open, so he'd driven around for a while, familiarising himself with the route between Henley and Twyford. It was sunny, the roads were reasonably clear and the view of the Thames Valley flashing between the cottages and vast riverside mansions was picturesque. In Twyford he parked up and looked at houses for sale in the area. Lee worked out that if he sold his flat in London and was careful with money, he could probably put down a deposit on a studio flat round there. Harry Venus was going to be a very rich man one day. If he survived.

When he went back to the Flowerpot it was open, so he checked in. He was given a comfortable room overlooking a big beer garden that was the definition of idyllic. It had two bars, one large and modern, the other small and filled with dusty taxidermy and early risers with local accents. Lee ordered a coffee under the gaze of a dead stag, and called Tina Wilton.

'Come over when you're ready.' She gave him an address on the Wargrave Road. It was minutes away.

Lee finished his coffee and left.

Sleep had never been a realistic option. He'd watched the sun set and then rise again over the streets of Islington without so much as a snooze. Paul Venus felt like shit.

In a sense, getting Lee Arnold involved had made his state of mind worse. Harry was in the hands of people who had threatened to kill him if the police became involved. And even though Arnold was no longer a serving officer, he was ex-job. So he knew the ropes, the signs, the tells that could give away even the most cautious. Like Paul Venus.

When it had first happened, he'd called people – bar those in the job – that he knew. Significant people. He'd shouted at men who had other men who looked like Staffordshire bull terriers, ready to kill for them. But no one had known anything, or so they said. And Paul owed no one anything any more. He was straight with the world, as far as he knew. Except for occasionally taking the odd gift . . .

But to stand a chance of finding out who had Harry, Lee Arnold should be told he'd spoken to such people at the very least, because the men with the other men who looked like Staffies lied all the time. Their women didn't know what the truth was even if it slapped them. They didn't want to. But how was Paul going to tell him? He wasn't because he couldn't. Even talking to such people was wrong, and he'd done much more than that in his time.

The money drop on Monday would have to work. It would work.

Tina Wilton was posh.

'When I started in the theatre back in the seventies you either had to be a debutante type, like Joanna Lumley, or a bit of a slapper,' she said as she put a glass of iced tea down in front of Lee Arnold. 'I opted for the latter because it seemed like more fun.'

She sat down and lit a cigarette. They were in a large conservatory that overlooked the River Thames. Just like the Flowerpot,

Tina Wilton and Paul Venus's house had an idyllic garden and views across the river that probably ramped up the price of such a place by at least a hundred thousand quid. The house itself was very tasteful if rather ordinary. Harry's bedroom had been surprisingly tidy and free of personality for a teenage boy.

Lee got his cigarettes out. 'Mind if I . . . ?'

'Oh, go ahead,' she said. 'I'm not my husband, Mr Arnold.'

Paul Venus was a virulent anti-smoker, which was one of the reasons he disliked the chain-smoking Vi Collins so much.

'In the seventies all slapper actresses had to smoke, it was the law,' she smiled. 'Now . . .' She shrugged. 'Bad for the skin, I know, but that's what Botox is for isn't it? And Rita isn't exactly an ingénue, is she?'

Rita was the character she played in *Londoners*. A hard-bitten East End matriarch who loved her thuggish 'boys' in spite of their crimes and doted on her spoilt young granddaughters. On one level, Lee was offended by what many felt was a caricature of East End womanhood, while on the other hand he had to admit he had known women like the awful Rita.

He lit his fag. 'Tell me about Harry,' he said.

The facade of tired bonhomie she had been maintaining since he arrived slipped. As did parts of her face. Tina Wilton aged ten years in a second.

'Harry's our only child,' she said. 'Don't know what Paul's told you.'

'I want to hear what you've got to say, Miss Wilton.'

Parents often had different takes on their children, which could be useful.

She said, 'We've spoilt him, materially. It's classic, making up for not being there for him. We've both always worked and so Harry was raised by a succession of nannies and au pairs until he went away to school, when he was thirteen.'

'Boarding school.'

'Reeds in Ascot,' she said.

Lee was none the wiser, but imagined a large Gothic building, boys in boaters and 'fagging'. Of course he was probably wrong.

'Is he happy at school?'

'Yes,' she said. 'Harry's an A star student; his masters anticipates he will easily get a place at a Russell Group university. He's a good all-rounder, but is especially adept at languages. He took his French and German GCSEs when he was fourteen and now, at no small cost to ourselves I should add, he's having extra Mandarin and Arabic classes.'

'The future is Chinese.'

'So they say.' She looked out at the river for a moment and then said, 'Not good at games though. No coordination. It drives Paul wild. He can't understand it.'

'And yet Harry rides a bike.'

'Yes, he likes that,' she said. 'I just think he can't see the point of things like football and rugby, and I have to say that I agree.'

Lee Arnold, lifelong West Ham United obsessive, said nothing.

'But Harry's fit and healthy and, as far as I know, beyond the odd glass of wine and the inevitable experimentation with cigarettes, I don't think he's got any addiction issues.'

'Friends?'

'Harry has a small group of friends. In fact, I met an old friend of mine again through one of Harry's. We worked in a club together years ago. Harry shares a room with George Grogan, who he was going to visit the day he . . . when he went,' she said. 'George is a linguist too. They're close. It was George's father, Dr Grogan, who first told me that Harry hadn't arrived.'

'Tell me about that day, Miss Wilton,' Lee said.

She leaned back in her chair. She still had a good figure, if a little soft around the middle.

'Last Thursday,' she said. 'I wasn't at work. I was just hanging around the house. Harry, I thought, was going to spend the day with me, but at breakfast he said he was going to cycle over to George's house in Twyford. It was beautiful, like today, and the Grogans have a swimming pool. I quite envied Harry a day of lounging in the water. He left at about eleven.'

'What was he wearing?'.

'Shorts, trainers, a T-shirt. He took his blue rucksack, which I thought at the time was a bit big just for his swimming things and a towel. But then afterwards I discovered that he must've taken his Apple.'

'Apple computer?'

'Yes. Sorry, a MacBook.'

'Does Harry watch porn? I have to ask. In some abduction cases youngsters have been tempted out to places they wouldn't normally go by the promise of sex.'

'I've caught him once,' she said. 'But it wasn't what I'd call extreme stuff. Some bondage. What boy of his age hasn't looked at images like that these days?'

She had a point, but Lee knew not to trust what Tina Wilton thought she knew. What kids could access online, often with very few mouse clicks, was terrifying. He'd seen it and wished he hadn't. What had Harry Venus and his friends seen?

'Do you know how long it takes Harry to cycle to George's house?'

'No,' she said. 'Not long. It's only five miles. Dr Grogan called me just after midday, expressing his concern. He said that George had called Harry's mobile, but it had gone to voicemail.'

'What happened then?'

'I tried to call, but I just got voicemail. Then they phoned.'

'The kidnappers.'

'A voice, electronic.' She shuddered. 'Like Stephen Hawking. Obviously disguised. Said they had Harry and that they'd be telling us how we could get him back soon. They knew Paul. They were very specific. No using his police contacts to try and free our son, or they'd kill him. No telling anyone what was happening. I called my husband immediately.'

'You didn't think it was a prank?'

'Why would I? You can see for yourself that we have money. I'm a D-list "celebrity"' – she raised her fingers to represent speech marks. 'Paul's a prominent police superintendent. We are the sort of people who get targeted by lunatics and criminals wanting to make money out of us. Years ago, back in the eighties, I was stalked. We kept it quiet. The poor man was mentally ill, but these people who have Harry want a hundred thousand pounds.'

Which was not, Lee thought, a lot in the scheme of things.

24

Venus's Islington flat was probably worth five times that amount.

'Paul came straight here,' she continued. 'He followed Harry's route. Looked in every lane and driveway from here to Twyford, went to the railway station searching for signs of Harry. But there weren't any. Not his bike, his rucksack, nothing.'

'What did you tell George and his parents?' Lee asked.

'We had to make something up.'

'Which was?'

'Paul came up with the story. Harry had gone to see a girl and then he'd come home before going to stay with my mother in Malta. She really does live in Malta, but the girl was complete fiction. Harry's never been out with a girl. I don't know whether George believed that. I suspect that he didn't, but it satisfied his parents.'

'Have you spoken to George, Miss Wilton?'

'How can I?' She put one cigarette out and lit another. 'We can't tell anyone. And what's the point? Harry didn't arrive at George's house, so what would he know?'

Lee knew that George could potentially know a lot. Harry was bright, privileged, and he had to have some feelings about the way his parents lived and how that had affected him over the years, feelings he might have shared with his friends. The story Venus and Wilton told was based on the notion of a boy, his bike and a large rucksack disappearing into thin air. That wasn't possible. Maybe it was easier for a boy to 'disappear' in sedate, posh Henley than it was in Newham, where everyone lived crammed up against everyone else. But it wasn't likely. If Harry had been abducted, especially if that had happened on the main road from Henley to Twyford, then someone must have seen something. It had been the middle of the day. But Lee couldn't talk to anyone . . .

'Anyway, George has gone away for the holidays now,' Tina Wilton said.

All he could do was look again at the route Harry had taken, or probably taken, towards Twyford and stare at George's house from a distance. It wasn't much and, apart from having spoken to Tina Wilton, Lee felt that he was spending Venus's money poorly. Until the drop on Monday there was little he could do.

'If anything happens to Harry I won't be able to carry on,' Tina Wilton said. She stared out at the sunlit river again. 'I won't want to.'

Lee had glanced at the faded scars on her wrists and arms when they'd shaken hands. Now he looked away in case he fixated on them again.

After a pause she said, 'There is one person you can talk to: Harry's housemaster, Mr McCullough.'

'Does he know?'

'No. Although I imagine he suspects that something's wrong,' she said. 'I told him that Paul has put surveillance on Harry and would he mind talking to the investigator assigned to the job. He didn't ask any questions, but he's no fool. I'll speak to him and then let you have his details.'

'Hello Chronus, how are you?'

Mumtaz put a handful of seed in the mynah bird's food hopper and then gave him a piece of carrot and a piece of pineapple. He looked up at her with annoyance in his eyes rather than gratitude. She wasn't Lee and so he was pissed off. Thoroughly spoilt, Chronus was, she always felt, the son that Lee had never had. Constantly vocal on the subject of West Ham, he was probably better company for Lee than his daughter. Mumtaz had only ever met Jody Arnold once, but she struck her as a bit of a madam. A year younger than Shazia, Jody lived with Lee's ex-wife in Hastings where, it seemed to Mumtaz, she busied herself almost exclusively with shopping and fake tans. Obviously Lee loved her, there were photos of Jody all over the flat, but whenever they spent time together he seemed stressed. Maybe it was being dragged around high-end shops?

Mumtaz's phone rang. She looked at the screen and then turned it off. Naz Sheikh.

'I know what he wants,' she said to Chronus. The bird looked at her with a little more sympathy than before.

She sat down in one of Lee's immaculately polished leather chairs. As well as money, the Sheikhs now wanted information. They knew how close she was to DI Violet Collins and how well known she was up at Forest Gate nick. Everyone knew Mumtaz. Tongues might loosen around her and it was always useful to the Sheikhs to know what the coppers were doing.

Mumtaz had no intention of telling them anything. A strategy that would work until the police inevitably raided one of the family's slum lets or brothels. Then they'd probably give her the kicking of her life. Or harm Shazia. That was always a threat that was held over her head and it was, she knew, her one

Achilles heel. Once the girl was off to university, Mumtaz knew she'd finally be safe. Until then she had to play the game. But not today.

She looked at the blank-faced phone and put it in her pocket.

The public bar of the Flowerpot had a different atmosphere in the evening. Still largely patronised by locals, it was dark and conversation was generally muted. Drinking was serious and laughter, though rare, was loud and genuine. In spite of the entirely on-trend taxidermy, it was mercifully free of braying incomers clad in designer suits, tweed or 'quirky' casual wear.

During his travels around the area, Lee had come across a very firm divide between older locals with Oxfordshire/Berkshire accents and younger people who spoke more like incomers from London, and people who had moved there. The older locals, and many of the youngsters, while living in cottages that were probably worth more than they would ever earn in their lives, struggled to make ends meet. The newcomers, who had chosen to live in the area, were very comfortable, thank you. Their place was the big modern saloon bar where they gathered straight from golf courses or for post-river cruise drinkies.

An old bloke in a stained boiler suit had asked Lee where he was from when he'd first arrived. Lee had said, 'London,' and then added, 'Don't worry I'm not moving in. I'm skint.' That had caused a ripple of laughter. Then they'd ignored him, but they also talked freely in his presence.

'The house next door sold,' the old bloke said.

'Ah.'

The others, three of them, were elderly working men, probably gardeners, given the smell of grass that came off their clothes.

He carried on. 'Gone to that tit up the road's boy.'

'What, old Ferrari?'

'That's it. Kid's only just left university. The missus . . .'

'With the Land Rover Evoque?'

'Yup. She tells me he got a job up the City in some finance firm.' He paused for a moment, then he said, 'He'll move on in time, I expect. He's young, he'll be wanting some flat in Kensington or somewhere.'

One of the other blokes nodded. 'Then some other tosser'll move in,' he said, and they all laughed.

Harry Venus and his mate George were well-heeled 'tossers' of that kind. Tina Wilton had given Lee the names and addresses of Harry's two other local friends. Not Reeds boys, but they lived in houses called 'Riverbank' and 'The Boater'. There was his housemaster at school too, Mr McCullough, but he lived in a house with a number, which made Lee think that he must be more downmarket.

In the morning he'd cruise around and look at these places, then he had an interview with McCullough at ten.

Lee's phoned beeped. A text from Mumtaz telling him that Chronus had been fed. He smiled.

3

He opened the door to the safe as his front door closed. The girl had given him some relief, but Paul Venus was still nervous. He took the briefcase out of the safe and counted the money again. It was all still there. Why wouldn't it be?

His behaviour was paranoid, but was it surprising? Some greedy, evil bastards had his son and until he got him back he was going to be on edge. Tina hadn't helped. How could she taunt him with how good-looking she thought Lee Arnold had been at a time like this?

She'd said, 'He was very thorough, your Mr Arnold. Rather easy on the eye too, I thought.'

What did she care about Lee Arnold? Bitch. If it hadn't been for Harry, Paul would have divorced her ten years ago. Maybe longer. They hadn't touched each other for years and yet she still felt the need to hurt him. It was more than he felt for her. If she hadn't denied him his share of what they had both built up over the years, he wouldn't have had to resort to things that made him squirm when he thought about them.

His landline rang. Paul Venus closed his eyes for a moment before he answered. 'Yes?'

'So, how was little Sasha?'

The voice was foreign and familiar.

'She couldn't speak English,' Venus said.

''Did she need to speak?'

'No.'

'Then what's your problem?'

'I'm going to pay you for her,' Venus said. 'Tell me how much.'

'For a whole night? You are talking serious money there, my friend,' the voice said. 'But I told you, she's a gift. You've got trouble now, you need a gift. You are my friend and friends help each other. It's my pleasure.'

Paul Venus bit down on his need to scream. He said, 'That's kind. But I . . .' He wanted to say that he didn't want to be in the other man's debt, but he knew that he couldn't. And he didn't. 'That's awfully kind.'

Why couldn't he have sex like an ordinary person? Pick up a woman and just have sex with her? Because this was easier. It was professional, he always felt good about himself afterwards, and he had become addicted to it.

'Welcome. And of course, anything I can do to help you with the boy . . .'

'Thank you.'

'Anything I can do, Paul,' the voice said. 'You just have to ask.'

'Thank you.'

He put the phone down, then he looked at the money again. It still hadn't gone anywhere. It wouldn't until the next morning when it would buy Harry back.

*

Clarence Road, Henley, was a small street that led up to the local community hospital. Comprising identical red-brick Edwardian cottages, the street was a place where, once upon a time, Lee imagined, poor people had lived. Now, with its parking restrictions, bamboo blinds and tiny frontyard herb gardens, its demographic make-up had changed. The sight of a young woman wearing Birkenstock sandals and carrying her baby in a vast alpaca wool sling confirmed it. The middle classes had colonised the area.

But there was one house that wasn't as neat as the others. Lee knocked at the door and a grey-haired battered-looking man of about sixty answered.

'Mr McCullough?'

'Malcolm.' The man smiled. His eyes were tired but humorous, and he smelt strongly of bacon and cigarettes. 'Come in, Mr Arnold,' he said.

'Lee.'

'Lee.' He smiled again.

The front door led straight into a small living room that looked like something out of a fifties John Mills film. The heavy, faded brocade covered furniture that gave the impression it hadn't been moved for decades, the gas fire in the large blackened hearth was probably illegal. There was even an oil painting of a stag on one wall. Books, both loose and in cases, were everywhere.

Malcolm McCullough walked through into another room, which was much plainer though no less antiquated. But it was brighter. There was a TV set – albeit one that was probably thirty years old – and a pair of Ercol-style chairs that were almost comfortable.

'Would you like coffee?' McCullough asked. 'Bacon sandwich?'

'A coffee'd be nice,' Lee said.

The kitchen, which was a continuation of the second living room, reeked of pork fat, which did make Lee's mouth water. But he'd had his breakfast back at the Flowerpot.

'Sugar?'

'Two.'

As McCullough tinkered around in the kitchen, Lee wondered what his neighbours thought about him. Without so much as a window box or sea-grass mat in sight, he was the odd chap with the dirty net curtains who, it was probably rumoured, smoked with the windows shut. When he returned he carried two chipped mugs in one hand and a plate with a white bread sandwich in the other.

'There you go.'

Lee relieved him of a mug with a coat of arms on one side and watched as McCullough sat down, sighed and then looked, with great love, at his sandwich.

'One of the few consolations in life, a bacon sandwich,' he said.

'I don't imagine many of your neighbours indulge.'

'No. Alfalfa and organic tofu with just a touch of sea-salt.' He laughed. 'When I first bought this house, most of the people round here were ordinary. Had an electrician one side, teacher at the local comp on the other. I rather liked that. Now on the right we have a banker, his wife and a child called Pisa – I kid you not – and on the left a systems analyst and a woman who shops for a living. They all drink organic wine.'

Lee smiled. 'The smell of bacon and fags was a relief to me,' he said.

'Ah, then maybe you should tell Pisa's mummy and daddy that I'm not the devil after all. That child wears a crash helmet to play on a scooter. Believe that? There is no hope.' He stuck half a sandwich into a mouth of yellowing teeth. Once he'd downed the first bite he said, 'So what's this about Harry Venus? What's he been up to?'

Lee stuck to the story Tina Wilton had told him. 'Harry's a bit old to be chaperoned by his mum, but she and his father are worried about him,' Lee said. 'When he goes off, they're not always sure he is where he's saying he is. That's where I come in.'

'What's the worry?' Malcolm McCullough took another great bite and swallowed. 'Drugs?'

'Drugs, girls, booze, you name it. They have concerns.'

'Helicopter parents.'

'Pardon?'

'Helicopter parents, hovering over their young like droves of middle-class Sikorskys,' McCullough said. 'Dump 'em on us all term and don't give 'em a second thought. Then the holidays come and they realise they've got kids again. You're not from round here, are you?'

'I'm from London.'

Malcolm McCullough frowned. 'I heard that Harry was away in Malta,' he said.

That was the story that had been given to George and his family.

'Not at the moment,' Lee told him.

George Grogan was definitely away for the holidays and so he wouldn't be able to contradict him. If McCullough had, in fact, been in contact with the Grogans. Maybe Tina Wilton had told the boy's master herself and then forgotten? Or perhaps Henley was just a small place.

McCullough shrugged. As Tina Wilton had predicted, he knew there was something wrong. 'What do you want to know?'

'Harry's parents tell me he's happy at Reeds. I want to know if that's true.'

McCullough put what remained of his sandwich down on the floor beside him and drank some coffee. 'What do you mean?'

Now he was slightly guarded.

'I mean, is he properly happy?' Lee said. 'I'm not talking about academically, I'm talking friends or the lack thereof. I'm asking you if Harry's being bullied or whether he does the bullying. I want to know if he's a likeable boy or a little shit.'

'Do you.' He nodded his head and then put a hand in his jacket pocket and pulled out a packet of cigarettes. He lit up.

Lee didn't ask whether it was all right to join him. The mood in the room had darkened and he didn't want to tip its equilibrium. Not until he knew what it meant. 'Yes. I'm a PI, Malcolm, and although I work for Harry's parents, what you say to me now is between us and only us.'

McCullough breathed in. 'Harry Venus is a problem,' he said. 'Not that I can tell you that officially. Headmaster is clear on the issue. Harry's an excellent chap, grade A student, no trouble at all.'

'That's what his parents are told?'

'Yep.' He flicked ash onto his sandwich. Lee hoped he'd had enough.

'What's the truth?'

BARBARA NADEL

'Harry's a bit of a square peg,' McCullough said. 'At Reeds. I know it's not Eton, but most of our boys are either titled or they come from very well established upper-middle-class families. Doctors, lawyers – that sort of thing. But Harry? Dad's a policeman, mum's a soap star. Whichever way you swing it, he is not among the elite.'

'Does he want to be?'

'Of course he does. He's desperate to be in with the "in" crowd.'

'So what . . . ?'

'I've never seen Harry bullied, Lee,' McCullough said. 'I would never stand for that, whatever the headmaster said. But I do know that he's not always one of the gang. My reading of the situation is that if he doesn't toe the line, he gets punished. Not physically, but . . .'

'Is this like fagging or . . .'

McCullough laughed. 'Oh God no! No, that's much more Eton, *Tom Brown's Schooldays* . . .'

'I'm afraid I went to a comp,' Lee said.

'Which is perfectly marvellous,' McCullough said. 'But public school isn't what people think. Pastoral care is a huge part of our job these days, and as Harry's housemaster, as well as his English master, I do address issues like bullying. We discuss the notion of following the herd, popularity and bullying in English Lit classes. Harry isn't bullied, but he is excluded by the others – including his room-mate George Grogan – from time to time.'

'Why?'

'For being out of tune with them, mainly. Boys of this age are very conservative, with a small "c". They do what their peers do and if they don't, things can go badly for them. Gay boys are

36

particularly vulnerable. But Harry Venus isn't gay. He's just . . .'
He frowned, smoked and flicked his ash in the bacon again. 'Different. Likes things that other people don't like. Significantly, he
doesn't enjoy sport, which is a real handicap at public school. As
I said before, he's a square peg.'

'Is George Grogan a particular friend?'

'They room and they do share some interests, but Grogan is
really, I'd say, best pals with Tom de Vries. They were at prep
school together. Grogan, de Vries and Charles Duncan. Harry
Venus came later. He was the new boy and, to some extent, he's
stayed that way.'

'Does Harry get upset when he's excluded from the gang?'

'He used to. I've never seen him cry myself, but I have it on
good authority that he has. Now, although I have no direct proof
of this, I am told he takes his ire out on some of the younger
boys. Not that any boy would ever say a word against any other
boy to a member of staff. It's not done. But I've caught whispers.
Not enough to act, unfortunately.'

'So he can be a bully himself?'

McCullough nodded.

'Would you say that Harry is sneaky? Have you ever seen him,
for instance, meeting people not resident at the school inside or
near the premises?'

This was a double-edged question, designed to find out not only
whether Harry had extra-curricular contacts but also whether
people were getting into the school that shouldn't.

'No,' he said. 'Reeds may look like something out of a Monty

Python spoof but it is actually a very sophisticated place these days. We have CCTV and we employ a firm of security guards to patrol the grounds during term time. Parents pay a helluva lot of money to send their boys to us. We have to give them value and not squander it on silly things like staff pay.'

He didn't sound bitter, even if what he said was. Could a pissed-off, poorly paid teacher have spirited Harry away for the money? McCullough was based in Henley. But then his house, which Lee had looked up on Rightmove – or rather, houses like it – could sell for almost four hundred thousand pounds. What did he need a hundred grand for? DIY? Did he have a secret sexual vice someone was squeezing him over?

'Some boys have been caught smoking cannabis on school premises,' McCullough said. 'Ditto alcohol. And I know that all and any boy can make a mistake, but Harry and his group are high-fliers. Harry himself wants a career in academia, de Vries will join the diplomatic service, like his father. Duncan fancies a career in the air force and Grogan is hell-bent on following his brother into banking.'

'Not a doctor, like his father?'

'George likes money,' McCullough said. 'And yes, I know that doctors earn high these days, but not the stratospheric sums that bankers do. Henry Grogan, George's brother, was also at Reeds, I remember him well and George is, believe me, cut from the same cloth. Those two boys are going to be very rich one day.'

'They're not poor now.'

McCullough laughed. 'Ah, the Grogan Arts and Crafts pile, with swimming pool attached. You've seen it?'

38

'Yes. Through the trees.'

'Couple of million there,' McCullough said. 'But that's just normal round here, as I'm sure you've noticed. No, when I say rich I mean Friar Park, the massive Gothic pile where George Harrison used to live. I mean zipping around the lanes in a Lamborghini with a Rolex Oyster on your wrist and a girl with a title at your side. That's where the Grogans are going.'

Lee drank some coffee.

'I know it's closed at the moment, but if you want to see Reeds I can get you in,' McCullough said.

'I may take you up on that.'

'Anything I can do to help,' he said. Then he leaned forward. 'I have worked out that Harry's buggered off.'

'I'm watching him.'

He shrugged. Lee knew he didn't believe him. Yet he worked at the kind of school where parents having their children watched was probably quite normal.

'Harry's parents aren't the type,' McCullough said. 'His mother may be famous, but they don't have security.' And then he smiled. 'But that's my *opinion*, you understand. As I said, anything I can do to help.'

When Lee left Clarence Road it was with a sense of unease. The fact that Harry wasn't quite the perfect child his mother believed him to be, coupled with McCullough's conviction that the boy had 'buggered off', was stirring up eddies of silt around the edges of the case.

Before he returned to London, Lee went to a local beauty spot on the river called Marsh Lock. He watched the smart private launches vie with the slightly tatty canal boats for space in the picturesque lock. The lock-house garden and every other garden by the river was covered with flowers, and where those were in short supply then the lawns on their own were spectacular. One of them, all completely straight stripes, looked as if it were made of velvet. He thought about his own front garden, with its metre of grass and a half-dead hydrangea. Indoors he had a spider plant in the toilet.

Henley-on-Thames was a sort of paradise, if only for those who could afford it. Lee anticipated going home and then, on Monday, heading out to Tower Hamlets with something approaching trepidation. Why Tower Hamlets for the drop? But then, why not?

Some people reckoned that Baharat Huq was an anachronism. Mumtaz knew that her brother Ali believed that. He'd say, 'He's like some relic of the Raj, banging on about cricket and correct behaviour. Doesn't he understand that the world's changed?'

Mumtaz believed that he did, but he chose not to acknowledge it. At least not often. Occasionally, usually in response to some hate-filled piece of graffiti on Brick Lane, or if he saw youths hanging about on the street sneering at people who were not like them, he would let loose with a rant.

'Where does all this hatred of Jews come from and why?' he said as he put his spoon down on his empty dinner plate. Nobody had mentioned Jews and so the subject had come out of the blue. That was often the way with Baharat's outbursts.

'I think you'll find, Dad, that it's probably in response to the occupation of Palestine,' Ali said.

Baharat waved a hand. 'Ah, I know about that,' he said. 'But that is Israel. All the disgusting graffiti you see on every wall right down to Aldgate is about Jews – or homosexuals.'

'Israelis are Jews.'

'Yes, but they are not like Mr Stein,' Baharat said. Ronald Stein was one of his friends. Mr Stein, Baharat and a group of other men who had come to London from what had then been East Pakistan in the sixties met almost every day in a cafe three doors down from the Huq family home. They shared a passion for moaning.

'A lot of the young boys, particularly, feel alienated here,' Ali continued. 'They see the UK government doing nothing to curb Israel, they come across Islamophobia in their lives . . .'

'They should get jobs,' Baharat said.

'They have jobs.'

'What, the boys who hang about on street corners wearing shalwar khameez and talking about Hadith as if they know something? They have jobs?' He shook his head. 'Nah. They dream of Ferraris they will never have and about that silly American who married Russell Brand.'

Shazia mumbled, 'Katy Perry.'

Sunday lunch with her stepmother's family was an ordeal for Shazia. Mumtaz had no doubt that she loved the Huqs, who treated her like a blood relative, but Baharat and her mother, Sumita, could be very irritating.

'These mangoes are very ripe, so be careful,' Sumita said as she placed a huge platter covered in fruit on the table.

'I don't know what the bloody woman is called,' Baharat said. 'And it is beside the point. Either these boys should be studying or they should be married and working.'

'They do work,' Ali said. 'I told you.'

'Work at what?'

'That's the point, Abba. They work in curry houses and cash and carry. They can't get the kind of jobs that bring in real money and a sense of fulfilment.'

'Then they should have gone to college,' Baharat said. 'You did. You, your brother and your sister.'

'Yes, because you and Amma were always behind us,' Ali said. 'And you could speak English. Imagine how it must be to come from a family where only the kids speak the language, where the kids have to do everything for the parents and grandparents. What time is there for education when you have to go to the doctors with your mum, sort out council tax . . .'

'Then the parents should learn the language,' Baharat said. 'For their children's sake. I know of such families, of course I do! But this doesn't excuse hatred . . .'

'They see themselves, as Muslims, disadvantaged . . .'

'So what has that to do with Palestine? Eh?'

'Palestinians are members of the ummah. They're Muslims . . .'

'Not all of them,' Mumtaz said.

'Most of them. Abba, these kids see their fellow Muslims attacked all over the world and they want to do something about it, but they have no resources.'

'Nonsense! They might not have resources themselves but these mad grown-up men who hang about the streets and preach jihad to these children do. They also are uneducated. Jihad is the battle that takes place in the soul as it wrestles to follow the correct path.'

'It's also the armed, physical struggle against oppression, Dad. Do you think that Muslims should just lie down and take Zionist oppression in the West Bank and the Gaza Strip?'

'No. But writing "Jew pigs, Hitler was right" on the walls of the local school isn't going to help, is it? The old saying, two wrongs do not make a right—'

Ali threw his napkin down on the table and stood up. 'And us?' he said. 'We eat Bengali food at a table, sitting up like Europeans. Why? Why don't we sit on the floor? We used to.'

'We improved ourselves,' Baharat said. 'Sit down.'

'No! Improved ourselves? I can't believe you just said that! So if it's European, it has to be better?'

Sumita began, 'Ali, my son . . .'

'No, Amma! No.' He held up a hand. 'I can't listen to any more of this stupid Eurocentric nonsense. Muslim youth is in uproar, and quite right too. What is there for them? Eh? Where can Muslims feel pride? Look at Egypt! Muslims won in that country, but then there was a coup—'

'Because the Muslim Brotherhood were useless! Some people the world is better off without!' Baharat said. 'They killed. They burnt down churches and—'

'Oh Abba, that was just anti-Brotherhood bullshit.'

'Don't swear in front of your mother!'

He looked at Sumita. 'I apologise, Amma. Abba . . .'

'The Muslim countries don't help themselves,' Baharat said. 'Corruption and nepotism . . .'

'Because they're western puppets! Secular dictators . . .' He put a hand up to his head. Then he looked at Shazia. 'What do you think? You're young. What do you reckon to these boys who just want some respect?'

Mumtaz could see that Shazia was cringing. She said, 'Ali, let Shazia eat her lunch.'

'No!' he shouted. 'I want to know what she thinks! Well?'

Mumtaz already knew. But even she wasn't prepared for the answer the girl gave. 'What do I think? I think, Uncle, that such boys should stop calling out "whore" and "prostitute" to girls on the street. And I don't just mean uncovered girls like me, I mean decent, covered ladies like my amma.' Shazia looked at Mumtaz. 'They want women to stay in the house.'

'No, not . . .'

'They do! Men all over the world want that! Not just silly Muslim boys, this isn't a religious issue, it's about gender.' She looked at Mumtaz again. 'It's about men making victims of women. Men running women's lives through threats and violence!' She stood up. 'I'm sorry!'

She ran out of the room. Ali, still standing, didn't know what to do with himself.

Mumtaz said, 'You asked.'

'I didn't expect her to go all feminist on me,' he said. 'She looks so . . .'

'Empty-headed? Like a silly little fashionista?' Mumtaz stood. 'She's a bright girl and you'd do well to listen to her, brother.'

She'd also caught the message for her in Shazia's rant. By letting the Sheikhs blackmail her, Mumtaz was letting women down. She knew this, but, like the surly boys catcalling girls in the streets, the Sheikh family was a reality it was hard to do anything about. Mumtaz excused herself from the table and went to Shazia, who was crying in the living room, her eyes red and swollen. She sat down beside her.

'You know I'm really proud of you, don't you?' Mumtaz said. The girl looked up. 'You're a better woman than I've ever been.'

'Oh, Amma!' Shazia wound her thin arms around Mumtaz's neck and kissed her. 'Please, please, please do something about those vile men! Please!'

But Mumtaz said nothing. She just smoothed the girl's hair and kissed her. What could she do?

4

The door was so nondescript it was easily missed. Caked in filth, no one had even managed to tag it with graffiti. Just within the stretch of Brick Lane known as 'Bangla Town', it was on the left, before the Truman's Brewery bridge, where the Bangladeshi community and the young artists' territories divided. Lee, sitting in a small Bangladeshi cafe opposite, watched Paul Venus drop seven large envelopes through the letterbox. He'd never seen a hundred grand posted before. It was very ordinary.

Venus had put the street number and the name 'Mr B. Shaw' on the packages, as instructed. Also as instructed, he had left quickly without looking behind him.

Lee didn't expect anyone to appear at the door for some time, maybe not even that morning. He'd looked at the building on Google Earth when he'd got home the previous evening. Just as Venus had told him, it didn't have an obvious back exit. But whether it could be accessed via one or both of the buildings on either side he couldn't tell. On the left, a house was boarded up, while on the right stood a small electrical shop. Lee sipped his coffee, which was milky and quite tasteless, and watched. For good measure, and without Venus's knowledge, he'd put one of his casual operatives, another ex-copper, at the back of the building, just in case anyone slipped in or out. Amy didn't know what the case was about and she didn't care, as long as she was paid. Concealing as much of this as he could from Mumtaz wasn't going to be easy unless the case resolved itself quickly. Luckily, she had wall-to-wall appointments with potential new clients all day. But the Brick Lane area was her manor. Her parents lived on Hanbury Street and Lee knew that her father, Baharat, was often out and about. Running into him would be awkward.

He ordered another drink, tea this time, and half-read a copy of the *Guardian*. It wasn't his usual reading material, but he'd found it on the table and picked it up. The headline concerned a group of Islamic militants called ISIS who had just sprung 500 of their men from Abu Ghraib prison in Iraq. These men, loosely allied to Al Qaeda, had already conquered part of Syria. Lee looked around at the people in the cafe, who were all Asian, and wondered what they thought about ISIS. Apparently the group liked to be seen beheading people.

He looked at the door. He'd spent some time looking up B. Shaw, which was obviously not the real name of the person in receipt of Venus's cash. That could be anyone. However B. Shaw had almost certainly not been chosen at random. People rarely, even if they didn't realise it, chose names or numbers without reference to some sort of personal meaning. The obvious connection was the Irish playwright and socialist George Bernard Shaw. Were the kidnappers radical lefties? Even without the 'George', was it too obvious? Did it have anything to do with the London

School of Economics, which Shaw had helped to found? A student prank maybe?

Except that students didn't do pranks any more. Now that all the kids were plugged into their iPads, they barely interacted. He thought about his daughter. Jody was always staring at her phone, swiping it, pressing it, spellbound by the magic it could do. He had no doubt that in a straight contest between her phone and her dad, the phone would win. He looked back at the newspaper. But then when kids came off their phones, was this inevitable? A lot of the ISIS fighters looked as if they were little more than kids. It was said that some of them had gone over from European countries, including the UK. Fired up by a passion to die for Islam, the press said. But Lee wondered if it was also about the excitement.

When he'd been a teenager, mobile phones had been bricks carried by yuppies and computer games were played by kids. Almost as full of testosterone as of hatred for his pissed-up father, Lee had left home and joined the army. While he was in the UK he'd had a great laugh getting rid of his aggression in the gym, out in the park or down the pub. Then they'd sent him to Iraq, and all that had changed. Lee wondered what the kids who joined ISIS really thought once they got out there. Did they cry behind rocks for their mothers as bombs went off? He had.

It was a stupid fucking job. Fetching and carrying for Mr Bhatti. Pratting around Brick Lane like a prick. Imran knew he was worth more than just being Mr Bhatti's peon. He had an NVQ 2 in Social Care. He could look after mentals and kids.

'There's a lot of deliveries today,' Mr Bhatti said, while fiddling about with an old plug. He called his business an 'electrical shop', but he didn't sell computers or phones or anything cool. Just old bits of wire and plugs.

Imran walked up the stairs at the back of the shop and then through the hatch into the building next door. From the top of the stairs he could see that there was a lot of post, including some massive parcels. He sighed. He'd only brought a couple of plastic bags with him. He walked down and began picking it all up. No one lived in the flat, which was knackered even by the worst Brick Lane standards, but the address served its owner, Mr Bhatti, well. Dodgy people paid a lot of money for a secure address that couldn't be traced back to them.

So here was a letter to Mr Qazi's Haj and Umrah Tours, which took lots of very pious and sincere pilgrims to Mecca and then dumped them in overpriced doss houses full of fleas. The letter was probably a complaint; they usually were. Something for Mrs Korai, not to be seen by her husband, from her son who'd run away with a Polish girl, a raft of perfumed love notes and the usual weird little envelopes addressed to that artist who lived in a damp basement and spoke like he'd been to public school. Then there were the seven very large envelopes. These were a first. Addressed to B. Shaw, they weighed a bit, and when Imran retraced his steps back into Mr Bhatti's shop, he only just managed to stop them falling out onto the floor.

'What the—?' Mr Bhatti ran over and hustled him to the back of the shop. He told his son, cross-eyed Jabbar, to 'watch the shop!'

He took some of the packages from Imran and pushed a load of light switches off a table and into a box. 'Put them down!'

Imran let them fall onto the table.

'What are they?'

'I don't know! Why would I? Are those the only bags you brought?'

'Yeah.'

He clicked his tongue. 'Ach! I'll have to give you a rucksack. You can't take these in Asda bags.'

'Didn't know I'd have to take stuff this size.'

He never had before.

'This Mr Shaw job is very important,' Mr Bhatti said. 'They paid a lot of money to use the address.'

'Who?'

'Mr Shaw.'

Imran picked up an envelope. 'What's in them?'

'Not our business.' He took the parcel from him. 'Now listen, you must deliver these to an address in Navarre Street.'

'Where's that?'

'Up bloody Bethnal Green. Arnold Circus.'

Imran looked blank.

Mr Bhatti shook his head. 'Go up the top of Brick Lane and turn left, then right onto Club Row. You'll find it.'

He pulled a battered canvas rucksack out from underneath shelves loaded with screws, fuses and switches. 'The rest of the letters are regulars?'

'Yeah.'

There was a list. He kept it in his wallet.

'Mr Shaw are new customers . . .'

'How can Mr Shaw be more than one person? I don't know who or what Mr Shaw is. Neither do you. How am I to know? It's money, most of which I pass on to you.'

That was a lie and they both knew it.

'You go to Navarre Street, to a shop called Veg. I don't know what it is. Some hippy-dippy thing, it sounds like. You ask for Danish.'

'Then what?'

'You give the envelopes to him. Then you go,' Mr Bhatti said.

'What about payment?'

Some of the regulars, particularly Mr Qazi, gave Imran cash in an envelope. Others had some other sort of arrangement.

Mr Bhatti filled the bag. 'Don't worry about that. Just take this to Navarre Street. Veg. Danish. OK?'

'Yeah.'

'Then you can do your other deliveries.'

Imran picked up the bag. It was heavy and made him wish he had a car. Amir, his brother, had one, but then he had a lot of things Imran didn't. Like a girlfriend, a leather jacket and money. Their mother cried over him all the time, worrying about what he did and where he went. Whatever it was, it let him buy a Mitsubishi Evo, which was one of those cars that went very fast and made a lot of noise.

When he left the shop, Imran went north along Brick Lane and into the area where most of the hipsters lived. A bloke with a beard dyed blue looked at him. Maybe he wanted to take his 'look'. They all wanted to keep on finding new 'looks', those people. But what was to want about being a fat kid in shalwar khameez? Imran certainly didn't like it, even if it did make his mother happy.

'We all want to know who we are, don't we?'

'Of course.'

Mumtaz sipped her tea. When she had multiple appointments like this, she tended to get bombarded. This client, Alison, was no exception.

'I've always known I was adopted,' she said. 'Mum and Dad were open about that. What none of us knew is who my birth parents were.'

'Which is . . .'

'So far, so normal, yes,' Alison said. 'Trouble is, there was no way any of us could know, because I was found in a phone box in Chiswick. Newborn and naked. A nun found me and took me to her convent.'

'The authorities would have tried to find your mother, surely?' Mumtaz said.

'Yes. I've got press cuttings I can let you have. They tried. But nobody came forward. After the convent, I spent some time in a children's home in Essex until Mum and Dad adopted me.'

'Have you always wanted to try and find your mother?' Mumtaz asked.

Alison shrugged. She was a dark-haired, slightly plump woman in her early forties. She sat awkwardly on her leather sofa. 'Not until this turned up,' she said.

'Your illness.'

'I just started to jerk. I'd be making a cup of tea, like I just did for you, and suddenly the cup'd fly out of my hand. I went to the doctor and was tested for everything – MS, motor neurone disease, cancer . . . Then, eventually, they found Huntington's.'

Mumtaz knew of it. Mainly afflicting white Europeans, Huntington's affected movement, cognition, and eventually presaged a form of dementia. It was inherited and fatal.

'I could have a year, five years, ten,' Alison said. 'And because it's inherited I may have got it from my mum or my dad who could both be dead. But I have to try. I've a son who's only six-teen and I've a limited amount of time to spend with him. The only bright point in all of this is that Charlie, my son, is negative for the disease.'

'Are you married, Alison?'

'I was,' she said. 'Christopher. Very good to us financially – but then he works in banking so he bloody well should be – pretty useless as a husband and father. Likes a young girl or three, does Chris. Legacy of his youth as a dashing officer in the RAF. Twat.'

Often when people saw her headscarf, they behaved as if Mumtaz had to be protected from subjects like sex. It was a response she hated. Alison was refreshingly straightforward.

'I'd like my son to know who he is,' she said. 'I've spent a lot of time in Chiswick lately, looking around the area, but I haven't talked to the nuns at the convent. I don't seem to be able to do that. Probably to do with the fact I'm knackered all the time. The nun who found me, Mother Emerita, died back in the nineties. I've even put ads in local papers.'

'No luck?'

'Nothing. I was "baby unknown" when I was found and I remain "baby unknown" to this day. All I do know, because I had a DNA test last year, is that I'm of white northern European and Mediterranean heritage. Oddly though, there's also a Native American component. Isn't that a turn-up, eh?'

Mumtaz said nothing. Sitting in Alison's large, neat garden they could have been in the Cotswolds. That was weird. In fact, they were less than five minutes from Wanstead tube station. Probably via her banker husband, the 'baby unknown' from Chiswick had come into some serious money.

'If I were well I'd do all this myself,' Alison said. 'But I'm not, and you were recommended by one of my neighbours.'

Mumtaz smiled. A Sikh woman, if she remembered correctly, with a wayward husband.

'Even now I don't know much,' Alison said. 'I know where the phone box is, I can give you the address of the convent where I spent my first few days, and the police of course, but I think this is down to legwork. One thing the nuns at the orphanage in Essex where I eventually ended up did tell me about Mother Emerita is that she always said that people were looking at her when she found me.'

'What people?'

'In one of the houses on the street. Locals were questioned at the time and claimed to have seen nothing, but I wonder.'

'You know that it's actually more likely that your mother wasn't local,' Mumtaz said. 'If you think about it—'

'Oh yes, she wouldn't have wanted to dump me on her doorstep,

I accept that. But I wonder if anyone in the street recognised her.'

'If they did then why didn't they say something?'

'I don't know.' She shook her head. 'But if there is anything I can find out about my parents, I want to know while I still can. I'll pay you whatever rate you ask and if nothing comes of it, nothing comes of it. That will be no reflection on you, Mrs Hakim. I just have to try You understand that?'

'Of course,' Mumtaz said. 'I will take your case and do what I can.'

Unlike all the other work she'd been offered, this was not a matrimonial case that could probably be wrapped up in a couple of days. And it interested her.

DI Kevin Thorpe was a legend. An expert on East End gang culture, as a kid he'd sat on Reggie Kray's knee. As an adult he knew every gang, however big or small, in his manor of Tower Hamlets.

'Bloody hell,' he said when he saw Lee Arnold sitting in the grimy window of the Chittagong Cafe. 'What brings you—?'

'Just having a cuppa,' Lee said.

Everyone in Tower Hamlets knew Kev, and the bloke behind the counter was no exception.

'DI Thorpe, you want cappuccino? Latte?'

'Just a normal coffee, Riz, mate.' He sat down opposite Lee. 'So . . .'

It wasn't like Kev not to twig that he was working, but then he was getting on. Maybe he'd even forgotten that Lee was a PI? Lee leaned in towards him. The young Asian bloke who had walked into the electrical shop next to the drop site was standing on the doorstep, apparently looking at electrical components. 'Kev, I'm not being funny but . . .'

He smiled. A grin of recognition – finally. Kev moved to another table and picked up a newspaper. Lee photographed the boy. He'd gone in with some plastic bags and come out carrying a rucksack. It probably meant nothing. The boy turned right up Brick Lane.

His phone rang. 'Yeah.'

'I'm being stared at by a bloke I think may have designs on my body,' Amy said. 'He's also wondering what I'm doing.'

Even in the busiest parts of London, the yards and lanes behind shops were often creepy and unsafe.

'Move off for a bit,' Lee said. He ended the call. Like Lee, Amy was ex-job. If the geezer tried it on with her, she could look after herself.

No one went near the drop site. Bangladeshi men came and went from the electrical shop next door, but that was to be expected. Maybe the shop had some sort of connection to the door. But what? The proprietor of the electrical shop didn't own it. According to Venus, who'd contacted Tower Hamlets council as soon as he knew the address of the drop, it was listed to an owner who was resident in Bangladesh. It was empty and unin-habited. Except that now it contained a hundred grand.

Lee finished his drink and went outside. Aware of the owner's eyes on him as he left, he cursed Kev Thorpe for queering his pitch. He stood underneath the bridge slung over the street from one side of the old Truman's Brewery to the other and watched the scarred doorway. Someone had to come to it some time.

'Old Mr Bhatti cheating on his missus?' Kev Thorpe appeared beside him and smiled. 'I told Riz in the Chittagong that I arrested you for car clocking, back in the eighties,' he said. 'What's so fascinating about Mr Bhatti's electrical shop? Or are you scoping out the flat next door?'

Lee said nothing.

'Ah, I see,' Kev said. 'I suppose these days if you told old plod anything, you'd have to kill old plod, wouldn't you? Well, far as we know, Mr Bhatti's only vice is mucky videos from Holland. Old school, women and Alsatians. Place next door is a postal address. We think. We know the postman puts letters through but we don't know who collects them. I've never seen anyone go in or out and, more to the point, neither's my mum.'

Lee looked at him for the first time.

'She lives in Hanbury Street,' he said. Where Amy had been watching the back of the address. Where Mumtaz's parents lived. 'She can remember when a load of Irish lived there, she's so bloody old. Now, according to mum legend, the "Pakis" use it to arrange romantic assignations. But then she is a racist with dementia.'

He began to walk away. 'Nice to see ya.'

Lee's phone rang. It was Venus. 'Anything?'

'Nothing so far.'

Except that, possibly, there could be an Asian connection . . .

*

57

Veg didn't look like a shop. Not a proper one. There was lots of wood everywhere and for some reason, hay lay on the floor and ordinary things like apples and tomatoes were nestled in tissue paper. There were no prices on anything. A young woman in a wet dream-inducing mini-kilt came towards him and said, 'Hi.'

Imran knew his face was red from all the walking and his embarrassment. 'I've come to see Danish,' he said.

'Oh. Danish? Oh, *Dan*,' she smiled. 'Are you a mate?' She didn't wait for an answer, which was lucky because Imran didn't have one. 'Dan!'

He wasn't like anyone Imran knew. Asian, but with blond hair, wearing jeans so tight you could see his balls. 'Oh, hi.'

He was ever so posh. 'Can I help you?'

Imran looked down at his own shoes. They were broken at the sides where his feet spilled out. 'I've got something for you,' he said. 'Parcels. For Mr Shaw.'

'Oh. Cool.'

Imran began to open up the rucksack, but Danish stopped him. 'Let's go through to the back,' he said. He called over to the girl, 'Can you manage for a moment, Clarrie?'

'Sure.'

Imran followed Danish through a doorway into a small storage room almost completely filled with boxes. It smelt sweet and earthy.

'This is for Mr Shaw, right?'

'Yeah.'

'Get them out then.'

He leaned against a stack of boxes, all his earlier bonhomie gone now that Imran was unloading the parcels onto the floor. As soon as they were all out he counted them. Then he said, 'Turn your back.'

'What?'

'Turn your back while I make sure they're genuine,' Danish said. 'Do you want to get paid or what?'

Imran did as he was told. He heard paper and plastic rip and then a short grunt.

'It's cool.'

When he turned back the parcels were gone. Danish reached into one of the boxes behind him and took out an envelope. 'Give this to your employer from Mr Shaw,' he said. 'A little bonus. With thanks.'

Imran took the envelope. He was used to this from his regulars. Bit odd that the posh did things this way though.

'And no opening it,' Danish said. 'Give it to your boss, sealed.'

'Yeah.'

Then he smiled again. 'Because if you don't, Mr Shaw will cut your fingers off,' he said. 'Fat boy.'

5

Tina couldn't stop crying. Why didn't Paul ring? It was five in the afternoon and not a word from either him or Lee Arnold. Nothing. What had happened and where was her son? Was Paul withholding information just to punish her? She knew he blamed her for Harry's kidnap. He hadn't said so in as many words, but he had told her that if she'd been more willing to drive the boy around it would never have happened. She'd countered by saying that Harry liked cycling, which he did.

Paul had answered, 'Cycling's not a proper sport.' Implying, as usual, that Harry was in some way effeminate. He had a thing about Harry possibly being gay. They'd argued about it and she'd called him a homophobe. Paul had responded by telling her about all the diversity courses he'd been on. Knob. What did it matter what Harry did in bed, if anything? He was sixteen, he was her son and she loved him.

She wanted to be held, but that wasn't possible. Nobody could know about Harry, and that included Cyd.

*

'When did they call you?'

'Just now. I've just got off the phone.'

Lee Arnold stamped his cigarette end out on the pavement. 'So what's the deal?'

'They want a quarter of a million this time,' Venus said. 'Otherwise same thing. Money or Harry dies.'

Why hadn't they asked for more money in the first place? Lee had wondered why the amount was so small. He walked past the drop site and ignored a man who tried to tempt him into a shabby-looking restaurant. 'We need to talk,' he said.

'I can get the money,' Venus said.

'I've no doubt you can, but that's not the point. Either these people have been bucked up by getting their hands on the hundred grand – not that I've seen anyone come and take it – or they're playing a game with you. I want to rule out the latter if I can.'

'How?'

He sighed. Venus was obviously panicking, but he was still a copper. 'By questioning the only people involved in this that I can identify,' Lee said. 'You and your missus.'

'But . . .'

'You both have to tell me everything. Or one of you does.'

There was a pause. Lee imagined him on the other end of the phone, sweating. He knew what he meant. Every dirty little secret he and Tina had ever had.

'There's nothing to tell.'

Lee passed the mosque and saw a throng of men talking outside.

61

'Yes there is,' Lee said.

'These people are not blackmailing me, except by holding my son.'

'I want to know anyway,' Lee said.

'Why?'

'You are not thinking straight,' Lee said. 'You know why. Get your copper's head on, for fuck's sake. They want a quarter of a mil now. What will they want once they've got that? I don't give a shit whether you're lying to me or not about what they do and don't know about you and your missus, but I have to know all your nasty little secrets if you want me to try and work out who they might be. Because at the moment, I know jack shit, and for someone to play with you like this they have to hate you. This is more than greed – in my professional opinion.'

Again there was a silence and then Venus said, 'Do you know the Princess Louise in Holborn?'

'Of course I do, I'm a recovering alcoholic. There's no boozer in London I don't know.'

'Not a modest man are you, Mr Arnold? Meet me there in an hour.'

'See you there.'

He ended the call, put his phone in his pocket and made his way towards Liverpool Street Station. He looked back just once at the drop site, but no one was there.

Shazia sat down beside her, but Mumtaz didn't look up from her computer. In 1971, the year Alison Darrah-Duncan had been born, there had been a telephone box outside a Turnham Green pub called the Tabard. This was where baby Alison had been found early in the morning on the fourth of September, by Mother Emerita from the local Convent of the Sisters of Mary Immaculate of Siena in Chiswick Lane. In those days it had been a hostel . . .

'Amma.'

She looked up. 'Shazia.'

Her eyes were wet with tears.

'What is it?'

The girl put her head down. 'I've been tough on you lately, about the Sheikhs,' she said. 'And I'm sorry.'

Mumtaz didn't say anything. What was there to say? They'd both been through pain because of the Sheikhs.

'When Uncle Ali was talking at dinner on Sunday I realised what we're up against,' Shazia said. 'I remembered the woman in the chemist.'

'In Spitalfields?'

'Yes. Do you remember, she was a Muslim but her boss was a Hindu? She didn't cover, but a gang of boys told her boss that if he didn't make her, they'd trash his business. He told her he'd support her whatever, but she felt so bad for him that she left her job.'

Mumtaz did remember. It had made her furious. She nodded.

'It suddenly got me that even if Lee or the police did support us, the Sheikhs wouldn't leave us alone because they're bullies who claim they have religion behind them. They don't, but they can fool themselves that they do. They can fool themselves into anything. That Naz says the word "slut" under his breath when he sees me, but even you get called a slut, and you cover. I bet he has sex with girls he picks up in clubs. I bet he thinks he's a good Muslim because he doesn't drink. If he actually doesn't. These men are just like Abba, and look what he did to us.'

What she was saying was true, but Mumtaz was disturbed by Shazia's pessimism. It took her back to the time when Ahmet had still been alive, when Shazia had been an unhappy, wounded child with no hope. Until Naz Sheikh had killed her father. Would she really fall apart if she knew about that? Would she hate Mumtaz for letting Ahmet die?

Mumtaz put an arm around the girl's shoulders. 'Shazia,' she said, 'when you go to university all this will end.'

'For me. But what about you? What will you do, Amma?'

'What I can.' She shrugged. 'Maybe go back to my parents.'

'With nothing?'

'When I have nothing, the Sheikhs will get bored. They are a powerful crime family with many business interests. The only reason they pursue us is because your father tried to cheat them. They do it to look hard and frightening.'

'Amma, you have almost nothing now.'

'Yes, but . . .' She couldn't tell her that the main 'thing' she had was Shazia herself. 'They're not bored with me yet,' she said. 'We will get through this, Shazia, I promise.'

Shazia hugged her. It was the first time Mumtaz had felt affection from her stepdaughter in months. She closed her eyes.

'When I become a lawyer I'm going to show the world what it means to be a strong, independent Muslim woman,' Shazia said. 'Islam isn't just for men. That's where *they're* wrong. Everything these men do who put women down is wrong. And I'm afraid that I don't agree with Uncle Ali about how all the boys are bored and don't have opportunities.'

'Some don't.'

'Some, but not all, and that's still not an excuse to call girls bad names.'

'No.'

'Amma, we have to live with the Sheikhs in our lives, so I want you to tell me everything from now on,' Shazia said.

Mumtaz frowned. What did she mean?

'Like, if we need some more money or something,' Shazia said. 'I can get a job and—'

'Not if it interferes with your studies you won't!'

'Oh, Amma, loads of people at college do bits of work. It's okay.' And then she laughed. 'Honestly, you know some of my friends think I'm a right spoilt princess because I don't work. And it's the holidays now, I'll be bored out of my mind by September. I want to work.'

Mumtaz kissed her cheek. 'We'll see,' she said. 'But I do appreciate what you've said, Shazia. Really. And yes, we will talk in the future.'

Just not about quite everything.

Shazia left to go and get online. Nearly all her friends were either working or away for the summer in places like Bangladesh, Pakistan or India with their families. The only way she could stay in touch was via the internet.

A happier Mumtaz went back to her computer and Chiswick in the seventies. She hadn't realised that the convent where

Alison had been taken as a baby had been a hostel exclusively for young girls.

The Princess Louise in Holborn wouldn't have been Lee Arnold's first choice for a quiet chat. On weekday evenings it was full to bursting with business types talking about things like 'hedge funds' and 'futures', whatever they were. But then maybe Venus knew some-thing he didn't, because one of the small snug bars arranged around the ornate Victorian interior was all but empty. Just a couple of old theatrical types – a man and a woman – talking about musicals.

Venus already had the Diet Pepsi lined up when Lee arrived. He was on the whisky and was what Lee would have described as 'mildly plastered' already. Lee sat down.

'Do you know when and where the drop will be this time?' he asked.

'Not yet. They'll let me know.' He downed one shot of whisky and began sipping a second. 'Mobile number was dead when I called back.'

'Nicked.'

He shrugged.

'Mr Venus, do you have a quarter of a million quid in the bank?'

'No.' He finished his second whisky. 'Equity in the flat. Tina's got it in cash, but it's all she's got. I asked her.'

'Are you certain you don't know anyone called Mr Shaw?'

'Positive.'

'Old lags from your past?'

'No!'

The male theatrical laughed and said, 'Never even heard of Judy Garland!'

The female screamed. 'Oh, no!'

Venus reached for his wallet to go and get another drink, but Lee shook his head. 'No more booze until you come clean,' he said. 'I know that all you want is to get Harry back, but I think it's possible you're being played, Mr Venus. There was no need to demand such a small amount of money and then go in for a larger one unless they were either just testing the water or there was an element of psychological torture going on here. Because every minute these people have your son, they are in danger of discovery, whether the police are involved or not. A neighbour could see your boy through a window and wonder who he is, a passer-by – anything. Think about it.'

Venus looked down at the floor.

'Are you buying anything else, apart from Harry, with your quarter of a mil, Mr Venus? Like silence?'

'No.' He looked up. 'I know that DI Collins thinks I'm up to all sorts, but that is just her fantasy,' he said. 'She doesn't like me for the same reason she doesn't like anyone who came into the police via graduate entry. She's an inverted snob. Ditto her DS, Bracci. Dinosaurs, both of them. I am "in" with no one in the crime world, Mr Arnold.'

'And women?'

'Women are my business,' he said. 'Contrary, again, to rumour and supposition, I do not have affairs with my female officers. If I am occasionally caught looking appreciatively at a young PC then all I can do is own up. I am only human.'

'What about your wife? She told me she used to work in a club in the seventies. What sort of club?'

'Oh, she sang a bit,' he said. 'Nothing sleazy. Tina did a few topless shots for magazines, but that was long before I met her. And if you think we'd risk Harry's life for those antiques . . .'

'You're sure? I mean actresses can have a bit of a rep . . .'

'Not Tina, for all her bloody faults. Now I'm going to get a drink.'

He got up and walked over to the bar. Lee drank his Pepsi. Venus had a point. Maybe he had been influenced by Vi and Tony when it came to his opinions and beliefs about the superintendent? But this stringing out of the ransom did seem like a game. A simple opportunist would have asked for a hundred grand, given the boy back and then buggered off before he got caught. Greed could come into it, and yet Lee still felt that an amateur wouldn't take the risk. A true pro, with access to expertise and truly safe 'safe' houses, would have asked for a million – which Venus and his wife could raise by selling property – right from the start. He couldn't help feeling that this was someone who had an agenda. But what was it about? And where, if anywhere, did Brick Lane Asians come into the mix? Because the drop had been on their manor, and if Kev Thorpe's old cockney racist mum was to be believed, Asians used that address to communicate illicitly. When Venus came back, he told him.

'So make contact with the locals.'

'Just march up to one and ask him?' Lee shook his head. 'I'm not local, Mr Venus, and so I'm automatically suspicious. Why would a white bloke want to know about a dodgy Asian mailing address? I wouldn't. But I could ask my assistant, Mrs Hakim, to check it out.'

'You mustn't tell her why.'

'I won't. But her family live off Brick Lane, so they might know.'

Venus downed his whisky. He was getting arse'oled. 'OK. But remember . . .'

'I won't say a word. I've more respect for Harry's life,' Lee said.

Some businessmen came in to the bar, laughing. The after-work drinking sessions were starting in earnest now. One ordered a 'bottle of your best Pinot, barman!' Knob. Lee desperately wanted the comfort of his flat, Chronus, tea and a fag. Knowing he had to get home by tube and then the overground didn't fill him with joy.

'I'll get online and see what else I can dig up about the drop site and that part of Brick Lane,' he said. 'I suggest you get a taxi home and have some kip.'

'Sleep?' he shook his head. 'How do I do that?'

His voice had risen and people were starting to look. Lee stood and pulled Venus up with him.

'What . . . ?'

'Time to go home, Paul,' he said. 'I'm sure you've got a load more booze at your flat, but now it's taxi time.'

Venus resisted a little, but not vocally, and once Lee had managed to ease him through the crowds that now choked the Princess Louise, he hailed a cab and sat him in it.

The cabbie, a little bit dubious about the drunk in the back of his motor, said, 'Where to?'

'Islington,' Lee Arnold said. 'Highbury Place.'

It was amazing what unintentionally revealing photographs people took of their homes and put on their Facebook pages, even superintendents of police. Lee called up Tina Wilton's number on his phone.

'I can see you on Wednesday. Do you know where we are?'

Mumtaz looked at the convent's website.

'Chiswick Lane.'

'Turnham Green is our nearest station. Turn left when you arrive and walk down Turnham Green Terrace, then turn left again onto Chiswick High Road. Chiswick Lane is two hundred metres or so on the opposite side of the road. We are at the top on the right.'

The nun, Mother Katerina, had a slight accent, which given the name of the order, the Sisters of Mary Immaculate of Siena, Mumtaz assumed was Italian. She sounded young and business-like and said that she was happy to tell Mumtaz everything she knew about the late Mother Emerita and baby Alison.

'Thank you. I'll see you then.'

When she'd finished the call, Mumtaz put the phone down beside her on the sofa and looked back at her computer. The Siena Sisters building had opened as a girls' hostel in 1951. As far as she could tell, any girl could go there provided she could pay, but the place was favoured by Italian girls resident in the UK as students.

Her phone rang. She looked at the screen. Not Naz, but Lee. She picked it up. 'Hi.'

'Wotcha. Not interrupting *Londoners* am I?'

He knew she didn't watch any soaps.

'I'd rather have flu,' she said. 'Are you OK?'

He didn't usually phone her in the evening unless it was something important.

'Fine. Just wondering if you've got time to get me a bit of intel on an address on Brick Lane,' he said.

'If I can. What is it?'

'It's next to an electrical shop run by a Mr Bhatti. Near the old Brewery on the right going up Brick Lane.'

'Mmm. Aren't there some empty properties there?'

'Yeah. It's one of them,' he said.

'What do you want to know about it?'

'There's whispers it might be used as a contact address, possibly for Asian ladies and men who don't want the world to know they're communicating.'

'Ah.'

She'd heard of such things. In spite of the internet, illicit lovers still made assignations by letter, in the old-fashioned way. It was far more secure than computer or a mobile phone, which a suspicious husband could investigate. Letters could be burnt.

'I know such things happen, but haven't heard that address mentioned,' she said. 'Do you want me to try and find out?'

'Discreetly.'

'Of course. Why do you want to know?'

'Can't tell you.'

This wasn't the first time she'd been locked out. 'OK.'

'But I need anything you can get yesterday,' he told her.

'Then something bad is afoot.'

'Something that can't wait.'

'I'll give it my best shot,' she said. Then she added, 'Oh, how was your weekend away?'

'Very nice.' His tone forcedly casual. 'Out in the countryside, bit of fresh air. Can't beat it.'

'Good.'

She put the phone down. Lee hated the countryside. Why was he lying? Had he, as Shazia had reckoned, been off with a woman somewhere? Not that it was any of her business.

She had to decide whom to talk to about that address on Brick Lane. Her mother wouldn't know about anything so gossipy and trivial, and even if she did she would never own up to it. Her father might well know, but the thought of talking to him about it made Mumtaz cringe with embarrassment.

Why did Lee want to know? Was he planning to use the address to contact some woman?

No.

Could she ask her brothers? They both worked on the Lane, but Arif did his best to live his life as far away from home as possible. He had a western girlfriend and spent most of his time in Clapham with her. Ali was involved in the Lane and talked to everyone, but he had become more judgemental and austere in his religious practice in the last year, which made him hard to talk to. If he didn't know about the 'secret' address and she told him, he was likely to tell community leaders and get people into trouble. Mumtaz hated to think what the hostile street boys who called girls 'sluts' would say and do, about something like that. She frowned, wondering whether she was going to be able to help Lee this time.

And then she remembered Rajiv.

6

'Getting my son back has got nothing to do with Cyd!' Tina said.

She could tell that her husband was either very tired or hungover.

'So he's *your* son?'

'Oh, fuck you!' she snapped. 'Arnold phoned asking questions about any little secrets I might have, so I thought of Cyd.'

'He asked me the same questions last night.'

'Oh did he? Why didn't you warn me?'

'Because I told him we have nothing to hide. Which we don't.'

'Oh really? Were you in the pub when you told him?'

'I . . .'

'So I told him about Cyd. What did you tell him?'

'Nothing.'

'I can hear the booze in your voice, Paul. Do the keep-fit bollocks for everyone else, you've got a drink problem, that's one little secret you could've told him. Then there are your other . . . We've both had help up the ladder, haven't we?'

'In the past you and I have benefited from our connections,' he said. 'But it's over. Irrelevant. I told you, Tina, that I checked that out before I did anything. Whoever has taken Harry is completely unknown to anyone you and I have contact with.'

'Then let's just pay them, get him back and move on,' she said.

'Without knowing who they are? No.'

'Why not? I've got the money.'

'And if they ask for more?'

'Then we give it to them. Just fucking give it to them.' Tina took what she hoped was a calming breath. 'Paul, I just want him back. I want Harry back and I want to see Cyd and I want you to tell me the truth about what the kidnappers said to you.'

'What do you mean?'

'I mean,' she said, 'Lee Arnold, I get the impression, thinks that these kidnappers may also be blackmailing us. I know they're not blackmailing me. But what about you?'

'No!'

'I know you still mix with . . . people you shouldn't. Paul, be honest with me!'

'I am,' he said. 'I don't.'

What could she say? She knew Paul. Once something was said he would never contradict himself. Never.

'OK,' she said. 'Just remember that Harry's the important person here. Not you or me or your career – or your reputation.'

'I have to go to work,' he said. 'I imagine you do too.'

'Late,' she said. 'We're night shooting. I'll stay over in London tonight.'

'At . . . ?'

'Call me on the mobile if anything happens.'

She put the phone down and the tear dam burst. When she

cried she gave in to it totally. Harry was a sneaky little shit. Over-privileged and manipulative. But she knew she'd do anything to get him back.

There had been a time when Rajiv could be seen on Brick Lane in his full glory, in one of his late mother's saris, make-up courtesy of Boots at Liverpool Street. But people had complained. Not to Rajiv, but to his boys, Amaal and Farooq.

'They say that you should be stoned.'

'Who does?' Rajiv had asked.

Amaal had looked away. 'People.'

Rajiv knew who. He knew everyone on Brick Lane, and their secrets.

'Well maybe I should be. Stoned,' he'd said. 'It's years since I smoked dope. Why I gave it up . . .' He'd shrugged.

He'd started dressing in male clothes many years before. But the make-up had stayed, and that was what a gang of boys who called themselves the Brik Boyz had objected to. After forty years on the Lane, five beatings from shaven-headed white-power twats, the shop trashed by a disgruntled customer in 1989, and the nail bomb attack by a man called Copeland, a neo-Nazi homophobe, ten years later, it seemed as if it was going to be a group of kids in shalwar khameez who were finally going to put him out of business. Mainly because the fuckers would not go away.

The police had been called again and again. When one of the Boyz had spat in Farooq's face, Rajiv had almost taken matters into his own hands. But the police had come, eventually. They'd seen the gang, asked them to move along and then told Rajiv there was nothing else they could do.

'So I just have to put up with having my salesmen spat at? My shop plastered with homophobic graffiti?' he'd said, but got no answer. And when Mumtaz Hakim walked into the Leather Bungalow early that Tuesday morning, Rajiv was, as usual, marvelling at the fact that his two boys had yet again turned up for work.

'Miss Huq!'

Rajiv always used her maiden name. He'd known her since she was a child.

'Rajiv, how are you?'

The smart young salesmen that he called his boys looked at her from behind rails of leather jackets, skirts, trousers and some very risqué suede dresses.

Rajiv stood, ran over and kissed her on both cheeks. Her father had always said that he looked like an actor from the seventies who had been called Peter Wyngarde. 'He was also inclined to men,' he'd said.

'I'm fine, but you're looking even more beautiful than the last time I saw you,' he said. 'Now you must take tea. Farooq!'

The boy walked through the shop and out into the small lean-to kitchen behind the cupboard that passed for Rajiv's office.

He took her arm. 'Amaal, mind the shop.'

'Yes, Rajiv-ji.'

'I haven't seen you for ages, Mumtaz Huq. You must come into my office and tell me *everything*.' Rajiv took Mumtaz's arm.

'Most of all you must tell me what foundation you use. Your skin looks *flawless*.'

The woman, or rather the girl, sitting outside Venus's office was bottle-blonde, fake-tanned and had tits the size of a bulldog's head.

'If she got any cheaper she'd be in one of them bargain bins at Farm Fresh Foods,' Vi Collins said.

She didn't usually peer at her superior's guests from behind her computer screen, but this one was special.

DS Tony Bracci, sitting beside her said, 'She's gotta be from Essex.'

'You know I've always wondered whether Venus has got a thing about sleeping with the lower orders,' Vi said.

'We don't know he's sleeping with her, Guv. We don't know he's sleeping with anyone.'

Vi cut him off with a stare. 'Grow up, Tone.'

Detective Inspector Violet Collins had been a copper all her working life, which was a long time. Now in her fifties, the divorced mother of two grown-up sons had seen a lot of changes in her thirty-five years on the force. One of them had been the fast-track system for graduates, which had enlisted people like Paul Venus.

'He's no different from the rough old sorts we had thirty years ago,' Vi said. 'None of them could keep their hands off of women's bums. Same wandering hands, different accent, that's all.'

'S'pose so.'

'I know so.'

Vi didn't like Venus and the feeling was mutual. Everything about her irritated him. Her age, her old-school values, the fact that she smoked and swore. Just the sight of him made her cringe. She was used to the sort of Super who was just posh enough to be in charge but could also have a drink and a laugh with the lads once in a while. But Venus only had eyes for his statistics and women under thirty.

'Smelt booze on him again this morning,' Vi said.

Tony said nothing. Venus was always lecturing everyone else about their smoking and their drinking, so it had been a bit of a shock when he'd first come in after a heavy night.

'Maybe he's got problems.'

'Like I give a shit.' Vi said.

'No, but . . .'

'You seen Lee Arnold lately?'

Vi was inclined to change the subject abruptly.

'No.'

Although they had never discussed it, Vi knew that Tony had lived briefly in their old colleague Lee Arnold's flat when his marriage had gone through a bad patch. For that period she'd been forced to keep away from Lee, which hadn't been easy. Although not lovers in the conventional sense, they had an occasional casual sexual relationship, which she found gave her life a sparkle. Lee was ten years younger than Vi. She'd never liked what she called 'old' men – men her own age – and that had included her ex-husband.

'So you don't know what Arnold's up to?'

'No, Guv.'

She was bored. Apart from the inevitable minimart robberies and the constant monitoring of the borough's gangs, Newham was unusually quiet and Vi didn't like it.

'Would you like to come in, Mrs Green.'

Venus, his face blotchy as an old woman's chilblained leg, was out of his office and shaking the tart's hand.

'Thank you,' she said.

When she stood up she unintentionally flashed her knickers. Vi wasn't surprised. 'Fuck me.'

Venus took the woman into his office and closed the door.

Vi frowned. 'Mrs Green,' she said. 'You don't think . . . ?'

'Guv, Brian Green's almost seventy and has not long been widowed,' Tony said.

'Yeah, but she's his type,' Vi said. 'Young, blonde, a plank.'

Tony shook his head. 'Oh, Guv, don't . . .'

'What? That's how it is, Tone,' she said.

'That can't be Brian Green's wife. God help us.'

'Old gangsters can always get young kids like her because they've got money,' Vi said. 'Someone like Brian Green can buy you a lot of plastic surgery and all the fake tan you could ever dream of. Anyway, I don't suppose he can get it up anymore.'

'I do hope not,' Tony said.

'Polarisation is what's to blame,' Rajiv said as he pushed another digestive biscuit on Mumtaz. 'Eat. You're too thin.'

She did as she was told.

'I was born here,' Rajiv said. 'In the fifties, but don't tell *anyone*.'

She smiled. She knew.

'Then we were very mixed here. Hindus, Muslims, Jews, Irish. We had a Spanish family lived next door to us. In the seventies some, what we felt were weird people, came. White from rich families, they wanted to save the old houses. I knew them. All very lefty radical, you know.'

Mumtaz had asked Rajiv about the postal address, but he had to weave it into a story. That had always been his way.

'Then we had the racism of the National Front and that lunatic who set a nail bomb in 1999 and now suddenly we're fashionable. Well, part of the area is. I don't have to tell you.'

But he would.

'Beyond the old Truman's Brewery you're too cool for school. You're probably white; if you're a boy you probably have a beard and you ironically experiment with cross-dressing from time to time. But only vintage clothes.'

Mumtaz laughed. She recognised the type.

'And then here we have Muslims.'

He put a hand on her knee, but Mumtaz didn't flinch, this was Rajiv.

'You know I mean no disrespect,' he said. 'You know that.'

'I know.'

'I've got a thousand Muslim friends. I have my two boys, both Muslims. But these characters who want the sharia law here . . .' He shook his head. 'I told them, I said, "I am Hindu. You do what you like and leave me to do what I like." But they won't. Kids, most of them, but there are adults behind them. Gone my mother's saris!' He threw his arms in the air. 'Gone my jewels! A man with make-up is all I am now. And what is that? So there is a climate of fear, Mumtaz.' He raised a finger. 'We come to that address.'

She nodded.

'Men and women are attracted to each other, it's natural,' Rajiv said. 'But in this climate, can you express such a thing? No.' He clapped his hands. 'Everyone looking at everyone else's phone, peering over your shoulder when you're on the computer. How can people communicate without the world knowing? The world that will hurt you if you get found out? The old ways is the answer. A postal address. You send a letter to your lover and someone gives it to you when your husband is out or you're in the park with your children. You use a postal address already in use by dodgy businesses who offer work to pretty girls or cheap trips to Mecca. You pay a lot of money to the man who has your life in his hands.'

'What about the owner of the address? He's registered in Bangladesh,' Mumtaz said.

'Maybe the owner is, but he doesn't run that address. That's someone else.'

'Who?'

Rajiv said nothing. As usual he had got carried away with his story. Of course he knew.

'If you've used the address I won't tell anyone,' Mumtaz said.

There was a pause and then he said, 'Is it important that you know who runs the address?'

'About as important as it gets.'

81

Rajiv lowered his head. 'You can't tell him you got it from me.'

'Would I?'

'I hope not.' He looked up. 'But how will you have got his name if not through me?'

'Perhaps I will have noticed something myself,' Mumtaz said. 'Maybe once I know who he is something will occur to me. But I promise you Rajiv, I will not reveal your name. I absolutely promise that. You and I have always been friends, and so even if he saw me come in here, I'll explain it away.'

'Mmm.'

He wasn't sure. When she'd arrived she'd seen a couple of kids in the local gang, the Brik Boyz, outside the shop. They'd sneered at her, but said nothing. Rajiv was a target. A middle-aged, gay, cross-dressing Hindu. Just about everything the Boyz loved to hate, in one body. These were the kind of kids her brother had almost been excusing. Little thugs.

'Rajiv . . .'

'Mr Bhatti from the electrical shop,' Rajiv said.

'The shop next to the address?'

He nodded. 'He pays that idiot son of the Ullahs, fat Imran, to do the deliveries.'

'How does he get in there?'

Lee had told her he'd seen nobody enter or leave the address. But he had seen a fat Asian boy go into and come out of the electrical shop.

'I dunno. He has a key . . .' Rajiv shrugged.

Maybe he did. Maybe Imran Ullah, who wasn't what Mumtaz

would have called an idiot, more of a rather dreamy boy, went and picked mail up in the middle of the night.

'Imran brought mail to you?'

'Yes. The secrecy was more for his . . . the man's benefit than mine,' he said. 'He lived in that world, your world.'

Mumtaz shook her head. That wasn't her world. But she knew what Rajiv meant.

Venus had asked Mrs Green what she wanted to drink. He hadn't been expecting her and had been entirely unprepared. Unfortunately she'd asked for a latte, which meant that a PC had to be dispatched to the nearest Starbucks. One didn't upset a wife of Brian Green's, even if he'd only been married to her for a week. One didn't upset Brian Green, especially when he was doing you a favour. But he wished she hadn't come. He also wished he hadn't called her 'Mrs Green' in front of Vi Collins.

'Brian wants you to know he has asked everyone he knows about . . .'

'Yes, thank you.'

Venus stood, as the PC they'd waited almost half an hour for returned with a fresh Starbucks latte.

'Thank you, PC May,' he said.

'Sir.'

The young man left, closing the door softly behind him.

'Kidnapping kiddies is sick,' Taylor Green said. 'Brian said to tell you that if he finds out who's got your boy, he'll deal with him.'

'That won't be necessary, but you can tell your husband that my wife and I appreciate his concern,' Venus said.

'We had a paedo on our estate once.' She drank her coffee, looking down at it through a forest of fake eyelashes. 'Some boys give him a right kicking. He never come back.'

Venus wondered whether Taylor knew what her husband Brian, owner of gyms and health clubs all over Essex and east London, had done to people when he'd been in charge of one of the capital's foremost crime families. Years ago, he'd told Venus about the blindings himself, during one of their little 'chats'.

'So, Brian sends his best and says when all this is over he'd really like to come out to your place on the river again one day. He's told me all about it. Sounds lovely. But he can't help you with your boy,' she said. 'If he hears something, though, he will let you know, he said. He'll do anything to help. Not that he mixes with them type of people.'

In spite of himself, Venus smiled. Brian Green had indoctrinated her well. Not all the previous Mrs Greens had been so unaware.

'Please do tell Mr Green that I appreciate it,' Venus said.

'I will. My Brian's very worried about your boy, Mr Venus. He likes him. And all Brian's mates are worried too. So much crime these days. All these foreigners about.'

She left.

Venus watched his staff follow her with their eyes as she walked out of the station. He wondered how many of them knew or suspected who she was, or thought he was having an affair with her. For himself, Venus was just cold at the thought of how close he'd been with Green and wondered how many old lags around Brian knew about Harry. He told himself it was unavoidable. He'd had to speak to Brian Green when Harry had been taken. Green could have taken him. Green had sent his new wife, unannounced, possibly to humiliate him. But Venus could say nothing and Brian Green could do anything.

7

'Imran Ullah is overweight and yes, spotty too,' Mumtaz said.

Lee nodded. 'That describes the kid I saw going into the electrical shop.'

'He has an older brother who looks like a Bollywood star. Drives a flashy car, wears a lot of gold chains . . .'

'Drug dealer?'

She just smiled.

'But if this kid's part of a private mail service for lonely hearts, why didn't I see him go into the address? I saw him go into the electrical shop. Now if you can access that doorway from the electrical shop . . .'

'I don't know,' Mumtaz said. 'But Lee, you have to understand that if people are using this address to conduct affairs, anyone connected to that doorway will deny that they have any involvement with it. Mr Bhatti who owns the electrical shop and who is, according to my source, involved, will be the loudest denier. He is a pillar of the community. The survival of his business is entirely down to his good name.' She paused for a moment. 'Can't you tell me anything about why you are interested in this address?'

'No. I wish I could. What I can tell you is that it's not about an affair. It's actually about packages delivered to that address. That's all I can say. Look, if I did tell you, would you be able to get these men to talk to me?'

'Me? No,' she said. 'My dad or my brothers maybe, but it would have to be serious, Lee. I mean, really, as serious as it gets. Mr Bhatti is a rogue, he's making a lot of money from the misery of others.'

'So why doesn't the community blow the whistle on him then?'

'What? Those who are using his service? Or those who get discounts at his shop?' She shook her head. 'Lee, the Asian world runs just like the white British world. You scratch my back, I will scratch yours, and outsiders can do their own thing provided they don't affect us. And anyway, if this thing is so serious, what about the police? Bhatti would talk to *them*. He's a coward.'

'No.'

Lee looked away.

She wasn't used to him being so guarded about a job. Obviously he had promised someone complete anonymity. But if whatever he was involved in was so serious, how could he do that?

'I'm over in Chiswick tomorrow,' she said.

'At the Little Sisters of the Wotsit.'

'You shouldn't be so flippant,' she said. 'I'm sure the nuns are sincerely religious women.'

'Who handed a baby over to an orphanage that probably employed paedophiles.'

Sometimes Lee could express a disdain for religion that bordered on hatred.

'My client hasn't told me anything about any abuse,' Mumtaz said. 'She just wants to find her birth mother. She's got Huntington's Disease, which is accelerating. She's living on borrowed time.'

His mobile rang. He picked it up, listened for a moment, then left the office for the back stairs. Probably to have a cigarette. Mumtaz had noticed that he hadn't eaten that morning. Although slim, Lee usually devoured a bag of cakes for his breakfast, but not on this occasion. And being so slim, when he didn't eat he quickly looked gaunt. Whatever he was working on wasn't making him happy. She wondered whether he was being coerced into doing it. She couldn't imagine it. He had always been very clear that nobody who worked for him had to do any job they felt uncomfortable about. But did he apply that to himself?

When he came back inside he said, 'Can you give Amy a bell for me?'

'Yes.'

He sat down. 'I'd like her to cover the office tomorrow if she can. If she can't, give Ian a tug.'

'You're going to be out?'

'Yeah,' he said. 'All day.'

He didn't look happy about it. Mumtaz instinctively didn't like Lee's latest job. It was time, she felt, to enlist some extra help.

The previous Mrs Green had put a dancing posse of stone fairies around the garden pond, if Venus remembered correctly. This one had put up a Japanese pagoda.

'Taylor's got good taste,' Brian Green said.

They both looked down at the pond, which was, in Venus's opinion, rather overfilled with koi carp.

Green sipped from a large glass of red wine. 'Short notice,' he said.

'They called just after your wife left. I didn't know what to do. It's impossible for me or Tina,' Venus said. 'She has the money but the bank won't release it just like that. She emailed me this.'

He passed a bank statement to the elderly man at his side.

Brian Green put on a pair of glasses and nodded. 'I've always liked your Tina,' he said. 'Good little actress, nice singer, good friend. Handy with money too, always was. I hope you didn't mind Taylor popping in to see you. She's soft over kids you know. Can't bear to think of 'em being hurt. I wanted you to feel supported. Know what I mean? In spite of everything.'

'We can get it back to you next week,' Venus said.

'Have it as long as you like, Mr Venus,' Green said.

Venus suppressed a shiver. Brian Green had been one of the East End's most vicious crime bosses. In the late sixties and seventies he'd had his stubby fingers in just about every illegal racket going. But then, when he'd got enough money, Brian apparently went straight. He was always – apart from the odd glass of booze – a bit of a health nut, so he'd opened five gyms in east London and then another four in Essex. They were the sort of places that offered fake tanning alongside cardio workouts and only employed attractive instructors. They were very popular, very lucrative, and they allowed Brian to launder a lot of cash for an old friend or twelve from time to time. He also lent money. Paul

Venus had borrowed money from Brian Green in the past, but not for over a decade and not this much. Not a quarter of a million.

'Usual terms,' Green said.

Last time he'd borrowed from Brian there'd been no interest payments. Just a favour. What would it be this time? Had the old gangster manoeuvred this whole situation just to get him under his thumb again? If so, why?

'A quarter of a mil is a lot in cash,' Brian said. 'Where you gotta take it?'

Venus said nothing. If Green already knew, then he didn't appreciate the taunting. If he didn't, then it was none of his business.

'It's in the dining room,' the gangster said. 'Already counted. But if you want to count it out yourself, Mr Venus, that's your prerogative.'

They went inside. The dining room, a vast space, contained a big table that it dwarfed. On the table was the money. Two hundred and fifty bundles of twenty fifty-pound notes, arranged in a pyramid. Venus looked at Brian Green. Was he having a laugh?

The old man looked at it, smiled and said, 'Tasteful. Them eastern European bastards all involved in everyone's business these days would've just slung it in some old black dustbin bag.'

Shazia felt crushed. Her friend Anita had said there were some waitressing shifts going at a new cafe called Forest Floor just north of Forest Gate station. As soon as her amma had left the flat, she'd raced over there. But all the jobs had gone already, mainly, as far as she could see, to girls who looked like Kate Middleton. When she'd walked in they'd looked at her like a herd of gazelles sizing up a predator.

All the jobs in the local paper seemed to be in telesales, which she knew she couldn't do, and so she spent a few moments looking at cards in a newsagent's window. Badly spelled ads for 'cleaning' were interspersed with word-processed requests for 'models' on slightly grubby paper. There was a Siamese cat for sale in Manor Park and an illiterate claimed to be an 'imagration lawyer – citizenship guaranteed'.

'Wotcha, babe.'

She turned.

Wearing a pair of very stained shalwar khameez, his beard dripping with sweat, was her amma's cousin Aftab Huq.

'What you looking for, love? A used motor?' He laughed. Cousin Aftab, despite his appearance, was the most cockney bloke Shazia had ever met. A devout Muslim, he swore like a trooper, smoked like a fire and had an almost limitless capacity for kindness. 'Here, they've got a Siamese cat over in Manor Park,' he said as he peered at the advert. 'Fancy one of them, do you?'

Shazia laughed. 'No. Or rather, yes if I could, but Amma would kill me. No, I'm looking for a summer job.'

'Oh, left that a bit late, didn't you?'

'Yes.' She shook her head. 'Stupid.'

'Eye off the ball, love.' Aftab lit a cigarette. 'Mind you, there's a lot of that telesales in the paper.'

'I can't do that,' she said. 'Forcing old ladies to buy kitchens they don't want.'

91

'You tried your Uncle Ali? Brick Lane's always heaving this time of year.'

Shazia looked down. She knew she could probably get a few hours in the Islamic clothes shop her amma's brother ran. But she didn't want to work on Brick Lane. The hipsters made her feel out of place and the Muslim gangs gave her a hard time. And Uncle Ali was becoming more and more overtly pious. She imagined he'd want her to cover her head.

Aftab bent down to look at her face. 'No? Yeah, he's a bit of a stiff these days, old Ali. Don't suppose I'd like to work for him meself. Gotta love him though, his heart's in the right place. Mind you, there is another option, but you won't like it much.'

She looked up.

'Long hours, dirty, have to put up with all sorts . . . Me.'

'Working for you? Well, yes, yes. Yes!'

'Hang on! Hang on! It's three weeks to cover for me warehouse man, George. He does serve in the shop from time to time, but he mainly helps me load and unload the van and stack stuff in the warehouse. It's heavy work and you'll get proper filthy.'

'But it's work!'

'It's work you'll have to cut your nails for,' he said.

Shazia whizzed her manicured hands behind her back. 'Well, yes . . .'

'And we will have to get your amma's blessing. But if you think you can handle a twelve-pack of tinned cat food and sacks of rice . . .'

'I know I can!'

'You might, but I don't,' he said.

Shazia deflated. Why had he mentioned a job to her if he didn't think she was up to it? Did he know just how much she and her amma needed more money? Probably not.

'So if your amma's in agreement, we'll give you a bit of a trial,' Aftab said.

'You will?'

'You're family. You obviously want to get some dosh together and I'll pay you eight quid an hour. I'm just worried you might hurt yourself.'

'I won't.'

'Well, let's see,' he said. Then he wiped his brow. 'If I don't get someone in soon it'll bloody well kill me.'

Cousin Aftab had a disabled wife who couldn't work and two daughters who both had jobs of their own. Usually he was helped by George, a white octogenarian who had once, it was said, tried out for West Ham United. His life wasn't easy, especially when George went on his annual holiday to Great Yarmouth.

'That person's me,' Shazia said. 'Guarantee it.'

'I hope you're right, love,' Aftab said. 'And I hope you can put up with stroppy customers. One thing I'm not light on are bastards who give me a hard time in me own shop.'

Even tortellini *in brodo*, the only food she'd been able to eat for months, was becoming difficult for her. Mother Katerina spooned some liquid into the old woman's shrunken mouth and then attempted to follow that with a small amount of pasta.

'Come, Sister,' she said, 'just a little?'

But the old woman turned her head into her pillows.

'For strength.'

'No.'

Mother Katerina put the food down on the bedside table and stroked the old woman's head. Sister Pia was ninety years old and had taken vows back in Italy over sixty years ago. She'd lived in England since the early fifties and spoke the language well, but with Katerina and her other Sisters it was always Italian.

'Dr Smith will come tomorrow and she'll want to know that you're eating,' Mother Katerina said.

'I'm dying.'

'You have cancer. Whether or not your time is near is for God to know. Forcing His hand is a sin, as you know, Sister.'

She said nothing.

'When Dr Smith has gone, I will have to attend to a visitor.'

'Not a visitor to me?'

'Not if you don't want to meet her, no,' Mother Katerina said. 'But you may.'

'Why?'

'Because she is coming to ask about my predecessor.'

'Mother Emerita?'

'She found a child,' Mother Katerina said. 'You remember? In a telephone box? A long time ago, but now that child, a woman, wishes to find her mother, if she can.'

The old woman, staring at her counterpane, behaved as if she hadn't heard.

'You were here at the time, Sister, were you not?'

There was a pause. Then the old woman said, 'The little girl was left. Mother heard her crying and carried her from the telephone box. The Nazareth Sisters in Essex took her because she had no parents. We never found a mother. She was abandoned.'

'Well, now she wants to find her mother, and so she's engaged a private detective to help her,' Mother Katerina said. 'A lady called Mrs Hakim will be here at eleven o'clock tomorrow.'

'Why? Mother Emerita is dead.'

'She made a report of the incident at the time for the police. There's a copy in our files. I will tell the lady what I know . . .'

'What do you know?'

'Not a great deal. Mother Emerita found an abandoned child. An appeal for information was made at the time, but nobody ever came forward.'

'No.' She paused. 'Why are you inviting this detective? All this is known.'

'Mrs Hakim wants to see where the child, Alison, was found and where she lived for the first few days of her life,' Mother Katerina said. 'Maybe, Sister, as the only person here who can remember that time . . .'

'I don't want to speak to her. There's no point. I know what you know and nothing else.'

'People skilled in investigation can sometimes uncover information from people that they may believe they have forgotten. It will do no harm, Sister.'

'Reverend Mother, are you ordering me . . . ?'

'No,' Mother Katerina said. 'Not ordering. But I am asking you to consider meeting this lady. I know you are sick and that what you can and cannot do is dependent upon how you feel. I also know that time in your life was very challenging for you. But do please consider it. Our mission, remember, is to help mankind, and that includes Alison, who was given to us as a gift so many years ago.'

She left Sister Pia and went about her duties. The old woman told her, as she left, to extinguish the light in her room.

'Does your wife know where the drop is?'

He heard Venus sigh at the other end of the line.

'She should,' Lee said. 'If she knows, it's extra insurance for you if things go wrong. Where is she? At work?'

'There or at her girlfriend's place. I gather you know about Cydney Denton?' Venus said. 'Tina's phone's off.'

Lee knew about Cydney Denton. At least twenty years younger than Tina, Cydney played her flirtatious niece in *Londoners*. She'd told him they were an item.

'Just for the record, does your son—?'

'Harry knows his mother and Cydney are friends. That's all. There's no need for him to be told anything else yet.'

Harry was almost an adult and probably knew anyway. In Lee Arnold's experience, modern teenagers really did know everything most of the time. Which was depressing.

'Are you at the drop site?'

'Yes, I am,' Lee said. 'And if I was of a nervous disposition it'd give me the shudders. As it is, as a place to leave a large amount of cash, it makes some sense. But only some.'

Rippleside Cemetery in the London Borough of Barking and Dagenham was a grey, depressing place even on a bright day.

Bordered on one side by council houses and blocks of flats, on the other thundered the A13, one of the main arteries into London. The older parts of the cemetery were shaded by trees while the newer, often flashier, graves were left to take the full force of the odd, light grey sun that shone on the rain-starved ground. Lee Arnold's eye had been immediately caught by a massive floral display in the shape of the word 'Nan'. It was laid against a vast black granite memorial to a woman who, from the photograph that dominated the structure, looked like a serial killer. A car full of men with tattoos drove past slowly.

Did *they* have Harry Venus? Were they scoping out the site, just like Lee? But if they were, like him, they were in the wrong place.

'I can see where I think it is,' Lee said into his phone.

'A winged angel, eight feet high. You can't miss it.'

'No. But there's several of them,' Lee said. 'Angels were very popular in Victorian times as funeral monuments. Not like now when they sit on your desk and guard the BMW.'

'What?'

'Nothing.' His daughter had sent him a small 'guardian angel' model for his desk. Apparently she believed it would watch over him.

He began to walk over rough ground towards an avenue of trees. It led east to a very old part of the cemetery and the largest angel statue, as far as he could see.

'I'll leave the money behind the statue. They want it in a red sports bag. They specified that,' Venus said. Then, nervously, 'What did you mean by as a drop site it made *some* sense?'

'That angel is one of the most visible things around here,' Lee said. 'There's some cover from the trees, but cars can pull right up to it. So when you've gone, I'll be able to see who picks up the drop very easily.'

'That's good.'

Walking over rough ground made Lee puff. He had to stop smoking.

'Not for the kidnappers. And a *red* sports bag? Visible or what. That's stupid,' Lee said. 'And I don't believe they're stupid. They chose their drop very carefully last time. I don't get this.'

Now in front of the angel, he read the name on the plinth. 'Septimus Couch'.

'That's it,' Venus said. 'That's the right one. God, I know that statue! My granddad's buried just over by the fence. Terrible afternoons in November spent dressing the grave with my grandmother.'

Lee looked up into the angel's age-weathered face. It hardly had a nose any more. Its wings looked moth-eaten round the edges, battered by vandals. It was a sorry-looking thing. All that was left of Septimus Couch, 1851–1899, whose family had to have had a bit of dosh to put that thing up. Barking had always been a poor borough. Maybe the family of Septimus Couch went without to give him a grand send-off? Or maybe, like his daughter, they had believed in guardian angels?

Lee turned away from the statue. 'I'm not buying this,' he said into his phone.

'That's where they've told me to leave the money. What else can I do but what I'm told?'

There wasn't anything.

*

Sumita had said that he shouldn't get involved with Zafar Bhatti. She believed him to be a charlatan. But Baharat Huq had been insistent.

'It's for our daughter,' he said. 'There cannot be "no" when it comes to our children.'

'And yet you argue with Ali all the time,' his wife said.

'Only because he's a silly sod.'

Baharat had left before Sumita decided to make an issue out of his disagreement with his son about Islam. Ali was becoming very anti-western all of a sudden and Baharat wondered why. He also feared for his son. A respectable Brick Lane businessman, Ali could ruin his own reputation if the anti-terrorist police began to call. People informed all the time and Ali Huq was becoming ever more vocal about his opinions.

Now looking at strands of wire and electrical components he didn't understand, Baharat Huq wondered how he might open a conversation with Mr Bhatti about his little sideline as a purveyor of forbidden messages. But he hadn't thought it through.

'Can I help you at all, Baharat-ji?'

Zafar Bhatti had held a management position at the mosque until he had handed over to a younger man five years earlier. It was whispered that someone had seen him with pornography, but he was still very much a part of public life, and vocal in the anti-alcohol lobby. Baharat found all that unnecessary. If non-Muslims wanted to drink alcohol then that was their business, surely.

'Ah, Zafar-ji, I was looking for um, a . . .'

He looked at what he knew were plugs. Mumtaz hadn't said exactly *what* she wanted him to find out. Like almost everyone else, she knew what Bhatti did to earn extra cash. What was he supposed to do about it? And why?

'Ah . . .'

'Plugs? I have every sort,' Bhatti said. 'Very cheap. B&Q? Ah! Not even in the picture. Go to those places on those industrial estates and they will cheat you.'

'Ah . . .'

'But then you know it, Baharat-ji.' He put a hand on his shoulder. 'You know it!' Bhatti had to know that Baharat didn't do DIY. Not even in the early days when he'd first come to the UK. If he couldn't pay for someone else to do things, they didn't get done. He was frightened of electricity and everybody knew it.

Bhatti was about to praise his stock to the skies again when a fat, spotty boy walked in carrying a rucksack.

'Ah . . .'

Imran Ullah, whose brother wore leather pants and had a car that people stopped on the street to look at, didn't see Baharat Huq. But Baharat saw him. Mumtaz had said that the poor fat fool was Bhatti's postmaster. What she wanted to know was how and when the boy went into the house next door to pick up his deliveries. Baharat assumed that Imran went through the front door, a view underwritten by Bhatti, who quickly hustled the boy out of the shop.

After half a minute, Baharat also left the shop and found the pair of them outside on the street. He heard the boy say, 'He won't know where I'm going. What does it matter?'

Zafar-ji didn't see Baharat for a moment. In that time he said, 'Baharat Huq is a gossipy old woman! Do as you are told!'

Then he hit him.

Baharat cleared his throat.

'Ah . . .'

He didn't look at Mr Bhatti, but at Imran. 'Are you all right?'

'Yes, Baharat-ji. I'm fine.'

The boy had his head down. Bhatti used everyone around him badly, from his wife to his friends. Why should this dopey boy be any different?

It was then that Baharat Huq realised that he had been looking at his daughter's request for information from the wrong angle.

Briefly, he smiled at Zafar Bhatti, and then he said, 'I will come and look at plugs another time, Zafar-ji. The ones you have in stock are very nice, but I think I need to see a few more before I make my decision. Plugs are very important, don't you think? Decisions about plugs should never be taken lightly, I feel.'

'No . . .'

Zafar-ji was clearly nonplussed by this behaviour. But what could he say? He was the man who was hiding something, not Baharat. He was the one who had struck the boy and that, Baharat thought, could now be crucial.

8

Yet another day's unplanned leave. Venus knew that tongues at the station would be wagging. Especially in view of the fact that a blonde called Mrs Green had been in to see him. Now that old crocodile Vi Collins would be pairing them off. But let her. Paul Venus just wanted his son back. The boy hated him, but he was sixteen and boys of that age always hated their fathers. He'd told himself that all night long. It was normal. Except that the vitriol Harry spat at him every time they met was not.

The last time they'd met he'd asked his father which clubs he belonged to. A seemingly innocent question. But Paul had known that it wasn't. He was a Mason, and Harry knew it. So were most of his friends' fathers. But they were also in prestigious gentlemen's clubs like White's and Boodle's too. Places that only men of a certain social standing could go. Policemen were generally excluded.

'It's at clubs where jobs are given out,' Harry had said. 'Everybody knows that! How can I get a good job if you don't have connections?'

Paul had said, 'On merit?' It had just come out.

102

Harry had harrumphed, which was something he had taken to doing ever since he'd started at Reeds. Maybe all the boys there did it? Paul didn't know. It had been Tina's idea to send him to what Paul considered a Woosterish time capsule. They had money, but they'd both worked hard for it and what was wrong with a decent grammar school? But Tina had insisted. He still didn't really know why. She could have carried on working if they'd employed an au pair to look after Harry. Tina was ambitious for her son and Harry had wanted to go to Reeds, but had that decision also been influenced by her affair with Cyd? When Harry was at school, the woman lived in Henley almost full-time. But what could he say? He'd been having affairs even before they married.

Harry had pulled a face when his father had mentioned merit. People apparently didn't 'do' that any more. He'd turned into a nasty little snob, but he was still *his* nasty little snob and when Paul got him back he'd take him out of that school, full of over-privileged kids and supercilious 'masters'. The grunts at work laughed at him because he was middle-class, and he could take that. But to be looked down on by a bunch of toffs was too much.

Paul counted the money Brian Green had lent him again, just to make sure. It was still all there. Would he ever tell Harry his life had been saved by a man who used words like 'serviette' and 'lavvy'? Then again the boy didn't seem to mind those words when Brian used them. Why Tina still invited him to the house from time to time was a mystery. Did she still feel beholden to Green?

Lee Arnold had swapped cars with his assistant and so he'd be driving an old Nissan Micra. He was going to start following him from just up the road outside Finsbury Park. He had this notion, because the cemetery was an open space, that Paul was in danger of being carjacked en route. Paul Venus didn't know, or care. He hadn't slept again and all he wanted was his son.

He looked at his watch. In ten minutes he'd have to phone Lee Arnold to let him know he was leaving. He went to the bathroom to have a piss. As usual he didn't bother to shut the door behind him.

It was nice driving Lee's latest acquisition. An eleven-year-old Subaru Impreza, it was comfortable even if it didn't have much in the way of speed left in it. If she'd still had the Micra, Mumtaz wouldn't have even considered driving to Chiswick, but in the Subaru it was bearable. And anyway, driving gave her more flexibility than the Tube and it meant that she could be alone to think.

Shazia had twisted Cousin Aftab's arm into giving her a really unsuitable job in his shop. It was basically labouring. But the rent was due on the flat and her next payment to the Sheikhs was coming up. What could she do but agree to it?

The gangster Naz Sheikh was annoyed that, so far, she hadn't come up with any useful information for him from her police contacts. She'd already decided she was never doing that, but how was she going to keep Naz at bay while she dissembled? And for how long? Her father's words about the world being better off without some people kept on coming back to haunt her. He'd been talking about the Muslim Brotherhood in Egypt, but couldn't that sentiment apply to Naz Sheikh too?

Of course it could, and she didn't feel any sense of guilt about having such thoughts. That absence made her shudder. It was wrong to wish anyone dead, but she did and he deserved it. Just like she'd done with her husband. The similarity, coming to her suddenly, was a shock. What sort of person was she that she wanted people dead? And would the nuns at the Siena Sisters convent be able to see it on her face?

Lee called Venus's mobile again, just to be sure. But he got no answer, again. He hadn't called at the agreed time to say he was on the road and he also wasn't picking up his mobile.

Lee fired up the Micra's engine and headed for Islington, his phone on the seat beside him, just in case. But he knew he wouldn't need it. Something had happened to Venus. He didn't know what or where, but he kept looking out for a black Lexus as he headed down the Blackstock Road towards Islington. Venus lived down by Highbury and Islington station, near where ex-Prime Minister Tony Blair had once had a house the size of a small country. Islington was trendy lefty territory characterised by copies of the *Guardian* scattered on old sofas in fashionable independent coffee shops, which were patronised by hordes of yummy mummies. At least that was the tale they told at Forest Gate nick, when Vi and Tony and the others ripped the piss out of Venus. But working for him had given Lee some insight into the Super's character, and it wasn't all bad. Yes, he was a middle-class twat who made his preferences for younger women very apparent, but he loved his son, he at least tried to be civilised around his ex-wife, and he was scared. He was human – even if right now, he was making Lee very anxious.

Not that Venus was doing anything. As far as Lee was concerned he could be anything from unconscious to missing to dead. Whatever had happened, unless the whole thing had been some sort of double bluff, Venus wasn't responsible.

Looking out for Venus's car made Lee hesitate at a set of lights. The driver behind, in typical London fashion, sounded his horn long and hard.

'Yes, all right, impatient bollocks!' Lee yelled at no one but himself.

It was more likely that if Venus's car had been jacked it had happened outside his house or in a backstreet. Lee turned onto Highbury Grove and then looked at his watch. The drop was now ten minutes away – in Barking.

The Tabard pub, an arts and crafts-style building, was on Bath Road, Turnham Green. Amazingly, there was still a phone box with a public phone in it outside. Mumtaz checked. It even worked. It was also overlooked by a church and two houses across the road; two others had a partial view. Hopefully Mother Katerina might be able to tell her whether Mother Emerita had ever identified anyone rubbernecking.

It was a prosperous area, the houses large and mostly with sizeable gardens. The people were either very smart and fashionable, in a designer manner, or studiedly scruffy, a bit like the hipster kids on Brick Lane. Mumtaz didn't feel in any way at home, but she did like the place. Turnham Green was somewhere she wished she could be, for Shazia's sake. It felt safe.

Over the road a curtain twitched in a red-brick house with cottage garden plants growing in the front lawn. Probably someone pitying her for not having a mobile phone. Mumtaz left the box and made her way towards the convent. She'd cut it fine to get there, which meant that eventually she had to run. By the time she arrived, she was sweating and her face was red. In stark contrast, the nun who met her had the skin of a porcelain doll.

'Sister . . .'

'I'm Mother Katerina,' the nun said.

Mumtaz became redder. 'Oh, I'm so sorry,' she said. 'I thought you were a sister . . .'

'No matter.' She smiled. In her severe habit and wimple it was almost impossible to tell how old Mother Katerina might be, but Mumtaz imagined she was probably in her early forties. 'Have you been running, Mrs Hakim?'

'I was late . . .'

The large front door led into a wide hall with a curving staircase on the left-hand wall.

'Please.' The nun ushered her forwards, to a door underneath the staircase. 'This is my office. We can talk there.'

'Thank you.'

Mumtaz was still breathing heavily. How had she got so unfit? She didn't smoke, drink or even overeat. Well, not often.

Mother Katerina's office was entirely out of date, with the

exception of the computer on her battered Victorian desk. A state-of-the-art Mac amongst oak filing cabinets, hard chairs and dark portraits of women with halos. Only the chair that Mother Katerina offered Mumtaz had a cushion. And that was thin.

'Would you like some water? Coffee? Both?'

Mumtaz sat.

'Sister Sofia can make a wonderful cappuccino. I really recommend it.'

Mumtaz took a calming breath. Her face was, she knew, still like a furnace. 'Well, I do need water, but I'd love coffee too,' she said.

'That's good.'

Mother Katerina opened her office door again and called out something in Italian. Then she shut the door, sat down at her desk and opened the computer. 'I have been in the process of scanning our records into the computer for some years now,' she said. 'Many of the old files are almost unreadable, they are so faint.'

'You've been here long, Mother?'

'The order took over the premises in 1951. I personally have been here since 1997, which was when Mother Emerita died.' She looked up. 'What is it you say here? Big shoes to put your feet inside?'

'Big shoes to fill.' Mumtaz smiled.

'To fill, yes. She was very loved.'

The office door opened and a hand put a glass of water down in front of Mumtaz and then withdrew very quickly. The door closed again.

'But you are here to find out what you can for a lady called Alison.'

'Yes.' Mumtaz drank the water she'd been given in a couple of gulps. 'She is sick with something called Huntington's Disease, which is terminal. She wants to find her mother before she dies.'

'You told me, yes. May God have mercy.' Mother Katerina shook her head and then looked at her computer screen. 'I will do what I can. Now, the child that Mother Emerita found in the telephone box was called not Alison but Madonna while she was here,' she said. 'Maybe the name Alison came from the Nazareth Sisters she was sent to live with in Essex. I have a report on the child's approximate age and her health, which was good. She was at most one day old. And small. Maybe, the doctor felt at the time, a little premature.'

Mumtaz took out her notebook. 'If I may . . . ?'

The nun said, 'Of course.'

'Madonna . . .'

'Yes. Before the singer,' she smiled. '1971. I was a child. You, I imagine, were not born.'

'No.'

'She was here for seven days before being transferred to the Nazareth Sisters. This was a hostel for young girls in those days,' she said. 'From Italy mainly, for study. But also from Spain, South America, all over. Having a baby here was not right for the girls or for the child.'

'No.' Mumtaz looked up. 'Mother Katerina, the police must have been involved. Did Mother Emerita give them a statement or something?'

'She did. We don't have a copy, but . . .' She clicked the computer mouse twice and then pressed some keys on the keyboard. 'She wrote an account of what happened for our own records. It is in Italian, but I can read it to you if you would find it useful.'

'I would, thank you.'

Again the office door opened and two enormous cups of creamily frothy cappuccino appeared.

Mother Katerina did not look up. '*Grazie.*'

A voice answered, '*Prego.*'

The office door closed.

'Ah . . .'

'She says, "I found the child in the telephone box on Bath Road, Turnham Green at 6.45 on the morning of the tenth of October 1971,"' Mother Katerina translated. She looked up. 'I'm sorry, this is a little hard. I may be slow. Mother's handwriting is not easy, you know.'

'No problem,' Mumtaz said. 'I couldn't do it at all. It's very kind of you to.'

Mother Katerina waved a hand. 'Nobody else was on the street at the time and Mother Emerita saw no one walk away from the box. She was entirely alone. It was cold and so she brought the child back here and then she called the police.'

Mumtaz sipped her coffee. It had a slight cinnamon aftertaste and was sweet and creamy and delicious.

The nun watched her face. 'Good, as I told you, eh?'

'Fantastic.'

She smiled. Then she looked back at the screen. 'So the police came and they took the child to Charing Cross Hospital,' she said. 'Once she had been examined she was sent back here. There was an appeal for the mother to come forward in the newspapers and on television. But nothing.'

It was odd that Alison should have been taken to hospital and then returned to the convent.

Mumtaz said, 'Does she say why the baby was brought back here?'

The nun scanned the screen. 'No.'

'Usually such children stay in hospital.'

'I don't know.'

'Also, Mother, Alison seemed to think that Mother Emerita saw someone watching, a neighbour maybe, when she found her in the phone box.'

Mother Katerina sipped her coffee. 'There is nothing about that here.'

Alison had said the Nazareth nuns had told her that story.

'Chiswick police may still have Mother's original statement,' the nun said.

'I've left a message for them to contact me,' Mumtaz said. That had been a mission. Unable to speak to anyone who was able to help her, she'd eventually had to leave a message on an answerphone. If they didn't get back to her, she'd ask Vi Collins to have one of her famous 'words' with Chiswick.

Mother Katerina leaned back in her chair. 'And then there is Sister Pia,' she said.

Mumtaz looked up.

'Sister Pia is the only surviving member of the Order who remembers that time. She knew Mother Emerita very well.'

She hadn't mentioned a living witness on the phone.

'She is very old,' Mother Katerina said. 'And sick.'

'Oh. I'm sorry.'

She smiled. 'To be honest with you, Mrs Hakim, Sister Pia has been sick all her life. Diabetes, arthritis, unnamed illnesses. It has been one torment after another.'

'I'm sorry.' And yet Sister Katerina seemed more irritated than distressed by Sister Pia's suffering.

'And now at last, she is dying,' she said. 'Sister Pia has cancer.'

'Again, my . . .'

She waved a dismissive hand. 'The Lord in His wisdom saw fit to give her ninety years of life. We have an excellent doctor. Sister remains lucid.' There was a pause. Then she said, 'I have asked Sister Pia if she will speak to you, but she has refused.'

'I understand,' Mumtaz said. 'Very sick people don't want questions from the dim and distant past.'

The nun put her head on one side. 'Maybe. But maybe not,' she said. 'Mrs Hakim, I was not here when Alison was found, as I told you. But what I do know is that when the convent was a hostel for young girls, this was not an easy place to pursue a religious life. I see you cover your head as observant Muslim ladies do, so you will understand, perhaps, how hard it was to be in such an atmosphere. Young girls . . . Worries about their bodies, their studies, boyfriends . . .'

'I have a seventeen-year-old daughter,' Mumtaz said.

'Ah, then you will know. And the Sisters here, they were *in loco parentis*, you understand?'

'Yes.'

'They replaced the parents who remained in Italy, Spain, Brazil. Observant parents expected the Sisters to keep their daughters safe and pure. In those days, sex outside marriage was not the common thing it has become today. The Sisters here were expected to control the girls, and that was difficult. The world was changing. Some of the Sisters – Sister Pia was one – took a hard line. There were disagreements, complaints even.'

'About Sister Pia.'

She nodded. '*Si.* At the same time as Mother Emerita found the child in the telephone box, Sister Pia was the subject of a – I don't know how to call it, the girls would not talk to her. There was even an investigation by the diocese. Sister Pia was cleared of any wrongdoing. But it was a hard time for her.'

'Which she won't want to talk about.'

'No. But I think that she should.'

To Mumtaz this was a peculiar thing for a Mother Superior to say to a stranger about one of her own nuns. It felt as if she were being disloyal.

'For her soul.'

Mumtaz saw the nun's face harden.

'You think she has something to add to the story of Alison's first few days?'

She shrugged. 'Maybe. Maybe not. But I think that she should talk to you. In fact I will insist upon it.'

Smiling again now, she stood up.

Venus's car hadn't moved. Lee rang the doorbell once and then got ready to kick the door down. Then he saw that it was open.

Venus was on the floor of his bathroom. Just about conscious, he was sitting up in a wide smear of his own blood. When he saw Lee, he said, 'The money!'

'Where?'

Lee knew he should be calling an ambulance, but he repeated the question. 'Where?'

Venus shook his head. 'Kitchen. In the big sports bag.'

Lee ran down a white corridor and into a big space and a lot of granite. Apart from a coffee machine and one sheet of paper it was empty. As he dialled 999 on his mobile, he read the few words on the sheet and then said, 'Ambulance.'

He gave Venus's address to the ambulance service and ran back to the bathroom where Venus had now managed to haul himself up onto the toilet.

'The money?'

'Not in the kitchen.' Lee finished his phone call and bent down to take Venus's pulse. 'What happened?'

Venus shook his head. 'You're sure the money . . . ?'

'Venus, don't worry about that now.' Lee looked into his eyes, which seemed steady. 'I've called an ambulance. Someone hit you, yeah?'

'I don't remember anything. I was in the bathroom . . . Then I was on the floor . . .'

'When I turned up, the front door was open,' Lee said. 'Did you hear anyone trying to get in?'

'No.' He breathed unsteadily. 'Why are you here? You should be in Barking.'

'Yeah. With you.' His pulse was fast. 'And now you're off to hospital.'

When the ambulance had picked Venus up, Lee spent a few minutes looking around the flat. There was no sign of the sports bag Venus had packed with his wife's money. There was also no sign of a forced entry. Unless Venus had left the front door open, his attacker must have had a key. Then there was the typed sheet of paper in the kitchen:

GO TO THE POLICE AND HARRY DIES.

But that wasn't possible. The flat had to be examined. It contained forensic evidence that could lead to uncovering the identity of Harry's kidnappers. Venus had babbled to the ambulance crew that he'd been mugged in the street and Lee hadn't contradicted him. But whoever had taken his son and his money had a key to his flat.

They were playing a game and it was easy for them because they knew him.

'Sister Pia.'

The room, which smelt of sickness, was vast. And even where the sun came through the pale yellow curtains it was cold.

An elderly woman said something in Italian and Mother Katerina said, 'In English, Sister.'

For a moment there was silence and then a cough.

Mumtaz turned to Mother Katerina. This felt wrong. 'Mother, I don't think that I should be here.'

'You should. It's OK.' She left her and went over to the small bed that stood in front of one of the long sash windows. 'Sister,' she said, 'you must speak about that time. So much was happening

115

for you, maybe you forgot something about the baby? But tell this lady what you know. The woman who was the baby, she is dying, Sister, she needs to find her mother. Anything you can tell this lady may be of use. Try.'

The old voice said something Mumtaz didn't understand.

Mother Katerina shook her head. 'No one is saying she is your confessor. Sister, you talk to Mrs Hakim or you do not, but I think that you should. I think it may be good for you.'

The old woman whispered and Mother Katerina whispered back. Mumtaz could hear a clock somewhere in the room. The nun's faint Italian drawled in a vaguely sinister way and then the old woman called her over. Suddenly Mumtaz felt nervous. It was only an old nun for goodness sake! And yet her hands shook in just the same way as they had done whenever her husband had come in after a night of drinking and gambling. The room was cold, but Mumtaz began to sweat.

9

Tina Wilton came as soon as Lee called. When he left her at the Whittington Hospital she was at her husband's bedside, crying. Venus was going to be fine, he had a mild concussion and would only be in hospital overnight, but all the money had gone and there was still no sign of Harry. Lee had been given no choice about sharing what he'd found in the kitchen with Forest Gate nick.

'How long you gonna give these people money?' he'd asked the superintendent and his missus. 'Your front door wasn't open. They have a key to your flat, Mr Venus. They might have a key to your gaff too, Mrs Venus. They're playing a game with you. They've got three hundred and fifty grand with no trouble at all. What makes you think they're gonna stop there?'

She'd said, 'We just want Harry back! At any price!'

Lee had exploded. 'Yes, and because you've got so much bloody money, it makes you vulnerable! I'm telling you, you can't buy your way out of this! These people know you, it's personal.'

It had taken a lot to convince them that getting the police involved had been the right thing to do. Venus was like stone.

Tina had just cried. Lee said he'd done it as discreetly as he could. 'I've spoken to Vi Collins and only her, so far,' he'd said. 'I know she'll keep shtum.'

Then oddly, for him, Venus had said, 'Tell DI Collins to ring me. She can have this one.'

Chief Inspector Stone would take over the running of the nick in Venus's absence. But he was little more than a pen-pusher with a rulebook stuck up his arse. Vi would really run the show.

When he eventually tracked DI Collins down, in the Boleyn pub at Upton Park, Lee listened in to the call she made to Venus. Venus knew how fanatically Vi loved her two sons, she was always talking about them. Whenever they had problems or got sick, she was there for them. She understood what having children meant and Venus knew that in spite of their differences, she would not endanger Harry.

Knocking back a Diet Pepsi, Lee heard her say, 'I've got it, sir, trust me.'

When the call had finished they both got up without speaking and went to Vi's car. She turned the air-con on while short men in baggy shalwar khameez occasionally looked at them from the balconies of nearby flats. Then she made a lot of phone calls.

When she'd finished, Vi said to Lee, 'How did Venus think that he could get his son back on his own with just you riding shotgun? No offence intended, Arnold.'

He shrugged. 'I'd've done the same if someone took my daughter. And you'd follow the kidnappers' script yourself, Vi, if it were one of your lads. You know you would.'

'I s'pose so . . . But Venus knows that we have protocols for this kind of situation.' She shook her head. 'You left the flat clean?'

'As I could,' Lee said.

The place would be under surveillance all night and then, in the morning, a 'friend', or Scene of Crime officer, would drive Venus home from the hospital. And Venus's phones would be tapped.

'So, you out of work now then, Arnold?' Vi asked.

'No.'

'How's that then?'

She fired up the engine.

'Your Super wants us to work together.'

'Does he?'

'Reckons I can go to places you lot can't.'

'Like where?'

'Like Harry's school,' he said. 'I've already spoken to his form teacher and been offered a tour of jolly old Reeds.' He put on a really bad fake posh accent.

'Do me a favour!' She pulled away from the kerb.

'If you lot roll up mob-handed the world'll know something's up. Vi, whoever has Harry knows that family, intimately,' Lee said. 'They had a key.'

'Could've had one made.'

'True, but the graveyard where the money drop was supposed to take place is where Venus's granddad is buried.'

'Venus is from Barking?'

'No, don't be daft! But some of his family must've been.'

Vi headed down Green Street, back towards the nick.

'What about the first drop site?' she asked. 'Where was that?'

'Brick Lane,' Lee told her. 'The Bangla Town end. Used a PO box for Asian lonely hearts. Drop was made in the name Shaw. Clearly that bit wasn't Asian.'

Vi said, 'Mumtaz know about this?'

'She knows I'd like the skinny on a rough as fuck doorway on Brick Lane, but she don't know why. She's got her own caseload.'

'Yeah, but I bet she's done some digging,' Vi said.

Mrs Ullah had tears on her face. People said that her eldest boy, Amir, not only sold drugs but also drank. His father was dead and there were few family members in the area. There was, Baharat remembered, a cousin, but he was a wrong one too. It was all bad women with him. Which left only Imran. Fat, spotty and smelt of chemicals. Spot cream maybe?

Baharat watched the woman walk up the concrete stairs to her flat and go inside. He'd seen Imran slumping along Brick Lane earlier and thought he might find him with his mum. But he hadn't. The kid was probably off delivering love notes to Mr Bhatti's 'customers'.

But there was a small, pleasant park outside the block where the Ullahs lived, and so Baharat settled himself on a bench to wait out Imran's return. Unlike his brother, the boy wasn't big on going out and so he probably wouldn't be long.

Then the two of them would have a little chat.

*

'I saw the child, but I didn't hold it,' the old woman said.

'When?'

'All the time it was here. From the moment Mother Emerita brought it in until it left to go to the Nazareth Sisters in Essex.'

In spite of the voluminous nightgown and wimple she hid inside, Mumtaz could see that Sister Pia was very thin and bald. She was also confusing. Her smile, which was almost constant, was seraphic, but the face behind it had a hardness. According to Mother Katerina, Sister Pia had been ill for most of her life, which could explain a lot, and yet was it just Mumtaz or had the Superior implied that Sister Pia's infirmities were in some way self-indulgent?

'Why didn't you hold the child, Sister?' Mumtaz asked.

Sister Pia's smile widened. 'Because it would not have been the right behaviour,' she said. Then she looked at Mother Katerina. 'Mother?'

'Convents like ours were much stricter in those days, Mrs Hakim,' Mother Katerina said. 'This was a hostel for young girls. To bring them into contact with a baby, probably born to an unmarried woman, was not thought to be right.'

'But other people must have held her here?'

'That was their choice,' the old nun said. 'Except for the girls.'

'The residents?'

'Mother Emerita was very clear. The child was not to be passed around amongst our girls.'

'Did they want to see her?'

She put her head on one side. 'Some.'

'But they weren't allowed to?'

121

'No. Some saw it by accident. All of them heard it. It was a child born of shame.'

Mumtaz had heard such terms used among some Muslims that she knew. They weren't all fanatics and neither, probably, was Sister Pia. But she noticed that Mother Katerina looked embarrassed.

'So who did see Alison in those first few days of her life?' Mumtaz asked.

'Mother Emerita and Sister Concezione looked after the child. Our doctor visited every day to check on its health. It was not easy for Mother and Sister Concezione. If the child cried during any of our Holy Offices or when we slept, it was unpleasant.'

'Holy Offices are our prayers,' Mother Katerina said. 'They begin at six in the morning with Lauds. There are different Offices throughout the day and night.'

Mumtaz frowned. 'But if Lauds is at six and Mother Emerita found Alison at six forty-five . . .'

'Lauds is a short Office,' Mother Katerina said. 'Meditation usually follows, but maybe Mother Emerita had a visit to make that morning. Our mission is prayer, but we are also here for the community in Chiswick. Sister, do you know why Mother Emerita was out that morning?'

'I do not,' the old woman said.

'She didn't say?'

'Not to my recollection. As I have told you, madam,' Sister Pia said to Mumtaz, 'I remember the child and I remember those days, but it had little effect upon me.'

Mumtaz recalled what Mother Katerina had said about the trouble that had occurred for Sister Pia around that time. Her strictness with the girls. It explained her antipathy towards Alison.

'The police may know where Mother Emerita was going,' Mother Katerina said. 'The report she wrote for our files was not identical to her statement to the police. And Dr Chitty is still alive.'

Sister Pia said something in Italian and was chided for it. She switched to English. 'Mother, what would Dr Chitty know? He is old, like me. He came after the child was brought to us. What would he know about what Mother was doing that morning?'

'It is something to consider, Sister, that is all.'

It was. The police and this Dr Chitty could be fruitful sources of information. Unlike Sister Pia. In spite of that smile, her hostility was obvious, and it wasn't just because Mumtaz was a Muslim. What lurked in this old woman's background that had made her so bitter towards young girls that even now it made her refer to a baby as 'it'? Was it just the strictures that some said hid horrific abuse in the Catholic Church in years gone by, or was it something else?

Making a phone ring just by staring at it was not one of Paul Venus's skills, but it didn't stop him looking at the damn thing every five minutes. It got worse after Tina left his bedside. A quarter of a million pounds in the hole to Brian Green and no Harry to show for it. Tina would still withdraw two hundred and fifty thousand from her account and give it to him to pass on to Brian, who no doubt would be full of sympathy for his plight. But he'd probably still want a favour or two if the chance came up, and there was nothing Paul could do about that. He should have kicked Brian into touch years ago. He blamed Tina. Why did she still maintain contact with him?

A nurse came in and checked the pulse, blood pressure and temperature of the unconscious man in the corner. When she'd finished, he groaned and she turned back to look at him, but then left. Paul was glad she hadn't come to him. Making small talk was hard at the best of times, but with Harry still missing, it was too much to ask.

What the hell did the kidnappers think they were doing? They had three hundred and fifty thousand pounds! Did they want Tina and him to have to sell their property? And how did he even know that Harry was alive? He'd never asked for proof of life, which had been stupid. Lee Arnold had known it was ridiculous, he'd seen it on his face when he'd told him. And it was. Someone had taken a vast sum of money from him and he still had no idea who they were, or whether they even had Harry.

But the boy had gone somewhere. Even if he was dead, he was somewhere. That didn't bear thinking about, but with Harry still missing, it was possible. He'd never actually investigated a kidnapping. He'd read a lot of historical cases, but it wasn't the same.

'If I don't get home soon Amma'll go mental, innit.'

Baharat Huq didn't do young people-speak. He said, 'Don't be a silly boy. Your mother is of perfectly sound mind.'

He put a hand on the boy's knee and applied some pressure. 'Tell her you've been with Baharat-ji. I know your mother, she's a good woman, she will understand.'

'Whaddaya want?'

Baharat had intercepted Imran Ullah as he walked across the small park he had been sitting in opposite the boy's flat. The silly kid had been out for ages and it was starting to get dark by the time Baharat ushered him over to the bench he'd sat on for over two hours. He hadn't wanted to come.

'I want you to tell me what you do for Zafar-ji.'

'What?'

'Mr Bhatti,' Baharat said. 'You know, the deliveries.'

The boy shrank. The spaces between his spots reddened. Baharat wondered if he'd make up a lot of rubbish about delivering electrical goods for Zafar-ji, but he didn't. Although trembling, he said, 'Zafar-ji knows people's secrets and people are in debt to him. Me too. I need money. Amma won't take a penny from Amir. He even bought her a Rolex, but she just chucked it on the floor. She says his money's filthy.'

'She's a good woman.'

'She's soft in the head,' Imran said.

Baharat clipped him round the side of his head.

'Ow!'

'Don't speak about your mother like that! She took pain to give you life.' He took one of the boy's hands. 'Now young man, it's like this. What you do is not so clean, now is it?'

Imran just looked at him.

'Taking dirty messages from this man to that girl and what have you. I know how it is. "Will you meet me at dusk by the river, my own true love for whom I will give my honour?"'

The boy looked shocked. He said, 'They make arrangements of where to fuck.'

Baharat almost hit him again, but the boy cringed in anticipation. 'It's what they say!'

'I know. I know.' Baharat sniffed. 'Sadly. Now, I cannot believe that your dear mother wouldn't think such employment easily as dirty as the drugs that your brother sells, and yet you are the man of the house. Does your mother think that maybe you do something else for your living, young man?'

The boy put his head down but said nothing.

'Your silence tells me that she does,' Baharat said.

'You won't . . . ?'

The old man raised a hand. 'Ach! Quiet now! Of course I will not tell your mother, much as it upsets me to fall into the sin of lying. Your mother is a woman who has nothing and you provide for her. I have to say "Bravo". But in order to keep my silence, you must help me, Imran.'

'What? With messages to a girl?'

Baharat slapped him. 'No!'

'Ow! Baharat-ji . . .'

'No. All you need to do is tell me how you pick up the mail from the postal address,' he said. 'No one sees that door open or close. You emerge from Zafar-ji's shop carrying bags. Do you get in around the back somehow? Or through his shop?'

The boy looked away.

'I will say nothing to Zafar-ji, on my honour,' Baharat said. 'But I have to know.'

'Why?'

He couldn't tell him it was for Mumtaz. 'Because I have an interest in the property,' he said. 'If it helps, I can tell you that it has nothing to do with the courting couples you enable. It is more serious than that.'

The boy paled. 'What?'

'That is for me to know and you to not worry about.'

'It's not got to do with taking them packages to that weird shop up Bethnal Green, has it?'

'What weird shop, Imran?'

But then the boy reddened again. He mumbled, 'Nothing.'

Baharat took him by the shoulders. 'No it isn't,' he said. 'It is far from nothing. What do you mean, boy? What weird shop in Bethnal Green?'

The silence combined with the absolute darkness made for a total loss of orientation. All he knew was that he breathed. That he could feel the tightness of the FlexiCuffs around his wrists. Every time he pulled against them, they got tighter. He should have known better, but then maybe he welcomed the pain because it confirmed he was alive. They'd even put plasticine in his mouth to stop him making any sound through the gaffer tape that covered his face. They'd thought of everything.

Did his parents think he was dead? Harry Venus knew that his mum and dad had paid up, but where did that leave him? He couldn't go home. They'd never let him – or rather *he* wouldn't. They'd always wonder what he'd say. He'd told them he'd say nothing, but they hadn't believed him, though they should have done. Because Harry wasn't going to say anything. Ever. It's not what was done and they knew it.

'So what did the Little Sisters of Eternal Pain have to say?'

Mumtaz didn't often come to Lee's flat. She sat down.

'Lee, don't speak about them like that.'

'I'm forever blowing bubbles!'

Chronus the mynah bird liked to sing his West Ham United songs and chants at every opportunity. Lee and Mumtaz both ignored him.

'The Mother Superior of the Siena Sisters was very sincere,' Mumtaz said.

'Good for her.' Lee sat down. Religion, of whatever sort, was just beyond him. 'Anyway, useful?'

'Yes,' she said. 'I think I have a direction now. But Lee, I didn't come here about me. I gently put the word around that your postal address on Brick Lane was a bit of a mystery. Everyone knows what it is, as I told you, but how the post was being collected when the door never opened . . .'

'You found out?'

'According to my source, the electrical shop is connected internally to the house next door. To get in, one has to go up a flight of stairs and then through a hatch, which leads to the head of the staircase in the empty property. Whether the owner of the house knows or not, I haven't been told. The boy who collects the post cannot be seen from the outside, thereby ensuring some measure of security for Mr Bhatti's guilty clients, while also making sure that the owner can't be told about any comings and goings from his property. It's very Bengali – clandestine, but not.'

'And religion makes people behave like this?'

She shrugged.

'Sorry, Mumtaz, but it's like the nuns are behaving like, well, they're frightened to live.'

She leaned forward in her chair. 'Lee, forget religion,' she said. 'The point is that the boy gets in through the electrical shop. So when you observed him he could well have picked something up from the postal address. And there's something else. My contact . . .'

'Mumtaz, it's me,' Lee said. 'It was your dad, wasn't it?'

Mumtaz said nothing for a moment. They both knew her contact was Baharat Huq.

'The boy says that a few days ago – he couldn't be specific, he's not the brightest star in the sky – he took some parcels from the postal address to a shop in Bethnal Green. These were heavy packages and he remembers them because packages are unusual. In general he delivers letters to and from illicit lovers and final demands to unscrupulous businesses who like to remain hidden behind a PO box. But this was different. It was a series of heavy parcels addressed to an Englishman – a Mr Shaw. He has no idea who that is, but he does know that he delivered these parcels to a young Asian man.'

'In Bethnal Green.'

'He called it a "hippy" shop, but I suspect that is Mr Bhatti's word,' Mumtaz said. 'He couldn't remember the name of the shop or what street it was in, but I managed to deduce it was somewhere round Arnold Circus.'

'The old flats with a garden and bandstand in the middle. Know it well.'

'Once council-owned, now very chic,' she said. 'There are hippy shops all over the place up there now. By "hippy" I mean vintage, organic, you know the score. I thought you'd find it of interest.'

He leaned back in his chair.

Chronus yelled, 'West Ham till we die!'

'Useful,' Lee said.

'Good.' She made as if to go.

Then he said, 'Especially now the coppers are involved.'

'What?'

He could tell her now.

'If you sit tight for moment, I'll make you a cuppa and tell you about it,' he said. 'You got time?'

'Of course,' she nodded.

'Who are ya? Who are ya? Who are ya?'

This time they both looked at the yelling mynah bird and Lee said, 'Oh wind it in will you please, Chronus.'

When he'd gone to make the tea, Mumtaz took a small plastic container out of her handbag and gave the bird a piece of pineapple she'd kept from the Florida salad she'd had for her lunch. She'd spent a lot of time at Chiswick police station making an appointment to see someone who probably wouldn't be able to help her. The luxurious salad had been her reward. And the bird's.

10

Vi Collins looked at her boss, who, weirdly, blushed.

'You must think I'm a prize idiot, DI Collins,' Paul Venus said.

'What, for doing what you thought was right for your boy?' Vi shook her unnaturally dark-haired head. 'No, sir. Off course you might've been, but an idiot? No.'

'I've parted with a lot of money and I still don't have Harry.'

When Venus had been discharged from the Whittington, he'd been met by two SOCO officers who were now examining his flat. Out in the garden in the summerhouse, he sat with Vi Collins drinking Starbucks coffee and letting her smoke.

'Why'd Brian Green's new missus come and see you?' Vi said.

He sighed. 'I knew you'd recognise her,' he said. 'As you know, Brian was a villain long ago.'

'Still is.'

Venus drank his latte and didn't comment. Then he said, 'My wife knew him in the seventies. This is all on record, DI Collins. I called Brian as a friend of the family.'

'In case he could dig out some old contacts.'

'Yes . . .' He put his head in his hands.

'We'll know when the kidnappers call, sir . . .'

'They haven't called since they took the money,' he said. 'Presumably they still have my son . . .'

'Not necessarily. Sometimes kidnappers release their victims miles away from where they've been held, in order to put us off their scent. I've tapped up a few old colleagues to keep an eye open. No details.'

'And only you, Chief Inspector Stone and Tony know, apart from SOCO . . .'

'We're on a special assignment,' Vi said.

Venus managed a smile. 'Imagine us talking like this, DI Collins,' he said. 'Talking at all.'

Vi sat back in what she would have described as a 'posh' deckchair. No one was listening. She spoke her mind. 'You don't like what I am – sir,' she said. 'You never have.'

He didn't deny it. How could he?

'Might seem like I'm kicking you when you're down, but to be frank with you, I'm a bit surprised you chose a middle-aged, hard-smoking, drinking woman to find your son. Because you know that's how you've always made me feel.'

'Like a middle-aged, hard . . .'

'Like an old lump of sirloin, past its sell-by date,' she said.

He looked down at the floor.

'I've felt as if my job's been on the line ever since you came to us,' she said. 'Like I'm out the door for not being into Zumba and having unwhitened teeth. I'm guessing that in spite of that, you think I'm good enough at my job to find your son.'

'You're also a mother,' he said. 'And a good copper.' He looked up. 'I'm sorry, DI Collins. We're very different people. I'll be honest, your personal habits appal me. They have no place in the modern police force.'

'Your midlife crisis appals me,' Vi said.

In spite of his need to keep her on side, Venus bridled. 'Having my staff make up stories about affairs I haven't had doesn't help,' he said.

'And looking down young DCs' tops does?'

He knew he did that and he visibly deflated.

'But all that's bollocks at the moment, anyway.' Vi had had her say. It was time to get on with the job. 'We have to find Harry.'

'Yes.'

'Now Lee Arnold called me this morning and told me he may have a lead on that PO box in Brick Lane you took the first lot of money to,' she said. 'So he's checking that out. He's also planning to go to your son's school.'

'Why?'

'Invited by his English teacher, Arnold told me. Your wife gave him the bloke's details and they met up when Lee went to Henley.'

'Oh, yes. Mr McCullough.'

'Don't know the geezer's name, but Arnold reckoned he knew something weren't right and that was why he offered to help.'

Venus looked confused. 'Help? In what way?'

'Maybe someone at the school has your son,' Vi said.

'That's ridiculous! Why . . . ?'

'I don't fucking know, do I? But Arnold wants to check out every possibility and I'm with him on that score. And he has the contact with this Mr McCullough, so why not? You told Arnold yourself you were keeping him on because he can go places more easily than us coppers.'

He shrugged.

'You think it's a waste of time? Fine,' she said. 'But you've brought me in to run this investigation and you've retained Lee Arnold, so let us get on with it.' Then she added, 'You've not exactly covered yourself in glory so far, have you?' Then, regretting what she'd just said, she shook her head. 'That was uncalled for. Forget I said that.'

Venus said nothing for almost a minute. Then he shook his head. 'No, you're quite right, DI Collins,' he said. 'I either let you run this investigation or I don't. Please do what you think is best.'

Then he stood up and walked out into his small garden. Everything in it looked dead.

Mumtaz took the Tube back to Chiswick for her meeting with Sergeant Connolly. On the phone he'd portrayed himself as some sort of Chiswick historian, but he'd sounded as if he were only about thirty. And if that was so, then there had to be a limit to how much Chiswick history he had actually experienced. Not that it probably mattered too much. He'd said he 'knew of' Alison's case, which was more than anyone else had.

It was a long journey from Upton Park to Turnham Green and so Mumtaz had a lot of time to think. Normally she would have taken a book, but she had too much on her mind. As well as from Alison's case, she had a vision of Shazia trying to lift boxes of tinned goods out of Cousin Aftab's van. But the girl had been so keen to start, she'd had to let her. Aftab was paying her well and they needed the money, what was to argue about?

The thing that really disturbed Mumtaz, however, was what Lee had told her about Superintendent Venus's son. It had made her shake. That was her worst nightmare and the one that Naz Sheikh and his family exploited to the full. She hoped that what she'd told Lee about Imran Ullah would help in the search for Harry Venus, and when a young boy of about Harry's age got into the carriage at Tower Hill, she felt tears start in her eyes. Chastising herself for being so soft, Mumtaz looked away.

There was nothing she could do for Harry Venus except keep her ear to the ground with regard to the Brick Lane connection. Her job was to find Alison's parents, if she could. As the Tube pulled out of Blackfriars station, the ecclesiastical reference struck her and she thought about Sister Pia. She wasn't alone in thinking that the old nun knew more about Alison than she was letting on. She'd seen some doubt in Mother Katerina's eyes when Sister Pia spoke about the baby. And then, just before Mumtaz left, Mother Katerina had taken her to one side and told her that she would do what she could to find out where the old convent doctor was living. The last thing she'd said to her was, 'I've been told that Dr Chitty attended the baby every day during her stay with this Order. He may know things about her that the Sisters didn't.'

Lee had always liked Arnold Circus. A raised green space in the middle of an estate of council-owned mansion flats in Bethnal

Green, his mum Rose's friend Eva had lived there years ago. Built on the ruins of the poorest, roughest part of the Victorian East End, known as the Old Nichol, Arnold Circus, next door to the bars and clubs of Shoreditch, was very trendy. It also, he noticed, seemed to have been invaded by young men from an Edwardian photograph. Bearded and moustachioed, they seemed to like wearing old suit jackets that smelt of mothballs. They either rode or had bicycles with them, and very pretty girls too, in floral dresses.

Hipsters, the press called them. The sons and daughters of the rich who liked an urban vibe in their lives, who wanted to live in a flat in a tower block, or an old mansion building. Where Lee came from they were called twats.

He walked once round the bandstand at the centre of the circus. Old Eva had lived at the top of one of the blocks. She'd been a council tenant until her son bought the flat. Lee wondered how much money he'd made out of it, when he'd inevitably sold it on to a boy with a taxidermy collection.

Imran Ullah had told Mumtaz's 'connection' that the shop he'd taken those heavy parcels to sold food. He either couldn't or wouldn't say exactly where it was. It had been 'weird' because there had been sawdust on the floor and the fruit had been in wooden boxes. Lee took a stroll. It was hard to find a food shop that didn't conform to that description. Everything foodie was organic and wrapped in either paper or wood. If only Imran had been able to remember the name of the fucking place! He had given Baharat Huq the name of the man the parcels had been addressed to – a Mr Shaw – but he could hardly walk into every food shop in the vicinity of the Circus and ask. It was probably a pseudonym anyway. It was anodyne enough. According to Mumtaz's 'informant', the Ullah boy wandered about in a dream most of the time anyway.

There were more shops on Calvert Avenue than anywhere else, but there were also some on Navarre Street. They had names like 'Organiks', 'Apples and Pears' and 'Veg'. Names that made Lee have to face just how fucking cynical he was. Skinny daughters of Sloane Rangers carefully examined new apples in baskets and all Lee could think about was how much they all needed a bag of chips.

He walked down Navarre Street. An Asian boy with dyed blond hair and jeans that left nothing to the imagination strolled out of Veg and lit a cigarette. He was as far from Imran Ullah and his saggy shalwar khameez as it was possible to get. For a moment their eyes met and then the boy looked away, his nose in the air as if he'd just detected a bad smell.

She'd just brought a box of Brillo pads out of the storeroom to put on the shop floor when Shazia spotted Naz Sheikh. He was at the counter choosing a chocolate bar. Cousin Aftab, who had been at the back of the shop filling the bread shelves, walked over to help him.

'Yes, mate?'

Shazia made herself small behind the Brillo box.

Naz Sheikh said nothing. Cousin Aftab slotted himself behind the counter and waited. Time passed and Shazia began to wonder whether Sheikh had seen her and was hanging about intending to speak to her. But why? She saw Aftab look at his mobile phone and then scratch his head. Would he say something sarcastic about how long his customer was taking to choose a sweet? He could be quite rude sometimes, she'd discovered.

A blonde woman in a boob tube and a pair of skanky jogging bottoms was queuing up behind Naz Sheikh now, holding a carton of milk and a loaf of bread. She looked bored and then sighed. Naz Sheikh turned.

'Holding you up?' he said. He looked at the woman like she was shit on his shoe.

She said, 'I must get back to baby.'

She was some sort of eastern European, Shazia recognised the accent. There were a lot of young women from places like Poland and the Czech Republic in the area.

'What? Have you left your baby on its own?'

The gangster widened his eyes.

Shazia saw the woman freeze.

'Ludmilla, love, you take your stuff and pay me later.'

Naz looked at Cousin Aftab.

'Off you go, girl.'

The young woman smiled. 'Thank you, Mr Huq,' she said. 'I will pay.'

'I know you will.'

She began to walk away. Naz Sheikh picked up a chocolate bar, apparently at random. 'That slapper's left her baby,' he said as he handed over a pound coin. 'That not bother you?'

'It's why I told her she could pay later,' Aftab said. 'I know her. She works hard.'

'You know her.' There was a sneer in his voice and on his face. 'She's a whore.'

Cousin Aftab didn't react. 'Always in and out for bits and bobs, chief,' he said. He handed a couple of pennies back in change. The gangster began to leave.

Naz Sheikh and Shazia heard Aftab say to himself, 'Tosser.'

She walked out from behind the Brillo box.

'Oh, bung them down by the J Cloths,' Aftab said.

'OK.'

She walked between the narrow rows of tinned goods on one side and cereals on the other and made for the household stuff at the front of the shop. She'd just opened the Brillo box when Naz Sheikh walked back in and looked straight at her.

'There used to be some sort of performing arts school off Bath Road,' Sergeant Connolly said. He was a lot older than she'd thought he would be from his voice. He was probably in his mid-fifties.

'I can remember all sorts of dramatic types in the old Tabard,' he said, referring to the pub on Bath Road. Alison had been found in the phone box outside. 'Normal people'd go in there and have a pint, while they'd go in and share a Tequila Sunrise between four of them.' He shook his head.

'You remember the baby being found?' Mumtaz said.

Connolly tended to drift off into his own Chiswick memories whether they were relevant or not.

'Yeah,' he said. 'My old guv'nor interviewed the nun who found her.'

'Mother Emerita?'

'Don't remember her name,' he said. 'But I do remember Sergeant Piper, my old boss, saying how strange it felt to have a nun in the station. Wasn't like it is today, with all the security cameras and everyone going about as if they're on *CSI* or something. Designer clothes and all that. Back then everyone smoked and drank and the place smelt like a pub. He was quite embarrassed, Sergeant Piper was.'

'Did he tell you anything about the interview?'

'No. But I've dug out the paperwork for you,' he said. 'I scanned a copy.'

He pushed a sheet of paper towards her.

'Can I keep it?'

''Fraid not. But you can read it.'

Mother Emerita had been going to visit Dr Chitty, the convent's GP, when she found the baby in the telephone box outside the Tabard. Why she'd been going there wasn't divulged.

'People like Sergeant Piper didn't ask too many questions,' Connolly said when Mumtaz asked if he knew where Mother Emerita had been going. 'They didn't then. She was a nun, so how could she lie?'

The word 'easily' came into Mumtaz's head, but she said nothing and read on. Once she'd found the child, the Mother Superior had taken her back to the convent and called the police. She said that she had abandoned her trip to Dr Chitty's. But when the police had arrived, Dr Chitty had been at the convent. In modern times,

Mumtaz would have said that the nun had probably called her doctor from her mobile, but phones had been exclusively land lines back in the seventies. Maybe Mother Emerita had called him from the phone box? But if she had, he had turned up quickly. The police had taken a call from the convent before 7 a.m. and a WPC Martyn had been sent over immediately. Mother Emerita had been interviewed by Sergeant Piper that afternoon.

'There were pictures of the baby in the *Chiswick Herald*. I remember them.'

'Did the story make the national news?'

'Yes, when they were looking for the mother. Even back then it was all systems go for a while,' he said. 'But when no one turned up it all just sort of faded. The baby was taken to Essex, as you know. But going back to the drama school, there were a lot of students of all types staying in this area at the time. It was cheap to rent a room out here back then.'

'You think the mother could have been a student?'

'It's possible. People didn't used to talk about that sort of thing too much in those days but I know there were some not very politically correct things said.'

'Like what?'

'Like girls who wanted to be actresses were easy. And of course there were loads of crude comments about the girls who lived in the convent.' He shrugged. 'Some men have a thing about convent girls, like they're especially hankering after sex because they're in a place run by nuns. Sexist nonsense.'

'But the child wasn't found at the convent,' Mumtaz said.

'Exactly! Plods talk, what can I say?'

Mumtaz thought about Lee and what he said 'plods' had talked about when he'd been in the job. Even now it was mostly sex, sometimes booze, though modern plods wore nicer clothes.

'To be fair though, it was mainly Sergeant Piper who made the convent jokes,' he said. 'Kept on about the baby being born to a nice Catholic girl from a good family.'

'You don't think that he knew something, do you?' Mumtaz enquired.

He smiled. 'I don't think so. Sergeant Piper just interviewed the nun and then he was finished with it,' he said. 'He had what he'd call a bit of fun with the idea of some girl in the convent getting pregnant, then he found something else to laugh at. It was what he was like. He never took anything seriously, and that included the job.'

Mumtaz looked down at Mother Emerita's short statement again.

'What about WPC Martyn?' she asked.

'Didn't know her very well,' Connolly said. 'But I do know she did most of the work to do with Social Services.'

'You don't know how I can contact her, do you?'

'Not without a medium, no.'

'A medium?'

'She died the year after the baby was found,' he said. 'I remember it well. She just dropped.'

'Dropped?'

'She had a heart attack. Came out of nowhere. Funnily – or not funnily – Dr Chitty pronounced her dead.'

*

Lee's phone rang. It was Malcolm McCullough, Harry Venus's housemaster.

'Hi.'

'Mr Arnold?'

'Yes.'

'McCullough here, from Reeds.'

'Good to hear from you.'

'I've managed to arrange for you to visit the school,' he said. 'Bit short notice, but is tomorrow at two p.m. good for you?'

'Fine.'

'The gates will be open and if you drive up to the main building I can meet you outside the front entrance.'

'Great.'

'OK then. See you there.'

He ended the call quickly.

Lee wanted to see where Harry Venus studied, only partly in case it gave him any insight into his abduction. He also wanted to go to Reeds because he'd never been inside a public school, and in spite of what Malcolm McCullough had said when they'd first met, he still had a notion that cruel, weird, upper-class practices persisted. He knew he was almost certainly way off beam.

A laugh like a donkey's bray interrupted his thoughts. For a moment, stuck on top of the Circus mound, he couldn't locate the sound. Then he saw them: four young men, one in a business suit, two in hipster uniforms, and the fourth was that Asian boy he'd seen earlier. The brayer laughed again and he saw that it was one of the hipster kids, a nascent moustache on his lip,

143

wearing clothes that would not have looked out of place on a fifties bank clerk.

Lee heard him say, 'Well my little horrors, what would you say to champagne?'

The Asian boy said, 'Hello, champagne!'

The older man in the business suit raised his eyes to the sky. 'Oh, please, not that old chestnut.'

They all laughed. Lee grimaced. Pitiful. Obviously an in-joke or some sort of catch-phrase bollocks. Youth was a weird country that he found more and more incomprehensible. What were posh kids doing in the East End? Yeah it was funky and edgy and all that nonsense, but what was so good about that? Lee had spent most of his life living the funky-edgy 'dream'. It was overrated.

The other hipster kid, who was clearly going for a Victorian undertaker look, danced in the road for no apparent reason, and again, all the boys laughed, especially when he narrowly missed being killed by a white van. Lee wondered how the one in the modern business suit was putting up with them – and why.

The heat of the day had given over to the gentler warmth of early evening, and Lee could smell and hear people preparing their evening meals. He felt happy when he heard a few voices that had very obviously originated in the area.

'Shut the fuck up and eat your pie!'

But then the boys started again.

'I know,' the one with the nascent moustache continued, 'let's have a night out. There's this pub that does lock-ins round here somewhere.'

And then they all fell quiet for a moment – even grave. The Asian boy's face first contorted, then it laughed. 'Oh, God,' he said, 'that would just be so fucking exquisite!'

The undertaker shoved him and said, 'You are such a twisted bastard!'

'And you're not?'

Business Suit said, 'Look, if you kids get into trouble for underage drinking, you're on your own.' He looked at the undertaker. 'I'm off home, OK?'

'Whatever.'

He left.

They all howled with laughter again. Youngsters. Lee had no idea how old any of them might be and even less interest in finding out. But he did wonder whether Harry Venus was like them. He too was posh, moneyed and probably full of raging hormones. When they could go to Monte Carlo or Marrakesh for the summer, what were they doing hanging about Bethnal Green?

Lee watched the boys smoke joints and talk nonsense until finally they left the Circus. By that time the light had faded and what had once been the Old Nichol, the darkest slum in London, slipped back into something approaching Victorian gloom.

11

'And again please!'

High-pitched and hysterical, the voice sounded to Paul Venus like a maniacal clown.

'What?' He watched Tony Bracci pick up the extension.

'Money,' the voice said. 'Same as last time. That way Harry stays alive.'

He resisted the reflex to scream that he'd need time to sell things if they wanted another quarter of a million, and instead he said, 'I'll need proof. That Harry's still alive.'

Tony gave him the thumbs-up. Venus knew that he should have asked for proof of life right from the off, but he still felt that Tony was being patronising.

There was a pause.

'Are you there?'

Another pause. Could he hear whispering in the background at the other end of the line, or was it just in his head?

'Can you hear me?'

The panic built in his chest and created a pain. Oh, God a heart attack was all he needed now! If he dropped dead, what would happen to Harry?

'Hello?'

Tony Bracci moved one hand gently downwards and mouthed, 'breathe'.

He wanted to say, 'It's all right for you, with your tribe of kids safely at home,' but he didn't.

'Eeeerrrrr . . .'

The screeching clown was a new voice and it ramped up Venus's anxiety. He'd always found clowns sinister and this was like the Coco the Clown of his youth, but on crystal meth.

He made himself speak. 'You can have your money, but I must have proof that Harry's still alive first.'

'Mmmmm . . .'

The screechy noises caught the raw edges of his nerves.

'Well?'

Tony Bracci turned away. That had been a bit imperious. Had it been too much? God almighty, they knew who he was and what he did, wouldn't they be expecting that?

'We'll send you a little DVD, Mr Venus,' the voice said. 'Then the money. Now we've been chatting for far too long . . .'

The line went dead. Venus put the phone down.

Tony Bracci said, 'Let's see what the technical bods got from that.'

A woman with a rasping voice like a macaw was very firm about Dr Chitty.

'He's too old and sick to see anyone,' she told Mumtaz.

Early that morning Mother Katerina had phoned with the name and number of the nursing home where Dr Chitty was living. Mumtaz had called the place at once.

'I accept that,' Mumtaz said. 'But could you please let Dr Chitty know I called and take my number?'

'I've told you, he . . .'

'Tell him it's about baby Madonna. Just take my details and tell him that.'

Across the kitchen table, Shazia was stirring her scrambled egg without eating it.

The woman at the other end said nothing.

'If it wasn't a matter of life and death, I wouldn't be asking to disturb Dr Chitty,' Mumtaz said. 'But it is. Please just tell Dr Chitty and let him make his own choice.'

'We don't tell 'em what to do and when to do it here,' the woman said, obviously offended.

'I . . .'

'It's his doctor says he has to be quiet, not us.'

'Yes, but even so, if you could . . .'

'I'll do what I can.'

She sounded peeved, but she took Mumtaz's name and number, by which time Shazia had gone, leaving her breakfast uneaten. It wasn't like her. She'd always had a good appetite. She'd looked glum too, which was strange considering that according to Aftab, she was doing well in the shop. Maybe it was teenage stuff? As far as Mumtaz knew there was no boy on the horizon, but she did have a lot of work to do over the holidays and perhaps she was worried about that.

She just hoped that the girl wasn't still brooding over the situation with the Sheikhs. There was nothing anyone could do, least of all Shazia. Mumtaz automatically looked at her phone. Naz had rung her twice in the last twenty-four hours. He was trying to find out why, according to a rumour he'd heard, DI Collins and Superintendent Venus seemed to have suddenly disappeared from Forest Gate police station. He wanted her inside news. The Sheikhs had other sources in Forest Gate police station, but no one, they felt, as close to Violet Collins as Mumtaz. So if Collins and Venus were coming after the Sheikhs and their drug business or their rented flats, their money laundering or their people-trafficking activities, Mumtaz could find out about it. That was Naz's thinking. And of course she did know what was going on, but she wasn't telling.

She liked Vi and knew her socially, but what Naz and his family were counting on were indiscretions made by DI Collins while in bed with her occasional lover, Lee Arnold. Everyone knew they had a 'thing' from time to time and Mumtaz was sure that Lee had passed information on to her that had come unofficially from Vi. But she was never going to make that available to anyone, least of all the Sheikhs. She'd made a deal with Naz to let him know about any proposed police action against the family in return for some concessions on what remained of her late husband's debt to them. And on condition that they left Shazia alone. But she'd never planned to make good on that agreement.

Mumtaz put her phone in her handbag and made ready to leave. She was in the office all day because Lee was out on Harry Venus business. She hoped that the poor boy was discovered soon.

*

When he'd been a kid, Lee Arnold's parents had always told him that if he 'made it' in life he could go and live 'out west'. This meant anything from Earl's Court to Oxford, but didn't include Notting Hill, which was 'full of blacks'. Living in places like Chiswick, Henley-on-Thames or Windsor said to the world that you had arrived. Quite what Bracknell, the largely modern new town where Reeds School was actually based, had to say, Lee didn't know. There were a lot of traffic roundabouts and new houses, which put him in mind of Basildon in Essex.

He'd arrived early. Keen to get a jump on the often congested M25, he'd left his flat at ten for a 2 p.m. appointment. Now he was at Tesco in Bracknell and it was only one o'clock. He'd driven past the entrance to Reeds, which was in a pleasant green area called Bracknell Forest, but the gates had been closed. He got an impression of a large red-brick building in the middle of a lot of grassland. He wondered what the boys did in terms of sport in all that wide open space, and imagined tennis courts and stables. It was little wonder that the boys who attended such places did so well later in life. A rigorous education combined with loads of improving activities and the opportunity to meet other future movers and shakers beat the hell out of sleeping through French, playing football in the street and smoking in the toilets. He'd met a lot of good people when he'd been at school, but none of them had ever got him a job.

He had to keep an open mind. And a clear one. The purpose of his visit to Reeds was to see if he could find any clues as to who might have kidnapped Harry Venus and why. Money, of course, but Lee couldn't believe that it was just cash that had singled Harry out to whoever held him captive. Why him? His parents were wealthy, but he couldn't believe they were the richest mummy and daddy of a Reeds boy. Most of their dosh seemed to be in property, which meant that to release large sums would take time. The kidnappers had been in touch with Venus that morning, demanding more money. Tony Bracci had told him that this time Venus had demanded proof of life. But he'd also put his flat up for sale. The techs had got the phone number and traced it to the Paddington area. It had been nicked.

Lee wandered into Tesco's cafe and ordered a coffee and a piece of cheesecake. There was definitely more to this than money, but was there also an element of punishment too – aimed more at Venus than his son?

'Real, proper Indian curry!'

The boy smiled at the tourists and wiggled his head in that way they, no doubt, expected him to.

Baharat Huq shook his head. He said to the boy, whom he knew, 'What the hell you talk about India for? You've never been to India in your life.'

The boy dropped his fake subcontinent accent and said, 'You think you can get anyone in any restaurant down here without the Indian thing? They don't know where Bangladesh is, innit.'

'Ach.'

Baharat walked on. He knew very well that all the restaurants had to be Indian for marketing purposes, just as it was wise always to put a Hindu god in the window to attract punters. Preferably the elephant god Ganesh.

'Abba.'

His son Ali crossed the road. He'd come out of the Jamme Masjid. Still smarting from their last bad-tempered encounter, Baharat nevertheless let his son hug him.

'You've been at prayer.'

'Yes,' he smiled. 'I didn't see you.'

'You know I don't always go,' Baharat said. 'Allah is everywhere.'

His son looked down at the ground. In recent years his observance of his faith had grown directly in proportion to a decline in his father's outward piety. It obviously rankled. Baharat changed the subject.

'Young Shazia is working for your cousin Aftab in his shop in Forest Gate,' he said. 'Heavy work, but Aftab says that she is doing well. She has determination and strength of character, that one.'

'And my sister allows it?' Ali said.

'Your sister who worked in my shop when she was that girl's age and younger? With you and your brother?' Baharat said. 'Why not?'

He was goading his son and he knew it. 'Why not, Ali?' he repeated.

'You know why not, Abba.'

'Ah, because she is a girl.'

'You—'

'The thing you so-called "pure" Muslims always forget is that the Prophet, Blessings and Peace be Upon Him, took as his first wife a woman who had a job. Khadija was a merchant, but she was also the first Muslim. And people like you would put her daughters behind closed doors?'

'Women tempt,' Ali said. 'They can't help it, but they must be protected and men, in turn, must be shielded from the temptations that they bring.'

There had always been 'loose' women. Back home in what had then been East Pakistan, every village had at least one. They were generally shunned by all but their late-night, very guilty, customers, but other women were not looked upon with undue suspicion. Although there had always been a level of sexual violence in heavily populated areas like Dhaka, in recent years it seemed to have risen. Maybe it was because it was more widely reported, but Baharat felt that radicalisation was also to blame. Why were nice Bengali boys with good prospects going to Syria to fight jihad? And why, when they got there, were they turning into rapists and murderers? There was no excuse and there was no connection to religion that he could see. Oddly his son could, and it made Baharat sad.

'I don't know who you have been listening to these past years,' he said. 'But I worry that what they have been saying to you bears no relation to the religion of your ancestors.'

'Abba, you are behind the times. Islam is moving.'

'Ah, to kick the Crusaders out of the Middle East? The Jews out of everywhere?' He shook his head. 'Muslims have grievances. They are valid, but so are other people's. We all must accommodate each other.'

'No.' He looked up. 'Not anymore.'

The old man shrugged. 'We have to disagree, then,' he said. 'It makes me sad, Ali.'

'I can't help that.'

'What we must hang on to is respect,' he said. 'Me for you – although I cannot agree with your views – and you for me.'

Ali said nothing.

'What I'm saying, my son, is that you will not interfere in the life of your brother, your sister or her daughter. I will not tolerate it. And I tell you, I won't allow it.'

'Allow it?' Ali's face flushed. 'Oh, and will you not "allow" me to pursue jihad if it is the right thing for me to do?'

'Is it?'

He felt his heart squeeze.

Ali said, 'I don't know. I haven't made my mind up, but if I do then I have to know that you won't inform on me to the police. You're so in love with this country and its culture and—'

'I will do what I think is right at the time, my son.'

He shook his head. 'Your son?'

He walked away, leaving what should have been a statement hanging in the air.

Baharat wanted to cry. What should have united them – religion – had somehow driven them apart and he couldn't understand why. Why would anyone want to go and fight in a country far away that was not their own? And how could the jihadists in Syria even dare to claim that name? They were thugs. Ali was an intelligent man, what did he find to admire so much about these vile people?

Then he looked at the bored kid outside the 'Indian' restaurant, trying to tempt tourists inside. Such soul-destroying work. Baharat could understand how kids like that might think that war was preferable to their own dull lives. Maybe they were not bright enough to recognise that real war was not like a video game. But what was Ali's excuse? A well-educated, prosperous businessman who could go anywhere and do just about anything he wanted? He said that his life lacked direction, but Baharat didn't even know what that meant.

Buildings that were usually full of people were always slightly forbidding when empty. Lee remembered once visiting a deserted hospital. Admittedly he'd been looking for an escaped prisoner, but the place itself had made him shudder.

Reeds was a four-storey red-brick building with a clock tower at its centre. It looked like a grand version of a typical Edwardian school, like the one that Lee had gone to in Plaistow. It was only the size and the massive grounds that made it look different. Also there were no graffiti.

Lee pulled up right in front of the shiny wooden doors that were the main entrance, but he could see no sign of any other cars. A caretaker must have opened up, and McCullough was late. It didn't matter. It was another warm day and so it wasn't unpleasant leaning on the car, having a fag in the sunshine. He imagined, given McCullough's relaxed attitude to smoking, that no one was going to come and tell him off. The posh tended to do what they liked, so they'd probably respect him for having a puff.

How long it took Lee to recognise that the small white blob in the window above the main entrance was a face was something he would later wonder. He had been looking up into the sky for at least a couple of moments, so maybe he'd thought that the pale oval was some sort of after-image caused by bright sunlight. But he couldn't remember clearly. Then when his vision resolved he saw that the patch had eyes, pale hair and a mouth that moved. He pushed himself away from the car and walked closer to the building. There was no sound. Either the child – it could only be a small boy, as its head was only just visible above the windowsill – couldn't shout loudly enough to make himself heard or Lee's ears were playing up. He moved closer still. The pale head was joined by two white hands, which hammered silently on the window. Lee felt cold. There was still no sound and yet the boy was clearly in distress. He couldn't just stand there and do nothing.

He looked around for McCullough or anyone else, but the place was like a tomb, except for the white-faced boy. Then he saw what looked like a pair of hands on the kid's shoulders and the tiny mouth opened in what had to be a scream. Lee ran up the steps to the front entrance, tried first one then the other round handles. The fucking thing was locked! Just in case, he called 'Help!' to whoever might be able to hear him. He knew that if he shoulder-charged the doors he'd only injure himself, but he'd give kicking them a go. As he walked back to take a run at them, he called up to the kid 'I'm coming!' All he could do was hope that he was. Those doors were bloody solid.

'What you doing?'

The voice made Lee turn. More of a girl than a woman, she wore a dayglo lemon boob tube and very tight jeans.

'There's a boy,' Lee began. 'Up there.' He pointed.

She looked. She had some of the biggest hair Lee had ever come across, and one of the biggest bodies.

'What you mean?'

'There!'

Now he looked. There was no boy. Nothing.

She said, 'What?'

'There was a kid,' he said. 'A boy, up there, in that window. Yelling for help.'

'A boy? School's closed. No boys here. Who are you anyway? This is private property.'

Lee noticed she was chewing, which annoyed him. Gum made everyone who chewed it look thick.

'Who are you?' he said.

'None of your business,' she said. Then, suddenly, her face changed. 'Here, you that bloke Malcolm asked us to open up for?'

'If you mean Malcolm McCullough, yes,' Lee said. 'But about this boy—'

'Ain't no boy in there,' she said. 'School's closed, like I said. My old man'll be along soon with the keys. Once Mr McCullough gets here, then you'll see.'

Lee looked up at the window again and shook his head. There had been a boy up there. He'd seen him, even if he hadn't heard him. And someone had placed hands on his shoulders.

'Well, can I go in and check?' Lee said.

She adjusted her jeans. 'When me old man gets here.'

Seeing the look of impatience on Lee's face she said, 'There's no one in there. Big windows in an old place like this. Trick of the light. Boys see all sorts in them windows all the time.'

*

He'd shat himself. He didn't know how, he hadn't eaten for . . .
He didn't know how long. In such complete darkness there was
no point of reference and there had been no sound for a very
long time. Harry *knew* he had been left to die. What he couldn't
understand was why.

His parents would have coughed up. They *had* coughed up.
So what had gone wrong? Something must have. But then as
Harry began to shiver in the coldness of his own shit, he knew
the answer. They couldn't let him go. They'd never been able to.
And it was the perfect crime.

12

Baby Madonna.

The nurse with the red hair had yelled her name and then smiled inanely at him, as if she were talking to a moron. Admittedly, most of his fellow residents *were* morons. Looking at them now, lurking round the walls in plastic padded chairs, gurning at a TV show about cooking, it was difficult to see why any of the staff would think they were worth speaking to like human beings. They were barely alive, most of them. Francis Chitty was just the same on the outside. Inside, however, he knew what was going on and he was well aware of the fact that he was not dementing. He'd diagnosed enough of that in his time. He knew what it looked like and it wasn't like him. Hard of hearing, underweight and nursing a dodgy ticker, Dr Chitty still had his marbles, even if the staff of the Lilacs Residential Care Home chose to ignore that fact.

A woman wanted to see him about baby Madonna. It was a name he hadn't heard for decades, and for a moment his old heart had stuttered. Red nurse hadn't said why this nameless woman wanted to see him about Madonna, but he could hazard a guess. A lot of time had passed since those events of 1971, and although he had thought about them from time to time, he'd begun in recent years to think that he'd never hear about them again. But even with a brain softened by years of Eamonn Holmes, Jeremy Kyle and *Strictly Come Dancing*, he had to know deep down that the baby wouldn't just go away.

Was the woman who wanted to see him Madonna, all grown up? How had she found him? And why after all this time? She had to be middle-aged. Mother Emerita had died a long time ago. All the nuns from that time had gone, dead or back to Italy, except for Sister Pia. She, he'd heard, was dying. And death had a way of opening mouths, as he knew. It was natural for people to want to clear their consciences prior to death even if they weren't religious. One of his patients, a married man with five children, had told him he was actually gay as he lay dying in what had been his marital bed for over fifty years. Dr Chitty had never told anyone. Baby Madonna was the same. Since the moment she left the Sisters of Mary Immaculate of Siena to go to the orphanage in Essex, he had not so much as breathed her name.

Red nurse had said to him, 'You don't have to see the lady. Don't worry. I've told her Dr Saleh wouldn't like you to be bothered.'

So he did have an 'out'. Except that he really didn't. Now that Madonna had somehow moved into the light, he would have to deal with her. The only question he had to think about was when.

'Sorry to keep you waiting.'

Malcolm McCullough shook Lee's hand. Wearing a jacket with elbow patches and cords, he looked every inch the archetypal teacher. He also reeked of fags. 'Hope Lila's been keeping you entertained.'

Lee just smiled. Lila, the boob-tube girl, was the caretaker's wife. Her 'old man', Bob, had turned out to be just that. It had taken him a while to find the right key to open the school front entrance, mainly because he couldn't see much without the glasses he needed but didn't possess. As soon as the door had opened, Lee had dashed inside and up the stairs that were straight in front of him. The window where he thought he'd seen the child let light onto a landing that was completely deserted.

Lila and Bob had let Lee run through Reeds' corridors looking for his pale boy, until McCullough had turned up.

Now they all stood inside the main entrance. Lila lit a fag. 'Been looking for some boy,' she said to McCullough as she nodded towards Lee.

'What boy?'

Lee told him what he'd seen. Malcolm McCullough nodded. 'Old buildings like this can do weird stuff to our perceptions,' he said. 'Boys are always imagining they're seeing ghostly faces at these windows.'

'Trick of the light,' Lila reiterated.

'Yeah, but I'm not a hormonal fourteen-year-old,' Lee said. 'What I saw was a real face of a real boy in trouble.'

'So where is he?' the caretaker asked. 'Mr McCullough, soon as I opened up, this bloke runs in all over the place. Never found nothing though, did you?'

'I ran down a few corridors,' Lee said. 'Couldn't get into any of the rooms. Can we go and do that now, please?'

McCullough smiled. 'Of course.'

He took two bunches of keys from the caretaker. 'I promised you a full tour and that is what you're going to get. Would you like to start upstairs, Mr Arnold?'

'Yeah.'

They left the caretaker and his wife at the main entrance. The girl was smoking and whispering in her husband's ear.

'Traffic in and out of Henley was atrocious,' McCullough said. 'We're on the countdown to the regatta and so the town's full of rowers and boaters doing their prep. And tourists. If I'd been on time you wouldn't have had such a fright. I do apologise.'

'I saw what I saw.'

'It's hot today,' McCullough said. 'And you'd been driving. Believe me, Mr Arnold, no one can get in here when school is closed. As well as Bob we're also bristling with alarms, CCTV cameras . . .'

'At the front entrance?'

'Of course.'

'I'd like to see what it caught,' Lee said.

'Well, it won't have recorded the window where you said you saw something,' McCullough said.

'Then which one would?'

'I don't know. We'd have to ask our security providers and the headmaster.' He opened a door to a large room that smelt of paint. 'If anyone had been in here the motion sensors would have picked it up. Alarms would have gone off and Bob would have called the police. This is one of the art rooms.'

There were two half-finished canvases on easels. Oil paintings of what Lee knew were called 'still life'. A pear, a bunch of flowers and a wine glass. A nice picture for a proud mother to display over her fireplace. Painting materials of all sorts – oils, water-colours, pastels – were ranged in neat drawers beside reams of paper, buckets of pencils and felt-tipped pens. There were clay ovens too. Surrounded by the usual array of deformed pots and surreal attempts at modelling dogs. Possibly underneath there were a few clay penises. There always had been at Lee's old school.

'The boys also work with textiles, wood, metal and whatever other medium they feel inclined to explore,' McCullough said. 'Most of 'em will end up in business or the military and so this is often the only chance they'll get to explore their creative poten-tial. A few of 'em opt to take the GCSE, but art is generally an extra-curricular.'

'Does Harry Venus like art?'

They walked out and McCullough locked the door.

'Not unduly.'

'What does he like?'

'Can't say I really know. He's not one for interests or hobbies; he's academic. History, English, but his real talent is for lan-guages. French, German, Arabic and now Mandarin. One day he'll become an academic or a diplomat. Mind you, Tom de Vries is the one who really has a shoo-in for the diplomatic corps because of his father. Bit of a waste really.'

'Why?'

'He's got great literary skill. Most talented boy I've taught for years.'

They passed the glazed doors leading to more art rooms. In

the third one, something caught Lee's eye. It made him step back and look inside.

'Ah, yes,' McCullough said. 'That is one of the mannequins the boys have made for the Harvest Festival service next term. There are four of them, representing earth, water, fire and air. I believe that one's meant to be air.'

The figure was blond, its face contorted in what looked like pain. The hands of the figure behind it lay on its shoulders.

'That one is fire, I believe,' McCullough said.

Shazia froze. He was in the shop again. What was he doing coming in twice in two days? He was messing with her head. But then how did he know she knew who he was? Had she made her feelings apparent to him in some way? Maybe scowled at him in the street? She didn't think she had. He'd abused her under his breath, yes. But then maybe he was just watching her for his own purposes? Maybe he'd come to try and abduct her, as Amma always feared?

Cousin Aftab was out picking up toilet rolls. He said he'd only be a mo and had left her in charge of the shop. She'd have to serve Naz Sheikh.

She walked up to the counter. 'Can I help you?'

He smiled. He *was* good-looking. But he was also a monster, so it was difficult for Shazia to smile back. She gave it a go, but she was sure what resulted was weird.

'Owner about is he?' Naz asked.

'No, at the cash and carry,' she said. 'Can I help you?'

He stared at her. Shazia began to feel her skin heat up. She knew what a man's lust felt like and she lowered her eyes.

'I need to speak to Mr Huq on his own,' he said. 'Much as I'd like you to be able to help me.'

'OK. I don't know when he's going to get back . . .'

'Just tell him I called.'

Ludmilla came into the shop with baby Tomasz in her arms.

'Tell him who?' Shazia even picked up a pen and a Post-it note.

His smile vanished. 'Don't play games, little girl,' he said. 'You know exactly who I am.'

He pushed past Ludmilla, almost treading on her feet as he left. Shazia shook with fear. What did he want with Cousin Aftab?

Ludmilla, shocked at Shazia's appearance, walked behind the counter and hugged her. Baby Tomasz giggled.

'Who is that pig?' Ludmilla asked. 'I see him yesterday. I hear him call me bad names. What he want?'

'You don't want to know,' Shazia said.

Was he being led into believing he'd seen a mannequin at the window? But then had he? At which window had he actually seen the boy? He couldn't remember now. The mannequin certainly looked like the kid he'd seen at the window. It had to be.

Vi had just called to say that Venus's Islington flat was already under offer. He'd put it on the market at eleven. The London housing market was insane and getting worse every week as people scrambled to get on the property ladder at any price. Lee felt cold and then hot as McCullough took him into the small bedroom that Harry Venus shared in term time with George Grogan.

There wasn't much to see. Two small single beds, a couple of desks.

'The boys take all their personal possessions home at the end of the academic year,' McCullough said. 'But I can tell you that this room was quite sparse. Youngsters don't seem to go in for posters and photographs these days. They're allowed to put them up if they want to, but they don't. All on their laptops or tablets these days.'

Magnolia-coloured and anodyne, the room gave nothing away. 'Malcolm, you said before that Harry Venus wasn't really a member of the in-crowd,' Lee said.

'Yes. Awkward. But he isn't the first to feel like that and he won't be the last. We're still quite old-fashioned here at Reeds, inasmuch as most of our boys are British and from upper- or upper-middle-class families. Next year a large proportion of our intake will come from the former Soviet Union.'

'Oligarchs' kids.'

'Indeed. But as for Harry, he'll grow into his own man eventually. A bit of adversity at school is no bad thing, toughens a boy up.'

Lee had heard this excuse for allowing bullying to happen before – when he'd been in the army. It hadn't worked for him, just as it probably hadn't worked for Harry Venus. Unhappier than he let on, had he organised his own 'kidnap' to punish his parents for sending him to a place like Reeds?

He would have to have had help. Maybe he'd had it from his

mates. But then they weren't really mates, were they? And also, if he had arranged his own abduction, how cruel was that to his parents? He didn't know Harry, but he was finding it hard to believe that any child could be that vile to its parents.

They walked through what McCullough still called 'dorms' but were in fact all single or double rooms, and into the refectory. Not in use for now, it was just a large empty space with stacked tables and chairs at one end and a service counter at the other. The only other thing in the room was a large glass trophy cabinet.

'Reeds does rather well at cricket and we've got a couple of really good tennis players,' McCullough said. 'I was always a rugby man myself, but Reeds, for some reason, doesn't produce many really good players. Tom de Vries was a good bat at one time, but his creative work takes up all his time. And he's a bit of a character, if you know what I mean.'

Lee frowned.

'Oh nothing awful,' Malcolm said. 'Not for these days.'

There was a variety of silver or silver-plate cups, vases and shields in the cabinet, some of them accompanied by photographs of the teams who had won them. However, the tennis trophies were for singles tournaments and accompanied by the winners' portraits. There were two: one for under-fourteens and the other for older boys. The latter, although it took Lee a few moments to work it out, was apparently George Grogan.

He looked very different when he wasn't arsing about in Bethnal Green dressed as a nineteenth-century undertaker.

*

Brian Green hadn't contacted Venus at home, which, given that it had been tapped by Vi Collins, was a mercy. But the Superintendent knew that the old lag would want to know where his money was soon. Brian was not the type to allow his business affairs to slide. But having Tony Bracci on his heels was not conducive to making contact with someone he should only be on the most casual terms with. Trying to save his son and preserve his career was taking its toll, and Venus found that thinking straight was difficult. Eventually he called Tina and told her to contact the 'bank' about the money they'd borrowed. Tina knew what he meant. It was after all Tina who had first introduced Paul Venus to Brian Green. When she'd been in lots of cheeky-chappy tit comedies in the seventies, Brian Green had been one of her escorts. Later, he'd helped her get the part of the granite-faced Rita in *Londoners*. He'd been disappointed when she'd 'gone queer' after her marriage fell apart, but by that time he was cosy with her husband, which was where he'd always wanted to be since he'd first met Paul. A copper in the pocket was always worthwhile, even if the relationship didn't last.

Paul put the phone down.

'Your lady wife all right, Superintendent?'

'As well as can be, thank you, DS Bracci.'

'Would you like a cuppa, sir? I'm gasping.'

'Yes, that would be very nice.'

Tony went into Venus's kitchen and riffled about for cups because he'd forgotten where they were. He really wasn't a bright man. But at least he was out of the way.

Venus looked at the piece of paperwork the estate agent had handed to him before he'd left the flat. It said that an offer had been made to Mr Venus for his flat by a Mr Adlam, which he had accepted, of six hundred thousand pounds. With two hundred and fifty thousand going to the 'Harry Fund' he'd sure as hell never be able to live in Islington again. He'd either have to settle for some ex-council flat, or go and live in somewhere like bloody Newham. There was of course a third way, but he didn't want to think about that now.

The Grogan family had the type of home that was very well protected from view. McCullough had called it an arts and crafts house, which meant, because Lee had googled it, that it had probably been built in the early twentieth century and that it looked a bit cottagey. He knew there was a swimming pool round the back because Tina Wilton had told him about it and because he could hear people splashing about and shouting from his car.

When he'd left Reeds he'd driven straight over to Twyford and parked across the road from the Grogans' house. It was a hot late afternoon and he hoped to be able to see the family outside, so that he could confirm that George was who he thought he was. People who lived this close to London rarely went there for their holidays. George and his mates had to have been on a day out when he saw them. But then they'd talked about staying out all night . . . Staying out as opposed to going home to Twyford, or somewhere else? George did have an older brother who lived in London. Could that have been the young man in the suit? And was any of this relevant to Harry Venus anyway?

Lee phoned Vi.

'What's happening?'

He told her about Reeds, his weird experience with the blond boy on the landing, and about George Grogan.

'Well, thanks for the tip about George,' Vi said. 'We're gonna have to interview him now he's back.'

'You're still keeping Harry's disappearance under wraps?'

'Officially. But if we're gonna find these kidnappers we've got to get more info, which means very carefully tapping up contacts and suspects. I'm getting an impression of Harry as a bit of a disconnected kid. Clever, but not really involved in much. No sport or clubs going on.'

'It's like he's got no personality,' Lee said. 'Certainly couldn't find any evidence of one in his bedroom in his mum's house. At school he's taken up and put down by his posh mates as and when they feel like it. Only bit of spark about him is when he goes and gives some of the younger kids a hard time.'

'What? Like fagging?'

'No. Well his teacher says not, but what do I know? He's a lost kid, Vi, and I don't just mean because he's missing. In fact, I've been wondering if he is missing. I don't know that he didn't kidnap himself. With help, you know.'

'Well, if he did he's likely to end up giving his dad a heart attack,' Vi said. 'Tone said Venus looked proper rough.'

'I would if my daughter was missing and I had to sell the flat to get her back. Not that what my flat's worth would get me far. What did Venus get for his?'

'Six hundred grand.'

'Fuck.'

'Do you think this George might have helped Harry to kidnap himself?'

'I don't know. He was hanging around Bethnal Green/Shoreditch with a gang of other posh hipster kids when I saw him. But then all that type gravitate to that area now.'

'One of the ransom drops was in Brick Lane.'

'Yeah, but in Bangla Town to an Asian lonely hearts PO box. There was a kid who looked Asian with George and his mates in Bethnal Green last night, but again, he was posh. He wasn't local. He certainly wasn't one of the shalwar khameez-wearing brigade. Maybe I'm wrong, Vi. Maybe some really bad-ass gangsters that Venus has really pissed off have got Harry. Or some mental fan of his mum, or something. But the whole thing's so chaotic, I can't help but think that kids are involved somewhere. And Harry Venus is a sad kid. His parents are separated, neither of them really have much time for him. Tina Wilton admitted that they both spoil Harry materially to make up for the time they don't have with him, and the poor fucker's at a boarding school where he's a social misfit. That's a creepy fucking place.'

'Mmm. And yet, all the voices the kidnappers use, the drops, the changes of plan, the violence, it's all a bit adult, bit clever,' Vi said.

'True. Oh, hang on, someone's coming round the side of the house.'

Lee put his phone down beside him and watched as a large, sopping wet black Labrador and a stark-naked skinny boy ran into the front garden. The boy, screaming with laughter, was definitely George Grogan.

13

'Sister?'

Mother Katerina put a hand on Sister Pia's shoulder and shook her very gently. The old nun opened one eye and said, 'What is it, Reverend Mother?'

'You have a telephone call,' Mother Katerina said.

'A telephone call?' Slowly and in some pain, she sat up in bed. 'Who wants to call me at this hour, Mother?'

'Sister, it's ten o'clock, you were sleeping so soundly I didn't want to disturb you.'

'Oh.'

Mother Katerina put the phone into the old woman's hand.

For a moment Sister Pia looked at it and then she put it to her ear. 'Hello?'

'Sister Pia?'

She didn't recognise the voice, which was old, male and British, but she thought she should know it.

'Yes. Who is this?'

There was a slight pause, which made her put a hand to her chest.

'It's Francis Chitty,' the voice said.

'Oh.' Had that Asian detective woman been to see him? What had he told her?

'Dr Chitty, Sister.'

'Yes. Yes, I know. Doctor, I haven't heard from you in many years. How are you?'

He laughed. She could hear shouting in the background. He was in a home with crazy old people, poor man. 'I'm old, sick and I watch far too much television,' he said. 'And you, Sister?'

'I am ready to go, but God has not seen fit to take me yet,' she said. 'Cancer grows slowly in old bones.'

'It does. I'm sorry.'

'There's no need. This life has become a burden. I look forward to being with Our Lord.'

In spite of being in a care home, the doctor was as lucid as she was. Sister Pia feared what he would say next.

'And it is with the afterlife in mind that I call you today,' he said.

Mother Katerina was listening from across the room. Sister Pia wished she would go, but then in all probability it was the Superior who had told the Asian woman where Dr Chitty lived. If his call was about that. She still hoped that it wasn't . . .

'Oh?'

'Sister, I have just today been made to think about something from the past, something I took part in, which was a mistake.'

She said nothing. She couldn't.

'Remember the baby girl, Madonna?'

For a moment her voice wouldn't work. Then she said, 'Yes.'

'A woman telephoned here, asking to speak to me about her,' he said. 'At first I thought it might be Madonna herself, but this woman has an Asian name.'

'I know her, she's a private detective. Mrs Hakim. She is employed by Madonna.'

'Ah, that makes sense.'

That one day, someone would come about the baby was as inevitable as death, and she knew that she should welcome it. She was dying and one of the things she needed to do was cleanse her soul of all her sins. But she still felt cold and afraid.

'Has she been to see you, Sister?'

'She has.'

'And what did you tell—?'

'Nothing,' she said. 'I repeated what is known by everyone.'

'Ah.'

'I said that you attended the child when she was here at the convent.'

'I gave Mrs Hakim Dr Chitty's address,' Mother Katerina interjected.

'Mother gave the lady your address.'

'I see,' he said. She heard him clear his throat. 'Well, Sister, I am going to meet this lady and talk to her. Madonna must be forty-two now and I think that the time has come for her to know.'

'She's dying.' It just came out. She hadn't wanted it to. She reached for her rosary on her bedside table.

'Madonna?'

'Yes,' she said. 'Mrs Hakim told Mother.'

Across the room she saw the Superior gravely nod her head.

'Then she must be told,' the old man said. 'Sister, I will tell her everything. If you would like to be present . . . ?'

'No.'

'But you don't—'

'What good will it do after all this time?'

'What, the truth?' he said. 'Maybe no good at all, but if the poor woman is dying she deserves to know. Sister, I probably know what she is dying from, and so do you. I will see this lady and I will tell her. I call you now out of courtesy only, I don't need your blessing or your permission.'

'No.'

She ended the call and put the phone down on her bed.

Mother Katerina walked over to speak. 'I don't know what happened back in 1971, Sister, but I do know that what was done was wrong. If Dr Chitty is now going to try to put that right to some extent, then you should support his actions. And you should confess because, I may be wrong, but I don't think that you have done so.'

She left. Alone in the heavily curtained bedroom, Sister Pia felt as if she were about to cry. But she couldn't.

'Harry often changed his mind, about all sorts of stuff.'

George Grogan had spectacular cheekbones. Slim and self-assured, he was the result of good breeding. A doctor for a father and apparently a baroness for a mother. The whole family looked like racehorses – sleek and slightly disapproving.

Vi Collins fought not to feel like a hobbit. She smiled. 'So he often made arrangements to do things and then didn't?'

'Sometimes.'

'He not turn up to your house before?'

'Once or twice. But he rang to say he was doing other things.'

'Not this time, though.'

'No. I called him once, but just got voicemail. Thought he was probably cycling.' He looked over at his father. 'Then Dad rang Mrs Venus. To be honest, I wasn't worried. The next thing we heard was that Harry had gone to Malta for a holiday.'

'Didn't you try to ring him?' Vi asked. It had been a treat driving high above the Thames to get to this house full of good taste. But she comforted herself with the knowledge that she only ever really liked to see the countryside from afar. It was nice as a view, but to live in it was something else.

'In Malta? No.'

'Still seems strange to me that Harry blew you out and then you didn't contact him.'

'I was due to go away myself the following day,' George said.

'Where to?'

'I spent some time in London.'

'Before you get the idea that George went to London alone, DI Collins, he actually stayed with our eldest son,' Dr Grogan interjected.

'Where's that?'

'Shoreditch. Henry works for a merchant bank and so he's got one of those rather dreadful industrial-looking apartments in an old mansion block.'

Vi thought about her eldest son and the crumbling wreck he'd bought in Romford just to get a toehold on the property ladder, but she said nothing. He'd paid nearly two hundred grand for that. God alone knew what Henry Grogan had shelled out for his flat.

She looked at George. 'So you went to see your brother the next day?'

'Yes.'

'What did you do while you were waiting for Harry?'

'What? The day before?'

'The day he disappeared, yeah. Where were you, George?'

'Waiting for Harry. Here. Where else would I have been?'

'But you only phoned him once?'

'I started swimming. Time passed. I thought maybe he'd forgotten.'

Vi turned her attention to Dr Grogan. 'Where were you, Dr Grogan? And Mrs Grogan?'

The missus spoke for the first time. It was a bit like listening to Joanna Lumley, which was nice.

'Oh, I'd gone off to London to meet a girlfriend,' she said.

'I took Helen to the station on my way to the surgery,' Dr Grogan said. 'I got back here just before midday.'

'What time'd you leave home?'

'Seven thirty. I had an early surgery that day.'

'And when you got home, you found George alone in the pool?'

'Yes. I asked him where Harry was and he said he hadn't turned up. He wasn't worried, but I called Mrs Venus out of courtesy. Then Henry arrived to stay over and take George back to London with him the following day. Mrs Venus called later to say that Harry had gone off with a girl, apparently. Then he was off to Malta. To be honest with you, I thought no more about it,' he said. 'Now—'

'No reason why you should've thought about it, Dr Grogan,' Vi said. 'Superintendent Venus wanted it kept quiet for the reasons I've told you about.'

She looked at George as she spoke, who looked straight back at her and smiled. She wondered what he thought of her and imagined him telling his friends he'd just been interviewed about Harry Venus by some rough old cunt. Kids liked that word, she'd noticed.

After speaking to Lee Arnold, Venus and Tony Bracci, Vi had decided to keep the fact that the PI had spotted George titting about the East End with some mates and, possibly, his brother earlier in the week to herself for the moment. It could mean nothing, but Dr Grogan had just told her that his son had been in London when the first ransom for Harry Venus had been paid, to an address in Brick Lane. Not more than ten minutes' walk from Shoreditch.

Instead she said, 'What'd you do in London then, George? Your brother take time off to be with you, did he?'

For a moment he said nothing. It was a question he hadn't been expecting. 'No. He has to work. I did some shopping . . . Wandered about . . .'

Mrs Grogan sat down elegantly beside her husband. 'Young people are so macabre these days,' she said.

Her husband looked at her as if displeased and then said, 'George collects taxidermy, don't you?'

'Yes.' The boy smiled again.

'And he has the most awful clothes,' his mother said. 'All black and . . . with a distinct smell of mothballs. But I'm not allowed to wash them . . .'

'Bit of a Goth are you, son?' Vi said to George.

'No.'

He looked offended now.

She smiled. Then she asked, 'What you got in your taxidermy collection, George?'

'Couple of voles. A meerkat. Got sparrows this time.'

'Nice.'

The Grogan parents looked embarrassed.

Then Vi pushed. 'You see any schoolmates up in town when you was at your brother's?' she asked. 'Must've been a bit lonely for you just hanging about the streets?'

'No.'

'What, you didn't see any mates, or you weren't lonely?'

'Neither,' George said. 'Everyone talks to everyone round there. All you have to do is go into a shop or a gallery. There's loads to do.'

'George has been very taken with that area ever since Henry bought his flat,' his mother said. 'Personally, I find it claustrophobic and, well, a bit dirty, you know.'

Vi smiled again. 'Do you?' Compared with what it had been like in her youth, Shoreditch was pristine. Which was more than could be said for Mrs Grogan's son. Who had just lied.

When Shazia had first told Cousin Aftab that Naz Sheikh wanted to speak to him, he'd said, 'Oh fuck!' Then he'd apologised. Now he was smoking out the back of the shop after receiving a phone call from the Sheikhs telling him to be ready, whatever that meant, at eleven. Shazia, stationed at the counter, knew that Naz could either come in through the shop door or via the alleyway round the back. At eleven, he chose the latter.

It was a warm day, but Aftab shivered as the gangster walked up beside him. He'd been in business for over twenty years and not once had he had to deal with organised criminals. He'd been lucky, but that luck had just run out. He knew why.

'What do you want?'

Naz hunkered down beside him. 'You shouldn't be employing Muslim girls. It's not decent.'

He should've given Shazia's need for work more thought. Mumtaz was mixed up with the Sheikhs in some capacity – he'd never asked – but he should have borne it in mind. He'd just wanted to help his cousin and her kid.

But he wasn't going down without a fight. 'My girls used to work in the shop when they were Shazia's age,' he said.

'Ah, but your daughters were whores.'

Aftab wanted to hit him so hard his eyeballs fell out. But Naz Sheikh wanted violence, it was what he traded in. Aftab breathed. 'What do you want?'

'I want you to get rid of Shazia Hakim, now.'

'And if I won't?'

He shrugged. That could mean anything from 'I'll torch the shop' to 'I'll rip your head off and shit down your neck.' And Aftab knew it.

'She's only temporary,' he said. 'While George is away on his holidays.'

'I don't care. I want her gone.'

'Why?'

'I told you.'

'There's loads of Muslim girls working in shops, it's—'

'They should be covered,' Naz instructed.

In common with most people, Aftab had seen Naz and his brother in company with scantily dressed young girls, both Muslim and non-Muslim. He didn't give a shit about religious observance, what he wanted to do was deprive Shazia of money, from which Aftab deduced that Mumtaz was probably in a lot of debt to him. And if she owed him, she was in his power. Aftab had no doubt that her ex-husband had to be at the root of all this. Mumtaz had always been very good with money.

'I'll get her to cover.'

'Too late,' Naz said. 'People are already offended.'

'What people?'

'Good Muslims.'

He wasn't going to say, because no one had complained.

'And what am I supposed to do without the girl until George comes back, Mr Sheikh? You gonna provide me with some lad to do all me heavy lifting, are you?'

Naz grabbed Aftab by the front of his kurta shirt. 'You usually do it on your own. What's the matter? Too old now?'

His breath smelt of onions and tobacco.

'No. I am . . .'

'And anyway, you had better get used to it.'

Aftab felt all the blood drain from his face.

'Because when your old white man comes back, you're going to sack him too, unless you do what I tell you.'

181

'What, sack the . . . ?'

'Sack the girl, agree with me that you need security and then pay me what that service is worth.'

Protection money. Aftab didn't have to ask whether something 'unfortunate' would happen to him, his family or his shop if he didn't comply.

'But if you don't want my services, all you have to do is get rid of that girl,' Naz said. 'Plus a charge for my time with you today.'

This could be any sum of money that came into Naz Sheikh's head. Five hundred quid, five thousand, a hundred thousand. Anything.

Aftab looked into the handsome, smiling face of his tormentor and he knew what he had to do.

Lee watched Mumtaz replace her office phone on her desk. She looked thoughtful. He'd spent the last ten minutes talking to Vi about young George Grogan, who had lied about being with friends in London. Mumtaz's call had also given her something to think about.

'What's up?' he asked.

'That was the old convent doctor,' she said. 'Wants to speak to me tomorrow about Alison. He says he wants to tell me "everything", whatever that means.'

'Maybe he's going to drop your nuns in it,' Lee said.

'I get the feeling you'd like it if one of the sisters turned out to be her mother.'

'Not really. It'd be no good to the poor woman to have a nun for a mum. But I'm a realist, and as a realist I know that babies have been getting born in convents for years. Celibacy doesn't work, period.'

'Oh, well, we'll see,' Mumtaz said. 'I'm meeting Dr Chitty at eleven tomorrow morning at his care home.'

'Lucky you.'

'I just hope I can get some closure for Alison. One way or another. Do you know what your plans are yet?'

'No,' he said. 'You know, what would be really helpful would be if your "contact" could get that Imran Ullah to let on exactly where the shop he took Venus's money to was. Is there any way . . . ?'

'The boy doesn't want to lose his job and so he will withhold information,' she said. 'What I was told last night . . .'

During what he knew was her routine phone call to her parents.

'. . . was that Imran thought it might have been on Navarre Street.'

'His way of saying it was.'

'Possibly. But my memory of Navarre Street is that it contains several "hippy" shops.'

'Mmm,' said Lee. 'It was in Navarre Street I spotted the Asian boy I later saw with George Grogan and his mates. You know Vi said that George lied about being in London with mates. Said when his brother was at work he just wandered about on his own.'

'Were his parents there while he was being interviewed?'

'Yeah.'

'Then he could have been lying for their benefit. I mean he's sixteen, right?'

'Yes.'

'Then his parents will want to know he's being good up in the big city, won't they,' she said. 'But if he's with his mates . . .'

'Yeah. Right.'

'Also the boys he was with may not have been school friends.'

'True.'

Mumtaz's mobile rang. She said, 'Oh, hi sweetie.'

Shazia.

For the next fifteen minutes she said nothing, Lee heard crying on the other end of the line.

The time had finally come. The pain was building and, instead of calling for one of the sisters to administer her morphine, Sister Pia gritted her teeth. Successive doctors over the years, including Chitty, had told her that her heart was weak. If she took the full force of the pain she could die.

Wasn't that suicide? Which was a sin? The old woman rocked backwards and forwards in her bed, silently begging her god to take her life. But nothing happened. Dr Chitty was seeing the Asian woman in the morning, when it would all come out, and she couldn't face it. To be bought like that, like Judas for thirty pieces of dirty silver . . .

She'd never confessed, Mother Katerina had been right. She was either a woman of unusual astuteness or she knew something. But who would have told her? The pain no longer came in waves, where one could rest in between breakers. There was just one, solid mass, a monolith that sat on her body like the lid of a stone tomb.

For reparation, forgiveness and God's mercy to be enacted, one first had to recognise one's sin and then confess. One also had to suffer. Not like this, but in one's mind, through one's heart and in the wreckage of a ruined reputation. Sister Pia's hand shook as she pressed the bell to summon Sister Sofia to her side with her morphine.

14

He put the phone down. Then he lit a fag and sat in his favourite chair. Over the years Dr Flanagan, the headmaster, had annoyed him in many and various different ways. But never as much as in the last year.

Malcolm knew it wasn't personal. Reeds wasn't wealthy by public school standards and certain financial realities had to be faced. But if the trend towards taking vast amounts of money from Russian and Chechen oligarchs in return for educating their over-indulged children continued, then in a few years' time Reeds could be dominated by sulky blond boys playing on their diamond-studded iPads and telling people like him to 'fuck off'. And people like Malcolm McCullough and his forebears were people who had once had servants with more taste and grace than the Roman Abramoviches of this world.

He was also concerned by how this new influx would affect the existing boys. They had their own internal order, their own codes; they always had. The school had never interfered unless it had to. But how would these Slavs, Chechens or whatever take to the nuances of the social hierarchy of an English public school? Would they complain?

Dr Flanagan wanted him to take on a couple of Chechen boys as part of his pastoral duties next term. Albek Umarov and Sultan Shishani. The headmaster had said he'd be emailing their CVs and photos over to him. Malcolm fully expected them to be clad in army fatigues and carrying Kalashnikovs – Umarov's father openly described himself as a 'warlord'. But his 'donation' to Reeds was going to completely renovate the gym and buy new computers for the IT suite. Malcolm was going to hate Albek and Sultan because they were going to be nouveau riche and sarky. They'd have a good laugh at his shonky old sports jackets.

He would have to suck it all up and take on Albek, Sultan and their like without complaint. The only consolation was that, with any luck, he wouldn't have to do it for very much longer.

Aftab Huq's home was the sort of house the neighbours always talked about. In the far distant backwaters of Manor Park, it had a huge hedge running wild in the front garden and hadn't been decorated on the outside since Edward VII was on the throne. But with a sick wife, a business he ran only with the help of one old man and, until very recently, university fees for his two daughters, Aftab didn't have a lot of time for home maintenance.

Mumtaz knocked on the door. It was only 7 a.m. and Aftab had said he could talk for a few minutes before he went to work. On the phone he'd been mortified.

He let her in and they walked down a hall lined with boxes of tins to a kitchen that was covered in a thin layer of grease.

'Sorry about the state of the place,' he said. 'Sit down. Far as

I know the chairs are all right. Cat might be on one of 'em but he'll soon shift.'

Mumtaz looked before she sat down on one of the Formica-covered chairs. It was OK – and catless. 'Aftab, I don't know what to say.'

He lit a cigarette. 'Nothing to say. Bastard wants Shazia gone and if I don't do what he says he'll trash me business and do who knows what to poor old George. Mumtaz, I know you've got some sort of issue with the Sheikhs that you won't talk about . . .'

'I can't.' She felt herself begin to cry. She put a hand up to her eyes to brush away the tears. 'I can't have family involved, not with them. Not . . .'

'Well, I'm involved now,' Aftab said. 'You can tell me.'

But Mumtaz said nothing.

'If you don't want me to, I won't tell Uncle Baharat or Dad or anyone,' he said. 'But Mumtaz, I've lost Shazia helping out in the shop until George gets back and Naz Sheikh wants eight grand in cash from me for the "time and trouble" he's spent protecting the local community from the sight of a young girl without a headscarf on.'

Now Mumtaz's tears came and she couldn't stop them. 'Oh, Aftab . . .'

When they'd spoken on the phone, he'd told her that Naz had threatened him, but he'd not said anything about money.

'I'm guessing it's something to do with your late husband,' he said. 'He leave you in debt to them bastards?'

She remained still, then slowly she nodded her head. This was the first time she'd owned up to involvement with the Sheikhs to a member of her own family.

'Your boss know?'

'Kind of. Not really.'

'Shit. 'Scuse my language. Mumtaz, Lee's an ex-copper, you know coppers yourself.'

'If I get the police involved with the Sheikhs I might as well give Shazia to a group of rapists,' she said. 'Because the Sheikhs don't threaten me if I don't give them what they want, Aftab, they threaten her. I give them almost all my money in lieu of Ahmet's debts that seem to have no end, and now they also want me to alert them in the event of a police raid on any of their disgusting rented properties. I'm supposed to "keep my ear to the ground". But how can I? How can I ask DI Collins about the Sheikhs on a weekly basis? I can't, and yet if one of their dumps full of starving eastern European sex slaves gets raided then it will be me who pays.'

'How much in the hole to the Sheikhs are you?' he asked.

She told him and he visibly baulked. Then he said, 'As a whole family we could probably get you out of that.'

'No!'

'But better would be to bring the bastards down.'

'I know. But how? If I told the police about their criminal activities and they somehow managed to wriggle out of the charges, they'd take my daughter.'

'If—'

'I can't take that risk, Aftab!'

What she couldn't tell him was about the other risk she couldn't take. If Mumtaz told the police what she knew about the Sheikhs, they'd tell Shazia how her amma had let her father bleed out on Wanstead Flats. And she couldn't have that.

Aftab reached inside his pocket and took out a roll of bank-notes. He pushed it across the kitchen table. 'Take this and give it to Shazia,' he said. 'It's what I owe her for her work and a little bit extra for some clothes or something.'

'No, I . . .'

'Take it,' he said. 'For her.'

She sighed. Briefly their hands touched as she took the money.

'I need to think about what we can do about the Sheikhs—'

'Nothing!'

He held up a thin finger. 'Not strictly true,' he said. 'I don't know what we can do because I haven't thought about it till now, but there's nothing can't be fixed. I know there's people round here who'd say it was your fate to be bled dry by them twats, 'scuse me again. They say it's ungodly to resist your fate. But I don't buy that. God's good, right? Then why would He want the innocent to suffer at the hands of people like the Sheikhs? I need to bend me mind to it and I will need to talk to George when he gets back from his holidays.'

'George? Oh no, Aftab, you mustn't tell anyone!'

'Except George, I promise,' he said. 'But as well as having a trial for West Ham donkey's years ago, George was also a bit of a fist for hire in the old days. He worked for several firms of hard men and still knows one or two.'

Mumtaz put her head in her hands. She knew old George and recognised him as a bit of a villain, but she couldn't see what he could do to help her. But in the end she said, 'OK.' Then she remembered the money. 'But Aftab, what about the eight thousand pounds?'

'What about it?' he said. 'What do you think this cash cow's for, Mumtaz?'

He held his arms up to encompass much of the greasy kitchen.

'Three hundred grand and counting,' he said. 'Thank you very much London property bubble.'

Should he call Vi or shouldn't he? The Asian kid he'd seen with George Grogan definitely worked at an organic shop called Veg on Navarre Street. There was him and some posh girl in a mini-kilt and some slightly older bloke, probably in his thirties, who seemed to run the place. Was he the Mr Shaw that Venus had addressed all that money to?

Lee had been in and bought a couple of organic apples, which had tasted like cotton wool. He'd poked around for as long as he could and had learned that the Asian boy was called Danny. Up close he was camper than he'd been when he was with the other boys. He wore eyeliner.

Lee's phone rang. It was Vi.

'Wotcha.'

'They've made contact with Venus,' she said. 'Two hundred and fifty grand this Saturday, drop location and time TBA on the day. They say they've put proof of life in the post.'

'Taking no chances. Venus back at work?'

'Yup. All apparently normal on the western front,' she said. 'What you up to?'

191

He told her.

She said, 'I feel an obbo coming on. Can you hold on, just for now?'

'Course,' he said. 'The first lot of cash almost certainly passed through here, but whether the people working in the shop knew what it was . . .'

'I can also feel a visit to the owner of that electrical shop on Brick Lane coming on,' Vi said. 'Saturday'll be upon us before we know it.'

'Have to be careful with the dirty PO box owner, Vi. If he finds out the Ullah boy's been talking to us, it could go bad for the kid.'

'Like I care? Arnold, a life's at stake here, remember? If one Asian boy gets shunned by his neighbours for a bit, I really couldn't give too much of a fuck.' As far as Vi was concerned, religious and ethnic differences didn't matter a toss when weighed against the possibility of criminal activity.

'But, Vi, you can't just go steaming into Zafar Bhatti's shop, all guns blazing.'

'Oh, do give me credit, Arnold!'

'So what you gonna do?'

'First I'll speak to old Kev Thorpe, it's his manor.'

Lee had seen DI Thorpe when he'd obboed the first drop site in Brick Lane. Thorpe, or rather Thorpe's mum, had given him the original lead on the PO box.

'I'm sure Kev can come up with some reason to go and have a chat with Mr Bhatti,' she said. 'Maybe he can pick up a couple of batteries for his hearing aid while he's there.'

Thorpe could sometimes drift off when someone was talking about something that didn't particularly interest him, hence the myth that he was a little bit deaf. He'd never actually had a hearing aid, but the East End rumour machine had never been bound by details like the truth.

'Keep me in the loop,' Lee said. 'Kev's always good value.'

'Will do.'

'What you up to now?' he asked.

'On my way to visit a flat in Mark Street, Shoreditch,' she told him. 'Belongs to Henry Grogan, George's merchant banker brother.'

'Mmm. Expect exposed brickwork and ironic furniture. Back in the good old days it probably used to be a crack-house. And tell me what he looks like,' Lee said. 'Told you I saw a suit twatting about with George and his mates. George Grogan's one of the "in crowd" according to his tutor at school.'

Danny came out of Veg and put two apples in one of the baskets on the pavement and then went inside again.

'That school they all go to made my fucking skin crawl. I'm sure I was being spooked on purpose.'

'Why?'

'Don't know,' Lee said. 'Maybe it's because I'm common.'

'Or an inverted snob.'

He laughed. She was the biggest inverted snob he'd ever met.

'Her mother was called Rosa Alvarez,' the old man said. 'She was eighteen and came from Buenos Aires in Argentina.'

Dr Chitty had turned out to be small, pale and very lined. But his eyes, which were a very bright blue, still sparkled in the sunlight, reminding Mumtaz of Paul Newman. A gracious man, he had taken Mumtaz's hand as soon as they'd met and organised tea and cake for both of them in the small visitors' room, far away from the day room and the blaring TV set.

'Rosa came to London to study English at a language school in Earls Court,' Dr Chitty continued. 'Her family was, it was thought at the time, a religious one and so it seemed natural they should look for a Catholic organisation for her to stay with. And they found the Siena Sisters. Unfortunately, shortly after arriving here, Rosa found a young local man too. She became pregnant, but she either didn't know what was going on, or she ignored it.'

Mumtaz sipped her tea. Still upset by her visit to Cousin Aftab, she couldn't bring herself to eat more than a few mouthfuls of the lemon drizzle cake.

'Eventually and inevitably, Rosa went into labour in her room at the convent. Thinking she could deliver the baby herself, she locked herself away for five hours, until Mother Emerita heard grunts and squeaks from outside the door and let herself in. She could see immediately what was happening and that Rosa was in trouble. She wanted to call an ambulance, but the girl wouldn't let her. Rosa said that she'd rather die than go to hospital and face the shame of being an unmarried mother. She was very vocal about that. Emerita was a kind, good woman, but she always found decisions difficult. It was Sister Pia, who can speak Spanish, who called Rosa's parents. She spoke to her mother. A little later it was discovered that Rosa didn't actually have a father. Or rather, she did, but he was not living with her mother. At the time he wasn't even in the same country. But what was significant was what the mother said, which was, "Get rid of it."'

'The baby?'

'Yes. Now, not only as a good Catholic could Sister Pia not even contemplate such a thing, but the baby was already being born. Rosa's mother said that she would speak to the girl's father, but the sisters had to deal with Rosa themselves, and it was then that money came into the story. And me.'

'You delivered Alison?'

'I did. At just gone one a.m. the following morning. At first I doubted whether Rosa could give birth naturally, but she managed even though she was completely exhausted at the end of the process. Both mother and baby were well. But I wasn't happy about what the sisters had asked me to do. I was even less happy when they asked me to take part in the pantomime they had devised in order to distance Rosa from her baby. Mother Emerita was to take the child out and then claim to have found it abandoned. I would then be called back to the convent to assess the child's health. I asked why this was being done and I was told it was at the request of Rosa's mother, who wanted the child to be adopted.' He smiled. 'Shame was still quite a big thing in people's lives in those days, especially in Catholic families.'

'Unmarried parenthood remains a big no-no in Muslim communities today,' Mumtaz said.

'So I agreed to the mother's request,' he said. 'Mother Emerita "found" the baby in the telephone box, even at one point embroidering the story with some nonsense about having been watched by an unknown person when she discovered the child. It was only when the child the nuns called Madonna had been sent to an orphanage in Essex that I learned the truth. Rosa had returned to Argentina, but I was still in and out of the convent as and when the sisters needed me. I couldn't help noticing that the building was becoming very smart, the accommodation for the nuns and the girls much more comfortable. I remarked upon it.'

Mumtaz felt cold. There was something very bad in this story, something she would soon have to tell Alison.

'Due to complaints that had been made about her by some of the girls, Sister Pia had been dispatched to Rome in order to contemplate her future, but Sister Concezione, another Spanish-speaker who had also spoken to Rosa Alvarez's mother, as well as to her father, was in the convent. She heard what I said and then, according to her, spent some weeks wrestling with her conscience.'

'About whether to tell you something?'

'Yes,' he said. 'Eventually she came to me and said that she had something to confess. I told her that she'd better go and see Father Tucci, our parish priest, but she said she couldn't speak to him, it had to be me. It was bizarre. I had to meet her outside Chiswick House of all places, on a Saturday morning. Later of course I realised she couldn't say anything in front of the other nuns because they were all in it together. And it was low, Mrs Hakim.'

'Money.'

'That's what it came down to, of course,' he said. 'The old demon himself.'

'The parents had paid the nuns to hush Rosa's pregnancy up.'

'The father,' Dr Chitty said. 'To be honest, from what Sister Concezione said, the mother didn't really care. A drunk, Sisi Alvarez was a woman only in her very early thirties and had actually sent Rosa away so that she could enjoy her career as a nightclub singer and have a lot of men in her bed.'

Mumtaz frowned. If the woman was only in her early thirties, then how old had she been when Rosa had been born?

'Rosa was illegitimate, but that didn't mean that her father had to like the idea of his only child giving birth out of wedlock. The convent was in dire need of repair in those days,' he said. 'Parts of it were positively unsafe. So when the money came from Spain . . .'

'I thought that Rosa was Argentinian.'

'She was, but her father was living in Spain at the time. In exile. Juan Perón, Rosa's father, was actively seeking re-election as president of Argentina and the last thing he needed was an illegitimate daughter and grandchild coming out of the wood-work. Keeping Rosa's mother quiet about bearing him a daughter at the age of thirteen had already cost him quite enough money.'

Mumtaz gripped her teacup to her chest.

'Your client is the granddaughter of Juan Perón, the Argen-tinian dictator,' Dr Chitty said. 'Deprived of her name by a bunch of poor nuns and a greedy old doctor.'

'You?'

'When Sister Concezione told me who the child was, I went to see Mother Emerita. I was going to go to the police, but in those days the Catholic Church wasn't routinely dragged through the courts. I couldn't do it. And she gave me money. I used it to buy equipment for my surgery and I've been telling myself it was all for the good ever since. But it wasn't. That money came from an anti-Semitic dictator who got a thirteen-year-old girl pregnant.' He paused for a moment, then he said, 'Mrs Hakim, I understand from Sister Pia that your client is dying. Is that correct?'

'Not entirely,' Mumtaz said. 'She has a terminal disease, but it's one of those that involves a slow decline . . .'

'Huntington's,' he said.

'How did you know?'

'Ah,' he said, 'the internet is a wonderful thing isn't it, Mrs Hakim? I was an early adopter, in other words I got online as soon as I could. And as soon as Google came along I began to look up all sorts. Bored old man syndrome. But it wasn't all messing around. One day I googled Argentinian nightclub singer Sisi Alvarez, Rosa's mother, and saw that she had died back in the 1980s. Cause of death was complications arising from Huntington's Disease. Whether Rosa had it, we will never know.'

'Why not?'

'She predeceased her mother back in 1973. Shot on the streets of Buenos Aires; the gunman was never found. Her father was president of Argentina again at that point and sometimes I wonder if he had a hand in it. People can do terrible things, even to their own children, when their ambition or their pride are under threat.'

Mumtaz knew this only too well.

'Maybe Rosa, pining for her baby, tried to blackmail him. Maybe she tried to persuade him to buy the child back for her. I don't know. But she's dead, so is her mother and so is Perón, so we'll never know. I am also aware that you only have my word for any of this. I have spoken to Sister Pia and she may or may not corroborate my story, depending upon how she feels. She still thinks that any criticism of religious figures or communities is wrong. But that is my truth, Mrs Hakim, and I am prepared to meet my god with it on my lips.'

She believed him. His manner was simple and sincere and the old nun had been evasive.

'I will go and visit Mother Katerina,' she said. 'Just to thank her for her assistance. If Sister Pia sees me also, then that's good, but if she doesn't . . .' She shrugged. 'We – Alison and myself that is – did wonder why a DNA test she had done some time ago threw up some Native American heritage.'

'That was Perón's mother,' the doctor said. 'From a local tribe. His father was of Spanish origin.'

'Which just leaves Alison's father.'

The old man shook his head. 'Ah, but if only we knew who he was,' he said. 'Of course the nuns weren't interested, but I asked Rosa. All she said was that the relationship was over. She wouldn't say who the boy was. Maybe he never knew he had a child. The nuns were of the opinion that he was local, although I don't know what evidence they had for that. If Sister Pia will see you again, maybe you can ask her. I've told her I'm telling you everything.'

Mumtaz shook her head. 'What can I say? I already have so much to tell my client. Where to start? Is Mother Katerina aware of all this history?'

'I doubt it, unless Pia has told her,' he said. 'But if she is as astute as I think she is, she may wonder how an effectively bankrupt convent back in the 1970s managed to completely renovate. You know, if Alison wants to come and visit me, if she's well enough, she's welcome to do so.'

'Thank you, Dr Chitty. I'll pass that on.' Then she said, 'Can I ask you one more thing?'

'Of course.'

'The young policewoman who was called to the convent when Alison was "found" . . .'

'WPC Martyn?'

'She died.'

'I know, I attended her. You think maybe she found something out.'

'Oh, no!' Mumtaz felt herself redden.

The old man put a hand on her shoulder and said, 'I've committed many sins, Mrs Hakim, but I can assure you that WPC Martyn died of natural causes. Sometimes people just die. We don't know why.'

'Fate.'

'Maybe. But she died naturally. I wouldn't lie, not at this late stage in my life.'

'No.'

Suddenly Mumtaz was hungry, and so she ate some more of the lemon drizzle cake and talked to the old man about his long life as a doctor and what he described as his 'failed' Christianity.

Before she left, she said to him, 'You did what you thought was best at the time. Now you have told me, I know what I've learned here today will give Alison some answers.'

'I hope so. And tell her she may use this information however she wishes. If she wants to make it public, then I will support her. The only thing I will say is that the sisters at the convent now are not to blame for what happened in the past. Only Pia, and she's dying.'

They shook hands and then she walked out of the care home in the direction of the convent.

Lee Arnold hadn't been wrong about Henry Grogan's Shoreditch flat. On the ground floor of what had once been a tenement building for those described as the 'underclass', it was all about exposed brickwork, wooden floors and two large film posters for old Hitchcock movies. Gracious to a fault, Henry offered Vi any number of coffee choices, but she just said, 'Instant's fine, black, ta.'

The seating consisted of a weird, metal-framed chaise longue and some very low-slung leather bucket chairs. In the middle of what was a very big living room – which had probably been three little rooms back in the day – was a vast metal trunk that he used as a coffee table.

'That came from a decommissioned car factory in Leipzig,' he said.

He handed her a square cup of coffee. The whole room smelt of what Vi recognised as patchouli oil. Had Henry been smoking dope? Back in her youth everyone who smoked doused themselves in patchouli to cover the smell. Apparently patchouli was in fashion again.

He must have heard her sniff because he said, 'Sorry about the air spray. There's an awful smell in this room I've been trying to track down. I'm just swamping it for the moment. Hope it doesn't make you cough.'

Vi sat down. 'No problem.'

'Now, what can I do for you, DI Collins?' He sat down.

'I'm trying to get a handle on what happened the day Harry Venus was abducted,' she said. 'Your brother George says that he was in or around your mum and dad's swimming pool all morning, until your dad got home at midday.'

'If that's what he said . . .'

'Where were you?' Vi said. 'Your dad told me you came to pick George up that day.'

'Yes, I stayed with my parents that night and then drove back to London with George in the morning.'

'What time'd you arrive at your mum and dad's?'

'Arrive? Oh, I suppose about three,' he said. 'I took the afternoon and the following day off. Don't get much time off, but I wanted to see the parents and get George settled into the flat. He loves it here.' He smiled.

'I bet he does, on the loose in the big city, all on his own.'

'He amuses himself.'

'Does he?'

'Yes.'

The atmosphere had become tense, which would be unhelpful. Vi looked around the room and said, 'Like your Hitchcock posters, Mr Grogan.'

He smiled and the atmosphere lightened. 'Presents. When I left Reeds. I was never a literature buff – not really academic at all – but I've always enjoyed film. Not as passionately as Georgie does though. He's crazy about books and film and Hitchcock was the master.'

'He came from Leytonstone,' Vi said.

'Yes. Just goes to show, if you really want to do something, you can do just about anything, can't you? Given the discipline and the will.'

'Back in those days, yes,' she said.

'You don't think it's possible now, DI Collins?'

'I think it's harder these days, yes. Mr Grogan, can you tell me what your brother does when he's staying here with you? You said he likes it here, but you're out all day. What's he get up to?'

'What, apart from not getting out of bed until midday?' he said. 'Georgie strolls. He's wandered all over the East End in pursuit of unusual items of taxidermy – it's his hobby.'

'I know.'

'He goes to galleries; they're all over the place round here.'

'And friends?' Vi said. 'My recollection is that when you're sixteen having mates is the most important thing in the world. Being Lonnie Loner ain't the place to be.'

'I think you'll find that being solitary is considered cool these days,' Henry said.

'Yeah, but your brother isn't on his own all the time when he's here, is he?'

It was a statement rather than a question.

'Because, Mr Grogan, I know that George lied to me when I interviewed him at your parents' house. He told me that he doesn't see his mates when he's up here in London, but I know that he does and I know that you've seen them too.'

She was taking a punt on Lee Arnold's observation. But Arnold had also told her George was a popular kid at school, and of course she knew the boy had lied to her.

Henry Grogan shrugged. 'Well, DI Collins, I don't know how you know, but you do indeed "have us", as it were.'

'So he does meet his mates?'

'Some of them live in London; it would be strange if he didn't. And yes, I've met up with them too. They're rather young and silly, but amusing in small doses.'

'So why'd your brother lie to me?'

'Well, my parents were in the room, weren't they?'

'Yes.'

'Explains it all,' he said. 'With the exception of Harry Venus, probably because he's a policeman's son, Mummy and Dad can't stand Georgie's friends, they think they lead him astray. Personally I think that my brother is perfectly capable of getting himself into trouble, but . . . Their particular *bête noire* is Tom de Vries, who has, it's true, been busted by the school for smoking weed in the grounds.'

'Didn't he get expelled?'

'Oh no,' he smiled. 'I gather you didn't go to public school, DI Collins.'

Vi said nothing. The bleeding obvious wasn't her forte.

'These things are dealt with at places like Reeds,' Henry said. 'Georgie and some of the others see Tom as some sort of hero. If our parents knew that Georgie was with Tom they'd have a fit. He's always with Tom and Danny Duncan at school . . .'

'And Harry.'

'And Harry, yes,' he said.

'Although Harry's not always in favour with your brother and the others, is he, Mr Grogan?'

She expected him to deny this. But he didn't.

'No,' he said. 'Sad fact of public school life is that first-generation boys have to work themselves in.'

'What do you mean?'

'I mean that most boys' fathers went to Reeds,' he said. 'If your dad didn't go then you're considered to be a bit nouveau riche. Mind you, that's all about to change now. School needs money so the headmaster's opened the doors to the Russians. It won't mean much any longer if your dad's a baronet. Whether your dad has oil wells and routinely executes his enemies will have far more cachet.'

Vi smiled. 'Afraid the old order's passing away, Mr Grogan?'

He smiled too. 'Oh, no, not me,' he said. 'I'm a merchant banker, DI Collins, shifting fiscal realities are my thing. As long as the barbarians from the east give us their money, how can we possibly complain?'

'Of course I've wondered how the convent survived during the seventies,' Mother Katerina said. 'The story is that Mother Emerita's predecessor had been diverting funds to her family in Naples for years. I knew that Mother had rescued the convent from bankruptcy, but I didn't know how. If I am honest, I did suspect that something not altogether moral had happened. To go from a deep deficit to a good surplus is hard. I confess I closed my eyes to it.'

'It's not really your problem,' Mumtaz said.

'Ah, but it is,' she said. 'What was done here was wrong, and I will speak to Sister Pia. Given her strong views on sexual morality, I am not sure she is even fully aware that what she did was a sin. I have known for many years that she has something on her conscience, but I didn't know what that was until today.'

'She is dying.'

'All the more reason for her to confess before it is too late,' she said. 'I will have to contact the Bishop. What do we do with this money from a dictator that we have already spent?'

'Perón is dead. You can't give it back.'

'No. But maybe we can make a donation to charities in Argentina. He robbed his people and some of that money came to us.'

'Do you have spare money these days, Mother Katerina?' Mumtaz asked.

'No. But a sin is a sin, Mrs Hakim, we have to pay. If Alison wants to visit the convent and speak to me I will be happy to receive her. I will apologise to her. Whether Sister Pia will see her is another matter, but she is welcome. Her mother gave birth to her in this place. Tell her this will always be her home.'

15

The man who owned Veg was called Jethro Nutt. He described himself as an 'organic warrior'. The Veg website said he was also engaged in bringing 'rural values to an urban environment'. In other words, Lee thought, he was some tosser from the Cotswolds whose name was really Sebastian. But it was unlikely that Jethro was a kidnapper. Mumtaz agreed.

She'd come straight over to Lee's flat from Chiswick with a story that came from a past neither of them could remember.

'I've not even seen *Evita*,' Lee said. 'All I know about Argentina is the Falklands War.'

'Same here,' said Mumtaz. 'But Mother Katerina was mortified when I told her that Alison's mother had been Juan Perón's child. She described him as an evil dictator. He used to have people tortured, his opponents would just disappear. And of course he got Alison's grandmother pregnant when she was just thirteen.'

Lee lit a cigarette and sat down. 'That's so messed up.'

'Lee, this is going to be a lot for Alison to take in. She's divorced, there's just her and her young son. When I tell her she'll need support. I mean, I can't just drop all that on her and then leave.'

'She got adoptive parents?'

'No,' she told him. 'She was adopted, but they're both dead. Any ideas?'

'You're seeing her tomorrow?'

'First thing. I've got a prospective new client in East Ham at eleven.'

'Can you move that appointment?'

'I can try,' she said.

'I'm thinking that instead of trying to find someone else to support Alison, can you take it on yourself?'

Mumtaz frowned. 'Difficult,' she said. 'I'm going to be the bearer of bad news for her. The Perón thing aside, her mother is dead and no one knows who her father is, probably not even the man himself.'

'But you do know that there was Huntington's in the mother's family.'

'Yes, that is something. But what Alison will want to do with regard to the convent I can't imagine.'

'What would you want to do?' Lee asked.

Mumtaz exhaled. 'I don't know. Slap Sister Pia? Maybe not, but I'd want her to explain herself, even if she is dying.'

'Would you want money?'

'From the convent? What for?'

'To keep shtum.'

'What? No,' she said. 'What's the point? Alison is slowly dying and she is alone, but her ex is rich and by her own admission, he is paying for everything. No, the damage is done.'

'So what are you afraid of?'

'That she'll have a breakdown. She's sick and alone.'

'But you have to tell her.'

'Yes, I do.'

'So move your other appointment and take your time with Alison. It's not like she can't afford it.'

He was right and she knew it, but he saw her wince. 'We're not a charity, Mumtaz,' he said. 'I'm sorry.'

She looked down. 'I know.'

'I'm charging Venus for every minute – poor sod – but I have to. He's sold his flat in Islington to raise more cash, which is just as well because the kidnappers have been in touch again. They want another quarter of a million on Saturday.'

'But if he's only just sold, then he won't have the money for at least six weeks,' Mumtaz said. 'What will he do? Borrow from the bank against the sale of the flat?'

'I guess . . .'

'You know one thing that I really can't understand about this kidnapping is why target someone like Superintendent Venus? I know he and his wife have money, but they're not super-rich, are they?'

'It's not just about the money,' Lee said. 'It's a punishment. Trouble is there are a lot of people who have had problems with Venus, and I don't mean the coppers at Forest Gate.'

'Criminals he's put away.'

'And the rest. People who don't like his wife's character in *Londoners*. Harry could've even engineered the whole thing himself.'

Mumtaz looked doubtful.

'Daddy in the Old Bill doesn't go down well at posh schools

like Reeds. Maybe Harry felt that his pop was limiting his options. Maybe by releasing Venus's money he can have a better time at school with his mates. You know, I've been told that unless your dad went to Reeds, the boys basically look down on you as some sort of pleb. I tell you Mumtaz, that place gave me the shudders.'

'You briefly saw something that wasn't there and it upset you,' she said. 'I've told you what that was.'

He'd phoned her up in the middle of the night when he'd returned from Reeds. With her psychological training he figured she'd be able to unravel that mystery for him, and she had. Given the presence of life-sized mannequins on that floor, one of them had reflected onto the window. He'd even seen the one it had to have been. Why couldn't he let that go?

'Anyway, what about the proof of life the Superintendent requested?'

'In the post, he's been told,' Lee said.

'Caught ya.'

Zafar Bhatti almost jumped out of his chair. Then, when he saw who it was, he lowered the hip flask from his lips and said, 'Oh, Mr Thorpe you almost gave me a heart attack.'

The shop had a 'closed' sign up when DI Kevin Thorpe had walked towards it. But the door had been ajar. Probably left by Bhatti's son, cross-eyed Jabbar, the man with the mental age of a five-year-old.

'You're gonna have to bolt that door yourself Zafar, unless you want any more nasty surprises,' Thorpe said.

'Oh!' Bhatti made as if to move off his chair, but Thorpe stopped him.

'It's OK, I locked it on my way in.'

'Ah. Thank you.'

Thorpe looked at Bhatti's hip flask. 'Whisky?'

'Mr Thorpe, I am a good Muslim!'

But Thorpe sniffed the flask anyway. It wasn't whisky or any other kind of spirit.

'We call it karkade,' Bhatti said. 'Entirely non-alcoholic.'

Thorpe shrugged. 'Good for you, Zafar. On the booze front,' Thorpe continued. 'If I could say the same for the romance trade, you really would be a good Muslim. But you're not, are you?'

Zafar Bhatti shook his head. 'What?'

'Letting young Latife have illicit letter sex with Ali out the chip shop while she's supposed to be engaged to old Mr Khan the jeweller? The names I made up to protect the guilty, but I know you run a dodgy PO box for dodgy couples and even dodgier businesses out of that empty house next door.'

He stood up and waved his arms in the air. 'Who told you such a lie, Mr Thorpe? Who? Who says things against my honour in such a way? Who is so jealous . . . ?'

'I've known about your little sideline for years,' Thorpe said. 'You think the white people who live round here don't keep their ears to the ground just like you?'

'Of course they don't! They spend all their time riding silly bicycles and opening pop-ups . . .'

'Not the hipsters, you doink. The actual East Enders. The ones who live here because it's where they've always been. Me. I've known for years, and for years I've thought, "Well fuck it, in the case of the lonely hearts, he's not doing a bad thing." I was a bit more chary about the Haj businesses that run out of that place, but I thought why rock the boat when the boat's dead quiet? Know what I mean? But now you've crossed a line.'

'A line? What line?'

Mr Bhatti sat down again.

'Fourth of this month you sent seven parcels addressed to a Mr Shaw to a shop off Arnold Circus. Remember?'

'Things come into that address and I get them delivered by a boy . . .'

'Yes, I know. I've seen him. Where's he get in next door? Round the back?'

Vi Collins had emphasised the importance of feigning ignorance about the entrance through the shop, so as not to drop Imran in it.

'I don't know of a Mr Shaw! Parcels? We get parcels. Tokens between lovers.'

'We know parcels addressed to Mr Shaw came through your PO box on the fourth. We know, Zafar.'

Mr Bhatti drank from his hip flask of karkade.

'And just so we're clear, this is a matter of life and death, so you'd better tell me what you know, or it'll be a trip down the station and goodnight Vienna to your reputation as a man of clean morals.'

There was a pause before he answered, but it wasn't long.

'I have no idea who Mr Shaw is,' he said.

'So how'd you get his business?'

'A woman came into the shop, very elegant, maybe one week before. She said that she knew about my service and would I take delivery of some parcels for a friend of hers on the fourth. She said a man would come and put the parcels through the PO box in the name of Mr Shaw. All I had to do was take them to a place in Bethnal Green.'

'What place?'

'I don't know! Some hippy shop.'

'Where?'

'I don't know!'

Thorpe knew it was on Navarre Street. 'What was it called?'

'I don't remember.'

'Didn't you write it down?'

'At the time, of course. But then I threw it away. These things go all over the place, I can't keep note of all of them.'

'Do you have any idea what was in these parcels?'

'No. Why should I? I pride myself on my confidentiality. I wouldn't get the customers if they thought I couldn't guarantee their absolute security.'

'Unless the coppers come to call.'

Zafar Bhatti pulled a face.

'Do you think your boy'd remember where he took the parcels?' Thorpe asked.

'No. He's an idiot.'

'Then why do you employ him? Because he's cheap? I'm gonna talk to him anyway.'

Mr Bhatti flung his arms up again. 'It was just a job, DI Thorpe. Just a job.'

'Well now it's just a job that could have some serious consequences,' Thorpe said. 'What did this woman who came in look like? She Asian, white? You seen her before? What?'

'Asian. She was Asian but in western clothes. Pretty. I had never seen her before.'

'You seen her since?'

'No.'

'So how'd you get paid?'

'In advance.'

'How much?'

Now there was a long pause.

Losing patience, Thorpe said, 'Come on Zafar. Fess up.'

'Two hundred pounds.'

'Two hundred to deliver seven parcels to somewhere in Bethnal Green.'

'Yes.'

Knowing Zafar Bhatti of old, Thorpe knew that he was lying about the amount. He always knocked at least a few quid off whatever people were supposed to have paid for anything.

'Well then Zafar, I think we ought to go and talk with Imran Ullah, your boy.'

'If it was that idiot who told you . . .'

'Imran Ullah told me nothing,' Thorpe said. 'And just to be clear, Zafar, you're not to breathe a word of this to anyone, comprende?'

He nodded.

'Because if I hear you've spoken about any of this, even to Jabbar, I will make sure that your little sideline closes for good. I'll also make sure that all your mates at the mosque find out about it. Now get on your phone and tell your boy to come in and do a rush job for you.'

They propped him up against a wall. Still covered in shit, they put a sheet down on the floor before they thrust the camera in his face. Both their faces had changed. Now they were grotesque, but still silent. When they came to get him they were always silent now. And even when they put him back all he could hear was a sort of booming muffled sound. Was the film for his parents? Had they asked to see some proof that he was still alive? How much money had been asked for this time?

They made him swallow more tablets. He could have hidden them in his mouth and then spat them out later, but he knew that without them he would go mad.

Imran Ullah wouldn't stop crying. Even when Mr Bhatti yelled at him to 'Bloody stop it or I'll bloody kill you!' he just kept on.

In the end Thorpe had to yell over him.

'I just want to know where you took those parcels for Mr Shaw on the fourth,' he said. 'That's all. God almighty, you're not in trouble, but you will be if you don't shut up soon.'

The boy, shaking on one of Mr Bhatti's knackered high stools, tried but failed to get his sobs under control.

'Jesus!'

It was a good job he liked Vi Collins and Lee Arnold, because he didn't give too much of a toss about Paul Venus even if he felt sorry for his kid.

'I need to know where you took the parcels and who you gave them to,' Thorpe said. 'You ain't gonna lose your job . . .' He looked at Bhatti, who shook his head, '. . . honest.'

Snot and water ran down the boy's face. He wasn't the brightest button in the box, but to have to make a living conveying smutty messages between people when their spouses were out was pretty desperate. And Bhatti probably paid him a pittance.

'Imran . . .'

'I took them to a shop called Veg, like vegetables,' he said.

'Veg?'

'Yes,' he gulped.

Thorpe hunkered down beside him. 'That's good, now we can find it. Who did you give the parcels to, Imran? Was it a man? A woman?'

The boy, whose sobs were calming now, said, 'A boy.'

'A boy. How old?'

He shrugged. 'My age . . . He was Asian, but he had blond hair.'

'And what was his name?'

Imran looked at Bhatti and said, 'Zafar-ji told me to ask for Danish.'

'Danish?' Thorpe said. 'As in Danish pastry?'

'I didn't remember that name until now, DI Thorpe,' Mr Bhatti said. 'I swear on the grave of my mother . . .'

'Your mother's still alive, I see her all the time in Tesco,' Thorpe said.

'DI . . .'

'Shut up, Bhatti. Imran – what happened with, er, Danish?'

'They called him Dan,' he said.

'Dan. The people in shop called him Dan.'

'Yes. I gave him the parcels and he gave me an envelope of money for Zafar-ji.'

Thorpe looked up at the shop owner. 'Thought you said some girl give you cash up front?'

'She did, DI Thorpe, she did.'

'But then this "Danish" give you more on delivery, yes?'

'Well, yes, it was a complete surprise . . .'

'And he said that if I opened up the money Mr Shaw'd come for me and cut my fingers off,' Imran said.

Thorpe said, 'Did you know the kid was threatened, Bhatti?'

'No!'

'I never told anyone,' Imran said. 'I was too scared. I'm only telling you because you're a copper and I'm scared of you too.'

Thorpe said, 'Mr Bhatti, do you have the envelope you got your little extra payment from Mr Shaw in?'

'The envelope?' He shook his head. 'I don't think so.'

'Well can you look? Or rather, look or I will.'

'OK.'

Mr Bhatti scuttled out of the shop and into the small space that passed for his office. When he'd gone, the boy said, 'Did Baharat-ji tell you about this?'

Strictly he hadn't, so Thorpe said, 'No.'

217

'What sort of serious is this?'

'It's bad, Imran,' Thorpe said. 'But don't worry about getting into trouble, 'cause you won't. Anything you can tell me . . .'

'If it's so serious then why aren't we at the police station?'

The kid was supposed to be thick, but it was a good question.

'Imran, you know this is very serious, so we can't take it down the nick.'

'Like a secret.'

'Yeah. It's a secret I need you to keep, Imran,' Thorpe said. 'You haven't even seen me. Right?'

Bhatti came back into the shop holding aloft an envelope. 'It is amazing what one can find in that office,' he said.

He'd either just grabbed the first envelope he'd come across or he'd known exactly where to lay his hand on the right one.

'You sure that's it?'

'Yes.'

He went to put it in Thorpe's hand, but the policeman took it only when he'd got a handkerchief out of his pocket.

'Ah, to preserve prints,' Bhatti said. Probably relieved that his little sideline wasn't at risk, he was now putting on a great act of helpful bonhomie.

Thorpe shook his head. 'No, they'll all've gone long ago.'

'So, DNA?'

'Don't try to guess, Bhatti, I'm doing what I'm doing, all right?'

'Oh, of course.'

Thorpe stood. 'Now, like I've just told Imran here, you tell no one what's happened here tonight. Not your wife, your kids or even your dead mum. Got it?'

'Oh, yes.'

'If I find out you've not done as I've told you, there'll be consequences.'

Venus jumped. Something had hit the window in the front door, and when he went to look he saw that the glass was cracked.

Tony Bracci pushed in front of him. 'Keep back.'

They couldn't station a copper on the front door, or even across the road, in case they were twigged.

Tony approached the door slowly.

'Sometimes kids throw things. I've had several broken windows in the past,' Venus said.

But Tony Bracci insisted upon treating what had happened as a suspicious incident.

'These people know you live here, sir.'

But when he opened the door, no one was there. What had cracked the window had clearly bounced off elsewhere. But there was something. Catching the light from the hallway it was a disc – a CD or DVD – and it had been very carefully placed on Venus's front path.

16

'Thorpe says the boy's called Dan,' Vi said.

She was wearing a very skimpy summer dress, which made her look ten years younger.

'But we can't move in until we know where he's going and what he's doing. We know he took Venus's money from Imran Ullah, but whether Dan knew what he had, we don't know. That name doesn't ring a bell as one of Harry's friends from school. But I'll text it to Mumtaz.' He took his phone out of his pocket. 'Her dad might know of an Asian kid called Dan who works in Veg.'

'Henry Grogan reckoned his brother had a friend called Danny,' Vi said. 'Don't know if it's the same one. Seems likely.'

Lee shrugged.

Alone with Vi in her office, Lee felt the absence of Tony Bracci's avuncular presence. He'd gone home to rest after a night at Venus's flat, much of which had been spent watching a DVD of Harry Venus propped up against a wall.

'With all these limits on us because of the situation, if you could carry on obboing Veg for the moment, that'd be good,' she continued.

'Venus is still paying me.' Lee finished his text and put his phone away.

'Yeah, but I know you, Arnold. Know what a soft touch you can be.'

'Not these days.'

'Harry Venus is a kid,' Vi said. 'And in spite of who his dad is, everyone who's working on this is a bit bonkers. Thinking what could happen . . .'

They both looked across at Venus's office. Behind his desk, shielded only by glass, he looked completely unruffled. Only those who really knew him would occasionally see the left corner of his top lip twitch.

'Kev Thorpe also said that some woman paid the electrical shop owner up front to take delivery of Mr Shaw's parcels,' Vi said. 'Elegant Asian woman. Shopkeeper claims he'd never seen her before. And there could be forensics.'

'How?'

'When the kid gave Dan the parcels for Mr Shaw, he gave him an envelope for this Mr Bhatti the shopkeeper. Kev got it off him.'

'Result.'

'Could be.'

'So come on, Vi, let's see this DVD then.'

She slotted a disc into the laptop and turned it around so that he could see.

Silent, it lasted less than a minute, although it seemed longer, lingering on a crumpled face that was Harry Venus, but in an altered state.

'Looks drugged.'

221

'Well done, Sherlock,' Vi said. 'Techs reckon they can enhance the background given time.'

'What, a blanket?'

'No! You can see a bit of wall and if you look carefully there's a darker patch at the top of the image. I dunno if it's a hiding to nothing, but it has to be worth a shot.' Then she said, 'You sure the suit you saw pissing about with the kids in Arnold Circus is George Grogan's brother?'

'The description you gave me fits,' he said. 'He was with George, this Dan, whoever he is, and a boy their teacher seems to rate called Tom de Vries . . .'

'Ah, Henry Grogan told me that Tom de Vries was let off smoking cannabis on school grounds,' Vi said. 'Seems like Reeds doesn't like to upset its boys' rich parents. What was de Vries doing?'

'Twatting about, talking about champagne.'

'You think they could've kidnapped George's mate?'

'I think if they did, they did so with Harry as a partner in crime,' Lee said. 'He's an unhappy boy who feels out of place with his peer group. He could well blame his parents for that. He might want to punish them.'

'Well, he looks even more unhappy now,' Vi said. 'Anyway, I thought that you saw an adult hand behind this. I do. I can see kids running about maybe getting involved for the craic . . .'

'What about George's brother?'

'The merchant banker? You think? Arnold, he's already a criminal and it's bringing in a lot of cash. Why would he risk his career for less than what he gets in bonuses?'

'Good point.'

'But, good news is that Kev Thorpe's chat with the owner of that electrical shop on Brick Lane may bring about some forensics for us.'

'Yeah.'

Her phone rang. 'Just a minute.'

She picked up.

'DI Collins, can you come into my office please,' Venus said. 'Bring Mr Arnold with you.'

'Yes sir.'

She ended the call. 'He wants us.'

Lee narrowed his eyes as he read the email again.

'I know naff-all about tech, Superintendent, I'll be honest,' he said. 'But I can tell you that that address looks well dodgy to me.'

'I'll have to get the techs to look at it,' Venus said. He put his head in his hands.

Lee looked at Vi, who shrugged and pulled a face.

The email said that whoever had written it knew who had Harry and where. If Venus wanted to see his son alive again, he had to wait for further information, which would come in the form of another email later that evening. But he'd need to pay. A quarter of a million pounds for the information. How had this person, or people, known that Venus's son was missing and that he was already in the hole for exactly that amount to the kidnappers? Was this the kidnappers again, trying to get their hands on his money more quickly? Or was it just an opportunist? And if it was, then who?

The Grogan family knew what was going on, and possibly George's friends. But who else? That teacher, McCullough, had to know something was seriously amiss with Harry by this time. But what else did he know? Then there was Venus himself, who was being bled like a halal lamb by people who knew him – well.

Lee sat down in front of Venus.

'Now look,' he said, 'I know you're gonna go up the wall, but Mr Venus you have to be honest with me now. This is . . . Look, I'm aware of the fact you always complain that people like DI Collins make assumptions about your personal life . . .'

'I do not have sex with my constables!'

'I never said you did. I want to know about Brian Green,' Lee said. 'His missus came to see you.'

Venus looked up at Vi.

'We have to know everything, sir,' she said.

'As I told you four days ago, DI Collins, Green is an old friend of my wife,' Venus told her. 'Yes, he has a criminal past, but I have never had any involvement with him in my capacity as a police officer. All this is documented. There is nothing more to know. I contacted Brian Green because he is my wife's friend. He put some feelers out amongst some old contacts . . .'

'So a load of old crims know that Harry's missing.'

'No! Mr Green made discreet enquiries, Mr Arnold.'

'Maybe I need to see about that myself,' Lee said. 'You know, Brian's an old mate of mine too, Mr Venus, but only since I left the job and only when I need him. He's as bent as a nine-bob note, and when I was a young copper I heard things about Brian that'd make your toes curl.'

224

'Mr Green would not have put Harry's life at risk,' Venus said. 'He likes him.'

Vi Collins leaned down onto Venus's desk and said, 'Your boy knows Brian Green?'

His face reddened. 'Through my wife,' he said. 'Since I left . . .'

Vi looked at Lee and then back at Venus. 'Strange company for a public schoolboy to keep, if you don't mind my saying.'

'I don't live with my wife, Mr Arnold, as well you know. I can't tell her who to see.'

'No. But I'll have to speak to Brian, Superintendent. Just to make sure.'

Venus paled. Brian, it was rumoured, was not a happy bunny these days. Lee didn't know why, but he was keen to find out. Because when Brian Green was unhappy, people tended to get hurt.

Mumtaz read Lee's text and put her phone away. 'We can talk for as long as you like, Alison,' she said.

The woman she had been due to see in East Ham had seemed happy to meet the following day.

'This doctor was sure that he didn't know my father?' Alison said.

'You can speak to Dr Chitty yourself if you want to. He's happy to meet you. But no,' Mumtaz said, 'he is certain that he doesn't know your father. Alison, he may be dead by now. What we do know is the identity of your mother.'

'And where my illness came from.'

'Yes.'

She shook her head. 'So I'm touched by fame.'

'I'm sorry it's in such a negative fashion,' Mumtaz said. 'And I'm so sorry I've not been able to find any of your relatives. Your mother was an only child and we are a long way from Argentina. But you now know where your Native American blood comes from.'

'A dictator.'

She looked out into her garden. She'd not cried or exhibited any outward signs of great emotion. In spite of the heat, she looked pale and cold.

'My son Charlie, he's very dark,' she said. 'My husband's mother was Indian, a Parsee. You know them?'

'Yes,' Mumtaz said.

'We thought he took after her.' She pointed to a photograph above the fireplace. 'That's my son.'

Mumtaz walked over and looked at an image of a smiling boy who could have come from Dhaka, Mumbai or Islamabad. Slim, with delicate features, he bore no resemblance she could see to the stout, full-lipped pictures of Juan Perón she had googled on the internet.

'He's a handsome boy. You must be proud.' She sat down again.

'I'm just grateful he doesn't have Huntington's,' Alison said. Then she closed her eyes for a moment. 'Mrs Hakim, do you think that Perón had my mother killed?'

Mumtaz didn't know. 'Those were violent times in Argentina.'

'How could anyone kill their own child?'

'No one knows whether Perón had a hand in Rosa's death or not,' Mumtaz said. 'We probably won't find out. Not now.'

'He raped her mother, he wanted his grandchild aborted. He must have been capable of anything.'

Mumtaz saw the first, very slight, shake of Alison's head.

'Where is Charlie?'

A shake became a pronounced twitch. 'Oh, er, he has a little summer job . . .'

'Would you like me to call him? Do you want . . . ?'

'No!' She began to cry. 'How can I tell him about this? I can't!'

It was like watching herself. A woman holding herself up with great difficulty in the face of a secret. In this case it had only just come to light, but Mumtaz knew that, for a while at least, Alison would keep it to herself. Or try to.

'Alison,' she said, 'you can talk to me about this whenever you want. If you want to talk through what you might say to your son . . .'

'He can't know about this! He can't! He can't grow up knowing he could do things that are mad and wrong and . . .'

Mumtaz sat beside her and put an arm around her shoulders. The shaking continued, but there was also a slackening as she let herself lie against Mumtaz's chest.

'Alison, this is not a source of shame. Not for you. The truth is what it is, but except for your illness it has nothing to do with you or with Charlie. There's no reason it should have any effect on your son.'

'My grandmother was thirteen. Thirteen!'

Mumtaz moved Alison's head so that she could look into her eyes. 'And one of mine was twelve,' she said. 'It happened. Women and children were, and sometimes still are, just a man's property. All we can do is make sure it doesn't happen any more.'

'I let my husband send my son away. How am I better than a girl who gives her baby to bloody nuns?'

'I'm sorry Alison, I don't know what you mean,' Mumtaz said. 'What do you mean, your husband made you send your son away?'

She wiped a trembling hand across her nose. 'To boarding school. Chris, my husband, had been there. He wanted Charlie to follow in his footsteps.'

Or Mr Darrah-Duncan had wanted the best education he could get for his son. Vile though he had been, Ahmet had sent Shazia to a private school in Essex with the best of intentions. He'd wanted her to be educated. Sometimes Mumtaz felt that because white British people had been offered free education for so long, they didn't value it in the same way as the Asian population. But how could she articulate that to someone like Alison? And was that even appropriate to the situation she was in right now?

'I didn't want him to go,' Alison continued. 'Then when I got ill, I didn't want him here.'

'That's understandable.'

'No, no, you don't understand.'

Her head was shaking violently now.

Mumtaz said, 'Alison, do you need me to get you medication?'

'Oh, for fuck's sake I'm full of antidepressants, antipsychotics, anti this, that and everything!'

A trembling arm pushed Mumtaz away.

'Charlie is a little shit, Mrs Hakim,' she said. 'I love him to pieces, but he treats me like a handicap. All he wants is money!'

'But he works?'

She thought about Shazia, at home, turning Cousin Aftab's unearned money over in her hands.

'Chris got him that job,' Alison said. 'Oh God, I thought I'd have something to tell Charlie to make it better. How can I tell him this?'

'You don't have to—' Was she really counselling keeping a secret? 'No, forget that,' she went on. 'You have to tell him one day, Alison, but maybe not now. He's sixteen, an adolescent. My own daughter is that sort of age and . . .'

And Shazia was now suffering because of Mumtaz's secret life. It was because of secrets that they were at the mercy of the Sheikhs.

'I bet your daughter doesn't look down her nose at you,' Alison said.

'No, but she did. I think it's all part of the adolescent angst they all go through.'

'Maybe, but at least you've never had to listen to all the puerile snobbery that passes for friendship at a boys' public school. You know the other boys call my son "Dan"? I've no idea why, he won't tell me, he just says it's a "Reeds thing". That's the name of the school. Reeds has "things" and "traditions" for everything.'

'Reeds?'

'Charlie's public school,' she said. 'It's in Ascot.'

Lee hadn't seen Taylor Green before. When he'd first spotted a young girl sunbathing beside Brian's pool, he'd thought for a moment that it was the old man's previous wife, Amy. But she'd died in a hit-and-run incident. When it came to women, Brian chose a type. Blonde, young, girly, spilling out of a bikini that was little more than a cobweb.

'Taylor's a student,' Brian said once the silent 'help' had given Lee a cappuccino.

Lee quelled the urge to ask what Taylor studied.

'If Harry Venus's kidnap gets out, whoever has him could kill him.'

There was no point holding back.

'The kid's dad told me that he told you so you could put the word out. I need to know who you've tapped up, Brian.'

'Why'd you need to know? He never asked me.'

'His son's been kidnapped, his brain's dead. I'm trying to watch his back, and that includes finding out who knows what.'

'No one I know'd do nothing like that,' Brian said. 'I don't mix with scumbags.'

'You mix with ex-scumbags.'

'I socialise with businessmen like myself.' He smiled.

Lee drank some coffee. His phone rang. It was Mumtaz, but he didn't answer. It could wait.

'Yes, and we all know what you and your fellow businessmen used to get up to, don't we? Money's tight.'

'What, for people like George Micaleff? Fuck off.'

'Yeah, Brian, pick the exception.'

Brian Green had gone legit through health clubs, but his old mate George Micaleff had a property development company specialising in creating very small, very expensive flats in old houses in Hackney.

'Tom Manners? Pat Tabor?'

Brian batted the names away. 'Oh, do me a favour. You think anyone's interested in them old fossils? Pat's got Parkinson's. They're nothing. We're all nothing now. I put the word out for Venus out of courtesy and because I like his boy.'

'Yeah, so he said.'

'Tina started in my Clerkenwell club back before the Ark,' Brian said. 'She was always a good girl and a lady. I've always helped her when I could. I spoke to George Micaleff and my cousin Benny and that was it. They knew nothing. None of us do because, if you've noticed, Mr Arnold, the game's changed in recent years. Foreigners.'

'You gonna give me your UKIP speech, Brian?'

He shook his big, round head. 'Look, me granddad come from Poland. If he hadn't, I'd've snuffed it in a concentration camp. I am a bloody immigrant. But this lot from eastern Europe, now, well they ain't playing fair.'

Lee knew something about the Polish, Bulgarian and Romanian gangsters on the manor. Hooky fags, loose women and booze that sent you blind were some of their products. He also knew it went deeper. People-trafficking, whispers about home-made heroin substitutes.

'Brian, you say you're legit now. What're they to you?'

'Nothing.'

'So why mention them?'

'Because if anyone has taken Harry Venus, it'll be them.'

'Why?' Was Brian going soft in the head? 'How would they even know Paul Venus, let alone his son? These are people who work out of shonky taxi offices and run girls from the back of fag shops.'

'George and Benny'll keep shtum.'

'Unless they see a few quid in it.' Lee leaned forward. 'Brian, we think that someone else knows now. Unless the kidnappers are playing a very risky double game, A. N. Other is claiming to know where Harry is and is trying to squeeze Venus for exactly the same amount of money as the latest ransom demand, except they want the cash sooner. Now if that info's kosher, fucking marvellous. But if it isn't, Venus is in the shit to two lots of villains. Understand?'

He took a moment to take it in, then he said, 'Yeah.'

'Meantime, you don't even tell Venus you know that. And you make sure of George Micaleff and Benny Zimmer, or I'm telling you, I will be coming for them.'

'They won't have told no one. They know nothing.'

'What made Venus even come to you, Brian?'

'I told you, Tina.'

Lee shook his head. 'You know Venus is not trusted don't you Brian?'

'He's got a woman problem . . .'

'No, I don't mean that,' Lee said. 'Tina bats for the other side these days, so I don't blame him for getting a bit of extra-curricular when he can, but there's something wrong about that man. Ask any copper at Forest Gate. What's he into, Brian? Because one of the theories going about in my head is that he's been having dealings with people he shouldn't and they've turned on him.'

'Like who?'

'I dunno. Like you?'

'Oh, for fuck's sake.'

'All right, then who? You know his wife. Tell me about Venus. If you care about Harry, tell me. Because if that kid is missing because his old man is bent, then the only way to get him back is to get his old man to own up, and I don't know how to do that.'

Brian shrugged. 'But Venus ain't bent.'

Lee sagged back into his chair. Of course Brian Green wouldn't give him Paul Venus while there was still something in their relationship for him. Maybe they did just know each other through Tina Wilton. Venus could easily have asked Brian Green to put out feelers with no strings attached, given the nature of their connection. But, although Lee knew intellectually that the kidnappers could have sent that email purporting to be from someone else, somehow he couldn't get himself to believe that was true. And why was Brian so stoked up about eastern European villains? They had to be nothing to him.

'Have you been out today, Shazia?'

She didn't look as if she had. Pale and watery-eyed, the girl looked like a classic female consumption victim from the nineteenth century.

'No.' She leaned against the living-room doorpost.

'It's lovely and warm in the garden,' Mumtaz said. 'And nobody's out there.'

She'd spent an hour in the garden when she'd got home from Alison's. It had been a tough day and her head had been pounding when she'd got in. She was also a little worried that she hadn't been able to contact Lee.

'OK.'

Shazia left. Mumtaz heard the back door open then close and then dug in her handbag for her phone to try to contact Lee again. Then the doorbell rang.

'Oh my God,' she said when she saw him on the doorstep. 'I've been trying to ring you.'

As he slumped down in one of her old leather chairs, Lee looked almost as washed-out as Shazia.

'I'll make a cup of tea in a minute,' Mumtaz said, 'but I've got to ask you something first.'

'Yeah?'

'The school where Harry Venus goes, it's called Reeds isn't it?'

'Yes.'

She sat down opposite. 'My client, Alison . . .'

'Oh, how'd that go?'

'Terrible. Car-crash. But look, her son Charlie goes to Reeds. Charles Darrah-Duncan. He's the same age as Harry. Heard of him?'

Lee asked if he could have a cigarette.

He said, 'A Charles Duncan is one of the boys Harry is, and isn't, in with.'

'I didn't see him while I was with Alison, but I did see a photograph,' Mumtaz said. 'He looks Asian.'

'Not South American?'

'No. His father's mother was a Parsee, from Mumbai. Lee, he looks like my brother Ali when he was that age. And, he's got a holiday job in a little shop called Veg off Arnold Circus. His school friends call him Dan, his mother has no idea why. But that's why I was trying to call you.'

'Why do people call you Dan?'

Charles Darrah-Duncan looked into the hollow eyes of his mother, who said nothing. He turned to Vi Collins.

'It's a school thing.'

'What is?'

'The Danny thing.'

Vi glanced at the duty solicitor. It was late and he was on edge. Probably wanted his dinner. So did she, but when Lee Arnold had told her just who the Dan in Veg actually was, she'd had to bring the kid in.

'Explain it.'

The boy looked at his mother again. Then he said, 'It's after Dannii Minogue.'

'Kylie's sister?'

'Yes.'

'Why?'

He seemed to wrestle with his thoughts for a moment. 'Because they reckon I'm gay.'

'Who does?'

'The other boys. It's sort of a joke.'

'Bit homophobic isn't it? So are you? Gay?'

His hair was dyed blond and he was wearing very tight trousers. Vi tried to be politically correct about him, but it was hard.

'No.'

'So why'd they give you a girl's name?'

'It's only a bit of ribbing. It doesn't matter.'

'No?'

She would have laid bets that it did, or used to, but she changed the subject. 'Who's Mr Shaw?'

The boy frowned.

'You took delivery of seven parcels for him eight days ago from an Asian boy at your place of work,' Vi said. 'You gave this boy some money for his employer in an envelope in return and then told him that if he creamed off any cash for himself, Mr Shaw'd break his fingers. Who's Mr Shaw, Dan, and what have you got to do with him?'

'Nothing. I don't know any Mr Shaw. I didn't say anyone would break anyone's fingers. Why would I? It's a lie! What's this about?'

'Oh, hasn't your mate George Grogan told you?' Vi said. 'You have seen him around Arnold Circus, haven't you?'

He shrugged. 'Once or twice.'

'And his brother.'

'He stays with Henry at his flat in Shoreditch.'

'And what about Tom de Vries?'

There was a pause.

Alison Darrah-Duncan said, 'Please tell me you're not seeing that awful boy.'

Charlie's lowered head said it all.

'So,' Vi said, 'you, George Grogan, Henry Grogan and Tom de Vries have been living the hipster dream in Bethnal Green.'

'I work there. My dad's friend David owns the shop.'

Vi looked down at a document in front of her. 'Aka Jethro Nutt.'

'It's kind of rustic,' the boy said.

'Ah. And is Mr Nutt also Mr Shaw?'

'No. I don't know who Mr Shaw is. I've never heard of him.'

'And yet you took delivery of a load of parcels for him,' Vi said.

'I didn't.'

'You do take deliveries though don't you? As part of your job?'

'Yes, people order products through the shop all the time, but I don't take any notice of who they're for.'

'What do you do with them?'

'I put them in the store room for David to sort out when he comes in.'

'And yet David, Mr Conway-Middleton, has told me he has no knowledge of anything for a Mr Shaw,' Vi said. 'Mr Shaw is not a regular customer at Veg. And when a young lady came into Mr Bhatti's electrical shop on Brick Lane and asked him to do a job for Mr Shaw via his PO box service, Mr Bhatti, who owns that business, had never heard of him either. So all we have is you, Danny. Oh, and the envelope you gave to the Asian lad to take back to Mr Bhatti.'

Kids were very aware of things like DNA testing. Dan was a bright boy, he'd see the implication.

But he said, 'I don't know anything about a Mr Shaw.'

'Well then, we'll have to see what that envelope turns up,' Vi said. 'Just for the record, Dan, can you categorically state that you never handed an envelope to an Asian boy eight days ago in return for parcels for Mr Shaw.'

'No, I can't,' he said.

'Ah.'

'Because like I say, I take deliveries in the shop all the time and sometimes we pay suppliers.'

He was right. According to Mr Conway-Middleton that happened a lot. But Dan was also a friend of a missing boy for whom those parcels had been a ransom.

'Dan,' Vi said, 'I want you to tell me about Harry Venus. Mainly I want you to tell me why you had your hands on envelopes that contained money demanded by his kidnappers.'

17

It was weird seeing Tina at his flat. She'd only ever come to deposit or pick up Harry. Now she was in his living room, watching him eat breakfast. Paul was grateful she'd not brought her hair-extension-decorated lover.

'So these new people claim to know where Harry is. Right?'

Venus swallowed a gobbet of muesli. Keeping healthy was hard work. 'Yes.'

'And they emailed last night?'

'For the second time, yes,' he said. 'They want the money tomorrow.'

'And the next drop to the kidnappers . . .'

'Day after tomorrow.'

'So it's easy,' she said. 'Pay the people who can lead us to Harry.'

She sat down and lit a cigarette.

'Please . . .'

'Oh, fuck off, you've sold the flat!'

'We don't know who these people are,' he said.

She shook her head. 'Just hand it over! You'll get the money. Get it off Brian. I don't know why you don't get on with it, Paul.'

'Oh, and I should go to visit Green with a police tail on my bumper? Or he comes here? The phone's tapped. Come on, Tina!'

'So I'll get it!'

'Yes, and where do you think my colleagues will imagine the money came from? Tina, it's under control. Brian's not to know. Now my colleagues know . . .'

'Harry is in more danger than ever.'

In a way she was right. Venus had no reason to suspect the kidnappers knew he'd informed the police. However, now one of Harry's friends was in custody. Could that little idiot Charles Duncan really be involved?

He'd taken the first lot of ransom money from the fat Asian boy Lee Arnold had seen trudging up Brick Lane shortly after the drop. Of course, at that stage Arnold had no way of knowing whether the boy had the money in his bag or not. That had been before they'd known how Mr Bhatti in the electrical shop accessed his PO box. But the fat boy, so he said, had delivered packages addressed to Mr Shaw, which was the name Venus had written on the front of every envelope. They'd been taken from him by little Charlie Duncan. Venus felt the ground shift underneath his feet as he walked across the room. He sat down. His mobile rang. He looked at the name on the screen and turned it off.

Tina said nothing. On her way to work she'd just 'popped in'. Together with fat Tony Bracci still sleeping in his spare room, she made the place feel overcrowded and claustrophobic. Venus resented them both. What he needed was time alone. DI Collins said that Charlie Duncan was denying everything. He didn't know where Harry was and neither did George or Henry Grogan. Why would a merchant banker in his mid-twenties hang around with a load of teenage boys? Collins was going back to question Grogan. And where was that de Vries boy?

'I don't know how I'm going to function today,' Tina said.

Drama. But then she was an actress. What did he expect?

'You will. You're a professional.'

'Ha!'

She got up and walked out.

Venus switched his phone back on and returned the call he had ignored.

'Hey, you!'

Shazia turned, looking back at Forest Gate station. At first she didn't recognise anyone.

'Hey!'

Blonde hair, bare midriff, baby.

'Ludmilla!'

She walked over and put out a finger for baby Tomasz to grab. 'Hiya.'

'I'm sorry, don't remember you name,' Ludmilla said.

'Shazia.'

'Shazia,' she smiled. 'Why you don't work at Mr Huq shop now? He say when the old man is on his holiday you can do his job. You like it. I see this.'

'Ah . . .'

'Mr Huq don't give you sack?'

'Oh, no,' Shazia said. But then why had she left if Cousin Aftab hadn't sacked her? 'No, it's just . . . Oh some Asian people, you know, they don't like girls working and—'

'Your mother? Your mother say no to working? Your father?'

'No, not my mum. And my father is dead.'

'I am sorry.'

Shazia shook her head. 'No, some other people,' she said. 'I didn't want to upset Mr Huq's customers and so I left.'

Baby Tomasz giggled.

Ludmilla shook her head.

'Just the way it can be sometimes,' Shazia said. 'Religion, you know.'

'I know. Pain in the ass.'

In spite of herself, Shazia laughed. 'That's one way of putting it!'

'Before we have communist in Poland, now the Church. Which is worse?' She shrugged. 'I think maybe Church. But you know, I think this is not many people who don't want you in Mr Huq shop.'

'I don't know.'

'No, really,' Ludmilla said, 'I think it is just one man.'

Shazia began to feel her flesh creep. Oh God, she didn't want any more trouble with Naz Sheikh, she didn't even want to think about him.

'That man who came that day and treated me like a whore,' Ludmilla said. 'I see the way he look at you, how he speak. He think I'm not there, but I watch him.'

'Oh, I don't know,' Shazia said. 'I wouldn't think about it. He's just . . . one of those intolerant men.'

'Maybe.' Ludmilla shifted the baby further up on her hip. 'But to behave badly to people you do not know is such ignorance!'

'Yeah, but . . . So where are you going Ludmilla? Are you—'

'I tell Janusz. He doesn't like such behaviour. He will speak to this man I think.'

Shazia's heart hammered. 'Oh, I wouldn't do that. Who's Janusz?'

'My husband. He come to UK to work in Russian gym in Wanstead.'

'Ah.' And Naz Sheikh had called his wife a whore. Shazia imagined some huge Pole smashing Naz's skull against the pavement, but she knew that was wishful thinking. In reality Naz would probably stick a knife in little Tomasz's daddy's guts.

She took one of Ludmilla's hands in hers. 'Oh I wouldn't make trouble with that man if I were you, Ludmilla,' she said. 'He's not a good person. I wouldn't like your husband to get into trouble.'

But Ludmilla just smiled. 'Ah, Shazia,' she said, 'but you don't understand. This man he called me a bad name and my husband, he is a Polish man. There have to be trouble.'

Henry Grogan looked completely relaxed. It was his solicitor, a tiny woman in her mid-twenties, who looked as if she were about to have a stroke. Her eyes bulged. But then maybe, Vi thought, that was simply genetic.

'I've told no one that Harry Venus is missing,' Henry said. 'He's my brother's friend. Why would I put him at risk?'

'I'm not saying you told anyone,' Vi said. 'We're searching your flat, Mr Grogan, because we think Harry might have been there.'

'Well, he has. When I first moved in. He came with my brother. Why do you think I've got anything to do with his disappearance?'

'The whole thing's a mystery to me, sir,' Vi said.

'Are you looking for his DNA in my flat?'

'Amongst other things, yes,' she said. 'Although you'd be surprised how often we solve crimes without involving scientists or even big transparent marker boards.' She leaned across the table at him. 'People leave things about. Bits of clothing, some of them bloodstained . . .'

'I haven't done anything to Harry Venus! Why would I?'

Vi leaned back in her chair. 'I dunno. Money?'

'Money? I'm a banker, DI Collins. I've probably already earned more in the course of my short life than you will ever see in yours.'

'It's all right, you can call me old . . .'

'I wouldn't presume to be so rude!'

Now he *was* rattled. His face was red and his breathing had grown erratic. The bug-eyed solicitor saw it too and put a hand on his arm. He ignored it.

'As you know, we have another of Harry's friends in custody,' Vi said.

'Charlie Duncan. Christ! He couldn't harm himself, much less anyone else!'

'Mr Duncan is not accused of harming anyone,' Vi said. 'Mr Duncan does, however, have a connection to Harry Venus's disappearance.'

'What connection?'

Vi looked down at her notes. 'You don't live far from where Mr Duncan works, do you Mr Grogan?'

'He's got some little holiday job on Arnold Circus, yes,' he said. 'What of it?'

'You've been seen with Mr Duncan, your brother and Mr de Vries around Arnold Circus.'

'I know. You said when you came to my flat the first time. So what?'

'Mr Duncan, as I've told you, has a connection to this incident.'

'What?'

'Mr Grogan, can you tell me anything about someone called Mr Shaw, please?'

Sometimes, to get more information, you just had to trust that those you were tapping up were on the level.

'Malcolm?'

'Hello.'

'Lee Arnold.'

'Oh.'

It was weird for Lee being back in the nick again, especially sitting opposite Tony Bracci. At the nick he was on the spot.

'Malcolm, I hope I can rely upon your discretion,' Lee said.

'You mean over Harry Venus going AWOL? Of course. I've not

uttered a word. You don't have to say anything, Lee. I imagine the family want to keep it quiet.'

'I'd like to know about Tom de Vries,' Lee said. 'I'd specifically like to know why you didn't tell me he'd been caught with cannabis on school premises.'

'Ah.'

'Malcolm, I know your kind of school looks after its own. I get that. But de Vries is the only boy in Harry's group we haven't spoken to yet. I'm sure he knows about Harry, but reaching him seems to be hard.'

'Oh?'

All Lee could remember about Tom de Vries was an image of a boy with a bum-fluff moustache who dressed like an old-fashioned bank clerk and brayed about champagne. Since then, he seemed to have disappeared.

McCullough cleared his throat. 'His father, also a Reeds boy, is a diplomat. Azerbaijan, I believe. Parents divorced. Mother had a bit of a drink issue. Of course this is just between you and me.'

'Of course.'

'I'm not breaking any confidence when I say he's got the highest IQ in the school. Belongs to Mensa. From my own point of view, he's a gift.'

'In what way?'

'Tom understands story,' he said. 'His own creative work is extraordinary. When he creates characters they have real depth and they don't just do things randomly. So many boys, when they attempt to write, just have their characters suddenly burst out with inappropriate acts of violence or heroism that don't make any sense. Tom's work is nuanced. You don't think that Tom's mixed up in Harry's disappearance do you?'

Lee wondered whether what had kept Tom's dope-smoking quiet was his talent or his father. When he got off the phone to McCullough he looked at Tony Bracci and said, 'Well?'

'Tom and his dad live on Princelet Street in Spitalfields,' Tony said. 'Very on-trend these days, as we know. But they've been there a long time. Bought by the family back in the seventies.'

Lee shrugged. Upmarket types had been in the area for a long time, colonising the old Huguenot houses.

'Dad also has a place in South Ken,' Tony said. 'Bought with new wife.'

'Ah. When?'

'Last year.'

'We need to get this kid,' Lee said. 'He's been seen with Charles Duncan, who took those parcels for this Mr Shaw from Imran Ullah.'

'He's still saying he never knew what was in them. And even if that envelope Kev Thorpe got from the electrical shop owner has got Duncan's prints all over it, doesn't mean that he knew what he was doing or why.'

'Oh come on, Tone: he knows Harry, he handled ransom money intended to free the kid. He's in this somewhere.'

'Yeah.'

'The Grogan parents are on their way down here with George and we know where de Vries lives now. I'm going to have a word. With my PI hat on. Nice and gentle.'

'Clear it with the Super then.'

Lee looked across into Venus's office. He had his head in his hands.

The anonymous figures in the white SOCO coveralls looked at the metal trunk in the middle of the floor. It was padlocked and the owner was in an interview. The one on the right stuck a short crowbar behind the lock and prised it off.

'Easy.'

They opened the lid. Then they both stepped backwards. The one on the left said, 'Fucking hell!'

The girl was beautiful. Asian by the look of her, dressed in very fashionable and expensive clothes. Kev Thorpe had told Vi about a stylish Asian woman who'd gone to the electrical shop on Brick Lane for the mythical Mr Shaw.

'Mr de Vries is rarely here,' she said as she stood in the doorway of a house that appeared to be in complete darkness.

'I know, he's a diplomat,' Lee said. 'Who are you?'

'I'm Mr de Vries's housekeeper. What do you want?'

'I'm a private investigator,' he told her. 'I have some information for Mr de Vries.'

'There's no one here.'

'What, not his son? Mr de Vries has a son, doesn't he?'

'Not here,' she said.

'You know where I can find him?'

'No, I don't.'

'So you're here on your own?'

'Yes.'

'You know you're doing a really bad job of lying, don't you?'

'Mr de Vries is out of the country.'

'Oh, I'm buying that,' Lee said. He knew for a fact that Marcus de Vries was in Azerbaijan because Tony Bracci had phoned the Foreign Office. 'But his son'll do, and I think you know where he is.'

'I don't.'

'He lives here, doesn't he?'

'Yes.'

Her face was blank, but there was a tension behind it, as if she were trying to hold some emotion in check.

'Then where is he?'

'I don't know.'

'Do you have his phone number?'

This time she said nothing.

'Well, do you or don't you?'

'I don't have to tell you anything,' she said. 'You're not the police.'

She began to close the door. Lee jammed his foot inside.

She shrieked.

He pushed her back and found himself in a hall lined with dark-red wallpaper. The only light came from a candle beside a long, dingy staircase. The woman, whose eyes he could just see through the gloom, made no sound.

'Now, look,' Lee said, 'I'm not the police, but the reason why I'm here is because someone's life is in danger.'

'Tom . . .' Her eyes were wet. 'Is it Tom?'

She loved him.

'Why should it be?' Lee said. 'What's the matter with him?'

'Oh, God!'

'Tell me!'

When she spoke, her whole face trembled. 'He's gone,' she said.

'Gone where?'

'I don't know.'

Lee moved away from her. But she didn't try to run. She just cried.

He said, 'Did he take all the money with him?'

And for a moment, he expected her to say, 'What money?' But she didn't. She just said, 'Yes.'

Vi sat down opposite Venus. He was white.

'It's all right sir,' she said. 'It wasn't blood.'

'Then what was it?'

'Shit, er, faeces,' she said. 'Don't know whose or what, but SOCO said there was a lot of it.'

'In a tin trunk?'

'Henry Grogan uses it as a coffee table. Very industrial-looking, very on-trend.'

'God, do you know, DI Collins, I don't think I ever want to go anywhere that has been gentrified again. Faeces! Where did Grogan say it came from?'

'I haven't asked him yet, sir,' Vi said. 'Waiting for his parents and his brother to arrive. To be honest with you, talking to Henry and little Dan, Charlie or whatever he's called, is like trying to ice skate on shag-pile carpet.'

'Public schools prepare boys for careers in professions like the law and so, though young, they are extremely articulate, DI Collins. Harry has run verbal rings around me for years.'

Vi wanted to say something along the lines of how it served him right for sending Harry to the type of school where people were trained to be superior, but she had better things to do.

'Sir, the science bods'll be able to lift DNA from all sorts of things in Grogan's flat, including . . .'

'Yes of course, comparisons must be made with my son's profile.'

'Thank you, sir.'

'Any news about the envelope DI Thorpe sent off for analysis?'

'No, sir,' Vi said. 'I wish we were like *CSI Miami* here in East London, but, as you know, in the real world of overworked technicians and budget cuts, things are a bit more leisurely.'

For the first time in a long while, she saw him smile.

'Thank you, DI Collins.'

18

Mumtaz walked into a shuttered room lit by candles. Two faces were familiar, one was not.

'The electric's off,' Tony Bracci said.

Mumtaz looked at Lee. 'What's going on?'

He'd called her away from a night in front of the television. She'd had to leave Shazia at her parents' house. She was disorientated and where she found herself now didn't help.

The candle-lit room was empty except for a wing chair. In it sat a perfectly still woman, about her own age.

Lee took Mumtaz to one side. 'I think this woman's boyfriend, Tom de Vries, may have Harry Venus,' he said. 'I don't know where. She seemed to think that her lover was missing before she went into this state, whatever it is.'

'She's silent? Motionless?'

'As you see.'

Mumtaz looked at the woman.

'I know she's in some sort of shock,' Lee said. 'De Vries, who she loves, took their money . . .'

Tony Bracci joined them.

'The guv'd just give her a slap round the face,' he said.

Mumtaz nodded. 'Which may work. But what do you want me to do?'

'We need to know what the fuck is going on here as soon as we can,' Lee said.

'Clearly.'

'I mean, this is like something out of Dickens,' Tony said.

The old Huguenot house was strange. Unlike most of them, which had been sympathetically restored, this one looked as if it hadn't been touched for centuries.

'What do you want me to do?' Mumtaz asked.

'When she did the silent thing on me I went through her handbag,' Lee said. 'I know she speaks English, but everything I found in her bag is like this.' He handed her a stack of papers. 'What is it? Arabic?'

'It's Urdu,' Mumtaz said. 'Her family are probably from Pakistan. You think that hearing her native language might wake her up?'

'I dunno. Might reassure her. Is this psychologically all right or . . . ?'

'Psychology is not an exact science,' Mumtaz said. 'I studied it for three years. I know.'

'You can do that language though, right?'

'She's called Laila,' Mumtaz said as she looked down at the paperwork.

'So you can.'

She smiled. Then she walked over to the woman on the chair and squatted down on the floor. She took one of the woman's hands and watched her blink – once.

'Laila, you know there is a line in the rock,' she said. 'I know you know what that saying means. To stay silent is a sin.'

253

The woman looked at her as if she didn't understand. Mumtaz wondered whether it was the language, or the old proverb that basically meant that the 'game was up' that was eluding her. She switched to English. 'Do you have any idea where Tom might have gone?'

She looked away.

'Why do you think that Tom left you without any money?'

The silence continued. She had to be at least thirty and yet Tom de Vries was the same age as Harry Venus. Had they actually been lovers and, if so, for how long? While Tom was still under sixteen?

Lee said something to Tony, who flexed one hand.

Mumtaz said, 'Now Laila, or whatever your name is, if you don't speak to us soon you will be arrested. These men are involved in a missing person investigation, which they think you know something about. If you try to obstruct them, you'll be in even more trouble than you're in now. And you are in trouble. Tom is sixteen.'

The woman looked back at her.

'What has Tom done?' Mumtaz asked. 'If you tell us, maybe it will help your case when you are asked to explain how you came to be in love with an underage boy.'

'He has no mother. His father left him.'

'Tell me about it.'

It was a start. But Mumtaz could see that Lee and Tony wanted her to get back to the subject of Harry Venus.

'The new Mrs de Vries didn't want Tom,' the woman said. 'Such a beautiful boy! But she didn't.'

Mumtaz gripped her hand encouragingly.

'Mr de Vries moved to a new house and left me to look after Tom when he wasn't at school. We fell in love. He may only be young, but you have to know him.'

'I'd like to know him,' Mumtaz said. 'Can you tell me where he is?'

She tried to speak, but her throat closed.

Mumtaz saw Lee take his phone out of his pocket and walk out of the room.

Henry Grogan saw his parents and his brother walk across the station car park and made a sound like a growl.

'I shouldn't say this to a police officer, I know, but I want to kill the little bastard!'

His solicitor put a hand on his arm.

In spite of herself, Vi Collins smiled. 'Take your point. Although I must say I'm finding it hard to believe what you've just told me.'

'Oh I can assure you it's true, DI Collins.'

'I'm not saying it's not.'

'That smell's haunted me for days,' he said. 'In the trunk! In the fucking trunk!'

'You're sure it was your brother, Mr Grogan?'

'Oh, yes. Or one of his friends. Who else would shit in an improbable place except an old Reedian? It's a school custom called "depositing", DI Collins. The chap who can deposit his faeces in the most obscure or dangerous place gets kudos, which is, of course, what Reeds is all about.'

'You didn't like your old school?'

'Loathed it,' he said. 'Full of boys who think they're special because their snobbish masters and their parents tell them they are. You may hate bankers, most people do, but at least we work.'

Luckily, Vi didn't have to respond, because her phone rang. 'Excuse me, Mr Grogan.' She left the interview room.

'Vi.'

'Lee,' she answered. 'You got the de Vries boy?'

'No,' he said, 'but I do have his girlfriend.'

'His girlfriend?'

'Almost old enough to be his mum. De Vries has gone missing, according to this Miss Malik. And he's gone with money. Vi, I think that Tom de Vries knows where Harry Venus is. We're bringing Laila Malik in now, but you've gotta make those other kids talk. That Dan had the ransom money in his hands.'

'All right,' she said, 'will do. Let me know when you get here.'

'Tony and Mumtaz'll bring the woman back. I'm gonna stay here, if that's OK. See what I can find. You have to see this place to believe it.'

'All right.'

She went back into the interview room.

Still very obviously fuming, Henry Grogan said, 'And you know where the little swine got the idea to shit in my trunk from, don't you?'

'No.'

'Bloody Alfred Hitchcock,' he said. 'Mr Malcolm McCullough and his obsession with Alfred effing Hitchcock. Another sod I could cheerfully murder.'

'I didn't know,' Vi said, 'that Alfred Hitchcock ever shat in a trunk.'

Henry Grogan laughed. 'I don't think he did,' he said. 'But he was in every one of his films, which I do love. That's partly down to Mr McCullough. He gave all his house groups Hitchcock posters when we left school. But McCullough had acolytes and still does. Boys who hang on his every word.'

'Your brother?'

'Yes. And I've no idea how this got started, but somehow the old "depositing" game became part of a Hitchcock homage. Georgie's proud of the fact that in the past he's dumped in a shower and on the school roof.'

Vi frowned.

'*Psycho* and *Vertigo*, DI Collins,' he said. 'Their plots are engraved on my memory for all time. The aim is to appropriately "deposit" for every one of Hitchcock's films. And there are a lot.'

'Does Mr McCullough know his boys do this?'

'Oh, I'm sure. I think he probably revels in it,' Henry said. 'McCullough is very old public school. He tells all his boys about his own "golden days" at school. He's some sort of title. Laird or something.'

'Does the school know? The headmaster?'

He laughed again. 'Oh, probably,' he said. 'They won't do anything about a "tradition", however disgusting.' Then his face straightened. 'But it's supposed to stay in school. Doing that in my home is outrageous.'

'But how do you know that's what it is?' Vi asked.

'A shit in a trunk? It comes from Hitchcock's *Rope*. Two vile American rich kids kill a younger school friend. They want to commit the perfect crime. They don't, but before they get caught they amuse themselves by putting the boy's dead body in a trunk they use as a table for a buffet – to which they invite their victim's father and his fiancée. It's actually based on a true story, I believe. Google it.'

Alison Darrah-Duncan had only ever met the Grogans once before. Still, she smiled at them and they smiled back. The glass wall that divided them made verbal communication impossible. But then what was there to say?

As far as Alison was concerned, she'd been innocently researching her parentage, which had proved to be a poisonous subject, when she'd been thrown into this nightmare. She wanted to blame Mumtaz Hakim for putting her through this stress, but she knew it wasn't her fault.

Shaking, she said to her son, 'It's gone midnight now, they're not going to let you go any time soon. You need to tell them the truth.'

Charlie looked down at his hands.

'You handled money intended for kidnappers. Whose idea was that? Tom de Vries's?'

'Why do you always think that Tom's involved in anything bad?'

'Because he usually is,' she said. 'I don't know what he's got over you, Charlie, but if it's that you're gay then it doesn't matter. But you have to tell the truth, because if anything happens to Harry and you were involved, the police will throw the book at you.'

He looked up. 'I'm not involved. If I touched any envelopes then it was just a coincidence.'

Alison's shakes intensified. She took a tranquilliser. 'And what will George say? Will he say it was a coincidence too?'

'George has got nothing to do with it.'

'Then why do the police think that he has?'

He shrugged.

'And where is Tom de Vries?' she said. 'You were all seen together weren't you? Where is he?'

'I don't know.'

She looked at him and watched his eyes fail to meet hers.

'Even if you did, you wouldn't tell me would you?' she said. 'When all this is over, provided you're not in some young offenders' institution, I'm taking you out of that bloody school.'

The alkie was a good idea. His inclusion created a story.

He took a knife out of his pocket and watched it gleam in the moonlight. The drunk snored.

He looked down at the alkie's fire. An empty tin sat in the embers, occasionally throwing up a dart of red and yellow flame. What remained of the alcohol burning off. He stuck the knife into the thin chest. He hadn't thought there'd be too much resistance, and there wasn't. Skin and bone like most seasoned drinkers, he just grunted once, softly, and then it was over.

He looked down at the corpse. An ember from the fire flicked up and caught one of his trouser turn-ups. Did people who died under the influence even know they were dead? It was a good philosophical point. He'd have to ask.

What he didn't feel good about was where the drunk had died. Underneath a statue dedicated to kids who'd been killed in an air raid in the First World War. That was unfortunate. That would upset people.

He hefted the sports bag up on his shoulder and felt in his pocket for the car keys. He knew he'd taken them. Obsessive compulsive disorder was a bastard.

'Do you know George Grogan, Harry Venus or Charles Darrah-Duncan – you might know Charles as Dan – Miss Malik?'

Laila Malik hadn't wanted a solicitor, but as soon as they'd left the de Vries house, she'd held on to Mumtaz.

Tony Bracci repeated, 'Miss Malik?'

Mumtaz squeezed the woman's hand. She was beautiful, her accent was cultured and educated. Why had she fallen in love with a schoolboy? But then why had *she* been briefly dazzled by Naz Sheikh?

After a pause she said, 'They're Tom's friends. Have you found him? Tom?'

'No, but we're looking. You know that Mrs Hakim isn't a solicitor, don't you, Miss Malik?'

'Yes.'

Mumtaz said, 'Laila, you really do need a solicitor.'

'No.'

Her refusal was absolute.

'Miss Malik,' Tony said, 'have you been having sex with Thomas de Vries?'

'We love each other.'

'So that's a yes?'

She nodded.

'For how long?'

Mumtaz felt herself cringe. It was bad enough that Tom de Vries was only sixteen, but if she'd been sleeping with him before his latest birthday, she was in all sorts of trouble.

'Just over a year.'

Mumtaz briefly closed her eyes.

'I was employed by Mr de Vries to be his housekeeper when he moved to be with his new wife two years ago,' Laila said. 'Tom was only home at holiday times. Mr de Vries would come and see him if he was in the country.'

'What about his mother?'

'No one talks about her,' she said.

'Why not?'

She shrugged. 'Tom was so alone,' she said. 'A beautiful boy rejected. But he was proud! He wanted nothing from his father.'

'Who pays his school fees.'

'We could live without electricity. We made fires . . .'

'You had sex with a boy who, you admit, was fourteen,' Tony said.

No one moved. Mumtaz hardly breathed.

Tony Bracci looked down at a stack of notes on the table and said, 'Tom de Vries turned sixteen on the second of August this year. Which means that if you were having sex with him just over a year ago, he was fourteen. You're an intelligent woman, Miss Malik. You have to know what trouble that puts you in.'

261

She said nothing.

'So is that the truth? Or isn't it? Because if you're telling me you had sex with a child then you're in a lot of bother. Think carefully.'

She looked at Mumtaz.

'Mrs Hakim can't help you. Look at me.'

Her face blanched.

'Well?'

'Tom needed love,' she said.

Mumtaz felt the need to take her hand away from Laila's, but she resisted. Instead she squeezed her fingers.

'So you did.'

'Yes.'

Tony cleared his throat. 'You've admitted committing a serious offence against a minor that, under the Sexual Offences Act 2003, will mean that you will be subject to arrest. If found guilty you will receive a custodial sentence and your name will be entered on the Sexual Offenders' Register.'

She didn't seem to hear.

'But where is he? Where's Tom?'

Tony leaned forward across the desk. 'All you can do is answer all my questions truthfully,' he said. 'We'll keep on looking for Tom, but you've got to help us. Now tell me about these friends of Tom's. When did you last see them?'

She swallowed. 'Tom left with Harry yesterday.'

'Harry Venus?'

'Yes.'

Mumtaz felt her skin prickle.

'To go where?' Tony asked.

'I don't know.'

'Didn't you ask?'

'No.'

'So what was said?'

She shook her head. 'Tom just said he'd be back as soon as he could. Then we'd go away.'

'And how did he and Harry Venus leave?'

'I gave Tom my car,' she said.

Tony clicked his pen. 'Registration number?'

The electricity supply was still connected. Down in the basement there was a great big state-of-the-art junction box. Lee threw the switches and then walked back up to the kitchen. He plugged in the computer he'd found in one of the bedrooms and watched it boot up. He was no expert when it came to technology, but the thing was a MacBook, the same computer Harry Venus had on him when he'd gone missing.

When it asked for a password he'd probably be fucked, but then he also knew how obvious a lot of passwords could be. Kids, in particular, were notorious for using their own names or the name of their favourite band or even just the word 'Apple'. He'd give it a go.

He tried 'Harry' and then 'Venus' but it threw him out. The boy was such a fucking cipher he didn't have a clue what bands, if any, he liked. If he shared any interests with de Vries then it wasn't obvious what he liked either. There was another computer, a tiny

MacBook Air, which had been lying on the bed Laila Malik claimed
to have shared with Tom de Vries. But even if it did turn out to be
de Vries's machine, Lee still had the password problem.

There was so little in the house. How could de Vries's father let
him live like this? He looked at the MacBook and went upstairs.
Now that the lights were on he could see the place properly. It
wasn't in the bad state he'd imagined it to be when he'd seen it
by candlelight. It was nicely decorated, there were radiators for
central heating, there was just sod-all furniture. No carpets at all.
A load of old and probably valuable books, just thrown around
in almost every room. He started to look through a pile in the
bathroom, then went back to de Vries's bedroom and booted up
the Air, just for the hell of it. Getting Laila Malik out of the house
had taken a long time. First she'd refused to move, then she'd
been sick, then finally she'd clung to Mumtaz, who had only then
been able to, slowly, get her outside. Then he'd had to call Vi.

Soon the fucking sun would be rising. Lee tried the password
'de Vries' once and gave up. Tom's bedroom had been nice, once,
probably when it had been used by his father. But now he looked
closer, Lee could see that the boy, or someone else, had scrawled
on the walls. He looked closely at a crude drawing of a woman
sucking a man's cock. Underneath was written, 'Tru 2 U'. De Vries
and Laila Malik? Whose handwriting was it? What did a woman
like her see in a kid? But then something else caught his attention. Something familiar.

He heard the front door open.

19

Vi threw her dog-end into the dew-soaked grass and walked over to a group of coppers, some of them in SOCO coveralls, crowded around a tent.

Although not on her patch, she knew Poplar Rec. She liked the old church at the back of the park, mainly because she thought it looked like a location out of a Dracula film. There was something eastern European about it.

Kev Thorpe was chewing on a sandwich. Vi smelt bacon.

'This better be something,' she said. 'I've got two minors in custody with extensions coming up. I need to get myself to court.'

'Vi, it's a kid,' Kev said. 'If it hadn't been a kid, you wouldn't be here.'

'I know.' She rubbed his shoulder. 'Want to show me?'

He held the tent flap up to one side and Vi held her breath.

Shazia pretended to read Baharat Huq's newspaper.

Her amma's brother, Uncle Ali, had arrived just before breakfast and was talking to the old man, who Shazia called her 'dada' or grandfather, in the kitchen. Both of them had loud voices, so it wasn't hard to grasp what was going on.

'Aftab wants to borrow eight thousand pounds and I have no problem with that,' Ali said. 'He will pay me back and I know he is a man of honour. But I wonder why he needs it.'

The old man cleared his throat. 'Business isn't easy for mini-marts these days. So much competition from supermarkets! I've been telling him for years he should move into something the young trendy people want. Old clothes . . .'

'In Manor Park? It's not that kind of area, not yet. But Abba, there is something else. I wouldn't be here if there wasn't.'

'Religion again? If your mother heard you speak the way you do, it would break her heart,' her dada said. 'Religion should not be a wedge between us . . .'

'I don't want to discuss that.'

Uncle Ali sounded angry.

'What do you want to discuss?'

Her dada tried to sound frosty, but he failed. He just sounded upset.

'I saw Ghazal.' Aftab's eldest daughter, who worked in banking, was not the sort of person Uncle Ali would approve of. 'We spoke and I asked after her family and she said that she is worried about her father.'

'Why?'

'Because he has been asking her all sorts of questions about remortgaging,' Ali said. 'How long it might take, what it will cost. I didn't tell her that he has asked me for money, but I get the impression he needs the cash quickly, that he is ultimately remortgaging his house to pay for whatever this is, and that my money is just a stopgap. Why would he want money so quickly?'

'To secure stock?'

'He should have enough cash to do that, and besides, he deals with suppliers he has known for years. They'll wait for money.'

'So ask him.'

'I did. He said he couldn't say. Abba, you were in business for years; you know what goes on. You know that there are people who want to provide services we don't need.'

There was a pause. Then her dada said, 'You think that someone wishes to protect our Aftab?'

'I'm afraid so.'

Shazia shuddered. Both Cousin Aftab and her amma had told her that getting rid of her from the shop had been the end of the matter. But it hadn't. She knew what 'protection' meant and how she had been the pretext for it. She could have said something about what she knew to her dada then, but she didn't. She'd started this thing between Naz Sheikh and Cousin Aftab and she was going to finish it.

Tina cried. Her husband watched her. He didn't want to touch her and he knew she didn't want to be comforted by him. He'd never known Adele de Vries. He'd seen her once at a party he'd gone to with Tina, and then a few times, at a distance, at Reeds. At the school, she'd usually been drunk. He'd felt sorry for her husband, who had put up with it for far too long. Only Tina ever seemed to speak to her on these occasions.

When she finally got herself under control again, Tina said, 'It took Adele years to conceive Tom.'

There had been a lot of abortions, Paul had been told. It had made him wonder about Tina and why it had taken her so long to conceive Harry. But now was not the time for that.

'Tina, we're struggling to find out what Tom de Vries was doing in a park in Poplar with an alcoholic,' Paul said. 'His father is out of the country and we can't find his mother . . .'

'Well, Adele's mum lived in Poplar,' Tina said. 'On the High Street.'

'Did you ever go there?'

He wished to God that his office had proper walls instead of glass. He'd never liked it. He felt as if they were on television. That was her career, not his.

'A long time ago,' she said. 'I stayed there for a few weeks when I was singing in the Grenadier in Clerkenwell. Adele was a dancer. That was how we met.'

Why Tina always tidied her friends' lives up, Paul didn't know. Brian Green had never employed 'dancers' back in those days. If you were female and you weren't a singer, you were a stripper.

'Where did she live, Tina?'

'A council block. Her mum used to put up some of the other artistes from the club too when I knew her, but the old lady probably died years ago.'

'And if she didn't? Or if Adele took over her mother's tenancy after she died? She's not lived with de Vries for five years. According to the woman who claims to be Tom's lover, his mother never visits. What was Adele's maiden name?'

'Well, she called herself Adele da Rosa but her real surname was Berger.'

'Right.'

She began to cry again.

Paul Venus picked up his phone and then put it down again. 'Look Tina,' he said, 'I'm sorry that Tom de Vries is dead, but Harry's still out there somewhere and we know that Tom, at least for a while, was holding our son against his will.'

'Why?'

'We don't know yet.' He picked up the phone again. 'I'm going to have to make some calls.' He punched in a number and waited for it to ring. When it didn't, he said, 'Where the hell is Arnold?'

Tom de Vries was dead. Found stabbed in Poplar Rec after what might have been a fight with an alkie, who was also dead. Although why a kid like de Vries would fight with an elderly alcoholic was a mystery. Lee looked across the road at the hardwood electric gates that hid Brian Green's house from view. The old git had gone to a lot of trouble to get a mobile phone number that ended in 007. He'd had it for donkey's years. What had it been doing scrawled on the wall of de Vries's house in Spitalfields?

Harry Venus had been in that house, Laila Malik had admitted as much, although she hadn't said why he'd been there. Harry knew Brian and so it was possible he would have his mobile phone number. But why had it been scrawled on de Vries's bedroom wall? And who by?

Only Vi knew where he was and why. If Brian Green was

involved in Harry's abduction in some way, then great caution was needed. Although nominally straight, Brian was not a man to be trusted or taken lightly. He had a lot of money and a lot of friends and some very hot lawyers.

He switched his phone on. No messages, but he recognised Venus's number as a missed call. He was wondering where he was. Tower Hamlets plods had turned up to secure the house in Princelet Street, and when Lee had left he'd told them nothing. What could he tell them? If Brian was involved he had to be sure of his facts. Because if he wasn't, Lee could find himself at the sharp end of the type of litigation that would put him out of business.

'You've gotta make this right now, George,' Vi said. 'I've just been to court and I've got you here for another twelve hours.'

Dr Grogan said, 'Oh, God!'

The boy's solicitor shrugged.

'It doesn't have to be this way,' Vi said. 'George, Tom is dead. I know that's upsetting, but we also know, from his girlfriend, that before he died, Tom had Harry Venus at his house. Do you know why?'

George looked away.

His father went to speak, but the solicitor put a hand up to stop him.

'Did you know that Tom had a girlfriend?'

The solicitor looked at George and just gently shook her head. Oh God, the 'No comment' game.

Vi took a breath. A different tack maybe? 'Good news is that your brother Henry's gone home,' she said. 'I don't know if your parents got a chance to talk to him . . . ?'

'Er, no,' Dr Grogan said. 'He just left.'

'Yes,' Vi said, 'he left because he was angry.' She looked at the boy. 'Tell me about "depositing", George.' Then she looked at his father. 'Dr Grogan? I ask because we don't have traditions like that here. Call us uncultured . . .'

Nobody said a word. The solicitor looked confused.

Vi smiled. 'Sorry Miss Whittle, "depositing" is a tradition at George's public school. It involves defecating in public places. It's, um, it's only done by, well, a certain type of boy, including George . . .'

The solicitor went to speak.

'Yes, it is relevant to the case,' Vi persisted. 'Because while looking for possible evidence about the disappearance of Harry Venus in Mr Henry Grogan's flat, we found faeces in a trunk. To be honest with you, it was so fantastic I found it hard to credit what Mr Grogan was saying. But we will discover whether it belonged to George or not, and from your reaction, Dr Grogan, I have to conclude that what Henry said was true.'

He tried to speak but ended up nodding.

'Mind you, Henry was not happy that you deposited in his flat, George. Supposed to do that at school, aren't you? But then this is a new game, isn't it? An Alfred Hitchcock game. Just like – what's that film where a couple of boys kidnap a kid and then kill him? – *Rope*.'

Now he looked her straight in the eye.

271

'I've sent for Mr McCullough,' she said. 'Because I'd like to know more about *Rope*. Wikipedia was a bit sketchy. Know what I mean?'

Tony Bracci hadn't met Tom de Vries, but he'd never imagined him to be related to someone like Rene Berger. Tony recognised the type. Skint, disappointed, lonely, in front of the telly. In the past there'd probably been some old husband who'd lost his job in the docks back in the seventies and eventually died of something smoking-related. It was an East End standard.

'She buggered off,' the old woman said.

'Your daughter.'

'Last year. Got in with some bloke supposed to have a place in Tenerife. He was a drunk, so who knows where she's ended up.' Hard. It was as if she were talking about the budgie that sat in a cage beside her chair. 'He broke her heart.'

'What, this fella?'

'No, her husband. Got fed up with her, got rid of her.'

She was fat and the flat smelt of tinned fish and piss. Most of the other places in the block had been sold, but Mrs Berger's was still owned by the council. Tony recognised the décor – circa 1975.

'My old man nearly died when she married one of them.'

'One of who?'

'Posh,' she said. 'Met him in one of the clubs she worked at. Sent our Tom to that school. Any wonder the kid turned out as he did.'

She didn't know that her grandson was dead. PC Rink was at his back, waiting to do the breaking-bad-news bit.

'I s'pose it's Tom you've come about,' she said.

'Yes.'

She looked up at PC Rink.

'What's happened?'

Tony moved across the stained chintz sofa and Rink sat down.

'I'm afraid, Mrs Berger,' she said, 'that your grandson was found dead in Poplar Recreation Ground this morning.'

Tony looked away.

'I'm very sorry . . .'

They'd had to tell her. There was still a missing kid out there somewhere. How long would it take to get the old girl to calm down enough to tell them anything she might know?

He heard a sigh and then she said, 'How?'

Tony looked at her. There wasn't a tear in sight. Just a resigned look on her large, grey face. East End to her swollen feet, her daughter had been little more than a brass from what he could gather, then a drunk. Now the only person in her life who'd ever had any sort of privilege was dead.

'We think he got into a fight,' Tony said.

Although if the skinny old alkie that Kev Thorpe had found with him had killed him it must've been a bloody miracle. Called 'Happy' by old-timers round and about Poplar High Street, Kev had discovered that most people had the idea he was dying of cancer. Unless that was just his shtick to con money for booze.

She nodded. It had affected her. But she was doing what she'd always done. Hiding it.

'He rung me yesterday afternoon,' she said. 'Out the blue. Said he had some business over this way and would I mind if he put his car in my garage round the back here. Hadn't heard from him for a year or more. Didn't know he could drive. I said yes.'

'Did he come in?'

'He had to, so he could take the garage key.'

'After that?'

'Oh, yeah,' she said. 'For quite a bit. Right chatty. But I knew he was in bother.'

'How?'

'Said he was going away, so I reckoned he had to have a reason. I never asked. You don't. You're not from round here, are you?'

'No. Newham.'

'I had a brother, Hyman. DI Thorpe still alive is he?'

'Yeah. Just.'

'Well ask him about Hyman Blatt. He was in and out – you know what I mean. Tom had that same look to him.'

No wonder Mr Marcus de Vries had seen the error of his ways with Adele. Tony imagined she'd been a looker before the booze took hold. She must've had something. Tom had been a good-looking boy, unlike his father, whose diplomatic profile included a photograph of a man with neither hair nor chin.

'Did Tom come here alone?'

'Yeah.'

'And when he left, did you see the car go?'

'No, I dropped off. He put the keys back through the street door like he said he would.'

'If you didn't talk about why he was going away, what did you talk about?' Tony asked.

'This and that,' she said. 'He talked a load of old pony about coming back and getting me, taking me to some Greek island. It was all cobblers. But I let him go on.'

'Did you think to tell his father what Tom had in mind?'

'Him? No. Up to the boy what he did. Dumped at that school, then left alone with some housekeeper. I thought good luck to him. Anyway, how would I know where his father was?'

'You could've asked Tom.'

'I hate his father. Why would I? You talked to him yet?'

Marcus de Vries, Defence Relations Officer to Azerbaijan, was on some sort of field trip in a remote part of the country where you could just about use a landline if you were lucky.

'No.'

'Well, there you go.'

The old girl was shaken, but she was holding up. So he asked her for her garage key. He looked at PC Rink for signs of disapproval, but she didn't scowl at him and so he couldn't have been too insensitive. He hoped.

What was he expecting Brian to do? If he looked around the side of one of those great hardwood gates, he could see that all of his cars, plus a few others he didn't recognise, were on the drive. Someone was in because he'd seen curtains being pulled back in one of the top windows, but that didn't necessarily mean that Brian was in the house.

Lee went and sat back in his car. Fuck it! He called him. 'Brian?'

'Whaddaya want?' He sounded groggy and grumpy. 'You found Harry?'

'No,' Lee said. 'But I've got a couple of questions for you. You home?'

'Well, you should know,' the old man said. 'You've been sitting outside me house for long enough.'

Lee ended the call, took a breath and then the fucking thing rang, just as he was getting out of the car.

Charlie Darrah-Duncan cried.

The police had put the family in what they called the 'soft' interview suite.

His father stroked his hair.

'I'm sorry about Tom, old man,' he said. 'I know you were close.'

Alison was shaky. She hadn't slept and her ex-husband's words made her furious.

'Oh for God's sake, Chris!' she said. 'We can't do anything about that!'

She sat down next to her son. She'd never liked Tom de Vries. Arrogant, pot-smoking little shit. He'd bullied Charlie, they all had. All except Harry Venus. Now it seemed that they'd done something to him. Or de Vries had. That was certainly the way it seemed to Alison.

'You have to tell the police everything you know,' she said. 'Whatever unnatural things were going on in that school—'

'Reeds is a bloody good school, Ali.'

'Oh, shut up Chris! Did you know about "depositing"?'

He laughed. 'Oh Lord, that still goes on does it?'

'You knew? You knew that boys competed to crap in the most unlikely places?'

'Well, it's a bit of an old Reeds tradition. Unofficial,' he said. Then he frowned. 'Has Charlie been . . . ?'

'I don't know! But one of them has.'

'What's that got to do with Harry Venus's disappearance?'

'I don't know! Ask the police. Because they'll be back and they'll want to ask him questions again and I don't think I can take any more of his silence.' She bent down so she could see her son's face. 'I know you know something. And even if they do, by some miracle, let you out of here without charge, you have to know that if you have a secret, you have to tell it. Secrets fester. I know.'

She'd told no one what Mumtaz Hakim had discovered about her parentage, but she would. There had been too much concealment.

'Charlie, for God's sake!'

'Ali, leave him be,' Chris said. 'He's upset.'

'And you who don't live with him ride to his rescue,' Alison said. 'Chris, I know you're trying to protect that bloody school of yours . . .'

'Don't be silly, Ali.'

'What you mean "silly", like I was being when I dropped that first cup? Fucking hell . . .'

'Ali! Please!'

'Oh, swearing "not on" is it?' she said. 'Don't get me wrong, I blame myself too. I should've taken him out of the bloody school myself. I knew he was being bullied.'

'No I wasn't. I'm not.'

'It speaks.' Alison got up and paced. 'Why is all this taking so long!'

'Ali, a bit of adversity's—'

'Oh, spare me!' She got up and paced the room. 'I—'

'Where's the Super?'

The voice came from outside. A yell followed by running feet. 'Where is he?'

Other, lower level voices made an incomprehensible jigsaw of sound. And then more running feet. Then more.

Alison, cut off mid-flow, looked at her husband and then her son, who had stopped crying.

'Something's happened,' she said.

The crumpled figure half asleep in the corridor outside the ward was Tony Bracci. Lee collapsed down on the chair beside him.

'How is he?'

Tony groaned as he sat up. 'Unconscious'.

'Why?'

'Don't know yet. He's hooked up to all sorts of machines.'

'Venus is with him?'

'And his mum. Coupla PCs. I was just gathering my wits to go back to the nick. Guv knows.'

'You have to tell me about it,' Lee said. 'Where'd you find him?'

Tony stretched. 'I will, but we'll have to go outside where I can have a fag or I'll crash out halfway through.'

They sat on the steps outside the old Royal London Hospital

facade. Tony took his warrant card out of his pocket. 'Anyone tells us off, I'll show 'em this.'

'I'm sure they'll be impressed, Tone.'

He shook his head. 'Whatever. We found the kid in a car in de Vries's nan's garage,' he said. 'In Poplar. You don't think about public school boys having nans in Poplar.'

'I wouldn't be surprised to find someone called de Vries in Poplar, these days,' Lee said.

'Oh no, she was Tom's mum's old girl. Proper old East End.'

'How'd you find out about her? From the father?'

'No, from the Super's wife. She used to work with Mrs de Vries years ago when she sang in clubs. Her mum, Tom's nan, used to put girls up from the club in her flat, including the Super's wife.'

When, Lee remembered, she sang in Brian Green's clubs. He said nothing.

'Tom de Vries went to visit his nan yesterday afternoon,' Tony said. 'He asked her if he could park his car, which was his girl-friend's, in her garage. She said yes and they spent a few hours together. Harry Venus must've already been spark out in the back, although we won't know for sure until he comes round. The old girl, Mrs Berger, hadn't seen her grandson for ages and so they had a good chat apparently. Adele, Tom's mother, buggered off to Tenerife with some bloke, his dad's off doing arms deals in Azerbaijan, Tom was pretty much alone.'

'Except for the housekeeper.'

Tony shook his head. 'Do you call underage sexual activity "care"? The kid told the old girl he was going away. Didn't say where, didn't say whether he was off on his own or with someone else, and she never asked. Comes from a bit of a hooky family herself, by all accounts, and so she wasn't surprised. Tom said he'd contact her when he could. When he left, he said he'd get his car and then put her garage keys through her letterbox. And he did, but she don't know when because she nodded off.'

'But he didn't take the car out of the garage.'

'Dunno. Maybe he did and then drove it back again.'

'Or perhaps someone else did. The person who killed him.'

Tony shrugged.

'Gotta disprove what Kev Thorpe saw first. Happy Agar the alkie and Tom with knives in their chests. Maybe they fought.'

'What about?'

'Money?'

'What about the money Tom took with him when he left Princelet Street? Must've had to put that in a big bag,' Lee said.

'Oh, there was no sign of big money,' Tony said. 'Only a coupla quid.'

'In the car?'

'Nothing.'

Lee frowned. 'I didn't get the feeling that Laila Malik was lying about the money, did you?'

'No, although she never said it was a large amount.'

'Well it must be,' Lee said. 'What I mean is that someone has to have Venus's ransom money. We know that Harry was at Tom's house. Malik wouldn't have mentioned money unless it was a significant amount. Her and Tom, she thought, going away together. You'd need some dosh to just disappear, especially when one of you is sixteen.'

20

'The boys who do want to understand the art of story are not many, but those we have are enthusiastic,' Malcolm McCullough said. 'And I do encourage them.'

'And Hitchcock?'

'As I tell the boys, he was the master,' he said. 'In my opinion there has never been a greater storyteller. Boys respond to film in a way they don't to books, DI Collins. It's the modern way. They relate to the world visually. Do you see?'

'Oh, yeah.'

Her own sons would far rather watch a film or play a computer game than pick up a novel.

'I don't necessarily approve, but one must use the tools that work in order to educate, and old Hitch has been working for me for years,' he said. 'It's all there. The human psyche *in extremis*, the philosophy of morality, murder and mayhem, which boys relish. Why do people kill? What beliefs, if any, inform a decision to kill? Can the destruction of another human being be a choice? Why are we fascinated by something so repellent?'

'All sounds very interesting,' Vi said.

'It is! But it's also a tool to get them thinking about how stories work,' he said.

'And what about *Rope*?'

'In my opinion, his masterpiece. It's based on a true story—'

'The murder of fourteen-year-old Bobby Franks by Nathan Leopold and Richard Loeb in Chicago in 1924.'

'Well, DI Collins, you have been doing your homework!'

'Wikipedia.'

Was it the way she looked at him that made his good humour disappear so quickly? Or was it, finally, the realisation that Harry Venus had been kidnapped and Tom de Vries was really dead? When she'd told him, Vi wasn't entirely sure that information had really gone in. The Much Honoured Malcolm McCullough, Laird of the Island of Balta, was not only lord of a place where nobody lived, he was also, she felt, a man who existed largely inside his own narrow view of the world.

'Well . . .' His upbeat mood and his smile returned. '*Rope* is a very loosely fictionalised version of the story. For instance, Leopold and Loeb never invited Bobby Franks's relatives to a meal. They abducted the boy, killed him and then issued an elaborate series of ransom demands to his family. They wanted to commit the perfect crime. Oddly, given later events, both these boys, from wealthy Jewish families, were fascinated by Nietzsche's concept of the *Übermensch* or superman, a superior being above both morality and the law, now, if a tad erroneously, associated with the Nazis. Of course, in spite of their extremely high IQs, they failed. They made schoolboy errors, because they were, after all, just schoolboys. In the film the pair are not Jewish and there

282

is a teacher involved, the teacher who introduced the pair to Nietzsche's ideas. He's played by James Stewart and—'

'The boys were renamed Phillip Morgan and Brandon Shaw,' Vi said.

'Yes. They—'

'The first ransom demand that was sent to Superintendent and Mrs Venus was in the name of a Mr B. Shaw,' she said. 'The Superintendent had to write that name on the envelopes where he put the first hundred thousand pounds he gave to his son's kidnappers.'

McCullough said nothing.

'Another very elaborate demand for money was made a few days later, not in the name of Mr Shaw. That drop was to take place at the cemetery where Superintendent Venus's grandfather is buried. But then the kidnappers gave up on that idea in favour of smashing my boss over the head in his own home and taking the money. Two hundred and fifty thousand pounds. Whoever had Harry knew his family well enough to know where Mr Venus's granddad was buried, and they had a key to his Islington flat.'

The laird stared. Half-smiling, unmoving.

'Now, we know that Harry stayed at Tom de Vries's house in Spitalfields for at least some of the time he was missing,' she said. 'What we also know is that their mate Charles Duncan was working in the area and their other mate George Grogan was staying with his brother in Shoreditch.'

'Henry.'

'Yeah. And Henry had a few issues this time. Not so happy to have George around.'

'Oh, I'm sorry about that.'

'Something called "depositing".'

She let it hang there, in the air. McCullough looked everywhere but at her face.

'George, or one of his mates, shat in a trunk Henry's got in his lounge,' she said. 'Poor bloke was tormented by the stink for days.'

'Oh, but depositing only happens at school . . .'

'Really?' She paused. 'And it has nothing to do with the films of Alfred Hitchcock?'

'No.'

'No? You sure? Henry Grogan wouldn't agree with you there, Mr McCullough. He reckons it's been going on for years among boys who worship the ground you walk on.'

'Nobody—'

'No, let me rephrase that,' she said. 'They don't worship you, these soft little arty boys, but they do worship the stuff you talk about. You put a positive spin on superiority. Must be so bloody easy. You in that school where the kids get top jobs because their dads have top jobs, because they went to Reeds and so did their dads.'

'Yes. And what of it? That's how it always has been. Although you'll be happy to know it's changing, DI Collins. Next term we have Russian boys, Chechens, people from an entirely different tradition.'

'But rich.'

'Oh, rich, but that's all.' If 'pissed off' could be embodied, it was Malcolm McCullough at that moment.

Vi leaned on the table between them. 'I'm not making a political point, Mr McCullough. I'm a copper, it's not my place.'

She knew she was lying and so did he.

'What I need is to find out who kidnapped Harry Venus and why. Can't ask him, because he's unconscious. This will not only lead me to who committed that crime, but it may also shed some light on who killed Tom de Vries.'

'A very talented boy.'

'As you say. Now, I've still got George Grogan and Charles Duncan in custody because we're pretty sure they know more about this than they're saying. We've pushed those kids as far as the law allows, but they ain't listening and they ain't talking. Me and my officers agree that this is beyond us. Public school. What's that? A whole set of loyalties we don't understand. But I think they'll listen to you, Mr McCullough. If I'm right, they've certainly listened to you in the past.'

He didn't say anything for a moment. Then he whispered, 'Do you think I may have inadvertently made the boys do something very bad?'

There could be no comforting Laila Malik. Her lover was dead and it was going to hurt.

Mumtaz had been asked to leave the interview room while a female PC broke the news. Out in the corridor, she could hear her crying.

'Mrs Hakim?'

It was Alison Darrah-Duncan. She had a cup of vending-machine coffee in one hand and a packet of cigarettes in the other.

'Alison.'

'Just trying to find a way out of here so I can have a smoke,' she said. 'Started again yesterday. After twelve years!'

'I'll get you out.' Mumtaz smiled.

'Thanks.'

They both leaned against the wall of the station car park and turned their faces to the sun.

Mumtaz said, 'I'm sorry you're having to go through this with your son. As soon as I made a connection between Charlie and Harry Venus I had to pass it on.'

'I know.' Alison's hand jerked as she took a puff on her cigarette. 'And I did feel resentful towards you at first.'

'I can understand that.'

'I thought, "That woman's brought me nothing but pain." But then, maybe that's not a bad thing.'

'Pain?'

'Because of you I know who my mother was,' she said. 'Her story's sad. But since when did life guarantee any of us a happy ending? God, she was Argentinian, a place I've never even thought of going. Now I'm thinking maybe I should, while I can.'

'It's a very different place to the country Rosa grew up in,' Mumtaz said. 'I think it would be a really good thing for you to do. Visit the convent too. Mother Katerina is a very nice woman who told me you'd be welcome any time.'

'Yeah. As for Charlie . . . I don't know what he has and hasn't done with his friends from that bloody school. But if he does get out of this unscathed, I will take him out of there, whatever Chris says. I know Tom de Vries is dead, but for a boy like Charlie there's always another Tom waiting round the corner to terrify and manipulate him.'

'You really think Tom bullied Charlie?'

'My son's gay in an environment where he can't even admit it to himself,' Alison said. 'But the elite, like de Vries, can sniff that insecurity out. When Charlie first met Harry Venus I had some hope. Harry came from a family with no history at Reeds and he seemed like a nice boy. But then he began to behave like de Vries and George Grogan and so Charlie just conformed. I don't know what they've all done or why, but I do know that it's good it's come to light. And I'm grateful that Charlie is safe. Do you know how Harry's doing?'

'The doctors are still trying to find out what's keeping him unconscious.'

'Poor boy.'

'Yes.'

Kids! According to Mumtaz's father, Shazia wanted to go back to the flat. She was still boiling with resentment about the loss of her job, and Mumtaz didn't like the idea of her sitting in the flat on her own, brooding. It wasn't healthy. And yet she knew that her parents would be forever bothering the girl with conversation, food and group TV-watching sessions. Baharat and Sumita had been raised in Bangladesh, where, Mumtaz always felt, it was probably illegal to do anything on your own. Being alone was 'odd' and really not understood and was frequently a bone of contention between those born in Bangladesh and those, like her, whose only home was the UK. But she'd told Shazia she'd have to stick it out if she didn't want to offend her parents, which was true. The girl had grumbled, but she'd finally agreed. Mumtaz just hoped she'd be home before dark so that Shazia didn't have to spend another night in Hanbury Street. She also wondered what Lee was doing. Last she'd heard he'd been with Tony Bracci at the London Hospital. But now Tony was back at the station, where was Lee?

'I appreciate your coming to tell me, that's very kind,' Brian said.

Lee sat down on one of the old man's many leather sofas.

'What I don't get is why you come earlier and sat outside the house.'

'Waiting for you to get up, Brian,' Lee said. 'Then when you were up, I got a call from DS Bracci at the hospital. So off I went.'

'Ah.'

He didn't believe that was entirely kosher, but he couldn't prove Lee was lying. Strictly speaking, he wasn't.

Lee leaned back into the thick luxuriousness of full-grain cow-hide. One of Brian's 'boys', Errol, kept it so shiny you could see your face in it. Brian liked to surround himself with people like himself. Obsessive.

'I've got some more details now,' he said. 'You know Harry was found in a lock-up garage in Poplar?'

'And he's still unconscious, you say.'

'At the moment, yes.'

'Mmm.'

'Odd thing is, he was found in a car that had been used by that boy who got killed last night.'

'What boy?'

'Didn't you hear? Young boy and an old drinker were found dead in Poplar Rec this morning.'

Brian Green shook his great meaty head.

'Oh yeah. I tell you I'm really glad that Harry's been found, but until he comes round this is going to be a puzzler.'

Just like the last time he'd visited, Lee could see Taylor Green sunbathing out by Brian's pool through the patio doors. He wondered if she ever did anything else.

'Harry might not remember nothing,' Brian said. He was already half a bottle of Rioja down and had just poured himself some more.

'Might not, but just between you and me, the boy who was killed and Harry were mates.'

'No!'

'At school,' Lee said. 'No connection between the two incidents as far as the coppers can tell.' He paused. 'Mind you, your name came up.'

He wanted to see something on Brian's face. He knew he wouldn't see much, but there was nothing.

'Yeah?'

'The garage where Harry was found belongs to the nan of that mate of his, Tom de Vries.'

Brian made a noise that could have been a laugh. 'How would I know anyone with a name like that?'

'Oh, you wouldn't know the kid,' Lee said. 'But you knew his mother.'

'How'd you know that?'

Not 'Who is she?'

'When Tom de Vries's body was found in Poplar Park, the police were trying to make a connection between the boy and that area. And because Tom was a school friend of Harry's, Superintendent Venus and his wife knew him.'

'So?'

'Mrs Venus, independently, knew Tom's mum. Through your clubs, years ago.'

'A girl from Poplar?'

'Adele Berger,' Lee said. 'Called herself da Rosa?'

'Oh.' He smiled, slowly. 'Adele, yes. Dancer.'

'As you say.' Lee smiled.

'So Tina Wilton brought my name up?'

'I think so, yes,' Lee said. 'But then, to be honest with you Brian, I wasn't really listening to anything about you. I was more concerned about Harry. Know what I mean?'

'Yeah.'

And he did, because now he did look a bit pale, in spite of his glassful of what he would have called 'good red vino'.

Everything that came out of Malcolm McCullough's mouth irritated Vi. It was like listening to a TV newsreader from the fifties. It also had very little effect upon Charlie Duncan, who just shook. Oddly it was George Grogan who cracked. By the time Vi eased the teacher out of the interview room, George was ready to talk.

'We wanted to help Tom,' he said. 'He needed to go away with Laila. But Harry reckoned that if we asked for enough money, we could all have a bit. Tom said we'd start off small and see what happened.'

'Why Harry's parents?' Vi asked.

George shook his head. 'He hates them.'

'Don't you all? At your age?'

'No.'

'So what's different about Harry's mum and dad?'

For a moment George said nothing. His father, Vi noticed, had reddened.

'They don't help him.'

'They pay his school fees and give him everything he wants, as far as I can see,' Vi said. 'What do you mean?'

George was obviously struggling to articulate what he meant. But Vi wasn't about to prompt him. What she knew to be the truth had to come from the boys.

'I mean his father isn't Reeds,' George said. 'Harry's never really been one of us. But he wanted to be. He was proving himself.'

Dr Grogan muttered, 'Christ.'

George looked at his father. 'Dad, it's not the sixties anymore. Class matters and so does money. Why do you think that all the people with the best jobs are connected or rich or both? If your father's a plumber, you won't end up being prime minister, will you?'

Dr Grogan looked at Vi. 'I apologise for my son, DI Collins,' he said. 'I should never have let him spend so much time with his brother.'

'Oh, I think you do Henry a disservice, sir. He might be a merchant banker, but I don't think he believes he's superior. No, that's Mr McCullough, isn't it, George?'

The boy looked up at the ceiling.

'Him and his *Übermensch*,' she said.

'Mr McCullough has nothing to do with what we did.'

'I know.'

He looked at her.

'He just made you little snobs,' she said. 'Planted the seed that made you and your mates feel justified in putting Superintendent and Mrs Venus through hell.'

'It was Harry's idea.'

'Sure it was. But I'm interested in why he came up with it,' Vi said. 'You said he was "proving himself". To you? To Charlie? Or was it especially to impress Tom de Vries?'

George's solicitor wrote something down.

Vi said, 'Don't think I'm trying to pin this on a dead kid. Don't you do it either, George.'

He took a deep breath. 'Tom always led. He was the best at everything. We all admired him. Couldn't understand why Tom's stepmother didn't want him. He said it was because she was a greedy, gold-digging bitch. Just young, you know. Tom's dad divorced his mother so he could marry her. Tom reckoned they were going to have more children and stuff.'

Mr de Vries clearly had a nose for 'gold-diggers'.

'Tom's dad was always out of the country. He left him in that house in Spitalfields with the housekeeper . . . Laila . . .'

Did he smile a little when he mentioned Laila Malik?

'Who was sleeping with him,' Vi said. 'Don't think his dad reckoned on that, do you? What did Tom say happened to his mum?'

'She's in rehab.'

Aka a council flat in Poplar. Tom had been quite the convincing fantasist.

Vi said, 'I ask again, did Harry arrange his own kidnap to impress Tom de Vries?'

George reddened. 'Tom wasn't a monster, you know!'

'I never said he was.'

'Harry knew his parents had money tied up in property.'

'That's where most people have their money.'

'No.' George looked at his father. 'You understand, don't you?'

Dr Grogan looked old. When she'd first met him, Vi had thought he was probably about fifty. Now he was looking bad for seventy.

'George, I have told you we are very lucky to have inherited wealth,' he said. 'I've also told you that unless you work, you won't get anywhere in life. I'm a GP—'

'Because you wanted to do that,' George said. 'But granddad was a stockbroker. You could've—'

'Did Harry want money from his mum and dad on his own account?' Vi cut in.

'No. Not really. None of us did.'

'So it was mainly about Tom de Vries wanting to run away with his housekeeper.'

'Yes.'

'And for Harry to prove himself and all of you to show off how clever you were. Just like the boys in *Rope*.'

George Grogan said nothing.

'It's a cocktail,' the doctor said.

For the first time in ten years, Paul Venus held his wife's hand. She didn't pull away.

'Present in your son's system we've found alcohol, ketamine – which I'm sure you've come across as a police officer,' the doctor continued. 'Cannabis and something called krokodil.'

Paul briefly shut his eyes.

'This is—'

'I know what it is, doctor.'

Tina pulled her hand away. 'I don't.'

Paul said, 'Doctor . . .'

'It's a cheap heroin substitute,' he said. 'Very rare in the UK, it's made and distributed in Russia by crime syndicates. Basically, it's codeine cut with household cleaners, engine oil, whatever comes to hand that has the capacity to get a person high.'

'And Harry's taken this?'

'Or someone has administered it to him. There are also signs of violence,' the doctor said. 'Which is why we're asking for your consent to operate. Harry's brain is swelling and we have to relieve the pressure.'

Paul said, 'Of course.'

But Tina needed to know more. 'Is it risky?'

'Every surgical procedure carries a risk, Mrs Venus,' the doctor said. 'But the reality is that if we don't operate he will die.'

21

'Shazia, you should go to bed, you look wiped out.'

'I'm OK.'

She was curled up in a chair, staring at the TV, saying nothing.

It hadn't been a nice day for her, locked in with the Huqs. They'd only left her alone when she'd said she had college work to do. Mumtaz remembered it well. One of the reasons she'd jumped into marriage so eagerly had been to get away from her parents and their stifling protectiveness. They were lovely people who meant well, but could drive a person who wanted to be alone a little mad.

Laila Malik had finally consented to be represented by a solicitor and so Mumtaz had got out of the police station at six. Then she'd had to go and pick up Shazia, and of course spend some time with her parents. It had been a long day. Then her phone rang. It was Lee, so she walked into the kitchen to make sure she wasn't overheard by Shazia. The girl knew her mother was involved in a kidnap investigation; she didn't need to know more than that.

She asked, 'What's going on?'

'Harry Venus has to have surgery to relieve pressure on his brain.'

'Poor boy. Where are you?'

'At home. Seems the kids cooked up the kidnap to get money out of Venus.'

'Yes. As far as I can tell, that does seem to be the case.'

'And yet, I wonder . . .'

'Wonder what?'

'Well, they can't have wanted it to end like this. I don't understand why it did.'

'I imagine we'll find out when DI Collins is finished with George Grogan. You know he's talking?'

'Yes. What about the woman?'

'Laila. She's got a solicitor now. I think she's finally realised how much trouble she's in. I don't think I've ever seen a woman look so hurt. When she was told what Tom de Vries told his grandmother about going away on his own, her face just collapsed. Why did he do that?'

'I don't know,' Lee said.

'Weren't they supposed to be in love?'

Mumtaz heard him sigh.

'Anyway, I'll be back in the office tomorrow,' she said.

'Good. I may be out most of the day,' he told her.

'Oh?'

'I've got to go over everything with Venus.'

'Won't he be at the hospital?'

'He's asked me to see him at nine. If he cancels he cancels. I'll let you know.'

'OK.'

'You all right?'

'Yes.'

'Good.'

He ended the call. When he'd gone, Mumtaz looked down at the phone for a little while and then walked back into the living room. Something wasn't right.

'Tom and Harry had a fight.'

'What about?'

The first ransom drop, via a dodgy PO box on Brick Lane and organised by Laila Malik, had gone well. But then things had soured.

'Tom's girlfriend,' George said. 'Harry groped her.'

'Did Harry tell you that?'

'No. Tom did. Harry said Tom was lying.'

'You believed Tom?'

'Yes.'

Laila Malik had told it differently. Tom, she'd told Tony Bracci, had wanted to get more money out of the Venuses. It had been so easy the first time and he'd got a taste for it. Harry had wanted it to stop. He'd told Tom that he could have all the money they'd already got, but he couldn't demand any more. He'd said it 'wasn't fair'. Tom had accused him of losing his nerve – which he had. Then when Harry had tried to leave the house in Spitalfields, they'd fought. That was when Harry had ended up confined in a wardrobe. Laila, by her own admission, had helped Tom tie him up.

'How'd that turn into an actual demand for more money from Superintendent Venus?' Vi said.

'We were angry at Harry.'

'You and Charles Darrah-Duncan?'

'Yes. Tom didn't deserve that. We went to see him.'

'At Princelet Street?'

'Yes. He'd tied Harry up. He wanted to go home but Tom said he'd rat on us if he did. Then we'd all be in trouble. Harry said he wouldn't and he denied groping Laila. But we didn't believe him.'

'Why not?'

'Because Laila said Harry had groped her. She was furious.'

'Where was Harry when you went to the house?'

'In a cupboard. He was a bit bashed up. It wasn't easy to see. But Tom said that if Harry was going to behave like a cunt then he deserved to be treated like one.' George looked at his father. 'I'm just saying what Tom said.'

'So what happened then?'

'Tom said that we could get more money out of Harry's dad. Then he could go away and Dan, er, Charlie and I could have some too. He said he'd keep Harry at Princelet Street and then let him go when he left the country. He said Harry would never know that Dan and myself had benefited too.'

'What, a kid who'd been accused of something he, and now Miss Malik, says he didn't do, was going to be allowed to go free to grass up the lot of you?'

George said nothing.

'Or do you believe that Harry would have kept shtum? Can't

work it out myself. Either he was an honourable Reeds man, not hitting on his mate's girlfriend, or he wasn't. What was he?'

George remained silent.

'Or can't you answer now you don't have Tom here to do your thinking for you? I think that once Harry had said he didn't want to fleece his own parents again, his days were numbered. And when Tom invested some of the money he'd made in drugs to keep Harry quiet . . .'

'I don't know anything about drugs.'

'He didn't even wait for Superintendent Venus to leave the next lot of ransom money at the drop site. He just took Harry's key, let himself into his dad's flat, assaulted Mr Venus and took the cash.'

'For me it was the thought of never having to come back,' Laila said. 'I just wanted to be with him, alone. Free to be in love. But for Tom it was different. I tried not to think about it. But I knew.'

'Different how?'

Tony Bracci was knackered, but the latest report on how Harry Venus was doing had been bad. He had to find out the truth for the boy's sake.

'He had this idea he could commit the perfect crime. He showed me a film.'

'Was it *Rope*?'

'I don't know. Maybe. It was about two men who kill another man and they think they're really clever. But they're not, I told him that. But he said that he could do better. He said the men in the film made mistakes. He said he wouldn't.'

'What did you feel about having Harry Venus locked up in the house?'

She shook her head. 'I didn't like it. But if Tom and I made enough money to go away . . . One night, when I went to visit my parents, they left him alone. All night. That was cruel.'

'And yet why should you care?' Tony said. 'He was going to be murdered wasn't he?'

She turned away. 'I didn't think about it,' she said.

'Making you as selfish as your boyfriend,' Tony said. 'Well matched, you pair.'

'Tom said we could do it once more,' George said. 'He was on a roll. Dan and I thought that we'd all go and get the money Superintendent Venus was going to leave in the cemetery in Barking. But Tom went on his own, and when he got back he told us he'd actually attacked Harry's dad in his flat instead. He laughed about it. He thought it was funny to use Harry's keys to get in. He didn't give Dan or me any of the money. That was when he said we could do it once more.'

'Greedy Tom.'

He ignored her.

'But then Harry's father wanted to see some proof he was alive before he parted with any more money. I hadn't thought about him being a policeman much before, but then I started to. I said to Tom that I thought we should just stop. It was getting too dangerous. I said that he could leave the country with Laila and I'd make sure that Harry didn't talk.'

'By killing him?'

'No!' He turned to his father. 'I wouldn't kill anyone.'

His father said nothing.

'No, I'd make sure that Harry didn't say anything. He was involved, just like the rest of us, so it was unlikely he'd talk. How do you tell your parents that you hate them enough to fake your own kidnapping? Harry knew his parents felt guilty about their separation and what it might have done to him. The truth is he doesn't care about that, but he knew his dad wouldn't go to the police if we told him not to because he would be too scared about what might happen to Harry.'

'Because he loves him,' Vi said.

'I guess.'

George was frightened, and so it was possible that he was coming over as cold because he was scared. It was also possible that he really was callous. Just not as callous as Vi knew Tom de Vries must have been. His father, who hadn't shown the slightest bit of emotion when she'd spoken to him, was finally on his way back to the UK. Maybe it was genetic.

'How did Tom react to your suggestion?'

'Not well.'

'How?'

'He cut me out. Said if I wasn't with him, I was against him.'

'What did you do?'

'I left. Went back to my brother's and then went home.'

'What about Charlie/Dan?'

'Oh he stayed with Tom,' George said. 'But only until they'd made the DVD of Harry, then Tom told him to fuck off.'

301

'Didn't Tom worry about Charlie alerting someone about Harry? Even if you didn't know that he was drugged up to the eyeballs, if your mate helped make that DVD then he must've known.'

'He knew Dan wouldn't blab.'

'Because Reeds boys don't, or because Charlie was terrified Tom'd tell the world he was gay? Is Charlie in love with Tom, George? Just out of interest?'

George said nothing.

'And now you're here,' Vi said. 'After you lied to me and your parents about who you were with in London. To be honest with you George, I'm inclined to go along with your mum and dad about Tom de Vries. God rest his soul, but he was not someone I'd want my sons to be mixed up with.'

She saw Dr Grogan very faintly smile.

'So state of play now is that Harry Venus is critically ill and at the moment we have to hold Tom de Vries responsible for that, because as far as we know he was the last person to see Harry before we found him. But you and Charlie Darrah-Duncan and Miss Malik also had a hand in this.'

'Harry wanted to be kidnapped! He offered! To kidnap himself . . .'

'And you helped him,' Vi said. 'I am going to charge you, George. I'm also going to tell you that you're about as *Übermensch* as I am, which is an insult and I'd like you to take it that way.'

'My parents live in Wanstead,' Laila said. 'I still go to the old gym I used to use when I lived there sometimes. These days it's full of Russians. They sell anything you want.'

'So you got the drugs?'

'Tom didn't want to go out on the street and get them.'

Tom de Vries, far from a heroic *Übermensch*, had just been manipulative, Tony thought.

'I thought it was better for him to be quiet.'

'What, giving him a drug that would rot his skin off? You do know what krokodil is, don't you?'

'He said it was a heroin substitute,' she said.

'What, your Russian mate?'

'He's not my mate. He was just some guy. Russians own the gym now, so they all go there and they all peddle drugs.'

'Bit of a generalisation . . .'

'They're quite open about it.'

'Whatever. You bought krokodil, ketamine . . .'

'That can really—'

'Don't care. And cannabis . . .'

'I already had that,' she said.

'Of course.'

He looked down at his notes. It was amazing how quickly the love goggles started to come off Laila Malik's face as soon as she realised that she was facing charges of child abuse. But Tony still felt that she was holding something back.

'What happened on that last day you were with Tom?' he said.

'What do you mean?'

'You said when I first met you that Tom had "gone". You didn't say where and you told us he was alone. But now we know he must've taken Harry with him. Why?'

'I don't know.'

'We also know that he went to his nan's, which is close to where he died. It was in her garage that we found Harry Venus.'

'Alive.'

'Just about.'

'Tom didn't ever say he was going to kill him. Not to me.'

'Which proves what?' he shrugged. 'Where did Tom tell you he was going, and why?'

She took a moment. 'He told me he was going to give Harry back.'

'To his parents?'

'I assumed so.'

'So why didn't you tell us that right from the start?'

She began to cry.

Tony, to her solicitor's disgust, showed his impatience. 'For Christ's sake!'

'DS Bracci!'

'I'm sorry,' he said to the solicitor, who was at least thirty years his junior, 'but between her lies and her boyfriend's lies . . .'

'I didn't know where he was going!' Laila Malik said. 'He said he was going to meet someone.'

'Who?'

'I don't know. But then he said he'd be back and we could leave.'

'For where?'

'We'd go to the airport and just go – anywhere.' Her eyes teared up again.

'And Harry? What would happen to him?'

'I don't know! But after he left, I realised that Tom had taken all our money—'

'Superintendent Venus's money.'

'Yes. And then he didn't come back.'

She cried again.

'And now he's dead!'

Vi pulled a face. 'Is this coffee or what?'

'I think it's "what", Guv,' Tony Bracci said.

'Fuck.'

They sat down at a random table in the empty canteen. Outside the sky was black. Vi didn't dare look at her watch.

'What do you think about this third-party thing then, Tone?'

'Well, someone killed Tom de Vries and it wasn't Happy the alkie, was it?'

'No, that would've been tough for him with a broken wrist,' Vi said.

'So who?'

'Brian Green's mobile number's on the bedroom wall . . .'

'Who Harry knows.'

'And which Lee Arnold must've seen when he was in the house on his own while you brought Miss Malik in,' Vi said. 'And he'd recognise it, because he knows Brian. We all know Brian. But he's not mentioned it to me.'

'Or me. But then Green wouldn't be involved would he?' Tony said. 'He knows the Super and his family.'

Vi shrugged. 'I dunno. Old habits die hard. If there was a few bob in it for him.'

'Guv, the kids, including Harry, kidnapped the boy. Tom de Vries, neglected by his parents, wanted to go away with his older woman – or so he said – and the other kids were into this superiority thing that teacher of theirs peddles.'

'McCullough, yes,' she said. 'Change of curriculum there, I hope. But I'm thinking about Green.'

'Maybe Harry scrawled his number on the wall?'

'Why? Harry's phone was long gone by the time he went into de Vries's house. He had his computer with him, which I suppose we'll find out about once the techies get stuck in. And de Vries's.'

'Perhaps Harry tried to ring Green, Guv. If he got hold of a phone . . . He could've copied the number down from his computer.'

'Why?' She sighed. 'Maybe there was no one else involved. Tom took Harry to his nan's garage intending to leave him there to die while he sodded off with a load of cash. But then who killed him?'

'Maybe he was mugged?'

'So who killed Happy?'

'I dunno.'

'And where's the money?'

22

As soon as her amma went to work, Shazia left the flat. She didn't know where any of the Sheikhs lived but she'd been told that they had an office behind a pound shop in Plaistow. And she knew Naz's car. It was a red Mitsubishi Evo X and it had one of those 'cherished' number plates. She knew it by heart.

Shazia got on the bus that would take her to the junction with the Barking Road. Then she'd walk. It wasn't a bad day and she wasn't the kind of person who got stopped and searched by the police – for a start she was a girl and she wasn't black. But having her father's hunting knife in her pocket made her feel uncomfortable.

'I need to pay you, of course, but also Mr Arnold, I wanted to thank you for all the work you did to get Harry back to us.'

Venus was grey. Not just a few flecks in his hair, but his skin. Lee sat down. 'How is he?'

'The operation was apparently a success, but he remains unconscious. At the moment his brain activity is minimal. That may change in the next few days.'

'I hope so.'

He exhaled. 'It's hard to see your child in such a state. And you know, what makes it even harder is that I'm angry with him.'

It was a rare fit of candour from Venus, and Lee realised he was probably its recipient because he wasn't a colleague or a relative.

'Of course you are.'

'To put us through all this pain . . .' He looked as if he were about to cry. 'If, *when*, he recovers, I'm taking him out of that school. Yes, we had enough money to send him to public school, but we had no knowledge about how those places work. Tina went to a convent and I'm a grammar school boy.'

'You went to Cambridge.'

'Yes, and I should have learned from that,' he said. 'There's Cambridge and there's Cambridge. Cambridge for those of us from state schools, and Cambridge for those from public schools. It's a much easier ride for them.'

'So you wanted an easier ride for Harry? I'd've probably done the same in your position,' Lee said. 'We all want our kids to climb that little bit higher up the ladder, don't we?'

Venus smiled. 'As you know, my grandfather was from Barking,' he said. 'I know most people in this station think I'm pure home counties, but that's only because my father pulled himself up by his bootstraps. I had it easy. But my father's parents were illiterate.'

'You have the East End ambition,' Lee said.

'We all find our way. What we don't do is listen to bizarre theories about superiority peddled by odd men obsessed by old crimes and their film interpretations.'

'Mr McCullough.'

'Yes,' he said. 'If I'd known he was, albeit inadvertently, giving those boys ideas like that, I would have had more than just words.' He bent down to pick up the briefcase, which was beside his desk. 'Now I owe you money . . .'

His mobile phone rang. He attempted to get to it on his desk, but it was actually closer to Lee, who passed it to him. Venus switched it off.

'That can wait.'

'Not the hospital?'

'No. Mr Arnold, I can write you a cheque or I can have the money transferred into your account electronically . . .'

Lee left Venus's office a lot better off. He also left with more questions. Venus had rejected a call from Brian Green when he'd switched his mobile off. By his own admission, Green was a friend of the family. Why had he done that? Had it just been because he was busy with Lee? Green's mobile number on Tom de Vries's bedroom wall still haunted Lee. He wanted to ask Venus why that might have happened, wanted to know whose handwriting it was. But when he looked back at the glass cube office, he saw that Venus was on his mobile and he was frowning.

'My mother is in a care home, in Tufnell Park. They have this room relatives can use when they visit.'

'So accommodation wasn't a problem for you,' Vi said.

She'd given Malcolm McCullough a couple of addresses of guest houses in Newham – mostly clean if a bit scruffy round the edges – but he'd done his own thing. Tufnell Park, if she recalled, was one of those areas of north London that had become colonised by literary and actor types in recent years. When she remembered it back in the seventies, it had been a grim, gothicky suburb. Before grim and gothicky turned funky.

'My mother is ninety,' McCullough said. 'She has every illness under the sun and so we all expect her to go almost at any minute. It was fine.'

Vi leaned back in her chair. 'So, Mr McCullough,' she said, 'we need to talk about your boys.'

He frowned.

'I'm not blaming you for what they did,' she said.

'Why would you?'

Malcolm McCullough had only been obliged to give a statement about what he'd known about the Harry Venus kidnap. And that was minimal. There was no proof he'd had any hand in it, but his influence on kids like George Grogan, albeit unintended, left a bad smell.

'This film, *Rope*,' she said, 'I'm not an expert, Mr McCullough, but I'm told it doesn't feature on the national curriculum.'

'No, it doesn't. But we are not a state school, DI Collins. Provided we teach the boys what they need to pass their GCSEs or their A Levels, we may add whatever enrichment to their classes that we please. They are boarders. In term time we are *in loco parentis*, which means that we must also entertain and inform our charges. That is what their parents pay for: enrichment. An educational experience that goes beyond the mere passing on of information designed to promote passing exams.'

'But my understanding of this Hitchcock thing was that it was part of your English Literature classes,' Vi said.

'Alongside their set books, yes.'

'Why?'

He sighed. 'Because, as I've told you before, DI Collins, some of our boys have an aptitude for story. They may become great writers. And I can think of no better model for them to follow than Hitchcock.'

'Not Shakespeare?'

'Even our boys are more engaged by the cinematic than the page these days,' he said. 'Hitchcock is my way of introducing the boys to story construction in a way they will relate to.'

'Not because you're obsessed with Hitchcock . . .'

'I'm not!'

'Or the notion of superior intelligence in *Rope*.'

'That film is anti-superiority! Good God, Hitchcock was a cockney! He was appalled by the Leopold and Loeb murder it was based upon. And like those real people, the characters in the film eventually come a cropper—'

'Yeah, they do, but I think that some of your boys looked at that film and saw an invitation to go one better,' Vi said. 'I watched it first thing this morning and you know what occurred to me?'

'No.'

'Well, you know that a lot of wealthy parents are buying up property for their kids in parts of the East End like Hoxton and Shoreditch? They're fashionable.'

'Yes.'

'So they come among ordinary people and they get hold of

property it takes most folk a lifetime to buy and they go to the type of universities that ensure they'll get good jobs, if they want them . . .'

'It's always been like that DI Collins. That's how our society is.'

'Yeah, I know. But there's a price, and I think we've just seen a bit of that being paid,' she said. 'Mr McCullough, what you did by introducing your passion for Hitchcock to these particular boys wasn't wrong in itself. But like the teacher in *Rope* . . .'

'Rupert Cadell.'

'Jimmy Stewart's character, yes. You gave these boys an image of flawed superiority that they felt they could better. Tom de Vries didn't need that, as he was already sure of himself from what I can tell. But he was also vulnerable, because he was unwanted. And so, for a different reason, was Harry Venus.'

'I wasn't to know they'd do *this*!'

'I know that. But they did, and Charlie Darrah-Duncan still won't talk. I dunno if he's got some misplaced loyalty thing going on, but Mr McCullough, you're going to have to think about what you teach these boys in the future. They don't need to feel better than other people, because they already have every privilege going. And those that don't should be counselled. Know what I mean?'

'Well, Reeds is changing anyway, so I don't think you'll have to worry about *that*.'

His face was white now and he looked as if he had a bad smell under his nose.

'What do you mean?'

'I mean that Reeds is taking in half of eastern Europe next term,' he said. 'Oligarch offspring.'

'All the more reason to be careful what you teach them,' Vi said. 'The very rich? The hereditary rich? I don't see the difference.'

'No, I don't suppose you do.'

'No,' she said, 'I just see poor Harry Venus who should never have been at your bloody school. I see a boy who could be dying because he wanted to fit in. Christ, Mr McCullough, doesn't it strike you as messed up, the way boys at your school have a tradition of defecating in unusual places? Who clears it up, eh? Do the kids even think about that?'

'Depositing is not approved . . .'

'No, and Dr Flanagan your headmaster told me that too,' Vi said. 'But I don't think any of you have really tried to stop it. Like I told your boss, all schools have an obligation to report drug offences on their premises to the police. But no one ever reported Tom de Vries, did they? What happened?'

McCullough turned away.

Either Mr de Vries had paid Reeds off, or someone had decided that a drugs charge against a boy would look bad for the school. Or both. Dr Flanagan had not been forthcoming about it.

'I know you'll disagree, Mr McCullough, but I think that your new boys from eastern Europe might shake the place up for the better.'

His face grew very ugly for a moment. 'Oh, and you'd know about the sons of oligarchs, would you?'

'Not a lot,' Vi said. 'But I do know that you should never blame the sins of the father on the child. Look what that did to Harry Venus.'

*

Lee barely heard her. Just off the phone from Vi Collins, his head was full of Malcolm McCullough, Alfred Hitchcock and a theory that was just starting to take shape in his head. Had she just said something about meeting some woman at Ilford Broadway?

'Her husband is a Salafi,' Mumtaz said. 'Which is a very strict, fundamentalist interpretation of Islam. He has divorced her according to sharia law, not British law, and now—'

'Yeah. Mumtaz, I'm gonna take the Micra. You all right with the Subaru?' He stood up. Either he was going to find out what Brian Green's number had been doing on de Vries's wall or he wasn't, but not knowing wasn't an option. It would drive him mad.

'Well, yes . . .' She looked surprised and a little alarmed. 'Lee, are you OK?'

'Yeah, fine,' he said. 'But I need to go out for a while.'

'Where?'

They always told each other where they were going, for security. Being out of contact was dodgy, they'd both learned that lesson the hard way. But he couldn't tell her. She'd talk him out of it. He put his jacket on.

'Keep your phone on.'

Avoiding those huge green eyes, he looked down as he loaded his pockets with keys and pens and change. He walked to the office door and then glanced back. And wished he hadn't.

Her face said it all.

'Don't do anything stupid,' she said, and turned back to her computer screen. He left, but he felt like a bastard.

*

314

She spotted his car on Balaam Street, outside a minimart just like Cousin Aftab's. An old man sat on a plastic stool outside, his fingers running though his prayer beads. His eyes were sad, and Shazia wondered whether Naz Sheikh had just threatened him.

But then she saw Naz come out of the shop, followed by a man who looked like a younger version of the old man. Shazia tucked herself in behind a boy holding a bottle of cider in the doorway of the Job Centre.

The man and Naz began walking across the road. One of the gangster's hands was on the man's shoulder. They passed her on their way to the Barking Road. She didn't hear either of them speak.

As soon as they'd gone, Shazia moved to follow them.

The boy with the cider bottle said to her, 'Do I know you?'

'Don't think so.'

He looked down at the ground and said something she couldn't hear. He was pissed. Whether it was because he didn't have a job or whether it was the booze that made him unemployable, she didn't know and didn't care. She followed Naz and the man and they went to exactly the place she thought they would go.

23

'My dad's buried here, somewhere.'

'Don't you know where?'

'I can tell you where Jack the Ripper's buried.'

Paul Venus didn't want to be sitting in Brian Green's stuffy Maybach. All his cars stood out, but this one was particularly visible. Even in a rarely visited cemetery.

'Open the window, Brian, it's like an oven in here!'

The old man shrugged and opened his window a crack.

'Aaron Kosminski, he was called,' Brian said. 'Died in the madhouse and they buried him here. A lot of people think he was the Ripper.'

'What are we doing here, Brian?'

He'd had to tell Tina he had work that just couldn't wait and he'd told his colleagues he had to go out to get spare clothes for his wife at the hospital. It all felt squalid.

'Well, you know, Paul, that I've had the best interests of Tina and Harry in me mind for bloody donkey's years.'

The gangster with a heart act had worn thin years ago.

'So I wanted to apologise to you personally, for not being able to do quite enough to help your boy,' he said.

If he'd dragged him all the way out to East Ham Jewish Cemetery just for this, Paul would be pissed off. But he knew he hadn't. Brian only went to the trouble of leaving his home and his child bride when he had to.

'In the boot you'll find something that belongs to you,' Brian said.

He'd asked Paul to park behind him.

'If I pop the boot then you can take it out and put it in your motor.'

'What is it?'

'Go and have a look,' Brian said.

Paul felt his legs shake when he opened the door. As he got out he saw a car pull up just outside the gates.

Venus's car was parked directly behind Brian's, but the BMW was empty and there were two figures in the Maybach. Lee watched. From that distance nobody would be able to see who he was, but he put sunglasses on anyway.

A second passed, no more. A figure, a slim, tall man, got out of the Maybach and went round to the back of the car. Lee couldn't see whether he was peering in the Maybach's boot or just staring at the rear to look for damage. Had the BMW back-ended the Maybach just before he got to the cemetery? Then he saw Venus lift something up and then put it down again.

It had taken Lee by surprise to see that Brian was not only being followed by him, but by Paul Venus too. He'd pulled up outside Green's house just over half an hour ago, in time to see the Maybach roll out onto the street. He'd kept his distance, but at Manor Park he'd noticed that a familiar BMW had inserted itself between Mumtaz's Micra and the Maybach and was clearly following Brian.

The original idea had been to go to Brian and ask him outright, 'What was your number doing on Tom de Vries's bedroom wall?' It was why he'd taken the Micra. Brian didn't know that car. He could park in front of his house and be completely anonymous to the gangster until he decided he wanted to go in. He'd known he could easily lose his nerve. Harry Venus was safe. Why stir up what could be a whole heap of trouble?

As he watched, Venus got back in the gangster's car. Quickly. They began to talk animatedly. If only he could hear what they were saying. Then Lee Arnold had an idea.

They went to the cashpoint on the Barking Road. Of course they did.

When they walked back down Balaam Street, the shopkeeper looked broken. As they stepped over the threshold into the minimart, the old man looked straight ahead as if he wasn't there.

Shazia wanted to scream. How many people did that family have in their pockets and how many more did they want? How could Naz talk about Islam and morality when he was the greediest man she'd ever met? Not even her late father came close, and that was saying something. Her abba had always bought himself everything he wanted, and he'd wanted many things.

It couldn't go on.

When a traffic warden came along and stood in front of the Mitsubishi and began writing a ticket, Naz Sheikh got out of it.

Whether he charmed, bribed or threatened the man, she couldn't tell, but he didn't get a ticket. Then he kissed the old man's hand, got in his car and drove away.

Shazia didn't know what to do. She couldn't follow him. She didn't have a car. She'd thought he'd be in that office the Sheikhs had, but it didn't seem that Naz Sheikh actually worked out of an office in the conventional sense.

She crossed the road and stood outside the minimart. She wanted Sheikh dead. Why hadn't she just stuck her father's hunting knife into his chest when he was standing beside the cashpoint, watching the minimart man take out money to give him? She didn't care what happened any more. What was her problem?

'Can I help you, young lady? Do you have a problem?'

The voice was old but very cultured in an intensely British way. Shazia looked around to see who had spoken, but could only conclude it was the old Bengali man on the plastic stool. She frowned.

He smiled. 'Yes I know, I'm awfully posh aren't I? Were you watching that young man who just came out of my son's shop?'

Shazia didn't say anything.

'You were, I know. I hope you aren't in love with him.'

'No!' Just the thought made her feel sick.

'Good. Because he is a bad man and you are a nice girl.'

'No, I . . . I hate him,' she said.

'Mmm. Hate is a very strong thing. But then he deserves it. What's he done to you, my dear?'

She didn't know what to say. Did she talk about her amma? Cousin Aftab? Her father? In the end she just said nothing.

'I can tell it's very bad,' the old man said. 'I expect you're wondering what an old bundle of rags like me is doing with this voice, aren't you?'

He was confusing her. Shazia said, 'Where did he go?'

'I went to one of the best schools in India,' he said. 'British-run, you know. My father was a very, very, very wealthy man.'

'Why do I want to know this?'

She began to feel her eyes tear up. Soon, people would start to look at her and then she'd have to run.

'And now my son is a poor man who is obliged to pay money to a character who is a stranger to art, literature and science. He pays this money for no reason at all, except that he wants to remain alive . . .'

Now she was crying.

The old man put a dry, crumpled hand on her arm. 'Go home,' he said. 'I don't know what you have in mind, but no good can come of it. Not for you.'

'I can't!'

A woman looked at her. Shazia glared back through her tears. The woman pulled her headscarf across her face and walked on.

'I don't think that lady deserved that.'

'If you know where he's gone, you must tell me,' Shazia said.

He took his hand off her arm and then looked her up and down.

'You must tell me!'

For a long time, maybe even thirty seconds, he held her gaze with his and then he said, 'If it is so important to you, he is going to the Lucknow Cafe in Forest Gate. You know it?'

'Yes.'

It was a nice little mum and dad cafe selling coffee, tea, hot samosas and not much else. She hoped he didn't have 'business interests' there. But he had to, otherwise why would he be going there?

'Go there if you must, but don't do a thing,' the old man said. 'Not to him. They bleed us these people, like sacrificial sheep. But when you fight them, they take your marrow. My father was once a very, very, very rich man and then he fought a man like Naz Sheikh and he lost everything.'

'I can't take it.'

'It's yours,' Brian said. 'It's clean.'

'No! No, I mean I can't take it, full stop,' Paul Venus said.

'But it's—'

'Mine? If it is, then where did you get it, Brian? Last time that money appeared on the radar it was in the hands of Tom de Vries, a boy who was stabbed to death. Where did you get it? I'm afraid of what you're going to tell me, but I want to know.'

'Do you?' the gangster chuckled. 'You've got your boy back.'

'I have part of him,' Venus said. 'Brian, you tell me what you know . . .'

'Or you'll do what?'

Paul Venus looked into Brian Green's eyes and saw exactly the same thing he'd always seen. Nothing.

'I didn't kill that posh kid, if that's what you think,' Brian said. 'Hand on heart I can say that.'

'So you had him—'

321

'Oh, I'd stop right there if I was you, Paul. I mean, what is the connection between me and Tom de Vries, eh?'

'Your mobile phone number scrawled on his bedroom wall.'

No change of expression or colour passed across the gangster's face.

'Well?'

'Harry was in that house wasn't he? His handwriting . . .'

'We don't know yet.'

'Think you'll find it is,' Brian said. 'Maybe he copied it down from his computer so he could use it if he got hold of a phone. Because he was in trouble. I'm touched and flattered, Paul, but it's news to me.'

The number had been written in a shaky hand and had not been instantly visible. But it had been there.

Paul Venus clutched at a straw. 'How did you know about Harry's computer?'

'Because you told me he had it with him when he disappeared,' Brian said.

He had.

'I never got a call from Harry or that posh kid, Adele's boy,' Brian said.

'So how'd you get my money?'

'I called in some favours. I did it for you, Paul, and Harry. It's all for Harry.'

'You called in favours with . . . ?'

'Does it matter?'

'Yes!'

'Don't seem to matter where favours come from when it

concerns you fucking Russian tarts,' he said. 'I know where you've got them from. I've even got photographs. It's dead easy these days . . .'

'No money has ever changed hands.'

'No, but you give a lot of support to Russian gyms and health clubs, don't you? Turning up to opening nights like a fucking Oscar nominee. Local bloody top cop saying "Come here and use this place, these people are kosher." But they're not. Places like that, full to bursting with drugs.'

'I don't know . . .'

'Oh, you don't think it's strange they give you free gash every time you get a hard-on? Think that's all just about wanting to have their own gyms?'

Of course he didn't, but then Brian used to pull the same sort of stunts back in the old days. Worse. He'd not taken women from Brian, but money. Then he'd needed it. And how did Brian know? What contact did he have with the Russians? Laila Malik had bought drugs to give to Harry from a Russian at a gym in Wanstead. Had de Vries told Brian? Why would he? Brian had known his mother. But had he known Tom? How could he? Adele had left the family.

'I've retired now,' Brian said. 'As you know. But I still have to earn, especially with Taylor to support, and it ain't easy with all these drug-pushing Ivans on my doorstep now. Can't have no more. Can't manage the ones that're already here.'

Brian lived outside Newham. He had to know that Paul couldn't do anything directly about this. But a phone call from Venus was all it would take to get the local police out to one or more of these gyms – on the Newham Super's say so.

The Superintendent's anger bubbled over. Brian was lying! 'I don't know how you got involved with de Vries and—'

'Who says I did?'

'When Harry regains consciousness what'll he say, eh?' Paul said.

'Harry? Poor kid'll be traumatised I reckon. Won't say much. Won't say nothing about me, I don't suppose. *You* can tell *him* his Uncle Brian has been thinking of him.'

Venus wanted to scream. Whether he took the money or not, he had to do what Brian wanted about the Russians, or his liaisons with girls like little Sasha would become public knowledge. The Russians were scum, he didn't care about them. They'd indirectly poisoned his son. What he did care about was where that vast holdall of money had come from – and who had died to make that possible.

'I can't touch that cash,' he said. 'And you know it, Brian.'

Unearned cash, even in small amounts, going into a serving officer's account would raise suspicion. And giving it to Tina wouldn't help. They were still technically man and wife and so the same rules applied to her.

'I said I washed it for you.'

'Yes, and you know I'll still refuse,' Venus said. 'I know that if I point the finger at you in connection with Tom de Vries's death, apart from the fact you have my reputation in your hands in the form of photographs . . .'

'Wanna see?'

Brian took his phone out of his pocket and dragged an image onto the screen. Venus frowned.

'Quite apart from that,' he continued, 'I can't prove any connection between you and de Vries except a phone number.'

'No. Well there ain't,' Brian said. 'Now, you want that money or what? Be like the old days, Paul,' He smiled. 'And if you think only the Ivans can get you women, you're very wrong.'

He had no trouble at the Lucknow Cafe. By the time Shazia got there, the old couple, from the expressions on their faces, had already paid Naz Sheikh and he was enjoying tea and samosas at a table in the window. She walked by on the opposite side of the road.

At first she thought that she'd missed him because she couldn't see his car anywhere. He had to have parked it in a side street. Shazia looked around. She was far too close to home and Cousin Aftab's shop for comfort. She knew that the Sheikhs were well aware of her address, but when she couldn't see Naz she could fool herself that he was miles and miles away. He finished up his samosas and left the cafe. Then he walked up the Woodford Road towards Wanstead Flats.

Shazia had never been able to pinpoint accurately where her father had died, except that it had been on the Flats somewhere. He'd been stabbed. Her amma hadn't seen who had done it. She must have been too shocked to take it in. Shazia wondered why she cared. Her father had beaten her and taken her into his bed to use like a whore. All he'd cared about had been her school grades – if they slipped it all got so much worse – so why did she give a damn where he'd died? Why did she always look out at the Flats and shudder?

325

Naz Sheikh turned right onto Capel Road and Shazia began to feel cold. He was walking in the direction of her flat. Did he know she was following him? Then she saw his car and she thought that he was going to get in it, but he just walked straight past.

Anxiety gripped her stomach again, Why hadn't he got into his car? Why had he even parked it in Capel Road? Then, just before the turnoff from Capel to Lorne Road, Naz went through a gate, up a path and rang the doorbell of a house that was only two doors away from Lee Arnold's flat.

'Hi, Bri.'

It wasn't often that Brian Green was shocked, but it wasn't every day that a bloke slipped out from underneath his car and looked through his open window.

'Arnold.'

'Hello.' Lee hauled himself upright and then opened the passenger door and got in the car. 'Just to satisfy your curiosity, Brian, I slipped in under the side of Superintendent Venus's motor first. Then I pulled myself along the ground so I was directly under you.'

'Christ.'

Venus had gone. Driven off like a boy racer with his pants on fire. Lee had reckoned that Brian would sit and ponder for a bit afterwards, and he had.

'So you, er . . .'

'Well, Brian, let's see shall we?' Lee said. 'Did I hear everything you said to Mr Venus or didn't I?'

24

It dawned on Shazia that her urge to stick a knife in Naz Sheikh's guts was turning out hard to fulfil. When she'd left the flat that morning, she'd just wanted him dead. She hadn't cared what it might cost her, and whether she did it in private or public hadn't mattered. On top of what she'd listened to Uncle Ali say about Cousin Aftab to her dada, she'd also overheard her amma apologising to her cousin. She hadn't said for what, but she'd been crying. Shazia had felt so guilty. Through her, the Sheikhs had got their claws into Aftab. She would rather have died than let that happen.

But now he was in some house on Capel Road and she didn't know what to do. A woman with blonde hair had let him in. He'd smiled at her in a way that left nothing to the imagination. He could be in there for, well, ages.

Shazia looked at Lee's flat and then at her watch. He was unlikely to come home in the middle of the day, but it wasn't impossible. What would she say if he did? He knew she didn't like to hang about around the Flats because of their association with her father's death. So why was she there? And could she really just go up to Naz Sheikh and murder him in the street when he finally came out of that house?

'When you've been in the army and then become a copper, a lot of people think you're just a thick thug who couldn't get a job in a bank, and there is some truth in that,' Lee said. 'I mean, I do still count on my fingers, but then could I have made a bigger fuck-up of the banking system than the management of the Royal Bank of Scotland did? Nah. I certainly couldn't have lived with myself if I'd wrecked my bank and then taken a big fat pension and a lump sum like that Fred Goodwin did. I'm not good at those things. You're not. We ain't all the same. But what I am good at is thinking through situations. Now I'm sitting here in your lovely Maybach, smoking a fag, which is irritating the shit out of you. I'm watching you sweat and wondering what the cause and the effect of this situation might be.'

Brian Green, who was sweating more heavily than Lee had ever seen him do before, said, 'What do you mean?'

'I mean, Brian, that you just gave Superintendent Venus three hundred and fifty thousand pounds,' Lee said. 'I heard you tell him yourself that it was the ransom money for Harry. Which of course makes me wonder how you got it, just like Mr Venus did. And I know you'll say you got it through a third party at great trouble to yourself and you're not allowed to say, blah, blah, blah. But like Venus, I saw your number on Tom de Vries's bedroom wall. Unlike Venus, I owe you nothing, and I know more than he does.'

Brian Green remained silent.

'Oh I realise you can have me killed,' Lee said. 'You've had lots of people murdered in your time. I think you had Tom de Vries killed. I can't prove it just from a telephone number scrawled on the kid's bedroom wall. Harry Venus knows you, that I can prove. Although why he should write your mobile number on the wall of a house where he was being held hostage, I don't know. Maybe he'll tell us when he wakes up? Did Tom de Vries get it out of him? Did he know that his mother once knew Harry's mum's friend Brian? Did Harry boast about his gangster "uncle"? I think yes to all those questions. The coppers know that Tom and Happy the alkie didn't kill each other. The old boozer had a broken wrist. Neither of them had the other one's blood on him. Sloppy, Brian.'

The gangster said, 'I think Venus needs to distance himself from these Russians.'

'As if it's your business.'

'It's everyone's business. They're drug pushers.'

'Not all of them,' Lee said. 'But too many for you eh, Brian? Want them off your manor. So why not just blackmail Venus with your photographs? Why all this?'

'Maybe the money's mine.'

Lee frowned.

'Personally,' Brian said. 'Maybe I gave him my own money, out the goodness of my heart. He'd only take money he thinks is his.'

'How can you say that? You know he's as bent as a nine-bob note.'

'Bent? Venus?' He laughed. 'Depends what you mean. He's never taken money from me without paying it back.'

329

'How? By covering your back? Turning a blind eye?'

'I understand he don't take money from the Russkis.' He paused, then he said, 'My relationship with Tina's another matter. I like to treat her from time to time, but she ain't a copper is she? And, well, back in the day I never gave her money without some sort of exchange of services going on.'

So somewhere, in all likelihood, there were mucky pictures of Tina Wilton.

'Spare me.'

'Venus has some money. Good for him. Maybe he can get himself another flat. That makes me happy.'

'All because you fucked his missus a million years ago and have a soft spot for her,' Lee said. 'How heart-warming. But you know, Brian, I have a better theory in my head than that.'

'Oh yeah?'

'Yeah. Wanna hear it?'

Brian said nothing.

'I don't think you knew who was behind Harry's disappearance when it first happened,' Lee said. 'I think you only knew about it when Tom de Vries called you.'

'I never knew the boy.'

'Bear with me,' Lee said. 'I think that Harry told Tom about his gangster "uncle" to curry favour with him. He must've tried everything over the years to get in with that kid. Fucking hell, he even kidnapped himself! Your name must've come up, if only because the boys' mothers both knew each other through you. But then they fell out, and when Harry didn't want to play Tom's game any more, Tom forced Harry to give him your phone number

330

because he had a plan. Silly Tom tried to blackmail you didn't he? High on this delusion he had about committing the perfect crime, he made you an offer. Harry for safe passage out of the country with all of Venus's money was it? Someone, from you, met him in Poplar Rec, someone who wanted it all to look tidy, just like you always do. The alkie was there so he killed him too. Nice and neat. But not before he'd found out where Harry was and got the keys to the car the coppers found him in. Then keys back to Tom's nan's, because you knew her, didn't you? Then off with the money, a quick peek in the garage to see whether Harry was still alive and away. You showed him who was boss, didn't you Brian? Then all you had to do was wait for Tina to remember where Tom's nan lived. And you knew that she would because you had. Whether Harry was alive or dead by that time wasn't your concern.'

'I loved that kid.'

'Maybe, but you loved having Venus's money more,' Lee said. 'Because you knew he was skint, you knew he couldn't refuse it when you gave it back to him, and you also knew it would give you power over him to break from his Russian friends, even close them down. So much more power than a few mucky photos. Venus is so dirty you could dig coal out of him, but then at least he's not thick.'

'What do you mean?'

'I recognised that sports bag Tom de Vries put the money in because it's the bag Venus bought for the second drop. The one that was supposed to be in the graveyard. Bright fucking red,' Lee said. 'De Vries nicked it from his flat. And I saw Venus take it out of your boot.'

'Prove it.'

'If de Vries's DNA's on it, and I'd bet it will be . . .'

'What do you want, Arnold?'

'Me? Nothing,' Lee said. 'I know you'll rip my eyes out, Brian. Now why would I want that? No, what we all need, you too, is Venus out of the job. From my point of view he's too bent, and from your perspective if he's no longer in bed with the Russians . . .'

'He won't be.'

'But if he's not in the job you can be sure he won't be because they won't want him endorsing their clubs. Why would they?' Lee said. Then he leaned in towards Brian and whispered, 'So have a word with him, Brian. On the quiet. I'm sure he'd get a decent pension.'

'Not my problem.'

'And if you're wondering how I can, as a man of the law, let you get away with it when I know you've murdered someone, Brian, then look at it like this. Cast your mind back to the eyes thing I just talked about. Always been very squeamish about eyes, I have. Squeamish enough to let me, just occasionally, hold hands with a devil like you.'

Now Lee Arnold sweated too.

Mumtaz's mobile phone rang. Her new client, the woman once married to a Salafi, had been hard work, and she was shattered. Illegally divorced and trying to get her children back, the client was now convinced her husband, who had taken them, was a terrorist. But was he? Or did she just want to blacken his name so she could get her kids? Mumtaz could understand completely, but could she help her?

She looked at the phone on the passenger seat of the car, dreading seeing Naz's name on the screen. But it hadn't come up. Instead it was another client.

She picked it up. 'Hi Alison.'

'Mrs Hakim.'

'How's things?'

The last time she'd heard from Alison Darrah-Duncan her son Charlie was still refusing to talk to the police about Harry Venus's kidnap.

'I just wish that Charlie would tell the police the truth,' she said. 'George Grogan has given them a statement. According to him, Charlie was involved with Tom de Vries and the kidnap for longer than he was, but I don't know if that's true or not. But because Charlie has some of the ransom money, there's enough evidence to prosecute him. It's only a few pounds! Not even a hundred!'

'I'm sorry.'

'Oh it's his fault, and I've told him that if he owned up it would be better for him in terms of custody. You know?'

She was hoping that if Charlie spoke up he'd get a shorter sentence.

'I don't know.'

'He doesn't seem to care that this is making me ill,' Alison said. 'I thought we had a bond, Charlie and me. You can be wrong about your kids you know, Mrs Hakim. But anyway I didn't call you to go on about Charlie. I'm aware I still owe you some money.'

'Yes.'

'Could I ask you to maybe come and collect it?' she said. 'I'm really not good on my feet, even walking to the postbox is a bit much at the moment. Could I ask you to call round?'

'That's fine. When?'

'Whenever you can.'

Mumtaz looked at her watch. She didn't have to be back at the office at any particular time.

'Now?'

'If that's OK it would get it done.'

'All right,' Mumtaz said. 'I'll be about half an hour.'

'Thank you.'

Mumtaz was just about to end the call when Alison said, 'You know, Mrs Hakim, my Charlie has always been a very quiet boy. Undemanding and easy, yet in these last few days I've been able to see his great-grandfather in him.'

'Perón?'

'Well, you don't get to be a dictator without being ruthless do you?' she said. 'And Charlie is ruthless. He will do what he wants to do and to hell with his parents. I'm finding it hard to even like him right now. He reminds me a bit of that awful boy Tom de Vries.'

Mumtaz put the phone down and shivered.

It took Shazia a while to realise that the front door of the house was open a crack. When had that happened? She was sure that

Naz had shut the door behind him when the woman let him in. But had he? He must've done. It had been clear, so she thought, that he had been going to have sex with that woman. So logically he would close the door behind them, wouldn't he?

No one else had gone in or come out of the house. She'd been there for just over an hour and the whole area had been quiet to the point of silence. That was why people liked living near the Flats. Locals, if they could afford it, and increasingly, people from outside. She'd seen a lot of very smartly dressed mothers out with their babies carried in expensive woollen slings in recent months. Well-spoken ladies, just like her. She'd tried to get rid of her private school accent since she'd been at college, but nobody was fooled and her friends accepted her for who she was. Nobody else mattered.

Shazia walked across the road and looked at that slightly open front door. Now she really studied it, she could see how dilap-idated the house was. The front path was covered in litter, the door was only just on its hinges and the windows looked as if they'd never been cleaned. It was silent.

Shazia put her hand in her pocket and felt the knife between her fingers. If the woman was still in there, what did it matter? She'd come here to do something, now she had an opportunity to do it. She put one foot inside the hall.

'Let's talk honestly, shall we? You knew Tom de Vries's mum, didn't you Brian?'

'You know I did. Adele.'

'And it's common knowledge Tom went to see his nan, Adele's mum, in Poplar on the day he died.'

'If you say so.'

Lee nodded. 'He was killed just round the corner in Poplar Rec at the same time as Happy the alkie, but not by him.'

'If that's what the coppers think.'

'They do now. There's lots of mystery around what happened that day, but what we do know is that Tom very rarely went to see his nan. She says she hadn't seen him for over a year.'

'Get away.'

'Weird he should suddenly take it into his head to go that day, don't you think? He told her he had business over that way. She doesn't know what. But what she does know is that he wanted to use her garage.'

'For his motor.'

'If there hadn't been a connection between Tom and Adele's mum's flat, Tony Bracci would have found it very hard to find Harry. It was such a stroke of luck – if you believe in such things. But I don't.'

They both heard the sound of cars entering the graveyard. Lee saw Brian look in his mirror.

'No one takes the piss out of you, do they Brian?' Lee said. 'And a kid like Tom de Vries . . . No one gets away do they? And that includes me, doesn't it?'

The old man took a gun out of his pocket.

'You don't disappoint, do you Brian? Always tooled up.'

Brian said nothing. Behind them a car door closed.

'Did Tom threaten to kill Harry if you didn't give him some

money? Was that the deal?' Lee said. 'Was that why Tom invented someone who claimed to know where Harry was before the last drop? To fit in with your timetable? So he could get out of the country faster? If you're going to kill me, Brian, you might as well tell me the truth. Dead men don't tell tales.'

Brian fired up the engine. 'Get out and get in the driving seat,' he said. 'Run and I'll kill you.'

'We're not alone, Brian. People come to cemeteries. They're public places.'

'Think I give a shit?'

'You should,' Vi Collins said. She was at Brian's window and she wasn't alone. What looked like a squad of robots surrounded the car. Lee had never been so glad to see an armed response unit in his life. 'Put the gun down, Mr Green, and get out of the motor.'

Lee watched Brian turn to face him. The old man said, 'Cunt.'

Lee's sweating increased. Green's gun was still pointed at his groin. 'Today I've learned that you can use a mobile phone underneath a car,' he said. 'And you've learned, Brian, that not even the fear of blinding can make me bent. Call me a fool to myself . . .'

'You're dead, Arnold.'

'Oh wind the macho shit in, Brian, and give me the gun,' Vi said. 'Because if you think this lot won't shoot you if you make a wrong move, then you're fucking wrong.'

The house smelt of damp and compost. Probably rotting food. What had once been a front room was empty, but there was an old fridge in the kitchen and a kettle which, when Shazia touched it, was still warm. And the back door was open. She looked out into the garden, which was full of old mattresses and dead electrical equipment. Just like her old house, there was an alleyway at the back that probably led out onto Lorne Road. The house was silent. Naz and the woman must have left through the back.

But his car was still outside.

She walked back into the hall and it was then that she heard what sounded like a gasp from upstairs.

'Get Venus?'

'On his way home,' Vi said.

'Did you get the sports bag?' Lee asked.

'We got it, but you'd better be right about this, Arnold,' Vi said. 'It's not every day a girl gets to arrest her own boss. On a scale of one to ten of fear I'd put it at a good twelve."

They watched SO19 armed response officers put a handcuffed Brian Green into a Land Rover.

Lee lit a cigarette. 'Keeping him talking wasn't a walk in the park,' he said. 'I've not sweated so much since Iraq.'

Vi put a hand on his shoulder. 'If you hadn't we'd never have got Venus,' she said. 'If he'd got home who knows what he would've done? Destroyed that bag.'

'At some point he would've done,' Lee said. 'Unless he actually believed Brian's lies, which I can't imagine he would.'

'Venus, for all his faults, just wanted his son back,' she said. 'He's not thinking even now. I wonder, when Harry wakes, if he ever does, what he'll say. George Grogan has admitted they all roughed the poor kid up pretty badly when he was supposed to have come on to Laila Malik. They all looked down on him, used him, took the piss. His mum and dad too busy with work and their various love lives to take an interest in him. Harry Venus was the real neglected kid in this, not Tom de Vries. He was horrible.'

'But he's dead, Vi,' Lee said. 'And far too soon.'

'So much for being an *Übermensch*,' Vi said.

'And so much for Alfred Hitchcock.'

She smiled. 'If only Brian had just done a bit of good old-fashioned blackmail on Venus, eh? What a fucking mess.'

There were four rooms on the first floor. She could see that one was a bathroom, albeit wrecked. Shazia could remember when her old house had an avocado bathroom suite like that. Her father had loved it, but his sister, nasty Auntie Veera, made him replace it with a pink one when she came from Bangladesh for a holiday. Only when her amma had first come had sanity intervened. When he had still wanted to impress her, her father had put in a new white suite.

She walked past the bathroom and looked in through the door of a small box room. Empty except for a few mouldering soft toys. The gasp she'd heard downstairs sounded again, but this time it was louder. It came from the far end of the landing. She wanted to say, 'Who's there?' but realised that people only said that in movies. Naz and the woman were probably shagging, that was the reality. She took her knife and her phone out of her pocket. If she lost her nerve the least she could do was take his picture having sex.

Why she crept along the landing, she didn't know. But she did. The door to the room the gasp had come from was open, so she could be heard whatever she did. As she approached, the thump of her heart began to interfere with her hearing. It wasn't every day that she killed someone. She'd often thought about it when her father had been alive. She had thought about murdering him all the time. But she had also loved him.

Shazia walked straight through the door.

25

There was only a mattress in that whole big room. It was over by the window and he was alone on top of it. Panting and gasping, he had both hands on his stomach. Had the woman kicked him? Punched him?

But he was too white for that, and when Shazia moved closer she saw that there was blood. But as she looked at it, she knew that she distrusted its provenance. Was it his? Or had he killed the woman and thrown her corpse somewhere? In that bathroom maybe?

She stood back.

But he'd seen her.

'Shazia!'

There was blood in his mouth. How had he managed to do that?

'Shazia, call an ambulance! I've been stabbed!'

And then she saw that blood was oozing from between his fingers. Had he really been stabbed? Was this some sort of elaborate trick to get her close to him, so that he could hurt her?

'Who stabbed you?'

Her voice was husky and strangled, not her own.

'Some eastern European bastard! Get an ambulance!'

'I only saw a woman,' Shazia said. Men usually only called other men bastards.

'She was the bait. Get help or I'll die!'

Shazia sat down on the filthy floor. She put her knife and her phone back in her pocket.

He knew a second after she did. 'You're going to let me die?'

She said nothing, just looked.

He moved his hands in the wet mush that was his stomach and then lifted his eyes to hers.

'Don't beg,' she said. 'It will do you no good.'

'What's happening with Malcolm McCullough?' Lee asked.

Vi put another chip in her mouth, chewed, swallowed and then said, 'Gone back to Henley. He'll have to give evidence when the kids are tried, but he didn't actually do anything.'

'That school did my head in.'

They were in the station canteen. Brian Green had been booked in and was waiting for his brief, while Chief Inspector Stone was conferring with senior colleagues about Venus. Vi and Lee had snatched at this hiatus to get some food.

'Too common for it, Arnold,' Vi said. 'School rejected you. God knows how it'll play out for all the eastern European kids rocking up next term. I think old Malcolm hopes his mum dies before that happens, so he can retire.'

Lee ate his pie. It was gristly and tepid, but he was sort of glad of it. Being up close to Brian Green had left a nasty taste in his mouth and an ugly smell on his clothes. Lee just hoped that he was right about de Vries's DNA being on the sports bag so that Green definitely went down. If he managed to wriggle free of any involvement in Tom's death then Lee would have problems. And Brian almost certainly hadn't killed the boy himself.

'The kids took McCullough's ideas and did what they did all on their own,' Vi said. 'Not that Charlie Darrah-Duncan's ever gonna 'fess up.'

'You don't think so?'

'Between what I can only interpret as a love/hate relationship with Tom de Vries and some loyalty to that school, Charlie is completely brainwashed, as far as I can tell. Not even self-preservation left. Probably comes of being gay.'

'Vi!'

'I mean in that environment,' she said. 'Public school's notorious for the persecution of gay boys. Not the teachers, the kids. Give them a well hard time.'

'How do you know?'

She shrugged. 'I know enough rent boys who've been with closeted old judges, all right? Damaged for life those geezers. Anyway, what does bloody Reeds think it is? Eton? We all know the only way to become anyone is to go there.'

He laughed. 'Commie.'

'Watch it!' She held up a warning finger. 'Anyway, we got equality in this country.'

'How'd you work that out?'

'Our crims are just as good as theirs,' she said. 'Brian Green.'

'I was bricking it when I had to keep him talking.'

'Not as much as I was when I had to get hold of Venus and then come and get you in short order,' she said. 'Stone was bloody brilliant.'

'New job opportunity for him,' Lee said.

'Nah. I think he feels sorry for Venus. We all do. If he's got a Russian girl habit he's been funding by turning a blind eye to what their boyfriends do, then he deserves what's coming to him. But what happened with Harry he didn't deserve, and I don't suppose he expected Brian Green to turn up in the middle of all that either.'

'He should never have been close to him in the first place.'

'Course not. But the Greens of this world get under your skin. When he sent his latest wife over here he must've known it wasn't good for Venus. And according to you, Green wasn't even in contact with de Vries at that time. Twisted old fuck! But then in his way I suppose you could say he was looking out for Venus on one level. He got his money back for him, even if poor Harry's still in a coma.'

'Do you think the kid'll ever be right?'

'Who knows? He's on life support. Could wake up tomorrow, next week, never. Poor little bugger.' She appeared to wipe a tear from her eye, but Lee said nothing. Vi didn't do sentimentality. 'Anyway,' she said, 'you need to get checked out at the hospital yourself.'

'Why?'

'You just nearly died, Arnold.'

'No, I never!'

'Yes you did. You've given me a statement. You can't do any more here now. Get off to Newham General and get checked out.'

He pulled a face.

She said, 'Doughnut!'

She put another chip in her mouth and chewed. Then she said, 'Do as you're told.'

He'd tried bribing her. He'd said he'd cancel all her amma's debts and leave Cousin Aftab alone. But she'd just laughed at him.

'Every word you say is a lie. When you talk about my family, about Islam, about anything!' Shazia said. 'I can't let you live. If you live you will carry on persecuting us.'

'No, no, I—'

'Yes you will! When you die I expect your dad and your brother will do that anyway. But I will at least have had the satisfaction of seeing you die. You know I came here to kill you myself?'

'You wouldn't have been able to.'

'Maybe I wouldn't,' she said. 'But I can watch you die and I can bless the man who killed you.'

'If I am dying then there's something you should know,' he said. 'About your stepmother.'

'More lies. Save them,' she said. 'I won't believe a word you say.'

'I think you will,' he said.

Mumtaz drank the tea that Alison had made for her in spite of the taste. God alone knew what she'd done to it, but it wasn't nice. Alison wasn't well.

'Charlie had become a horrible little snob,' she said. 'Not

having anything to do with the neighbours' kids when he came home on holiday, demanding all sorts of things I couldn't afford. And that filthy tradition they had at that school . . .'

'Hadn't your husband told you about it?'

'No, he had not!' She moved her body on the sofa to try to get comfortable. 'I think about the last week or so and I can't believe I've had to absorb so much negative information. I didn't have any preconceptions about who I might be when my search for my mother started, but I didn't think it would be . . . what it was. I feel tainted.'

'None of it is your fault, Alison.'

She smiled. 'I know. But where do I go from here, eh? Charlie facing kidnap charges. That poor Venus boy still unconscious in hospital . . .'

'Maybe when all of that is settled you should try and find some of your relatives in Argentina.'

'I can't go there!'

'Online,' Mumtaz said. 'Your grandmother had a family. Maybe you could trace some of them and find out more about her. She was quite famous in Argentina for a while.'

Alison frowned. 'I've spoken to Mother Katerina.'

'Good.'

'Sister Pia is very ill now, apparently. She says that if I want to speak to her I should go as soon as I can. But you can see how bad I am.'

Mumtaz's phone rang. 'Excuse me.'

She looked at the screen. It was Shazia's mobile.

'Hi sweetie.'

There was a pause.

'Shazia?'

Mumtaz got out of her car at the same moment she saw Lee leap from his. An ambulance, blue lights flashing, was in front of the house already. She ran up to the entrance. Lee, behind her, put a hand on her shoulder. Upstairs she heard voices.

'Let me go in first,' Lee said.

But she pushed him behind her.

'She's my daughter,' she said and ran up the stairs.

Sirens in the street signalled the arrival of the police.

The ambulance crew had placed some of their equipment on the landing. It led her to where they were. There were two of them. One was putting a mask on the patient's face. The other one stood up and walked towards her.

'Who are you?'

For a moment she couldn't see Shazia. Then she spotted a tiny bundle wrapped in a blanket in a corner.

Mumtaz pointed. 'Her mother,' she said. 'I rang you.'

Lee joined her.

'You her dad?'

'No,' he said.

'I'm Dave,' the man said. 'I'm ambulance crew. With the patient we've got paramedic Don. As soon as we can get your mate stabilised we can get him to hospital.'

'Will he live?'

Dave said, 'Look, why don't you take Shazia downstairs. She's

347

shocked but she talked to me quite easily. We'll have to take her to hospital, just to check her over, but she doesn't need to be here now.'

Mumtaz walked over to the girl.

'Come on, sweetie,' she said.

Slowly, Shazia looked up. Mumtaz put a hand out, but the girl didn't move. And now that Mumtaz looked at her, she could see that her daughter's eyes were not on her, but behind her.

'Shazia?'

'Lee.' She raised her arms.

Why did she want Lee? Why? Mumtaz turned to look at him.

'Lee, will you take me home, please?' Shazia said.

Mumtaz felt slapped. But she moved aside so that Lee could get to Shazia.

He crouched down and put an arm around her shoulders. 'No, not yet, babe,' he said. 'But I'll take you and your mum home once you've been checked out at the hospital.'

The sound of several pairs of running feet on the stairs caused Mumtaz to look round.

'Who's that?' Shazia said.

Lee said, 'It's just the police. Nothing for you to worry about, kiddo.' Mumtaz knew that wasn't true. When Shazia had called her, she'd been hysterical, but Mumtaz had managed to gather that Naz Sheikh had been stabbed and was at a house on Capel Road. That was when she'd called the ambulance. But Shazia hadn't said who had stabbed the gangster. Had she done it herself? And what about the other thing Shazia had said?

'I know, Amma, about you.'

Mumtaz looked down at her daughter, who was crying in Lee Arnold's arms.

Paramedic Don Phillips knew it was a losing battle. Once it was just him and Dave again, he said, 'He's all over the place.'

Dave knelt down beside his colleague and looked at the screen on the monitor attached to the patient's arm. At 150 beats per minute he was tachycardic, his blood pressure was falling and his skin was white and clammy.

'Do you think he's gone too far?'

'What do you think?' Don said. 'We can't move him while he's like this. We'll have to ride it out.'

Dave nodded. Extreme blood loss, or hypovolemia, was usually fatal. They'd both seen it as a result of gang warfare in the borough and Don had come across it in Afghanistan. This guy had been stabbed in the gut, and when they'd got to him he'd already lost consciousness.

'What did the girl say?' Don asked Dave.

He hadn't had a chance to speak to the teenager who'd been with the man, and it was, in his experience, best to keep Dave talking until either a doctor arrived or the man died. Not that any doctor would make any difference to the eventual outcome. The man was still breathing, but what his brain was doing was anyone's guess.

'Said she found him,' Dave said.

'How?'

'Didn't say. I didn't ask.'

'You think she did this?'

'I dunno. Not our worry.'

Don looked at the face behind the oxygen mask and knew what he thought. He'd seen things like this in Afghanistan. Girls who'd just had enough of their men. Although most of them had been covered up; they certainly hadn't been wearing miniskirts and ripped tights.

26

Shazia had always liked Tony Bracci, and he liked her. Unlike Vi Collins, he wasn't too close to the kid, but he could and did put her at her ease. He'd taken the knife she'd been carrying and her phone away from her at the scene. She'd seen a doctor and now she was in the soft interview room with her mother. She wasn't talking to Mumtaz, he'd noticed, but when asked whom she wanted in the interview with her, she'd chosen her mother.

'Shazia, I have to understand why you was in that house at that time,' Tony said. 'OK?'

'Yes.'

She looked down into her lap, saying nothing.

'Shazia . . . ?'

She was on a fair old whack of tranquillisers, but she was far from drowsy.

'Oh,' she looked up. 'I wanted to talk to him.'

'Who?'

'Naz Sheikh,' she said.

'What about?'

'He keeps calling me bad names,' she said. 'In the street. He's one of those men who think that all Muslim girls should be covered. I've told him to stop in the past, but he won't.'

'What type of names does he call you?'

'Horrible stuff. "Whore", "slut".'

'Do you know him?'

'No,' she said.

Mumtaz put a hand on her shoulder, but Shazia shrugged it off.

'If you just wanted to talk to Mr Sheikh, why'd you have a knife on you?' Tony asked.

'I always have a knife,' Shazia said. 'Most kids do. It's rough round here.'

Mumtaz looked as if she might be about to say something, but then seemed to think better of it.

'Well, we'll be able to see whether you used it or not once SOCO have worked their magic.'

'I didn't use it.'

'Did you see who did attack Mr Sheikh?'

There was a knock on the door. Tony said to Shazia, 'Just a minute.' Then he called out, 'Come in.'

A uniformed constable entered and put a slip of paper in front of DS Bracci.

'Shazia . . .'

'I didn't see anyone,' she said. 'When I found him he was already unconscious. I don't know what happened.'

'Why'd you go into the house in the first place?'

'I saw him go in and I wanted to talk to him.'

'So who opened the door for you if he was already unconscious?'

'No one; the door was open.'

'You must've seen him go in. Who opened the door for him?'

'No one.'

'So he went into a derelict house on his own, leaving the door open behind him, and you did what?'

'I waited for him to come out,' Shazia said.

'To tackle him about the verbal abuse?'

'Yes. I'd followed him. I saw him in the Lucknow Cafe . . .'

'By Forest Gate station?'

'Yes, but I didn't want to have a row in there.'

'You'd rather have a row in a deserted house?'

'No. But I didn't notice that the door was still open after he went inside for a long time,' she said. 'When I did I went inside. I went upstairs because I heard noises.'

'What noises?'

'Groaning . . .'

'So you went upstairs, you found Mr Sheikh lying on a mattress on the floor, and then?'

'I was afraid. I phoned my mum.'

'I called the emergency services,' Mumtaz said.

'And yet, Shazia, although you couldn't dial 999, you seemed to be able to call your mum and take a photograph of Mr Sheikh on your phone.'

He saw Mumtaz look at her quickly and then look away.

Shazia didn't speak for a moment, then said, 'I thought you might need it.'

'Me? What for?'

'The police,' she said. 'As evidence.'

Tony didn't say anything. Forensics would prove whether or

not Shazia was telling the truth about not stabbing Sheikh. What was harder to establish was whether, if she hadn't stabbed him, she knew who had. The Sheikhs were gangsters who had many enemies both inside and outside the Bangladeshi community. Tony could think of a lot of people who might want one of them dead, but he couldn't think of any who would actually do it. Because if the rest of the family found out who the culprit was and it turned out to be a member of a rival clan, that could cause all sorts of bother in Newham and beyond. Not that Naz himself was going to say anything. Not after Tony had read what Constable Mills had written on the note he'd handed him.

There was nothing he could do. The fucking street was full of police cars and 'Police Line Do Not Cross' tape, and although Mumtaz had told him not to wait around in the nick, he didn't want to go home. Lee sat in the office and smoked. Bollocks to not smoking in the office. George wanted them out anyway, what did he care? And what was Shazia saying to Tony Bracci? What had she done?

He knew someone had been hounding Mumtaz for money ever since her husband had died. Was that the Sheikhs? They were good candidates. Should he tell Tony? He knew the answer to that, but he also knew the situation was complicated. Mumtaz wouldn't want anyone to know about her involvement with the Sheikhs. He also knew that ethnic and religious loyalties that he didn't understand were in play. There was nothing he could do, not until he knew more.

Had Shazia known that her mother was being hounded? All he knew was that Mumtaz's late husband had owed money and she had inherited his debt. Families like the Sheikhs had expensive lawyers, and so he was sure that legally she was indebted to them. She was no fool and the Sheikhs were not the sort of outfit to leave anything to chance. Like any good crime family, they used the law. They rarely, if ever, fought it.

He'd have to speak to her. He'd have to somehow break through that brittle outer shell she always raised whenever her financial situation was mentioned and find out exactly what had been going on. Her husband had been murdered, but no one knew by whom. Had one of the Sheikhs killed him? Had Shazia somehow found out who had killed her dad? Ahmet Hakim had not, by all accounts, been a nice man, but his unsolved murder had to still rankle with his family. But could Shazia, even if she knew that, kill?

'You lied.'

'So did you.'

Mumtaz felt her stomach turn.

Shazia threw herself down into her favourite chair. 'Would you have wanted me to tell DS Bracci that we are slaves to the Sheikhs?'

Mumtaz sat down. 'No.'

'Well, there you go then. I lied about why I was following Naz Sheikh, not about what happened in that house.'

'You didn't see anyone?'

355

'No,' she said. 'I got there and he was lying on that mattress, and the rest you know.'

'But why did you have that knife with you?'

'Because I wanted to kill him! After what he did to Cousin Aftab, he deserved it! I know you tried to keep it from me, but when I was staying with Dada I heard Uncle Ali talking about how someone, he didn't know who, was demanding protection money from Cousin Aftab.'

'How did he know?'

'Ghazal told him. She was worried. I knew you wouldn't do anything. I thought enough was enough.'

'So you intended to kill him.'

'But I couldn't,' she said. 'All I did was watch him bleed and listen to him.'

Mumtaz knew that Shazia had become confused when she'd found Naz Sheikh bleeding out in that house. When she'd phoned her at Alison's she'd said she didn't know whether to let him die. Mumtaz had called the emergency services immediately.

Had he known he was dying? He must have had some sort of awareness.

'Did he tell you who stabbed him? Are you protecting—?'

'No, he didn't,' Shazia said. 'But he did tell me something else. About you.'

When she'd arrived at that terrible house, Shazia had rejected her in favour of Lee. Mumtaz felt as if her head were splitting. 'What?'

'What? He said you know who killed my father,' she said.

Mumtaz, her heart thundering, said, 'Who did he say that was?'

'He didn't know. So he said.'

'What else did he say?'

'Nothing. Should he have?'

'No.'

'Anyway, he's dead now and I'm not sorry,' Shazia said. 'Maybe they'll leave us alone now.'

'What, with you there, in the room where that family's most pampered son died? Shazia, they will never leave us alone now!'

'I didn't kill him!'

'You think they will ever choose to believe that?' Mumtaz said. 'Even if the police do find out who killed him?'

'Then you'll have to tell them what's been happening, won't you? And you'll have to tell me who killed my father.'

What could she do? Mumtaz knew she was facing some choices that could mean life or death for them both. 'Naz Sheikh lied,' she said. 'Why do you think he wouldn't?'

'He was stabbed . . .'

'He was a gangster, Shazia,' Mumtaz said. 'Lying was just one of the many bad things that he did. I don't know who killed your father.'

'You hated him.'

'So did you.'

'He was my father.'

They sat in silence for a moment and then Shazia said, 'Did Naz kill Dad, because of his debts?'

Mumtaz had to limit the enmity between Shazia and the Sheikhs. She said, 'No. A man ran up, he stabbed your father and then he ran away. It happened quickly. I didn't see him because

I was attending to your dad. I may not have loved him anymore, but I never sought his death, Shazia.'

The girl looked down at the floor. 'Neither did I.'

She'd said some hard things about Ahmet since his death. Sometimes it was almost as if she revelled in it. She'd always been good at bravado. Mumtaz wanted to go and hug her, but she knew that it was too soon. She'd heard a rumour that her mother was a liar, from a very bad man, and part of her had believed it. She would need time to absorb and totally believe Mumtaz's words. And in the meantime, Mumtaz herself would just have to pray that Shazia had not been lying to her.

Ah, but the world was a wicked place sometimes. Baharat pulled down a poster some moron had put on the wall of what was once the old Katz Paper and String Shop, which said 'Death to Zionists!'

He crumpled it up and put it in his pocket. That would do for the incinerator in the backyard. It had been a sad day. Somehow his little Shazia had found herself in a house with a member of a criminal family, the Sheikhs. He'd been stabbed. Later he died and now the police were investigating whether the girl had killed him. Of course she hadn't, but why had she been there, with him? Mumtaz said something about the man insulting her, but that didn't seem very plausible to Baharat.

He didn't know the family himself, but he had heard rumours. They ran illegal gambling parties where people became indebted to them. That terrible Ahmet Hakim had possessed a gambling habit that he'd kept quiet before he'd married Mumtaz. The building society had taken the house because of it. She'd been left with nothing. He was just glad that his daughter hadn't had to deal with such people on Ahmet Hakim's behalf.

Had Shazia somehow become involved in gambling, or worse? She was a very 'western' little girl and probably even believed in living in sin and all that. Baharat couldn't approve. But he couldn't condemn either. That was her choice and, just like the terrible fierce-eyed boy Ali was allowing to use his house as a base for who knew what mischief, it was personal. He'd seen the boy only that morning. An Arab of some sort. Who knew why he was in England? He'd smiled a lot at Baharat and been very respectful until Sumita had come into the room, then he'd averted his eyes. After that, conversation had been stilted and Ali had been very obviously embarrassed.

Was he one of this new breed of young, merciless jihadis? Baharat couldn't see him tolerating Mr Bhatti's sexy PO box number, but then that was lying low since the recent trouble with that poor boy's kidnapping. A policeman's son! Then he'd heard that a friend of the boy had been murdered in Poplar. He shook his head. No, Ali's new friend was much more likely to target old Rajiv for the tiny smear of eyeliner the poor thing was reduced to. Baharat remembered Rajiv's old sari-wearing days with great affection. Rajiv's father had been just the same, if not more flamboyant.

Lee gambled that Mumtaz would still be awake and that Shazia would be asleep when he called. It was one o'clock in the morning, but it had been an extraordinary day.

'She was given sleeping pills by the hospital to bring home,' Mumtaz said.

'Maybe you should take one.'

'Won't erase the image of that man dying in front of my eyes with my daughter crouching by a wall like a terrified animal,' she said.

'No . . .'

He asked her what they'd said to the police and she told him. He said, 'So not the whole truth?'

Silence.

He took a deep breath. 'Mumtaz, we've been here before. I know you're in hock to someone. I'm guessing it's the Sheikhs. I've left you alone to deal with it because that was how you wanted it. But this changes things. I don't think that Shazia killed Naz Sheikh any more than you do, but whether she did or not, she was there.'

'I know.'

'Well, also know there's a possibility they'll want to take revenge against you,' he said. 'Whoever is eventually convicted of his murder. You can't do this on your own, Mumtaz.'

Silence again.

'I won't let you.'

'Oh, so what will you do, Lee? Go to the police and tell them my statement was a lie?'

'No . . .'

'So how do you intend to do this?' He could hear anger in her voice. He knew he'd provoked her. 'You leave it alone, Lee, you leave it with me.'

'I care about you. Both of you.'

He heard her take a breath. 'Then leave it to me,' she said. 'Besides, we don't know what they'll do.'

'We know they're taking money off you right now!'

'Leave it.'

She could sound really snooty when she wanted to.

'Which you no longer owe.'

Yet another silence. 'I'll see you at work once this business with Shazia is . . . has clarified. I hope that's OK.'

'You know it is! Take as much time as you need!'

He heard her sigh. Then she said, 'I know about Mr Green and Superintendent Venus. What will happen to them?'

'Depends what evidence the police find,' he said. 'They're examining the sports bag I believe Green took from Tom de Vries with Mr Venus's money.'

'But the Superintendent didn't have anything to do with Harry's kidnap.'

'No,' he said.

'Oh well then, I will see you.'

She put down the phone, leaving Lee staring at his handset, feeling helpless. If that woman wasn't careful she could end up dead, and then how would his life be?

Chronus, rather appropriately Lee thought, came out with 'West Ham till we die!' then went straight back to sleep.

27

Two weeks later

'According to the doctors, it was the blows to the head that did for him,' Vi said.

'Fucking hell.'

Chronus copied his master and Lee told him to shut up. Vi had come to the flat to tell him about Superintendent Venus's son, and all the bloody bird had done so far was play copycat.

'If it had been just the drugs, he would've been all right,' she said. 'But those kids kicked that boy in the head like he was a football, and now he's never going to be able to do anything for himself ever again. He's awake, but that's all.'

'And his father?'

'Flung his hands up to all of it.'

'The Russians? Green?'

Vi lit a fag. 'I don't know whether Tom de Vries's DNA on that bag clinched it for Venus or whether it was just his own guilt. But he confessed to misconduct and he dropped Green right in it. You know he borrowed money from Green to do the second drop? I had wondered how he'd managed to raise so much so quickly on his flat.'

'What about George Grogan and Charlie Darrah-Duncan?'

'I think Grogan is truly sorry for what happened, but Charlie isn't. Looks dead behind the eyes to me. I wonder what de Vries was like. Some of the more intelligent lads have used the word psychopath. I wonder if Charlie's the same. Who else but a psychopath wants to commit the perfect crime?'

'You think that de Vries always wanted to kill Harry Venus?'

'He was superior, he was just killing a lower life form. How could he resist? Especially when that silly old twat McCullough was inadvertently feeding his fantasies.'

'He'll never include the work of Alfred Hitchcock in his lessons again.'

Lee shook his head. 'Christ.'

Chronus said, 'Christ!'

Lee pointed at the bird. 'Once more and I'll stick you in the spare bedroom,' he said.

Vi said, 'You won't.'

The bird looked at him knowingly.

'Mumtaz back at work?'

'No reason why she shouldn't be,' Lee said.

'I've been meaning to go round and see Shazia.'

'I'm sure she'd like that,' Lee said.

Then he offered her another cup of tea and changed the subject.

Once Vi had gone, he spent some time with the bird, stroking his feathers and talking to him. He hadn't given the poor sod a lot of his time in recent weeks. Waiting for the forensic report on the knife Shazia had been carrying had been nerve-racking. To his credit, Tony Bracci had thoroughly investigated the girl's story, so there could be no doubt. Shazia had not killed Naz Sheikh. A neighbour at the back of the house had seen a man walk down the alleyway behind the property around about the time Naz would have been inside, but she hadn't been able to describe him in any detail.

Maybe Naz's killer would never be found. His family had a lot of enemies. Maybe the Sheikhs knew who'd killed him and were going to deal with it themselves. Perhaps, in the near future, an unidentified decapitated body would be found in Victoria Dock? He only cared if the victim was one of those the Sheikhs had persecuted. If it was a member of another crime family, he didn't give a shit. People always focused on the street gangs that made life difficult for kids growing up in some parts of the borough, but the real power was still in the hands of the old-time gangsters, like Brian Green, and the crime families, like the Sheikhs, who had diversified their activities enormously in the past ten years. Connections ran through Europe across to the Chinese border as well as down into Africa. People-trafficking was the big thing. And property. His own shonky old flat had doubled in value in five years and yet it didn't make him happy. Underlying it was something rotten, and it reached right up from people like the Sheikhs to the very top of society. His mother's dad, a Jew from Lithuania, had been a communist. His father had always laughed at his ravings against the rich and powerful, but maybe he'd had a point. Because now the rich and powerful weren't just toffs, they could be anyone, and could frequently be out of plain sight. One thing the toffs were not was invisible.

He'd tried to talk to Mumtaz, but now that Shazia had been cleared of Naz Sheikh's murder, she was unreachable. She just came to work, talked about her cases and went home. Any friendship that had existed between them had evaporated. Not for the first time in his life, Lee Arnold wished he'd acted when he'd had the chance. What he felt for Mumtaz was neither easy to express, nor straightforward. But it meant something and it was more than just admiration.

Old George was back from his holiday in Great Yarmouth.

'The missus made me go and see the Chuckle Brothers at the theatre on the pier,' he told Shazia. 'I fell asleep,'

'Maybe you should go somewhere else next year, George,' she said. 'For a change?'

But George frowned. 'Can't do that. Missus wouldn't like it.'

He went back to stacking boxes of washing powder. It was nice being back in Cousin Aftab's shop. Aftab himself looked happier and Shazia knew that she could hang out there all day if she wanted. She didn't know what had happened about the protection money now that Naz was dead, and she didn't ask. But that wasn't why she was in the shop.

At eleven, Ludmilla came into the shop with baby Tomasz, and Shazia, apparently in a fit of kindness, helped her carry her shopping back to her flat on Forest Lane.

When they were out of earshot of the shop she said, 'How's your husband?'

'Janusz? He's fine.'

She gave the impression she didn't want to talk about him. But Shazia did.

'You know I saw you, Ludmilla,' she said. 'At the house on Capel Road.'

'Capel Road? Over by the park?'

'Wanstead Flats,' Shazia said. 'I saw you let Naz Sheikh into a house the day he died.'

At the time she'd hardly let herself believe it, but Naz Sheikh had told her. He'd tried to say something about her amma, about how she knew who had killed his father. But then his eyes had rolled and he'd said he had to tell her who had stabbed him before he died. 'It was that tart from your cousin's shop, and her husband.'

Then she'd known that she had to let him bleed enough so there would be no way back. Little Tomasz couldn't be an orphan.

'I was there,' Shazia said. 'I followed him.'

'Why?'

'So I could kill him myself.'

Ludmilla looked up at her. She had tears in her eyes.

'I was the girl they didn't name in the newspaper,' Shazia said. 'I found him.'

'You go to police . . . ?'

'Yes, several times,' she said. 'But I said I didn't see anyone. I won't say I saw anyone. Ever.'

Tomasz chuckled and Shazia tickled him under his chin.

Ludmilla's face whitened. 'What do you want?'

'Nothing.' She carried on gently tickling the baby. 'Look after Tomasz. Live your lives.'

'He was a bad man, yes?'

'He was a very bad man,' Shazia said. 'I'm glad he's dead.'

'You have, I think, more than just his rudeness against him?'

'Oh yes.'

Ludmilla stroked Tomasz's head. 'Us too.'

'I don't need to know.'

'You do.' She put a hand on Shazia's arm. 'You protected us. You must know.'

The house was ridiculous. Stone gryphons guarding the front door, two Ferraris on the drive, Viennese blinds – which Mumtaz had always thought looked like bunches of French knickers – at every window. It was new, this house, and vast and pseudo-Georgian. They might as well have put a sign outside the massive electric gates, 'Gangsters Live Here'.

The door was open and a small, elderly man stood on the threshold. She didn't recognise him, but she knew who he was.

When she approached, he stood aside to let her in. A hall painted in bright emerald green led into a white and gold room the size of her entire flat. It contained only a TV and four vast brocade sofas.

'You may sit,' he said. He spoke in English, but with a heavy Bengali accent.

She looked around. Was anyone else in the house?

'We are quite alone,' he said. 'As I said we would be.'

She sat.

'It is nice to meet you Wahid-ji,' she said. 'I appreciate your invitation to talk.'

He smiled. 'I have made tea. Would you like some?'

'Thank you.'

He served tea on a silver tray with salted nonta biscuits. Sumita had always made nonta biscuits on a Sunday and Mumtaz liked them. But her stomach was knotted with tension, which made eating difficult. She was in the Sheikhs' house, with Naz Sheikh's uncle.

'So, I summoned you,' he said.

The use of grandiose language made Mumtaz feel uncomfortable, but she said, 'Yes.'

It was true, he had phoned and 'summoned' her.

'Because now that my nephew is dead, we must renegotiate his agreement with you. My brother, his father, is too distressed to take on the work at this time.'

'I understand.'

'Mmm.' He drank his tea and ate a biscuit. 'Now, I have looked at the paperwork drawn up for my nephew by the lawyers we use here in the UK, and I must say that I find some of it a little irregular.'

He was going to ask for more money. Mumtaz put a hand up to her head.

'It was my understanding,' the old man said, 'that it was your husband who incurred a debt to my family.'

'Yes.'

'You sold your family home to pay this debt when your husband died.'

'I sold everything,' she said. 'And, Wahid-ji, my husband was murdered.'

'Oh, yes,' he said. 'Of course.'

If Wahid Sheikh was what he claimed to be, then he knew. Because he would have ordered it.

'You know that people wonder why I live in Dhaka, when most of the family live here in the UK,' he said. 'But then I say, "Our business is global." With the internet and wonderful innovations like Skype, what does it matter where one lives any more? Business is everywhere now, it is twenty-four seven, and as long as you have agents that you trust in your various territories, nothing can go wrong.'

Mumtaz's heart couldn't sink any further. He was the overall head of the clan. 'Wahid-ji.'

'But this is not always true. And in this case . . . yours . . .' He opened his arms. 'It is my belief that my nephew pursued you needlessly.'

For a moment she thought she had misheard.

Seeing the look of confusion on her face, he repeated. 'Needlessly, Mrs Hakim. We have obtained the monies from you owed by your husband. Agreements drawn up by my nephew subsequent to that may, I say may, now be deleted.'

Mumtaz was speechless. Did he mean that her debt to the Sheikhs was cancelled? He'd spoken on the phone about 'normalising' the relationship between their families. Was this what he had meant?

'I can see that you have no money or assets. You work, from time to time, alongside the police based at Forest Gate police station. It was my nephew's belief that you would be able to provide my family with intelligence from that source,' he said. 'But from what I can gather it seems that you would not have access to anything useful. You are a private detective, not a police officer.'

'Yes.'

'So it would seem to me that an obligation to report police activity on your part should also become redundant.'

Mumtaz was beginning to like this man. He was the head of the Sheikh family, but he was clearly intelligent and reasonable.

'However . . .' he said.

Ludmilla's flat was sparsely furnished, but very bright and clean. On the walls were pictures of relatives back home in Poland and of Ludmilla's late mother, who had been Russian.

When they got in, she put Tomasz down for his nap and made coffee for herself and Shazia. Sitting at the kitchen table, they looked out at the railway line that ran into the London Liverpool Street terminus.

Ludmilla said, 'What I told you about Janusz and the Sheikh man when I see you at the railway station, that was true. But that was not why he died.'

'Then why?' Shazia said.

'Because Janusz, he was told to,' she said.

'By who?'

She sighed. 'I tell you Janusz has job at gym. It is in Wanstead. It's beautiful, really. But the man who runs it, he's not so nice. He sells drugs to kids. Steroids. He is a drug-dealer, you know?'

'Yes.'

'He work with people all over the world,' she said. 'For drugs. Also that man, the Sheikh and his family. But they cheat him. They give him things not real drugs, something else. And this man, Russian he is, he says he will teach them a lesson.'

'So your husband . . .'

'Janusz says he will give the Sheikh man a beating. He wants to do this because of what names he call me. But then the boss, he say no, he wants Janusz to kill him. My husband says no! He is not a killer. But the Russian say he has said yes already, that he will lose his job, that I will be, um, what you say when someone makes you to have sex . . . ?'

Shazia gasped. 'Raped?'

'Raped. Yes.' She shook her head. Her eyes filled with tears. 'The Sheikh man goes to Mr Huq's shop and I see him. I flirt. He is easy to interest. The Russian knows a house on Capel Road we can use. I arrange to meet him there. Tomasz I put with my friend Kelly.'

'And Janusz . . . ?'

'It was so hard for him!' She cried.

Shazia didn't know what to do, and so she went to the bathroom and got a handful of tissues.

'Sorry! Sorry!'

She gave them to Ludmilla.

'It's OK,' she said. 'This is not easy stuff to talk about. I know.

Naz Sheikh made my family's life a misery. I'm glad he's dead. I really am.'

'But Janusz didn't want to kill him! When I take Sheikh upstairs to have sex – he thinks – Janusz is like a man about to die himself. And Sheikh, he laugh, you know? At first he laugh because Janusz he can't do nothing. It is only when I see him put a hand in his pocket, I think he have a gun, I jump in front of Janusz and push the man to the floor. Janusz had to kill him because he had the knife, but I hold him down.'

She cried again. 'We ran.'

'And then I went in the house,' Shazia said. 'I found him.'

Ludmilla put a hand out to her. 'I am so sorry.'

Shazia gripped her fingers. 'I'm sorry too,' she said. 'Until these people can be put away in prison, what can we do? We have to protect ourselves. You know I always thought that when I grew up I'd be a lawyer. I thought I'd use the law to help people like us, but the Sheikhs and your Russian have lawyers in their pockets, you understand?'

She nodded.

'That's why they're safe. I don't think I want to be a lawyer any more.'

'So what you do now?'

Shazia smiled. 'Now I have so much fury in me, I just want to punish them. I want them to hurt and I know I need to do that myself.'

'To hurt them?'

'If I join the police I can break their doors down, terrify their families – just like our family was. I want them to fear me,' she

said. 'Because when I was watching Naz Sheikh die on the floor of
that house, it made me feel good. I was afraid. I called my mum
and she called an ambulance, but I knew he'd bled too much. I
knew he was going to die and I didn't feel even one little bit of
pity or shame or anything. And I will go to hell for it, I know that.
Our religion teaches that taking a life is unforgivable, whatever
the reason. So if I'm going to hell anyway I may as well take a
few more of them with me.'

'Oh, Shazia,' Ludmilla said, 'that is such a terrible thing to say.
You are a good person, you—'

'No, I'm not,' she said. 'My mum is. You know, if she knew
what I'd really done, she'd want nothing more to do with me.'

'No!'

'Yes. And I doubted her, when he told lies about her,' she said.
'My amma, that's what we call "mum", she's the most wonderful
person in the world. And if I can become a police officer, I can
protect her.'

'When you are in a position like that of my family, honour must
be satisfied. And it must be seen to be satisfied too,' the old man
said. 'When your husband was promising and then failing to
pay his considerable debts to our family, it made my brother ill.'

Rizwan Sheikh had suffered a stroke during that time. Whether
it had come about as a direct result of Ahmet's failure to pay his
debts, Mumtaz didn't know. Naz Sheikh had always said that it had.

'That was why your husband had to die,' Wahid said. 'There
was a lot of anger in the family. Your husband's lack of respect

was appalling. If our competitors got to know about such things it could ruin our business. The modern world is not for the faint-hearted, Mrs Hakim.'

Mumtaz looked down at the floor. He wanted something. What was it?

'So when Ahmet Hakim's daughter was found at the place where my nephew died, well, some in my family felt that she should pay for her mistake.'

'Mistake? Shazia made no mistake, she tried to save his life,' Mumtaz said. 'She did not kill your nephew, Wahid-ji, and you know it.'

Ah,' he smiled. 'A spirited defence of a young girl you have sought to protect ever since you found out what her father did to her. We have her interests at heart, too.'

'Don't say that you saved her from abuse by killing her father,' Mumtaz said. 'I would have found a way. In the end, I—'

'Would have what? Killed him yourself?'

She looked away.

'Mmm. You're a dangerous woman, Mrs Hakim. I think you could kill.'

She didn't like him anymore.

'You don't know me. Get to the point,' she said. 'What do you want?'

'Ah, that western bluntness!' he said. 'I don't imagine that your father conducts his business affairs in such a fashion.'

Mumtaz said nothing. There was a form, a pace and a style of doing business that was entirely Bengali, but she'd been born in London.

'You don't know my father,' she said softly.

'No. But I know *of* him,' the old man said. 'I have also heard of your brother, Ali.'

Wahid wore traditional clothes. He had probably been to Ali's shop on Brick Lane. She shrugged.

'I know he currently harbours a boy some would call a terrorist,' he said.

She felt her heart jolt. Her face flushed.

'An Arab. He has been fighting in Syria, I understand. A very pious boy.'

Could Ali have such a person as a guest in his house? If he did it was nothing that she knew about. Ali was a bit more radical than he'd been before, but a terrorist . . . ?

'If you don't believe me, go and see who is sleeping in Ali's spare bedroom,' the old man said. 'It is important to people in business, like my family, to know as much as possible about those who are in debt, in whatever way, to us. So let us recap. We know you have no money, we know that your brother harbours a terrorist. Your stepdaughter was found with my nephew when he was dying—'

'And tried to save him.'

He shrugged.

'The point is, Mrs Hakim, you still owe my family. I may decide to cancel your fiscal debts. As I've said, they can be seen as not strictly fair. However . . .'

Mumtaz became cold.

'What is it?' she said. 'What do you want?'

Why had she liked this old monster, even for a second?

He smiled. 'Well, for some time now,' he said, 'I have been looking for a wife . . .'

People didn't usually hammer on his front door. Maybe the doorbell was broken? Lee sauntered through the lounge and into the hall. Whoever was out there was making a helluva racket for a quiet Saturday afternoon.

When he opened the door a flurry of trench-coat and scarves bowled in at him.

'Mumtaz!'

She was shaking and crying and her face was so white he thought she might faint. He put his arms around her and all but carried her into the lounge.

'What the . . . ?'

Chronus, who had been asleep, opened one beady eye.

Lee sat her on the sofa.

'I'll get you some water.' He ran to the kitchen. She was in shock. If she hadn't been a Muslim he would have dug out the brandy he kept for emergencies.

He came back with a glass of water and put it in her hand. She drank some, almost choking.

'Slow down! Slow down!'

He could see she was trying. But the tears kept coming and the choking continued. He put an arm around her shoulders. He was desperate to know why she was like this, but he had to calm her down.

'Ssshhh. Ssshhh.'

He felt her fall against the side of his body as her sobs began to subside. What could have happened to make her like this? Had her father died? Shazia gone missing? No, the kid wouldn't do that. Not after all she and her mother had been through.'

'It's Shazia.'

Maybe he was wrong. He looked down into her eyes and said, 'What?'

'The Sheikhs want her,' Mumtaz said. She closed her eyes briefly, probably in order to help steady her nerves. 'The head of the family wants to marry her.'

'What?'

'And if I don't agree to it, then they will take everything I have left and they will destroy my family.'

Overwhelmed by her sudden appearance, her panic and the fear that vibrated in her eyes, he looked down at the floor. Then he said, 'What do you . . . ?'

'I want you to help me,' Mumtaz said. She put a hand on his arm and squeezed it hard. 'I want you to save Shazia, Lee. And I want you to save me, too.'

Acknowledgements

Thanks go yet again to the people of Newham for sharing their stories – particularly friends at the Newham Bookshop. Thanks also to Sarah for showing me the joys of Broadway market.